A Jenetta Carver™ Adventure

A GALAXY UNKNOWN™

RETREAT
AND ADAPT

Book 10

BY

THOMAS DEPRIMA

Vinnia Publishing - U.S.A.

Retreat and Adapt
A Galaxy Unknown™ series – Book 9
Copyright ©2012 by Thomas J. DePrima

ISBN-10 : **1619310198**

ISBN-13 : **978-1-61931-019-3**

Cover by: Thomas DePrima

1st Edition

Amazon Distribution

Appendices containing political and technical data highly pertinent to this series are included at the back of this book.

To contact the author, or see information about his other novels, visit:

http://www.deprima.com

Many thanks to Michael A. Norcutt for his suggestions, proofreading, and for acting as my military operations and protocol advisor in this series.

<u>This series of novels includes:</u>

A Galaxy Unknown™…

A Galaxy Unknown ™
Valor at Vauzlee
The Clones of Mawcett
Trader Vyx
Milor!
Castle Vroman
Against All Odds
Return to Dakistee
Retreat And Adapt

<u>Other series and novels by the author:</u>

AGU:™ Border Patrol…

Citizen X
Clidepp Requital

AGU:™ SC Intelligence…

The Star Brotherhood

Colton James novels…

A World Without Secrets
Vengeance Is Personal

When The Spirit…

When The Spirit Moves You
When The Spirit Calls

Table of Contents

Chapter 1 — 1
Chapter 2 — 14
Chapter 3 — 25
Chapter 4 — 37
Chapter 5 — 46
Chapter 6 — 60
Chapter 7 — 70
Chapter 8 — 82
Chapter 9 — 94
Chapter 10 — 107
Chapter 11 — 121
Chapter 12 — 132
Chapter 13 — 145
Chapter 14 — 158
Chapter 15 — 169
Chapter 16 — 184
Chapter 17 — 195
Chapter 18 — 206
Chapter 19 — 218
Chapter 20 — 229
Chapter 21 — 240
Chapter 22 — 252
Chapter 23 — 263
Chapter 24 — 275
Chapter 25 — 286
Chapter 26 — 297
Chapter 27 — 308
Chapter 28 — 323
Chapter 29 — 335
Chapter 30 — 347
Chapter 31 — 360
Appendix — 368

Chapter One
~ February 15th, 2286 ~

"I should kill you," Strauss growled, each word dripping with unmistakable menace, "slowly and painfully, as a lesson to other fools who would disobey my instructions."

Nicole Ravenau squirmed nervously in her silken blouse and expensive business suit as she stood facing his large desk. She never doubted for a second that Strauss was capable of committing cold-blooded murder. She also knew that not a single trace of her perfect body would ever be found.

The Lower Council Headquarters Building was so secure that Strauss could talk openly, free from worry that anyone outside the room could overhear the conversation. Almost as sure was the fact that if he did commit a crime here in his enormous penthouse office, no witness would ever speak of it. If they did, they would probably not live out the day, and certainly not long enough to testify.

"You knew I wanted to temper Space Command's anger by keeping deaths on Dakistee to an absolute minimum," Strauss continued. "I stressed that repeatedly. Then, not only did you intentionally attempt to kill someone, but you selected one of the Carver women as your target! Just *what* the hell were you thinking, you dumb bitch?"

"It wasn't me," Ravenau whimpered defensively. The two burly bodyguards standing just behind her would kill her in an instant if Strauss preferred not to perform the deed himself. He would only have to make eye contact and nod slightly. And she was practically defenseless. A lecherous bodyguard at the executive suite entrance had meticulously checked her for weapons, examining her in places where no weapon could have been hidden, before she was allowed to proceed. A broach with a poisoned barb was the only weapon he had missed, but it could not save her life because it was a one-use weapon. At best, she might be able to start one of the bodyguards on a quick march towards death before the other ended her life. "It was that idiot archeologist," she sobbed loudly. "He shot her, not me."

"What were you doing in her bedroom?"

"We'd heard that the ancients on Dakistee possessed some incredible unknown stasis technology. I was hoping to steal Carver's computer, thinking she had probably downloaded the specs into it. But she had already returned from her debriefing session by the time we were finally able to infiltrate the Marine dormitory area unnoticed."

It was a lie, of course. Ravenau had been preparing her excuses ever since being summoned to Strauss's office, but he seemed to be buying into it.

"Even aside from the Carver assassination attempt, I should kill you for not telling us you had been successful in recreating the Age Prolongation and DNA Manipulation formulas, and finally developed an Age Regression formula."

Ravenau was prepared for this accusation as well, and was able to answer without hesitation. "I'm the final test subject, just as I was for the original project. If there are no medical complications, I'm ready to turn over the formulas and procedures to the Raider Central Laboratories group."

Formerly known as Mikel Arneu, Ravenau had once told the Lower Council that the formulas were lost when Jenetta Carver destroyed the Raider-One base, but that was also a lie. He had feared losing the enormous budget and subsequent power that had been his since development efforts had begun and which would be wielded by whoever else was chosen to administer the project in the future if it were taken from him. Arneu's promise to reconstruct the lost work had provided almost unlimited research funds for twenty years and finally enabled him to develop a formula to reverse the aging process— a primary goal since the age prolongation efforts had first begun. Thousands of test subjects had died, some horribly, since the work started some four decades earlier, but once the formulas were proven to be reliably safe, Arneu had been the first in line to undergo the changes. Now, instead of being a sixty-something, middle-aged male, his appearance was that of a shapely twenty-three-year-old female with a face and complexion to die for, or kill for.

The body designed by the geneticists for Arneu rivaled that designed for Jenetta Carver, although facial appearances were vastly different, but Arneu hadn't wished to be female and had continued to press the scientists for a workable formula for his male body. Once they proved that the process was consistently blocked by the presence of abundant male hormones in the body, a sex change was the only avenue to reverse aging. Having finally accepted that becoming female was the only way to restore his youth, he had spent a year in almost constant pain as his body was reshaped from toenails to scalp.

Arneu had planned to undergo the DNA Manipulation process and become male again once his age had been firmly established at twenty-three, but he couldn't bear the thought of another year of excruciating pain. Besides, once he was female, he'd found that he liked it, or rather that *she* liked it. Where before he had mainly used threats to get people to do what he wanted, she found that she could often accomplish the same things simply by assuming a practiced stance or talking seductively. Lately she had worked on projecting an appearance of weakness to exploit the tendencies of most males to act in a protective capacity. And if that didn't work, she still held enough power to force subordinates to do her bidding.

"So when will we see the final formulas?" Strauss demanded.

"I can send them any time you wish, but I strongly recommend you wait a bit longer before putting them into use. I'm still being closely monitored for possible health risks associated with the changes. My doctors continue to watch for signs of severe complications that would require additional laboratory work and more testing. To date, I'm the *only* successful test for all three formulas."

"The Central Labs scientists will determine when the formulas can be used. Send them tomorrow, and I'll forget about the Christa Carver incident. You're fortunate she survived." Strauss waved his hand dismissively and said, "That's all." In an angry voice, he added, "Now get out of my sight."

Ravenau didn't hesitate. Strauss's bodyguards followed along and watched every movement closely until the elevator door closed and the car began to sink towards the lobby level. She was well aware that she'd been lucky Carver survived, although she couldn't imagine how. The blood loss from three lattice rounds fired at close range had been incredible. Ravenau had attributed her recovery to the amazing recuperative powers of the DNA manipulation performed on Jenetta.

Every time Ravenau thought of the Carvers, she practically salivated over the power that could have been hers if she'd been able to get her hands on the cloning technology. That was the real motivating factor in going to Loudescott. She'd intended to personally oversee the acquisition of new technology. Her altered appearance gave her confidence that she wouldn't be recognized, and in fact Christa hadn't had a clue when they first met. Ravenau had believed that acquiring some incredible new technology would both allow her to get some revenge against the Carvers and avoid retribution from Strauss for violating his directive.

 Christa's recovery meant that Ravenau's appearance was no longer the great secret she had hoped to maintain, and surrendering her new identity had yielded nothing of value. She'd been crushed when she discovered that the only secret of the facility was the existence of people who should have died two hundred centuries ago. So now she was considering going through another DNA Manipulation process to get a new face. It wouldn't be nearly as difficult and painful as changing her sex had been, but it certainly wasn't something to look forward to.

As the elevator descended, she thought about the formulas she had just agreed to turn over to the Raider Central Laboratories. She knew that if she complied she would be losing control over the greatest medical discoveries in history.

She desperately needed to find a way to stay in the loop while receiving full credit for everything that had been developed thus far. She had named each of the processes after her former identity, and if that held, they would always be attributed to her, but once she turned the formulas and notes over to the lab rats, Strauss might decide that her usefulness to the Raider Corporation was over. He might have already made that decision and was only waiting until the formulas were in his possession before ordering it carried out. He didn't necessarily need to kill her. He might just wipe her mind and send her to the fate she had once planned for Carver. The prospect of spending her extended life in a Raider brothel as a mindless whore held no appeal. Ravenau knew that Strauss would have to go if she was ever to feel safe again, but Strauss was the darling of the Upper Council, so his death must not point back to her or implicate her in any way.

* * *

"General Ardlessel, give us your report," Prime Minister Pemillisa said.

Ardlessel rose to his feet in preparation for addressing the government officials and military officers assembled in the dimly lit War Conference Center. The centerpiece building of the Defense Complex, located in the Ruwalchu capital city of Pierrdoncu, had hosted this same large group every month since Admiral Carver defeated the Uthlaro armada. Senior officials and military officers had seats at the great circular table, while lesser officials and officers occupied available gallery seating or silently lined the walls of the chamber.

"Mr. Prime Minister, honorable members of the Gilesset, and my fellow officers, we continue to prepare for our upcoming fight with the Galactic Alliance. Over the past annual, we have positioned all available ships in the optimal defensive locations along our common border, as approved by this Council. New shipbuilding, previously delayed by budget cutbacks for many annuals, is now moving along at a furious pace, and the Weapons Research section has been promised almost unlimited funding as we prepare to meet the greatest threat to the peace and stability in this part of space that we've ever known. This annual we've inducted some four million men and women into the armed services and increased the size of the classes at the military academies by some seven hundred percent. We're doing now what we should have been doing annuals ago, and would have done if we had viewed Maxxiloth and the Milori Empire at the threat level we view Admiral Carver and the Galactic Alliance. That is all I have to report. I'll answer any questions you might have."

"General," Prime Minister Pemillisa said, "What's the latest word from the Intelligence section? Do they believe the enemy will invade before we're adequately prepared?"

"We're monitoring all broadcasts coming from the Galactic Alliance and to date have heard of no plans to invade our space. But our contacts in the former Uthlaro Dominion tell us that it's only a matter of time before Space Command turns its attention to our borders. And the enemy would hardly broadcast their military objectives openly on public airwaves. It's an immutable fact that we occupy territory that stands between them and the most densely populated areas of the galaxy, areas rich in resources and plunder. In all honesty, we don't know how much time they will spend organizing their new territory before they return to their expansionist goals of controlling the galaxy. If the Great Protector smiles down on us, we'll be ready for them when they come at us."

"From all accounts," Pemillisa said, "their weapons are most formidable and their ships nearly indestructible. You've talked about fantastic weapons being developed by our Weapons Research section. What progress has been made?"

"Thanks to information provided by the Uthlaro, we're primarily concentrating our efforts in three different areas. First and foremost there's the research into the indestructible hull of the Space Command ships. For a price bordering on insane, the Uthlaro have provided a complete laboratory analysis of the material developed by Space Command. They claim to have purchased it from the Raider organization. To date, they've been unable to replicate it, but they're continuing their work on it, and they experiment with newly produced materials each month.

"The agreement between us calls for us to provide a copy of all laboratory efforts if our research yields a proven formula and process before they discover one, at which time they'll return our full purchase price of fifty trillion credits. If they succeed first, our cost to purchase it from them will be an additional one hundred trillion credits."

"One hundred *trillion* credits?" one of the senior members of the Gilesset uttered aloud.

Glancing at the man, Ardlessel said, "Minister, it would be worth every credit to have indestructible hulls on all our warships." Returning his attention to the Prime Minister, Ardlessel said, "While we work to learn the secret of making the material Space Command calls Dakinium, we're also working on ways to render the material vulnerable to attack."

"I agree with the concentration of funds in this endeavor. What else, General?"

"The second most important project is to learn the secret of their incredible speed. We have offered enormous rewards to anyone who can supply verifiable information on how Space Command ships can travel beyond the former theoretical limits of FTL. And they haven't just broken through those former limits, they've shattered them. Our information is that they can attain speeds of Light-9790."

"Surely that's just propaganda," a minister uttered. "We've been hearing that farce for an annual."

"No, sir," Ardlessel said, "it's almost certainly fact. Admiral Carver was reported earlier this annual as being at her headquarters on Quesann. A few months later, she was seen on a space station near Earth. She couldn't have made that trip in less than five annuals at the top speed of our fastest ship. We must remain open-minded to new information and not allow ourselves to ignore the possibilities that new technologies offer. Our distant ancestors once thought this planet was flat. Where would we be today if we had continued to cling to that notion and not seek new knowledge?"

"And what is the third area where our funds are primarily being expended, General?" Prime Minister Pemillisa asked.

"A weapons-delivery system that can overcome the effectiveness of the Space Command system they call 'Phalanx.' According to the Uthlaro, Space Command is able to shoot down virtually ninety-nine percent of all torpedoes directed at their warships. We must be able to penetrate a ship's protection umbrella if we're to have a hope of damaging it."

"And have you had any success?"

"We believe so, Mr. Prime Minister. We won't know for sure until we actually have to face one of their ships, but we think we've found a method of overcoming their systems."

"So we must wait until we meet the enemy at our gates before we know if it's effective?"

"Not necessarily, Mr. Prime Minister. Several months ago, using the powers vested in me by this body, I authorized a bold plan to test our new Phalanx Destruction system. I hesitated to mention it earlier lest word leak back to Space Command."

* * *

It had been torture holding their tongues until they were assured of the secure privacy available aboard a Space Command ship, but once Jenetta and Christa were ensconced in Jenetta's VIP quarters aboard the SC battleship *Ares*, they opened up completely. Admiral Holt had specifically asked Jenetta not to bring Eliza with her to his office, and she understood once he explained the full details of Christa's *recovery* through the use of Project Springboard. But Eliza, third officer aboard the *Ares*, was able to join them now since it was second watch. The reunion behind closed doors had been spontaneous and heartwarming as they celebrated Christa's return to good health, then began to catch up on all the news they hadn't been able to share until now.

"You're kidding!" Jenetta said. "Mikel Arneu is a woman now? He's had a sex change?"

Christa was sitting on the carpeted deck pulling a brush through Tayna's thick fur, while Cayla, Jenetta's other Taurentlus-Thur Jumaka, lay on the deck next to Jenetta with her head in Jenetta's lap. Eliza was also on the deck, leaning against a sofa while she enjoyed a large bowl of delicious chocolate ice cream from Jenetta's well-stocked kitchen.

"Yes and no," Christa said. "It wasn't a regular sex change like anyone can have performed over the weekend at any large clinic or hospital. He went through the Raider DNA Manipulation process. He's a *real* woman now. Or I guess I should say *she's* a real woman now."

"Complete with uterus and ovaries?"

"Yeah, the works— as far as I know. He, I mean she, told me that she was in pain for a year while her DNA reconfigured her pelvis. I assume that included all the proper plumbing. She said it was excruciating, and she couldn't move without hurting."

"That's the first good thing you've told me," Jenetta said with a smile. "She deserved every second of it."

Between spoonfuls of ice cream, Eliza chimed in with "Yeah, and then some."

"I knew they intended to kill me before they left," Christa said, "so I'm lucky to have survived. I really, *really* thought I was dead when Kasim shot me."

"Uh, yeah, it was a close one," Jenetta agreed. "We almost lost you. We're lucky the doctor placed you in that stasis chamber when he did and that the Dakistee stasis chambers operate the way they do."

"Yeah, he saved my life. I'll have to thank him when I get back to Dakistee."

"And Kasim really told you he was responsible for drugging Jenetta and creating you and me?" Eliza asked.

"Yup. He said he did it to prove to himself that he understood the process well enough to produce new clones."

"Then he must have been successful in deciphering the Ancient Dakis graphics before we did."

"Yes. We hadn't reached that topic yet, but he'd had months to study the equipment before Jenetta arrived on the planet. For such an intelligent person, and considering his senior position in the labor force, he would have had no trouble sneaking into the facility to study the equipment at night. I can only imagine his frustration in having to play a subservient role to the young scientists there."

"I'm going to recommend you for a commendation for a job well done," Jenetta said. "The stasis technology alone is worth everything you went through. It's going to have far-reaching benefits for the Galactic Alliance. And discovering the sleeping Dakistians will change the face of that planet, and perhaps the Galactic Alliance."

"I'd trade the commendation right now for a ticket back to the *Hephaestus.*"

Jenetta smiled sadly. "I wish I could. But the Admiralty Board wants you on Dakistee for a while. Don't worry, you'll get back to shipboard duty."

"Isn't that what you always told yourself?"

"Yes, but you have a friend who's very highly placed. Do this job and I'll find a way to get you on a ship."

"Okay, sis. I hadn't really considered *not* doing it."

"I know," Jenetta said with a smile.

"So you'll be heading back to Region Two right away?" Christa asked.

"No. I'm going home to see mom first. And I'm going to talk to the Admiralty Board while I'm on Earth."

"Ooh. See if you can get me freed up from Dakistee," Christa said jokingly.

Jenetta smiled. "The job on Dakistee is an important one. I know it's not what you want, sis, but it'll be excellent experience. When I was the commanding officer at Dixon and then at Stewart, hardly a day passed when I didn't learn something new that would serve me well later in my career. And to paraphrase something Admiral Holt once said to me, 'You need a little rounding out.'"

"Okay, but I still think I'll be bored out of my mind."

"Only if you're lucky," Jenetta said with smile.

The SC battleship *Ares* departed for Earth a week after dropping Christa off on Dakistee. Jenetta had accompanied

Christa down to the surface and thanked the medical staff for the quick action that saved Christa's life and for their efforts in meeting the other medical emergencies following the attack at the archeological dig site. Madu, the pro tem president of the Dakistee people, was performing administrative duties on another part of the planet and so missed the opportunity to meet with Jenetta on this occasion, but Jenetta met with the diplomatic staff charged with handling public relations for the temporary government and toured the new-found facility. She also renewed her association with the Loudescott archeological staff and visited the Space Marine base at North Pendleton.

* * *

The *Ares* was just hours from Earth when a light chime seemed to sound next to Jenetta's left ear. It was followed by a message that a Priority-One communication had just arrived in her message queue. Already seated behind the desk in her office adjoining the Admiral's bridge, she held up a hand to silence her aide, Lt. Commander Ashraf, in mid-sentence and said, "I have an incoming Priority communication, Lori. Hold your thought for a minute."

Jenetta leaned into the area where the computer could perform a retinal scan for verification of identity and instructed the machine to begin.

When the computer was satisfied with the identity of the recipient, an image of Admiral Augustus Poole filled the screen. His voice could only be heard through Jenetta's CT so that anyone within range couldn't eavesdrop on the Priority-One conversation.

"Hello, Jen," the image of Poole said. "I'm sorry to disturb you while you're on leave, but I felt you should be aware of an incident. Three weeks ago, the *Yenisei* reported making DeTect contact with three ships and announced an intention to pursue and investigate. That was the last we heard from them. I've declared the ship officially overdue and ordered every other DS ship within two hundred light-years to immediately proceed to the *Yenisei*'s last reported position to begin a search operation. Unfortunately, the *Yenisei* was operating at the furthest reaches of Region Two, out near the Ruwalchu and Hudeerac border areas, so there were only two ships within range. One is the scout-destroyer *Thames*, and the other is the DS destroyer *Duluth*. Both ships should be nearing the area by the time you receive this message."

"Augustus Poole, Rear Admiral, Upper Half, Base Commander, Quesann SCB, message complete."

Jenetta sighed loudly as she sat back in her chair.

Ashraf, seated across the desk from her, could see the sadness in her admiral's eyes. "What is it, Admiral? Anything you can talk about?"

"Since we first entered Region Two to conclude our conflict with the Milori, we've only left twice. The first time, we were only gone a week before the THUG pack began to wage war to arrogate our new territory. We returned and saw an end to that conflict, and since then things have been reasonably quiet. Now we leave the Region again, and suddenly we have an incident reminiscent of the last time. I'm no sooner back in the vicinity of home when someone starts trouble."

"What kind of trouble? Another invasion?"

"The *Yenisei* is missing after reporting that it was pursuing three ships."

"Missing? For how long?"

"Three weeks."

"But the *Yenisei* is Dakinium-sheathed. No three warships should have been able to take him down before he could get a message off."

"That's why I sighed. No *three* warships should have been able to take him down. So how many warships are out there this time— twenty? fifty? a hundred? a thousand? ten thousand? And what are their full intentions?"

"Perhaps it's only a problem with the *Yenisei*'s drive, like the one the *Colorado* experienced where everything short-circuited and left you without propulsion and communications."

"I hope so, but it seems like too much of a coincidence. If the *Yenisei* was chasing after three unknown ships, a double-envelope shouldn't have been needed. Scout-destroyers are capable of speeds up to Light-487 without resorting to their maximum speed capability. No— I fear the worst."

"Then we should get back there as soon as possible."

"All that can be done is already being done. Admiral Poole is very capable of handling the situation. And I've already notified the Admiralty Board that I'm coming to Earth."

"But surely this new problem is far more important than a meeting with the AB."

"Perhaps, but we won't be able to establish that until we know what happened. We'll continue on to Earth. Now, about that issue with the Milori High Council…"

Chapter Two
~ February 25th, 2286 ~

The *Ares* received a straight-in approach by traffic controllers when it reached Earth. Captain Gavin hadn't declared an emergency or requested special treatment, but Earth Space Traffic Control had been advised that Admiral Carver was on board, and a supervisor decided it wouldn't do to keep Earth's greatest heroine waiting to disembark while the ship spent the better part of a day slowly following standard traffic protocols for approaching the planet.

When the *Ares* had established a stable position in Earth orbit, Jenetta and her aide, Lt. Commander Ashraf, made their way to the *Ares'* shuttle bay where a small ship reserved for her exclusive use was waiting. The flight crew had already completed the preflight and received Earth sub-orbit permissions and approach routes. They were ready to depart as soon as the shuttle was buttoned-up.

Gone were the days when Jenetta could pilot her own shuttle, but there was always that Marine fighter on Quesann with her name on the cockpit. Whenever the burden of supreme command in Regions Two and Three weighed too heavily upon her shoulders and she could get away for a few hours, she enjoyed a bit of full-throttle wave hopping and canyon skimming in the more remote areas of the planet. Her flights never failed to fill her protection details with near heart-stopping sensations of dread as they trailed from a safer height, but the occasional outings were sometimes the only way Jenetta could cope with the incredible pressures of a job she had never wanted and still remain sane.

Jenetta would have preferred to go directly to the Potomac Space Command Base where her family owned a home in the adjoining military housing subdivision, but she knew that would be impossible on this first trip back to Earth since defeating the four powers that attempted to arrogate Region Two. Annexation of the space formerly claimed by the Tsgardi had substantially increased the size of Region Two, and the space annexed following the defeat of the Uthlaro was so massive that it was designated as Region Three. Naturally, all unclaimed space between the conquered territories and the Galactic Alliance Frontier Zone had immediately been claimed and added to the two new regions. Jenetta's incredible victories had more than quadrupled the size of the Galactic Alliance. And since her promotion to full Admiral had taken place while she was still in Region Two, she couldn't possibly avoid all the pomp and ceremony hurriedly planned following notification of her return home.

The shuttle from the *Ares* touched down at the Galactic Alliance Headquarters Complex in Nebraska at the appointed time. Jenetta, her ribbons and medals shimmering brightly, looked resplendent in her dress uniform. She was even wearing the peaked cap she disliked so much. This was actually the first time she had worn either it or her medals since her last trip home.

At the same parade ground where she had first been honored so many years ago, the cloth emblem of every member planet in the Galactic Alliance was represented on one of the tall flagpoles arranged in five concave, semi-circular rings that faced a massive stage. The February wind gusts kept all of the flags flapping wildly and ensured that the heavy winter coats of the several thousand attendees seated in the folding chairs that filled the field were closed tightly to preserve as much body warmth as possible.

Owing to the unpleasantly cold weather, the ceremony began as soon as Jenetta arrived, and speeches by red-cheeked officials and dignitaries, spoken through billowing clouds of condensed breath, were kept to a minimum length. All members of the Admiralty Board were present, including Rear Admiral (Upper) Yuthkotl, the Nordakian officer who formerly held the rank of Admiral of the Fleet for the Nordakian Space Force. With the NSF now fully absorbed into Space Command, he had finally taken a rightful place on the Admiralty Board. Admiral Hubera's disgrace and subsequent retirement meant that the board was still composed of ten admirals.

When it came time for Jenetta to speak, her two jumakas accompanied her to the microphone and stood at her side, staring out at the audience while she spoke. Where in the past, the male spectators might have spent their time ogling Jenetta's gorgeous legs, on this occasion most eyes in the audience remained glued to the two magnificent beasts who never left Jenetta's side. Perhaps an occasional pair of eyes would have focused on Jenetta's legs if she hadn't opted to wear trousers on this cold February day instead of a skirt. Like the other speakers, she kept her comments brief.

Jenetta was already wearing the medal honors earned since her last appearance on Earth, as well the insignia of her rank, so there was no physical presentation of honors, but each honor was detailed in chronological order for the present audience and for the vid cameras capturing the event for nightly news programs and posterity.

When Admiral Moore, the Admiral of the Fleet for Space Command, closed the ceremonies, the attendees stood, clapped, and cheered for several minutes, then hurried away to warm vehicles or more weather-hospitable environs. Jenetta took a few minutes to shake hands and exchange greetings with the people assembled on the stage before they too dispersed to escape the frigid mid-winter Nebraska temperature and icy cold winds. As Jenetta hurried to a waiting vehicle, thoughts of the year-round pleasant weather at the Region Two Headquarters base on Quesann filled her mind.

Her shuttle was ready to lift off as soon as Jenetta and her small entourage were aboard. Flight-plan requests had already been approved, and they were on their way to the Potomac Space Command Base within minutes.

The commanding officer of Potomac had arranged for a small welcoming ceremony, and after disembarking from the small ship, Jenetta smiled and shook the hand of each senior

officer lining the shuttle pad perimeter as they were introduced. It was too cold to stand around, so Jenetta took her
leave as soon as possible. Three covered oh-gee vehicles
filled with Marines surrounded the VIP limo carrying Jenetta,
Lt. Commander Ashraf, and the two jumakas. Even though
access to the housing area was limited to military officers,
their families, and approved guests, there would always be at
least a dozen security people near the house while she was
there.

Jenetta received the expected ebullient reaction as the front
door of her family home opened. She barely had time to utter
the words, "Hello, Momma," before Annette Carver cried out
in delight and leapt into her arms.

As Jenetta bent to accept her, Annette coiled her arms
around her daughter's neck and showered her with kisses and
happy tears. Jenetta responded in kind, although a little less
demonstratively. The jumakas, having been here before and
understanding the familial relationship, knew there was no
danger from the parental attack. They merely stood and
watched in fascination.

"Mother Carver, let the poor girl come in out of the cold,"
Jenetta heard from inside the house. Her sister-in-law Marisa
came into view as Annette relaxed her arms and Jenetta was
able to straighten up.

Annette sniffled and wrapped her right arm around
Jenetta's waist as she pulled her into the house. The jumakas
moved inside as well, followed by Lt. Commander Ashraf,
who closed the door.

As soon as the wintery elements were once more sealed
outside, Marisa moved in to hug her sister-in-law. Although
they corresponded regularly by vidMail, this was their first
in-person meeting. Marisa had known that Jenetta was almost
as tall as her husband Richie, but the height still came as a bit
of a shock because she was used to seeing Jenetta in a head-
and-shoulders perspective only. But she didn't let the half-
foot difference stop her from embracing her sister-in-law like

a family member who had been away for a long time. "Hi, Jen," she said as they touched checks.

"Hi, Marisa. It's wonderful to see you in person at last. I wish I could have attended your wedding."

"We military families understand such things. Richie cryo'd a piece of the cake for you during the reception. And thanks again for the great wedding gift."

"You're most welcome. I'm glad the store had the pattern you posted in the bridal registry."

"The set is perfect. Richie and I both love it. I hope you have time to stop over to the house before you have to leave."

"Just try to stop me. I'm dying to see all the things I've only seen as small images on a vid screen. I've scheduled three weeks for vacation, so there should be plenty of opportunity to get together."

"You mean the Admiralty Board won't be commandeering all your time on this stay?"

"Not a chance. I'm naturally going to visit them, but this trip is as much a vacation as a business visit."

"Wonderful," her mother said. "Where's Eliza, dear? Isn't she still posted to the *Ares*?"

"She's trying to save some of her leave to spend with her latest boyfriend, but she'll be down in a few days. We visit and talk so often aboard ship that she already knows everything I'll be talking about over the next couple of days. So when she comes down she won't have to hear it all over again and she can just tell you her news."

"News? About her boyfriend?"

"I didn't mean *special* news— just the things that have been happening to her since she was home last."

"Is she serious about this new boyfriend?"

"As far as I know, it's not marriage serious, if that's what you mean."

"Okay, we'll wait to hear her news from her. Are you hungry? We were just about to sit down to dinner."

"You know me, Mom. I'm always famished. That's especially true when I smell your home cooking. Is that lasagna I smell?"

"Yes. Marisa and I spent the afternoon preparing it. I know it's your favorite."

"Then what are we doing here in the entrance hall?" To Lt. Commander Ashraf, she said, "Lori, you're in for a treat. My mom makes the best lasagna in the world."

"It sure smells great, Admiral."

"Mom, just give us ten minutes to put our bags upstairs and wash up."

"Alright, dear. Lori can stay in Billy's old room."

"We'll be down as soon as possible," Jenetta said as she picked up her suitcase and led the way upstairs.

As Jenetta and Lt. Commander Ashraf entered the dining room some fifteen minutes later, Jenetta paused to look at the family photos on the wall there. Many of the images had been replaced since her last visit. Billy was now a Captain, Richie was a Commander, and Andy, Jimmy, Christa, and Eliza were all Lt. Commanders. There was a recent photo of her father on the bridge of his new command and a copy of the official picture of four-star Admiral Jenetta Carver that hung alongside that of Admiral Moore in every captain's briefing room of every ship in the Second Fleet and in every administrative office in Regions Two and Three. Pictures of Richie with Marisa and Billy with Regina on their respective wedding days had been added to the family photos since Jenetta's last visit home. She wished she had been able to attend at least one of their weddings, but she had been far away in Region Two on both occasions.

"Come on, girls," Annette Carver said as she entered the dining area carrying a large baking dish of steaming lasagna and added it to a table already overflowing with food items, "take your seats. Everything is ready."

As they settled into their chairs, Marisa entered carrying a carafe of chilled wine and an insulated pot of coffee. After placing them on the table, she joined the others. A brief prayer of thanks for the food was spoken by Jenetta's mom before the food plates were passed around the table so everyone could take what they pleased.

It was amazing that anyone found time to chew their food because the conversations never stopped throughout the entire meal, but even Jenetta got her fill of the delicious home-cooked cuisine. Over coffee, the conversations turned to ship deployments.

"Jen," Marisa asked, "is Richie's ship going to be coming home soon?"

"The *San Francisco* is part of the First Fleet, so I'm not included in discussions regarding its deployment. I *can* say that the GA has expanded so much that we need many more ships in the new territory. But— with the situation worsening on the Clidepp border, it seems likely that some ships will be recalled from patrol in what we used to call the Frontier Zone to assist with interdiction efforts in the Clidepp border sectors. Perhaps the *San Francisco* will be one of them. Of course, that doesn't mean that he'll be able to come home anytime soon. The *San Francisco* is pre-Dakinium, so travel time to the Clidepp border from Earth is well over a year. Fortunately, the new DS ship transports cut that to just a couple of months, and they can carry up to four destroyers at one time, so they can zip around GA space, pick up the older ships, and deliver them to where they're needed.

"I understand what you're going through, Marisa. I haven't seen Hugh in years. He's deployed here in Region One aboard the *Bonn*, while I'm posted thousands of light-years away in Region Two. He can't get any time off right now so I don't even expect to see him while I'm here. We have to content ourselves with frequent vidMails. Say, how would you like a vacation from this cold weather?"

"Vacation?"

"Well, sort of. I've been trying to talk mom into visiting our estate on Obotymot for some time. I suspect she doesn't want to go because she'd be alone among a race of giants."

"Giants? You mean the Nordakians?"

"Yes. At her height of about a hundred fifty-five centimeters, mom would definitely be unique. As you probably know, Nordakian females are typically over a hundred eighty-three centimeters, and males range from two hundred fourteen to two hundred forty-four."

"I think I'd feel just as much out of place. I'm only a hundred sixty-eight centimeters."

"It's not that I'm afraid or anything, dear," Annette said. "I just don't think I'd feel comfortable among people who are all more than thirty centimeters taller."

"At least you wouldn't have to worry about hitting your head on doorways," Jenetta said with a chuckle. "I told you of our experiences dealing with the Arrosians and the Selaxians. Momma, as part of the family Carver, and the Azula-Mum at that, I can promise you that no one on our estate, or anywhere else on Obotymot or Nordakia, would denigrate you in any way for your size or coloration. In fact, I'm sure that once you arrive they'll alter their coloration to match yours so as to make you feel more comfortable and welcome. That's the kind of people they are."

"It *would* be nice to get away from this cold weather for a while," Marisa said. "What's the weather like on Obotymot?"

"It's pretty much like Earth in that it depends where on the planet you're situated. At any time of the year, you can find blistering heat waves and formidable snowstorms, but our estate has about the best year-round climate you're likely to find on the planet. We own most of an entire peninsula in a wonderfully temperate area, which is why it was selected as the place for the royal family to stay when visiting Obotymot. Of course, the king and queen have never actually traveled there, so the palace has been empty since its construction, with just a staff of servants to maintain it. Their job has been to keep it so pristine that it would be ready for royal occupancy with just one day's notice. In summer, the estate enjoys mild-to-warm breezes throughout the entire day. In winter, they have slightly cooler weather at night, with daytime highs around twenty-six Celsius. I've been told that some of the most magnificent vistas on the planet can be found on our estate."

"And the staff still keeps it ready for immediate occupancy now that *you* own it?" Annette asked.

"Yes. It's their home also, although the only one occupying quarters outside of the servant wing is my chamberlain. The palace is the focus for all the business functions of the estate. From the reports I've received, agriculture on our lands, and indeed the entire planet, has been steadily improving each year. My chamberlain believes the estate should turn a tidy profit this year for the first time since the meteor strike that devastated life on the planet so long ago. I'd love for you to visit the estate and stay there as long as you wish. My magnificent quarters on Quesann was fashioned after the palace on Obotymot, so it must be beautiful."

"I just don't think I'd be comfortable living somewhere where they speak a different language," Annette said.

"Mom, that's part of the fun. You get to learn a new language. And because our family originates on Earth, my chamberlain has had the staff studying Amer for years. According to him, they've become bilingual and quite profici-ent because two days each week they are limited to speaking only in Amer. For years, the royal family has been working to convince the citizens that knowing Amer will help their people tremendously as their involvement in galactic com-merce increases. Every school on Nordakia now requires that students speak Amer proficiently by their fifth year and most speak well enough to carry on a basic conversation by the time they enroll for their first year. Language is not the barrier it once was when the priesthood actively worked to isolate the planet. Besides, you can always carry a small translation device if you wish."

"Well, that relieves a little of my apprehension."

"If you're unhappy there, you can come back on the next passenger ship. There are weekly departures for Earth and other planets. You're a bit isolated here on the base, but if you were to visit the commerce centers and space stations on the planet, you'd be amazed at the number of Nordakian citizens you'd see, as well as numerous other species."

"I see them on the news all the time, dear. We're not *that* isolated here."

Jenetta chuckled. "Okay, I never have time to watch the news, and I don't trust the accuracy of ninety-nine percent of the reporting anyway, so I was forgetting that it does offer a lot of exposure to other cultures."

"If we went," Marisa asked, "how long would we really have to stay?"

"Only as long as you wished. There's no minimum or maximum. Perhaps you'd decide you like it so much that you'd want to sell the home here and move to Obotymot permanently. The Nordakian people are amazing. I know you'll come to love their culture as much as I do."

"I don't think I'd ever want to sell our home here and move there permanently," Annette said.

"You don't have to. It's entirely up to you and Dad. But if you wished to do that, there's always a place there for you. And you could have your friends visit whenever you wanted, for as long as you wanted. The palace is enormous and can house hundreds of people without being crowded."

"I have to think on this for a while," Annette said. "Packing up and leaving home for an extended stay on another planet is not something I feel comfortable with."

"I understand. Packing up and moving is something I've become quite used to since joining Space Command, but you've spent every night in this same house for fifty years. Perhaps it's time for a temporary change of address."

"After listening to you talk about the planet and the people," Marisa said," I'm beginning to warm to the idea. I'm certainly not ready to commit to a permanent move, but it might be nice to visit Obotymot."

"There's no pressure, Marisa," Jenetta said. "The palace is there and available for the use of any member of the Family Carver if and when they want to go. If you decide to visit it before I leave, I can offer you passage on the *Ares*. It will cut as much as a month off your travel time. And it will give me an excuse to visit the estate. I'm sure you know I've never been there. It would be nice to look over the estate and make sure everyone is being treated well by the chamberlain and other people charged with administration and security."

"How long will you be here?"

"I've scheduled three weeks' leave. Tomorrow I have to meet with the Admiralty Board, but then I should be free until it's time to return to Region Two. If you decide you want to go to Obotymot, we can leave before the end of my stay here and spend the time there instead."

"I'm thinking I'd like to go since Richie isn't expected home anytime soon, but let me sleep on it."

Early the following morning, Jenetta and Lt. Commander Ashraf climbed aboard the *Ares* shuttle for Jenetta's appointment with the Admiralty Board. The trip was uneventful and quiet. Lori was thinking about her trip later that day to her ancestral home on Symi Island in the Aegean Sea where she would spend a week, while Jenetta was planning how she should present certain requests to the Board. She expected to meet some resistance with at least one request—nay demand— she felt was imperative to her remaining in command in Region Two. She didn't like to make peremptory demands, but she was prepared to stand firm on this occasion.

Chapter Three
~ February 26th, 2286 ~

Newsies tried to crowd around Jenetta and Lt. Commander Ashraf as they walked from the oh-gee vehicle to the steps of the building where the Admiralty Board conducted its sessions. She chastised herself for not having foreseen their possible presence and had the driver take them to the underground entrance. There were no newsies on Quesann, so the memories of how annoying they could be had dimmed. Fortunately, the newsies backed off as soon as Cayla and Tayna bared their fangs and growled menacingly. Jenetta usually calmed them, but she allowed them to express their uneasiness on this occasion and would only intercede if her girls actually moved to attack someone. The newsies were rightly fearful and backed off ten paces, then shouted out their questions from there. Jenetta had other things on her mind and ignored them.

Rather than remaining in the waiting area outside the meeting hall until told she might go in, Jenetta simply walked past the surprised clerk and led her entourage inside. Lori took a seat behind the chair where visiting admirals always sat at the large table while Jenetta went directly to the office hallway door from which the admirals would emerge prior to the meeting. She had told her girls to stay with Lori, so they were peacefully sitting next to the chair she would occupy. She didn't have long to wait and she greeted each admiral as he or she entered the hall. She knew them all on a personal level, including Admiral Yuthkotl, whom she had met years ago when she was inducted into the Nordakian Space Force and again when she received the Nordakian Tawroole Medal of Valor.

Admiral Moore was the last to enter, and he and Jenetta chatted for a few minutes before it was time to start the meeting. The gallery was empty today, but the chairs behind the admirals were filled with their clerks and aides.

After a few of the formalities, such as the reading of the minutes, were completed, Admiral Moore said," We're delighted today to welcome Admiral Jenetta Carver as a visiting guest to this session. Welcome, Jenetta."

"Thank you, Richard. I'm happy to be here with all of you today."

"You mentioned that you had two issues to discuss. You have the floor."

"Thank you. First, I must mention that while on my way to Earth from Dakistee, I received a message from Admiral Poole in which he informed me that the scout-destroyer *Yenisei* was overdue and not responding to communication. Admiral Poole dispatched the only two ships within two hundred light-years of the *Yenisei*'s last reported position with orders to begin a search as soon as they arrived. Since the *Yenisei* is Dakinium-sheathed, the loss of all radio contact without warning is most distressing. The last message we received was that the *Yenisei* had DeTected three ships and was preparing to investigate."

"Do you suspect the loss of radio contact might be owed to an attack on the ship?" Admiral Moore asked.

"I fear that might be the case. I know you've been giving us every ship you possibly could, and I'm grateful. I'm not being critical of your efforts when I say that even with the Region Two Territorial Guard formed from the former Milori Empire forces, we can't begin to provide adequate coverage in an area of space that is four times the size of Region One. The *Yenisei* was out on standard patrol near the Hudeerac and Ruwalchu borders. That there were only two other Space Command vessels within two hundred light-years of the *Yenisei's* last reported position might give you some idea of what we're up against out there. If the loss of communications is the result of an attack, I can't begin to guess who might be responsible."

"We do understand your situation and will continue to give you every ship and resource we can," Admiral Platt said. "We hope the *Yenisei* and his crew are safe."

"Thank you. I'll keep you up to date with whatever new information becomes available just as soon as I learn it. My second issue today is one that I've been thinking about for some time. I'm sure you understand how overwhelmed I am with the job of governing both Regions Two and Three. The people I do have are doing an incredible job, but I need someone with special skills. I want to bring Admiral Brian Holt to Quesann to work with me."

"Brian?" Admiral Moore said with surprise. "He's near retirement age. We've been discussing bringing him here to finish out his career."

"I think everyone at this table knows that Brian doesn't exactly covet a post here at Supreme Headquarters."

Admiral Moore chuckled. "Yes, we're aware of his position on that."

"However, I think he might like to join me at Quesann, and I know I could use his talents there."

"You haven't addressed this possibility with him?"

"No. I felt I should discuss it with the Board first. Further, if you agree and he wishes to join me in trying to tame Regions Two and Three, I'd like to see him advanced in rank to Vice-Admiral."

"We've offered him advancement to Vice-Admiral if he'd join this Board."

"Quesann is a long way from Earth, politicians, and newsies."

"Uh, not so far as you might think," Admiral Moore said.

"What do you mean?"

"Just that for some time the GA Senate has been discussing the possibility of moving the government to Quesann. Naturally, we'd have to provide a press pool with local accommodations. And if the Senate goes to Quesann, Supreme Headquarters will have to go as well."

Jenetta remained quiet for a full minute as she looked at the admirals around the table. "I've wondered how long it would be before the Senate decided it should be more centrally located in GA space. Quesann has been center stage in Galactic Alliance space since we added Regions Two and Three. However, as evidenced by the issue of a missing warship, they have to understand that they would be giving up the margin of safety they enjoy here. I had that problem when merchants flooded into Stewart before the sectors were tamed."

"They understand, but they know that their lives couldn't possibly be in better hands with you protecting the planet and the Regions. None of this will happen immediately, of course. It will take time to construct the buildings and complexes for government, Supreme Headquarters, and residences for thousands of people."

"If Brian learns of this, he may refuse to come to Quesann."

"He already knows. He manages to keep pretty good tabs on what's going on here despite being ninety light-years away."

"Which is exactly why I need him on Quesann, and need him now. I'm hoping he'll agree to finish out his remaining years in Space Command while filling a position at Quesann."

"There may be more years available than you currently believe," Admiral Platt said.

"What do you mean?"

"Thanks mainly to your successes in battle against invading nations, our territory has grown far faster than our officer corps. Sometime this month the Senate will vote on a measure to increase the mandatory retirement age for Space Command officers to one hundred twenty-five. Ship posts will be increased to one hundred ten."

Jenetta chuckled. "I know a few officers who will be ecstatic over that change, including my father."

"Yes," Admiral Moore said. "With age spans now averaging one hundred forty and extending as long as one hundred eighty for some individuals, it was time for a change."

"So all of you on this Board will probably be coming to Quesann?"

"Not all," Admiral Platt said. "I'll be remaining on Earth. Quesann is too far distant for the Commander of the First Fleet to properly coordinate operations, especially given the current situation in the sectors along the Clidepp border."

"Once the move to Quesann is complete," Admiral Moore said to Jenetta, "you'll be expected to assume Evelyn's place on this board."

Jenetta was taken aback by this latest revelation, but she managed to respond with, "I'm sorry, but that's just not possible. My duties as Commander of the Second Fleet and Military Governor over Regions Two and Three consume every minute of my days."

"Once the Senate has moved to Quesann, they will take full responsibility for governance of all three regions. That will reduce your load considerably and allow you the time to participate as a member of this Board, just as Evelyn is able to do at present."

The changes that would take place with the GA Senate and Supreme Headquarters' move to Quesann, plus the extension of maximum retirement ages, had sent Jenetta's mind into overdrive. She needed time to consider things from all angles, so she simply nodded to this latest bit of information. She knew one thing for sure— she didn't savor the thought of becoming a member of the Admiralty Board. It appeared to be one more wedge being driven between her and possible ship command, although she had come to view that as a near impossibility for some time.

"Do you have anything else to present to the Board?" Admiral Moore asked.

"No, that was all. My weekly reports have included all other pertinent information."

"Very well. Then allow us to bring you up to date on several matters. The Flordaryn people are most appreciative that you freed them from the Tsgardi Kingdom, and they've requested member world status with the Galactic Alliance. They say they want to establish a cooperative sharing of technology now that they're a part of the GA."

"The Tsgardi vessels made by the Flordaryns are the most poorly made and most undependable in Galactic Alliance space."

"They claim to have made significant technological advancements, which they kept from the Tsgardi because they didn't wish to see them become more powerful. Their scientists and researchers continued to work under the very noses of the Tsgardi the entire time their race was enslaved, but new developments were never shared with their Tsgardi overlords, and the Tsgardi were too ignorant in scientific matters to know the difference. When you return to Quesann, we'd like you to deliver a delegation of political, scientific, and technical representatives to Flordarya and engage the Flordaryns in talks so we can better assess the situation and make specific recommendations to the GA Council."

"Of course, Richard."

"And lastly, we're going to construct new shipbuilding facilities around suitable planets near Quesann."

"To replace the Mars yard?"

"No, to supplement it. It will also require the creation of a foundry to produce Dakinium sheathing and other products."

"Until some other nation manages to develop Dakinium, that will be a major target for infiltration and attack."

"The responsibility for preventing infiltration will fall on the shoulders of Admiral Kanes and his intelligence section. You will only have to protect the foundry from direct attack."

"Unlike Earth's solar system, the Quesann system doesn't have a gas giant suitable for providing enormous quantities of hydrogen for fuel. Foundry operations will cost considerably more unless it can be situated in another system, one that does have a gas giant, but that would make defense substantially more difficult and spread our forces. Can't the Jupiter foundry continue to produce all Dakinium?"

"The foundry is running around the clock and still falling behind with demand. We must have an additional foundry if we're to step up ship and vital components production."

"Why can't we simply build another foundry at Jupiter?"

"With the GA Senate and Supreme Headquarters moving to Quesann, the planetary defense forces here will naturally be reduced, so the long-range plan is to have all Dakinium production take place in Region Two near the new heart of the GA. Expanded foundry facilities will be established near the new one once it reaches full production, and the foundry around Jupiter will be phased out. The exact location for the new foundries will be up to you and your scientific personnel."

"Yes, sir," Jenetta said, but her face clearly showed that she wasn't thrilled with the order. For a full minute there was complete silence around the table.

"On the positive side," Admiral Moore said, "The reduction of Earth defense forces means those ships can be reassigned to interdiction efforts, reducing the need to pull ships from other areas."

"With the Mars shipyard and Jupiter foundry still requiring protection, the cuts cannot be that significant."

"We estimate that we can free up ten ships."

"But those ships are among the oldest still in service. They never leave the solar system because they would be of little use in interdiction efforts these days. Look at the *Perry*. It barely survived that encounter with a Clidepp destroyer in the hands of untrained rebels. Granted, the Earth force isn't as aged as the *Perry*, but it's not even up to the modern standards of pre-Dakinium ships."

"Where possible, all Earth Force ships have been upgraded with the newer engine designs. Although the cost of sheathing them with Dakinium isn't economically feasible owed to their advanced age, they will have Light-487 speed capability."

"That will help, to be sure, but we're still talking about just a handful of ships. The rebellion brewing in the Clidepp Empire can't help but continue to increasingly spill over into our territory in future years. If we get pulled into that conflict and also have a new enemy attack in Region Two or Three, we'll be hard pressed to adequately defend our territory on two fronts."

"We can't properly address potential conflicts until they actually occur," Admiral Platt said. "We can only do our best to be prepared for any contingency. Moving Supreme Headquarters and the GA Senate is a logical move and can't be altered or postponed because of actions that might— or might not— occur."

"The GA Senate has made a decision to move the government center to Quesann," Admiral Moore said, "and it's our job to carry out their plan. Let's move on now. The next topic concerning Regions Two and Three is the creation of new space stations. Our planners and engineers have reached agreement that bases built inside asteroids offer the greatest safety by a wide margin. As shown at Stewart, they are far easier to defend than the space stations we built before the dangers from criminals and outside invaders became so prevalent. Higgins was very nearly destroyed by a Raider attack, where Stewart, with a much smaller protection fleet, suffered almost no damage and no loss of life. The asteroid form even beat out a suggested plan for a station covered in Dakinium plating because it could allow for the protection of hundreds of ships if we have a little advance notice of an impending attack."

"I figured the asteroid form might be chosen," Jenetta said, "so I've had my captains checking out asteroids during their patrols. We already have fourteen possible choices that warrant closer examination if the decision favored asteroid bases."

"Excellent. Have that information sent to the Marine's Corps of Engineers so they can begin their analysis of those asteroids. With that we can move onto other new business."

"There is an issue that hasn't been concluded," Jenetta said. "I asked if I might invite Admiral Holt to join me at Quesann. We got sidetracked onto other issues."

Admiral Moore looked around the table at the other admirals before saying, "I have no problem with it if a majority of this Board agrees and Brian wishes to go. All in favor of posting Admiral Brian Holt to Admiral Carver's staff at Quesann to fill a new position of Deputy Military Governor of Regions Two and Three with promotion to Vice-Admiral, signify by raising your hand."

Everyone at the table raised their hand without hesitation. Admiral Moore said, "The motion carries unanimously, subject to his acceptance of the position."

"Thank you," Jenetta said, then smiled as she looked around the table and made eye contact with the members of the Admiralty Board. "I'll stop at Higgins on my way back to Quesann and offer Brian the position. I feel confident he'll want to join me, so you might want to begin considering replacements for his current position."

"We'll do that. Is there anything else you need to discuss with the Board, Jen?"

"That's about it, Richard. Thank you for your indulgences today."

"Okay, let's continue with our regular business."

Jenetta sat and listened quietly through the rest of the session, but her mind was elsewhere. Among other things, she was thinking about how she would ask Brian Holt to give up command of his base and join her at Quesann.

When the morning session ended, Jenetta and Lt. Commander Ashraf joined the Admirals and their aides for lunch in their dining room. Jenetta sat at the large table reserved exclusively for flag and general officers, while Lori sat at one of the tables reserved for commissioned officers.

In the informal and relaxed environment, Jenetta related information about the situation at Quesann that she would never put into official correspondence. At one point, Admiral

Platt said, "Tell us about Christa, Jen. Is she completely well?"

Jenetta smiled and looked briefly at the four members of the Board whom she knew were aware of Project Springboard. She had no idea whether Brian Holt had informed any of the members that he had used the capabilities of that project for Christa's return to duty. Jenetta couldn't see any indication in their expressions that they knew, so she decided to assume they didn't. "Yes, thank you. Her wounds are completely healed. She couldn't wait to return to work so she could wrap up her business on Dakistee and get back into space."

"We need her talents on Dakistee right now," Admiral Moore said. "The discovery and awakening of the ancient Dakistee people has been like opening a Pandora's box. First, the archeological people have been screaming their heads off. You would have thought they'd be ecstatic to have an enormous reservoir of firsthand information about the distant past fall into their laps. I suppose they may have felt that way at first, but they'd also come to believe that Dakistee was *their* planet. They had expected to spend their lives uncovering the ruins of an ancient civilization. It's become obvious that the Dakistee people will not sit idly by as scientists slowly peel back the layers of time. They want their planet returned to their control as quickly as possible. Personally, I don't blame them, but they have to understand that we must dismantle forces set in motion on what we believed was an uninhabited planet. When we told the Archeological Expedition Headquarters on Anthius that they would have to return everything removed from the planet, they used their influence to have every member of the Galactic Alliance Senate demand we rescind our ruling. I informed the GA Council that we were only proceeding according to the laws passed by the Senate that clearly specify our response to such situations. I told them that if they wished us to behave differently, it was up to them to rewrite the laws. They've been arguing about the affected statutes ever since.

"Second, the awakened Dakistee people at Loudescott— or Camtolla, as they're calling the location now since that was its name in ancient times— aren't waiting for us to peacefully retire from the planet. They've formed a new pro tem government and begun pushing the scientists out of the way so they can begin awakening the still-sleeping citizens in other buried facilities.

"Third, the Dakistians aren't only pushing to get exclusive access to the locations identified as underground stasis facilities. Our intelligence people tell us that they are also looking for other buried facilities. As yet we don't know what they're searching for, and they haven't been forthright with information. We're hoping that Lt. Commander Carver's return to the planet might help us learn what they're seeking. They acknowledge that they owe her much for her role in awakening them and feel a unique kinship towards her since she was born on Dakistee."

"Their search must have something to do with gaining independence," Jenetta said, "since the stasis pods contain the brightest minds on the planet and the young people they'll need for reproductive purposes once a cure for their sterility is found."

"Yes, we're assuming they're trying to locate the wealth of the planet— probably precious gems and minerals since manufactured currency would be worthless," Admiral Bradlee said.

"By rights, it belongs to them, so we can't fault their actions," Admiral Hillaire said.

"The question is: Why the emphasis on recovery right now?" Admiral Plimley said. "No one is allowed to transport anything off the planet. It's not like it's going to be stolen from them if they don't find it first."

"As Jen said, it must have something to do with making themselves independent of the GA," Admiral Woo said. "Knowing the wealth is safely buried somewhere isn't the same as having it available for purchases."

"What sort of purchases, Lon?" Admiral Yuthkotl asked.

"That's the big question," Admiral Woo said. "I'd bet it has something to do with their number one problem— the sterility issue."

Following lunch, Jenetta said her good-byes and headed for the base's shuttle port with Lt. Commander Ashraf. As Jenetta boarded a shuttle with her pets for the trip back to the Potomac base, Lori boarded a shuttle for a flight to the Mediterranean island home of her family.

Chapter Four
~ February 26th, 2286 ~

"Today's meeting will come to order," Chairman Glads-worth said as he pounded the decorative gravel once on the equally ornamental sounding-block. He waited until the meeting hall was silent and all council members were seated and looking at him before he added, "We shall dispense with the reading of the minutes today because we have a visitor who is not authorized to hear Upper Council business. I welcome the chairperson of the Lower Council, Arthur Stephen Strauss. You have the floor, Mr. Chairman."

"Thank you, sir. And thank you to the council for allowing me to come before you today on such short notice. I have good news and I believed you would want to hear it as soon as possible. For four decades, this organization has lavished almost unlimited funds on a special project. I'm here to tell you today that the project is about to begin returning dividends on those expenditures."

"You're referring to the Age Prolongation Procedure?" Council member Whitely asked.

"Yes, sir," Strauss said to one of the oldest members of the council. For that matter, there wasn't a single member younger than one hundred forty. The advanced ages of the council members were probably most responsible for their continued monetary support of Arneu's project.

"As you all know, the formulas had just been proven successful when Ensign Jenetta Carver managed to destroy Raider-One, wiping out the development lab and killing all of the research scientists. The loss of the scientists alone far exceeded the value of the station and the other eighteen thousand employees. That fool Arneu had refused to turn over the formulas until they were proven, so we lost everything and had to start over. It's taken him almost two additional decades to recreate the lost work, but we once again have proven formulas, *and* they have been turned over to our Central Laboratories this time. Plus, we have an additional enhancement. We can now reverse the aging process completely."

"You say the formulas have been proven?" Gladsworth asked. "Is that definite?"

"Anyone who doubts the success of the procedures need only look at an image of Admiral Jenetta Carver or one of her clones, all of whom appear the same as the day she graduated from the NHSA in 2256. The ability of her body to heal almost any injury is legendary in Space Command. As you know, one of our people recently went against orders and tried to assassinate one of Carver's clones. He shot her three times at close range with a lattice weapon as she shot him with a laser. He died almost instantly while she survived her injuries and has already returned to active duty."

"But Carver was altered with the old formulas, the ones that were lost with Raider-One," Whitely said.

"The individual in charge of the project, Mikel Arneu, has used the new formulas on himself to change his sex and return his body to age twenty-three. That certainly indicates his confidence in the procedures. He, or rather she, is as healthy as a person can be and damned attractive to boot. I propose a return to our original plan of producing sex slaves for our brothels for a one-year test period. If no complications arise, we could then offer the DNA Manipulation procedures to anyone who has the trillion credits to buy it, but I further recommend that we alter our original plan and not offer the Age Prolongation procedure to anyone outside of senior company personnel."

"What's your reasoning behind that?" Gladsworth asked. "That procedure could make us an additional trillion on each sale."

"If we offer the Age Regression procedure and the DNA Manipulation processes, we'll still make those trillions. Then the patients will begin to age normally again. In ten or twenty years they'll be back to undergo the procedure again. *But* if we sell the Age Prolongation procedure, we've lost those trillions for possibly thousands of years. I suggest we reserve that one for ourselves."

"Good thinking, Strauss," Gladsworth said. "We can keep milking their vanity forever."

"I question the price," Whitely said. "If we get too greedy, we'll be limiting our market to just a few dozen people. Instead of a trillion credits for the procedures, I think we should establish a price of say ten billion credits. That way we'll have tens of thousands of potential customers.

"Yes, that makes sense," Gladsworth said. "All in favor of only charging ten billion for the two procedures, signal by raising your hand."

Everyone at the table raised his or her hand except Strauss, who didn't have the right to vote at an Upper Council meeting.

"The motion passes. Er, Strauss?"

"Sir?"

"You said that Arneu changed his sex?"

"Yes, sir. He's now a twenty-three-year-old female. And since he's used the Age Prolongation procedure on himself, or rather herself, she should live for possibly another five thousand years. At least that was the original projection for Admiral Carver."

"I didn't realize the DNA Manipulation procedure could be used just to alter *sex*," Whitely said. "We could market that process alone and clean up. We wouldn't be adversely affecting the size of the general population if we didn't combine it with the other procedures. The sex change clinics are always busy these days and the final result is not a true gender change. It's more or less cosmetic. We could easily charge a hundred times the sex-change rate for a full genetic conversion."

The other council members began talking among themselves about the merits of offering single-procedure packages until Gladsworth pounded the gavel.

"There will be plenty of time to discuss alternate possibilities later. The issue nearest and dearest to any of us here should be the use of the procedures on ourselves. I would love to be twenty-three again and have the energy of a youthful body."

"Uh, there's a small— glitch, sir," Strauss said. "Arneu says that the Age Regression procedure only works on women. That's why he changed his sex. It was necessary if he was to become twenty-three again."

"And you can't change back to male afterwards?"

"Yes, you can, but the process of changing sex is quite painful according to Arneu, and it takes a full year to complete just the basic changes. That's allegedly the reason she's procrastinated beginning the procedure to become a male again. Also, I think she likes her new form."

"That doesn't mean that everyone would prefer to remain a woman. And we could charge outsiders for every change."

"But if you are already female," Council member Paula Sorreto asked, "you wouldn't have to change to male first. Is that correct?"

"Yes, ma'am. The process requires you be female when the Age Regression procedure is performed. It has something to do with the percentage of male and female hormones in the body. There's no need to alter your body in preparation for the process if you are already female."

"Well, that's okay," Gladsworth said. "You'd only have to go through the Age Regression procedure once if you then go through the Age Prolongation process."

"What if we opt to only undergo the Age Prolongation procedure?" Whitely asked.

"At your age, sir, it would probably only extend your life by forty years at most, and repeated application wouldn't extend it further. The age at the time the process is first administered makes all the difference."

"Well, it seems that we all have a great deal to think about. That's all, Strauss. Thank you for coming in. And congratulations on your success with this issue. It's been a long time in coming, but it's worth every credit we've expended. And it clears the slate of your Dakistee blunder."

"Yes, sir. Thank you, sir."

* * *

Chairman Strauss leaned back in his sumptuous chair and stared out the full wall of glass in the penthouse apartment provided for his use by the corporation. An orange sun was setting over distant mountains that wore caps of white below a cloudless sky. Far below his domicile the 'little' people were struggling to eke out a daily living in the timeless tradition of the less affluent. Strauss had never had a moment's remorse about the role he played in the misery and suffering of so many. When he stood at the window and looked down at the tiny dark shapes moving in endless streams of traffic, he always thought of them as insignificant insects. If an action he took or was responsible for killed a few, a few hundred, or a few thousand, it didn't lead to any sleepless nights. His only concern was that their deaths not make his life or job any more complicated or difficult.

Strauss hadn't believed Ravenau for a second when she spun that lie about not having plans to kill Carver when she visited the military quarters on Dakistee, but he couldn't harm her until he had the formulas. Now he could dispose of her at any time, but killing her would be a waste of a beautiful body. Perhaps he should simply have her mind wiped and put her into one of the corporation's brothels where she would continue to produce income for hundreds, or maybe thousands, of years. Or perhaps he should let her live and serve the corporation in some more useful capacity. He couldn't deny that she had succeeded in providing a product that would make hundreds of trillions for the corporation in the years ahead, so the question was whether or not that was enough to forgive her past transgressions. Should he emulate the clemency exhibited by the Upper Council, who had just forgiven Strauss for the costs associated with the bollixed operation on Dakistee, even though the problems were beyond his control, or should he follow his instincts and condemn Ravenau to a life of sexual adulteration and degradation? He decided he should sleep on it some more.

A handsome face and tall, slim body meant that Strauss had no real desire to make use of the DNA Manipulation process for the sake of appearance, but the side benefits might be desirable. Having a body that repaired itself ten times faster than ordinary humans, even those with surgical nano-bots in their bodies, was surely an enviable attribute. That process and the Age Prolongation process would be the extent of his treatments. Now in his early seventies, he was just middle-aged and had the distinguished appearance of a wealthy power broker, so he certainly wasn't going to spend a year in pain just to change his sex so he could look thirty or forty years younger as Ravenau had, but he had no doubt that every one of the Upper Council members would soon begin the changes.

After ordering a drink from his automated servant, Strauss relaxed until the three fingers of bonded scotch whiskey was poured and delivered. He never drank until his business for the day was over, and even then he strictly maintained a limit of two. When he had drunk more than that in his younger years, he had tended to desire female companionship and sometimes gotten foolish and talked too much, leaving himself open to possible blackmail. He'd always regretted it in the morning and had finally outgrown the behavior after a woman had been dumb enough to try using his loose talk to her advantage. She'd disappeared very soon thereafter and was never heard from again. He couldn't even remember which whore palace she had been sent to after her mind was wiped.

After his second drink, Strauss walked to the bedroom and flopped onto his bed. His dinner, untouched, grew cold on his dining room table and eventually went into the disposal unit.

* * *

Nicole Ravenau stretched out languidly as she relaxed on the sofa in her quarters, an excellent bottle of wine from the Sebastian Colony chilling in a wine bucket on the side table. The DNA Manipulation formula she'd subjected herself to while at Raider-One had left her almost impervious to the effects of alcohol, and the most recent application, the one that changed her sex, hadn't altered her tolerance. Where in the far distant past she had sometimes used alcohol to intentionally dull her memory, that was no longer possible. Now she imbibed only in social situations or when she had acquired a particularly excellent vintage. On this occasion she was celebrating with a bottle of the priciest wine available in the online catalog. She had delivered the formulas to the Raider Central Labs and was still alive. What's more, she was still free. That was more than she had expected following her meeting with Strauss.

Of course, Strauss could still come after her, but every day that didn't happen lessened the chances that it would. Perhaps he had decided she still had enough value to the corporation as an administrator that he should keep her around— at least for now.

Ravenau was currently attired in the slinkiest lingerie she owned. She was trying to fully adapt to her gender change, and lingerie was the most pleasant aspect. She still hadn't been able to wrap her head around engaging in sex with a male, though. She had all the right equipment now, and there was no lack of admirers who would love to bed her, but more than sixty years of living as a male had left her with certain— prejudices. She had three times tried sex with female partners since her gender change, but it just wasn't the same as when she had been a male, and each encounter had left her more unsatisfied. She was alone at present and wasn't expecting company, so she was trying to drown her current sexual frustration in a fine wine.

Suddenly Ravenau sat up straight, her eyes wide. Then a huge smile played across her face. Perhaps it was the wine or perhaps it was just her baser instincts, but she had been struck by an idea, nay an epiphany, on how to settle the issue with Strauss once and for all and at the same time resolve several other longstanding issues.

* * *

"Sir," the controller at a Flordarya Planetary Defense Distant DeTect Grid console said to the lead controller via his com headset, "I'm getting some strange readings on the grid."

"What kind of strange readings?" Supervisor Caulliffyr asked.

"The grid indicates that there are five ships headed inbound towards the planet, but we're not expecting any arrivals this morning."

"Five?"

"Yes, sir."

"What kind of ships? Passenger or freighters?"

"Uh, the equipment puts them at about small passenger ship size, but…"

"But what, Azeallum?"

"Uh, there're no AutoTect signals."

"Do you think it's a ghost reading?"

"Negative, it's too strong. They're coming in slow and in tight formation. If I was going to guess, I would say it's five warships about the size of destroyers. They're moving like a task force."

"And no AutoTect?"

"That's correct, sir."

"I'm coming over."

Caulliffyr rose from his chair and walked to the steps that led to the lower level of the large room where the controllers who monitored the planetary DeTect grid were located. When he reached the console where Azeallum sat, he peered over his shoulder.

"Here's the cluster," Azeallum said, pointing to a spot on the screen. "As you can see, there's no indication that it might be a ghost reflection. It's hard and steady."

"Yeah," Caulliffyr agreed. "I wonder if they can be Space Command?"

"Space Command ships always announce their presence long before we can see them, and besides, they always use AutoTect."

"Not if they're on a mission. Since there's five of them, that could be the reason for not using AutoTect."

"But they'd certainly notify us if they were approaching the planet."

"They should, but they don't have to."

"Space Command always plays it by the book, sir. They'd notify us if they were coming here."

"So who do *you* think it is?"

"I don't know, sir, and that's what bothers me."

"Admiral Carver established a Territorial Guard unit composed of former Milori military units."

"But everything I've heard says they follow the Space Command rulebook as stringently as Space Command."

"It has to be one of them. There's nobody else operating warships in GA Region Two."

"Yes, sir. There's not supposed to be anyone else operating warships in GA Region Two. But if it was someone else, why would they be moving so slow?"

"I have to report this to the Commander. Continue monitoring them and advise me immediately of any changes."

"Yes, sir. Will do."

Chapter Five

~ February 27th, 2286 ~

With her Admiralty Board business concluded, Jenetta settled comfortably into vacation mode. Repeated requests for personal appearances from recruitment officials were declined without discussion, and she did her best to put aside thoughts of the *Yenisei* until new information became available. Jenetta hadn't been home in years and wasn't going to squander the opportunity to enjoy the company of available family. As much as she loved spending every moment she could with her mom, she relished the time she now had with Marisa. The numerous vidMails they had exchanged over the years were a poor substitute for direct contact where you could say what you felt without worrying that someone might be eavesdropping on the communication. She didn't initiate any calls to schoolmates or old friends, but she didn't refuse them either. She merely tried to limit them to a reasonable conversation length and put off all requests for visits.

"Marisa and I have reached a consensus," Annette announced to Jenetta one morning at breakfast.

"A consensus on what?" Jenetta asked after she had finished chewing and then swallowed the piece of pancake she had pushed into her mouth ten seconds earlier.

"Obotymot."

"What about Obotymot?"

"We've decided to travel there for a brief visit."

"Wonderful. I think you'll enjoy the trip. Do you want to go when I leave here or travel independently?"

"We might as well go with you. It appears that neither daddy nor Richie will be home for at least a year, so we want to go now. And this way you can show us around."

"I've never been to the estate."

"But you've been to the planet, right?"

"Not since '67. I'm happy to say that the face of the planet has changed dramatically since then. When I was there, the air was full of the dust and dirt kicked up from the meteor strike. The vegetation had died from lack of sunlight and the erosion of the soil was making the situation worse. The surface never got brighter than a sort of twilight, even at high noon. It took years of low-altitude scrubbing with air filtering and moisture release to clear the air, and then more years to get crops growing again."

"Then this will be your chance to see it as well," Marisa said. "The more I think about it, the more excited I become. What's the weather like on the estate right now?"

"From the reports, I would say our estate lands are like central California. It never gets bone-freezing cold like it does here at the Potomac base, but you might see a little snow in winter, and it never gets burning hot in summer like it does in parts of Arizona. The temperate weather, combined with a good average rainfall and dozens of enormous fresh-water reservoirs for irrigation in the event of a slight drought, makes it ideal for crop production. Now that the atmosphere is clearing, the farms have become productive again, with expectations that crop yields will continue to improve in coming years as the topsoil is replaced and improved. The tenant farmers have all returned over recent years and I expect we'll find a number of active communities on the peninsula."

"It sounds lovely," Annette said. "I admit that I've been warming to the idea a little more each year. I just didn't want to go there alone and be the only human among an alien culture."

"You should have said something, Mother," Marisa said. "I would have gone with you so you didn't feel alone."

"So, it's decided," Jenetta said, "we'll all go to the family estate on Obotymot. Do you need to do some shopping before we go?"

"Are you kidding?" Marisa said. "Of course we need to do some shopping before we go. We'll need new clothes suitable for the climate and, of course, a few new pairs of shoes."

"Okay, but let's not go overboard. I have no idea what the fashions are like there at present. Besides, there's a dressmaker on staff at the palace. She'll be able to assist with tailoring clothes we purchase on the planet or perhaps even prepare new clothing."

* * *

A week later, the *Ares* left Earth orbit. Its primary destination was Higgins Space Station, but it would make a quick side trip to Obotymot on the way. Two civilian guests, members of the Nordakian Royal Family Carver, had come aboard for the trip and been assigned quarters on the VIP deck.

The *Ares* reached Obotymot in just sixty-four GST hours. After establishing a stable orbit around the planet, Admiral Carver and her two guests boarded a shuttle for the ride down to the surface. Since this was a vacation, Lt. Commander Ashraf remained aboard the ship and would monitor communications in case something of importance arrived, but a large security team accompanied Jenetta. Planetary sub-orbit traffic control immediately cleared a route to the royal palace on the Gavistee peninsula, and the shuttle landed at the pad on the palace grounds within thirty minutes. Three oh-gee limos were waiting to accept the guests, cats, and security team for the short ride to the main house. They could easily have walked, but the luggage had to be ferried there anyway.

"Oh, Jen, this is soooo beautiful," Annette Carver said to her daughter as they pulled up in front of the palace.

"The palace or the countryside?"

"Both. Everything. It's all so grand. I can't believe it's all yours."

"Ours, Momma. It's the official estate of the Family Carver. Uh, don't show surprise by what happens next."

"What's going to happen next?"

"You'll see," Jenetta said as the vehicle came to a halt and someone opened the door.

Jenetta led the way, being the Azula. The entire palace staff, all of whom had already adopted Jenetta's skin color, had turned out to greet them. As Jenetta stepped from the vehicle, all but one of the entire staff of males dropped to one knee and bowed their heads, while the women bowed their heads and remained staring down at the ground.

"What are they doing?" her mother whispered.

"Showing their respect," Jenetta whispered back. "I'll explain later."

A very dignified Nordakian, whom Jenetta instantly recognized as her chamberlain, stepped forward and then dropped to one knee and stared at the ground.

"Chamberlain Yaghutol, please raise your head and stand up," Jenetta said.

The Nordakian rose and smiled. "Greetings, My Lady. It's wonderful to finally be able to welcome you home."

"Thank you, Chamberlain. I'm happy to be here. The palace and grounds look magnificent. You've done a marvelous job here."

"Thank you, My Lady. It's been my honor to represent you during your absence."

Raising her voice to address the servants, Jenetta said, "Thank you for this wonderful greeting. I'm delighted to be here among you at last. The reports I've received from Chamberlain Yaghutol have kept me informed of the progress here, and I know how hard you've all worked to restore the palace and grounds following the terrible event that devastated our planet, and then to maintain them since being presented to me by King Tpalsh and Queen Ckuhah. Although I will only be here for a week on this trip, my mother and the wife of one of my brothers will be staying for an extended visit. I recognize all of you from the files that have been sent to me, and I look forward to getting to know each of you on a personal basis."

"May I escort you inside, My Lady?" the chamberlain asked.

"Yes. I'm anxious to see the palace. Perhaps you could give us a tour."

"Of course, My Lady," he said. Gesturing towards the front entrance, he added, "Please come this way."

The palace tour lasted for hours, and they didn't enter even a quarter of the rooms. Since it had been constructed to serve as the main residence of the King and Queen of Nordakia when they were on Obotymot, the palace was as ostentatious as it was enormous. The royal court always traveled with the king and queen, so the palace was built to accommodate many hundreds of guests in spacious suites, all with the requisite private rooms for handmaidens. Separate suites for up to a thousand staff members were available on the lower floors.

The size of the palace necessitated use of an oh-gee cart if they were to see all the floors of living quarters on this occasion. Even with the cart there wasn't time to view all of the suites, so they only visited the more sumptuous ones on the top floor and then viewed a sampling of the lesser suites on lower floors. The tour of the ballrooms, dining rooms, sitting rooms, conference rooms, kitchens, and work areas, plus the numerous pools and gardens, added several more hours. They finished up and took their leave of Chamberlain Yaghutol in the area of the 'family' suites on the top floor.

"I'm beyond speechless," Annette Carver said to her daughter as they walked around the suite intended for the King and Queen of Nordakia. "You told me how large and impressive the palace was, but I never dreamed it was *this* large and *this* impressive. Our home on Earth would fit into this one suite three times over."

"I'm almost as speechless," Jen said. "When I first saw the governor's palace on Quesann, they told me they had modeled it after this palace, but I never knew they had downsized it so extensively. That palace would be dwarfed if they set it down next to this one."

"You did tell us that it was intended to accommodate the king, queen, and entire Royal Court on extended visits, so it's understandable that it would be this spectacular," Marisa said. "But it's going to take some getting used to. I've never slept in the middle of a football stadium before. At least the bed in the suite I picked is only the size of a small condominium," she added with a smile.

"I'm glad I don't have to sleep in this suite," Annette said. "Even the handmaiden rooms are larger than most homes. I hope you can sleep in here, sweetheart."

"I'm not going to sleep in here, Momma. I'll use one of the smaller suites on this floor."

"But you're the Azula," Marisa said.

"Yes, but that doesn't mean I want to sleep in a bed that's large enough for a thirty-person sleep-in. We'll reserve this suite for when the king and queen come for a visit."

"What did you say?" Annette asked in a shocked voice. "They're coming here? While you're away?"

"Not that I know of, Momma. As I've told you, they've never visited this planet." With a grin she added, "But if they do happen to drop by while I'm not here, I'm sure you'll have no trouble hosting their stay. They're both wonderfully nice people. The queen is someone whom I think you'd really enjoy talking to."

"But I don't know how to host royalty," Annette said.

"They're just like regular people," Jenetta said mischievously, but with a perfectly serious facial expression. "And I'm sure the staff has been trained in all the appropriate protocols. Just make sure the royal banquet outshines every dinner party you've ever attended, combined, and that the king and queen get anything they want, when they want it."

Annette just stared at her for a minute. "Okay, I know that look; you're pulling my leg. You haven't done that since high school."

Jenetta couldn't hold her serious expression any longer and her face broke into a wide smile. "The king and queen aren't coming here, Momma, so don't worry about it. But we'll hold this suite open for them simply because none of us want to sleep in it."

"I'm getting hungry," Marisa said. "What time is dinner?"

"Whenever we want. It's been a long day, so let me call the kitchen. Any preferences? Or would you like to take pot luck with Nordakian dishes? I love having a bowl of Queelish as an appetizer, or even as a whole meal."

"What's Queelish?" Annette asked.

"It's a vegetable stew made mostly from Nordakian brononako leaves. When it's cooked, it's like a thick Escarole Minestra soup on Earth but without the sausage or any meat products."

"I'd like to try it," Marisa said.

"So would I," Annette said.

"Okay, we'll have that as an appetizer, if they have the necessary greens, and then whatever entrée items the chefs have prepared."

After Jenetta had called the kitchen and arranged their evening meal, she said, "Dinner will be ready in an hour. They have the ingredients for Queelish, so that will be the appetizer. The main entrée will be a sort of vegetarian meatloaf, with side dishes of stuffed tubers, rice pilaf, and a mushroom soufflé."

"It all sounds delicious," Marisa said. "By the way, what activities did you have planned for tomorrow?"

"I thought that in the morning we'd take an oh-gee craft and tour the local area to see how the farmers are doing and how well the crops are coming back. I receive the monthly production figures from Chamberlain Yaghutol, but I'd like to see the progress in the fields firsthand. I can still remember how devastated the farms were on my first visit here almost twenty years ago— it was absolutely horrendous. The wildlife was mostly gone, and the winds constantly eroded the topsoil because there wasn't enough vegetation left to hold it. Now the wildlife is making a comeback and the land looks green again. It's wonderful to see nature coming back."

"I wonder how many species of wildlife managed to survive." Marisa said.

"I don't know. I heard that they did their best to round up all of the species they could and house them in impromptu zoos or aquariums all over the planet. But they must have lost a lot of the diversification in species and among subspecies."

"I'm sure we can learn a lot from the tenant farmers tomorrow," Annette said.

"Probably," Jenetta agreed. "Well, perhaps we should clean up and get ready for dinner."

On most populated planets, oh-gee vehicle flight was restricted to very low altitude levels and specific strata based on the direction of travel. Additionally, built-in governors enforced a maximum ceiling to prevent interference with government and commercial passenger traffic. Over the Gavistee Peninsula, there was little traffic except farm carts, so Jenetta had the palace mechanic disable the ceiling governor. Her position as a member of the nobility was enough to ensure that no mechanic would voice objections to her order about the flight governor. Besides being the Azula and therefore the final authority on all matters on the peninsula that did not fall under the purview of the royal family, she was also a military-rated pilot and qualified to fly above the normal height restrictions on any planet in GA space.

After breakfast the following morning, the three women set out to view the farmlands. Jenetta didn't allow either the palace security force or the security force from the *Ares* to tag along, but she knew the *Ares* security force had launched several small observation satellites when the ship arrived in orbit and would be monitoring her travel wherever she went. For personal protection, she had Tayna and Cayla in the vehicle. Chamberlain Yaghutol wanted to join them, but Jenetta said they were looking for a relaxing day as they roamed about in an oh-gee vehicle and that he probably had much more important activities waiting. He tried to insist, saying that they might get lost, but Jenetta held firm, saying she could always call for assistance if all instrumentation in the vehicle were to suddenly fail.

It was mid-summer on Gavistee Peninsula and the weather was wonderful. The air was crisp and clean, and the scent from abundant wildflowers floated on every breeze as the vehicle lifted off from the small parking pad near the palace. The warm day was especially pleasing after the freezing February weather recently experienced at the Potomac base.

Jenetta took the vehicle up to three hundred meters above ground level, a height that should guarantee they didn't encounter any other vehicles, and pointed the small craft north. The height gave them a great view of the farmlands as they covered the first of the estate's thirty-six million hectares. At roughly three hundred sixty thousand square kilometers, the estate was about the combined size of Kansas and Oklahoma back on Earth. While most of the estate was arable, it was still extremely under-utilized in many areas. As they began to pass over the farms, the scent of wildflowers mingled with an occasional whiff of fertilizer, but the scenery always remained pleasant.

It was wonderful to see the remarkable changes since her last visit to the planet. Where farmers had returned to their family plots, the fields were now mostly alive with healthy crops. When they overflew one farm where the crop seemed a bit undeveloped, Jenetta landed the vehicle.

As the oh-gee ship settled onto its skids, a farmer and a young boy who had been working in a field hurried over and dropped to one knee while adopting Jenetta's skin color. Cayla and Tayna stood by Jenetta's side as she stepped out of the vehicle but apparently didn't sense danger because they didn't adopt an overly protective appearance.

"Is this your farm?" Jenetta asked the farmer.

"Yes, My Lady. My family has farmed this land since Gavistee farmland was first allotted to tenants. My grandfather was the first tenant on this land, and the lease was passed down to my father when grandfather died. It has now been passed to me, and my son will take it over when I'm no longer able to farm."

"Raise your heads, please."

"Yes, My Lady," the farmer said as he looked up. The boy looked up without saying anything.

"What's your name?"

"I'm Gerravx Hthumakp, My Lady. This is my son, Beauxvu."

"As we overflew your farm, we couldn't help but notice that your crop seems to be a bit— stunted."

"Yes, My Lady."

"Do you know why? Are you getting enough water for irrigation?"

"The water is plentiful, My Lady. The problem is with the topsoil. The wind took the good soil away after the disaster. We've done what we can, but it will take many years to rebuild it. I fear it will be a long time before we'll have a good crop for you."

"The farms around this one all seem to be doing well."

"They've been able to get free allotments of fertilizer. They've each given me a little, or we'd have no crop at all."

"Why haven't you applied for your own free allotment of fertilizer?"

"I have, My Lady, but I haven't received any."

"Have you informed Chamberlain Yaghutol that you haven't received an allotment?"

"Yes, My Lady. He knows."

"And what has he said?"

"He's said he'll look into it."

"When was that?"

"Several times, My Lady. The last time was just before spring planting."

"But you've received seed assistance."

"Yes, My Lady. But the seed can't mature properly in such poor soil."

Jenetta looked around at the sickly looking plants in the fields. She wasn't a farmer, but even she knew that plants needed proper care, sufficient water, sunshine, and good weather, plus the nutrients found in soil or fertilizer, to grow strong and healthy. It appeared that the farm had only been getting four of the five things needed to produce a good crop.

"How long have you known Chamberlain Yaghutol?" she asked the farmer.

"Most of my life, My Lady. As young boys, we were in school at the same time."

"Were you friends?"

"Uh, we were when we were very young, but then later we had a falling out."

"What was the reason for the falling out?"

"Uh, we had a bit of a rivalry over a girl."

"A girl?"

"Yes, My Lady."

"Who won her?"

"Uh— neither of us. She chose another."

"And you've never reconciled your differences?"

"No, My Lady."

"Are you aware of any other farmers who haven't received a proper allotment of seed, fertilizer, or water?"

"Just one, My Lady. Kurthxl Werxziall has said that he hasn't received any fertilizer."

"And was he also a suitor for the same young lady?"

"Yes, My Lady. He was the one who won her hand. But she left him after the disaster struck. I heard that she's moved to Nordakia. Kurthxl farms the land with his three sons now, but his crops are as poor as mine."

"I see. I shall discuss the situation with Chamberlain Yaghutol and see that he gets the accounts straightened out so that you get your allotment of fertilizer. Perhaps it might be too late to help this season's crop, but it'll help with the next."

"Thank you, My Lady. I promise to produce better crops in the future."

"What did the farmer say?" Annette asked after they were airborne again.

"Oh, I'm sorry. I forgot you don't speak Nordakian. But even if I hadn't, the situation was such that translation would have made the discussion more difficult. Essentially, this farmer hasn't been getting the allotments of free fertilizer necessary to replace the nutrients in the soil. I'll have to speak to Chamberlain Yaghutol about it."

"And everyone else has been getting free fertilizer?" Marisa asked.

"Well, the farmer told me of another who hasn't received it. But everybody *should* have been getting it. It's absolutely necessary to rebuild the land and make the farms self-sufficient again. Once the topsoil is revitalized and the farms are profitable, the farmers will be responsible for securing their own fertilizer and seed, although water for irrigation will always be freely available."

The women stopped near the bank of a winding river at noon to enjoy the picnic lunch prepared by the palace kitchen. They were out quite far, and there were no farms nearby. Mother Nature was still struggling to gain a foothold here as evidenced by the small clumps of wild grasses sprouting around the area. Within a few years, the banks would probably be covered in green during the summer.

The peninsula was too vast to be seen in one day, but the women made it as far as the mountain range that formed the northern boundary before it was time to turn back. The highest peaks were still covered in snow, and water flowed down to the reservoirs in fast-moving streams that would probably continue all summer. By autumn, the snow would be falling again on the mountains and continue to provide fresh water until the high mountain streams turned to ice in winter.

Jenetta took a different route back so they'd overfly prev-iously unseen farmland sections. As on the trip out, most farms looked healthy, but a couple had sickly-looking crops. Since all of the farmers were using the same water supply and were getting seed checked by the King's Agriculture Ministry, it appeared that the problem might be a lack of fertilizer. Jenetta recorded the map coordinates of those farms.

As the oh-gee vehicle settled onto the skids, Chamberlain Yaghutol hurried over to greet the travelers.

"Thank Nallick you're safe, My Lady," Yaghutol said as the women exited the car. "We were getting nervous. We expected you back earlier."

"It was such a delightful day that we went all the way to the mountains at the north end of the peninsula," Jenetta said.

"Oh, I expected that you would only view the farms nearest the palace."

As they began walking towards the palace, Jenetta said, "We'll have time for more sightseeing, but there is something I'd like to speak to you about. While most farms seem to be doing well, we saw some where the crops appear to be suffering. Have you looked into that?"

"Uh, yes, My Lady. There aren't that many. Usually it's a matter of poor farming skills. Some of the tenants have grown too old to farm during the years since the disaster, and the younger family members aren't experienced enough. We're trying to establish training courses to improve their skills."

"I see. Then you feel that's the problem with the farm held by the Gerravx Hthumakp family?"

"Hthumakp? Oh, he's always got an excuse for everything."

"Really? He mentioned that he's the third generation to farm that plot, so I would have expected him to be quite knowledgeable. He also told me that he hasn't received any allotments of fertilizer. The soil appears to confirm that— at least to my untrained eye. Would you please confirm that he has received his allotments?"

"Yes, My Lady. I will check the books this evening."

"Thank you. Please check on the allotments to a tenant named Kurthxl Werxziall also. And while you're at it, have your staff check the allotment records against the names of every tenant to ensure that everyone is getting their proper allotment of fertilizer. I didn't have time to stop, but we overflew a number of farms where the crops seemed stunted. I want to make sure that the tenants can't claim incompetence on the part of you or your staff here. We must be able to show that poor crops are owed to their *own* ineptitude or the Family Carver will get an undeserved reputation for being uncaring. We certainly wouldn't want that to happen."

"Of course not, My Lady. I— uh— mean about the uncaring reputation. Naturally I'll have the records checked as soon as possible and make sure that every farmer is receiving the fertilizer he needs."

"Thank you, Chamberlain."

After dinner, Marisa asked, "Did you believe the Chamberlain tonight when he said the poor crops were owed to the inexperience of some farmers? He seemed nervous."

"Did he? Well, I'm sure he'll do what I've asked and ensure the farmers get their fertilizer because I suspect he knows I'll be checking up. Undoubtedly, a few very young tenants now hold the most senior position on their farms, but even among them most have probably grown up talking with others and learning about crops and farms. If inexperience is the problem, they'll pick up what they need to know if the farmers here are anything like I've heard."

"What have you heard?"

"Only that the farming community is often a tight-knit group, and most try to help their neighbors, expecting that the help will be reciprocated when they have a problem."

A Priority-One message from Admiral Poole at Quesann cut Jenetta's short vacation even shorter. After viewing the message, she made immediate plans to leave the tranquil life on Obotymot and respond to the new emergency situation in Region Two. As she packed her travel case she wondered if life on the planet could ever be fulfilling enough to sustain her after the constant challenges and life-threatening situations she'd faced in the military.

Chapter Six

~ March 8th, 2286 ~

The short time spent on Obotymot had been relaxing and refreshing. Jenetta had visited the farm of Gerravx Hthumakp just before she'd left and determined that he had received a full delivery of fertilizer the day after her first visit. He was most appreciative and couldn't stop thanking her and guaranteeing that he would produce a great crop for her by the following season.

Naturally, her mom was agitated about the situation that caused Jenetta to cut her vacation short, but Jenetta managed to calm her fears before departing the planet.

During the one-day trip to Higgins Space Command Base, Jenetta spent every spare minute thinking about the latest emergency and the other important business before her. She naturally took care of regular business, such as her hour-long morning briefing session with her aide, Lt. Commander Ashraf, and a morning discussion with Captain Gavin, but other than that, she isolated herself in her office.

As with Earth Space Traffic Control, Higgins Approach Control gave the *Ares* a straight-in approach vector. Admiral Holt hadn't yet had an opportunity to tour one of the new *Ares*-class ships, so Jenetta invited him aboard as soon as they docked at the station. Although the *Ares* was her flagship, Gavin was the ship's captain, so he conducted the tour while she trailed along with Holt. The Higgins SCB commanding officer was suitably impressed and was as shocked as most visitors when Gavin ordered the tac officer to remove the decks using the special Simage technology, although he hadn't ordered the deck removed until Holt was over the initial sensation of having the bulkheads melt away and had agreed to a further demonstration. Even though surrounded by almost a million tons of solid shipbuilding materials, the technology made it seem like they were encased in a clear plastic bubble in open space.

"Incredible!" Holt uttered as all but bridge personnel, consoles, and a grid of light lines on the deck used to aid orientation seemed to disappear.

"A commanding officer could never hope to have a better view for making maneuvering or attack decisions during battle conditions," Jenetta said. "The Admiral's bridge has the same capability."

"I have to say it again," Holt uttered as he looked at the other ships docked at the station. "Incredible."

"It is impressive," Jenetta agreed. "Well, that concludes the tour, Brian. Would you join me in my office? We have a couple of items to discuss."

"Of course."

Turning to Captain Gavin, she said, "I'm sorry, Larry. I have a private matter to discuss with Brian first. I'll let you know when you can join us."

"Of course, Admiral."

"Jen."

"Of course, Jen."

Jenetta smiled and looked at Holt, then tilted her head briefly towards the corridor.

Once they had prepared a beverage and were seated in her sumptuous office that adjoined the Admiral's Bridge, Jenetta said, "Brian, I'd like you to join me in Region Two."

"I know."

"You know?"

"Richard contacted me right after the Admiralty Board approved your request."

"Hmm, I thought it would be a surprise."

"He needed to know if I intended to join you so they could begin the search for someone to replace me."

"Of course. This base is too vital to have the top position left open for very long. And how did you respond to Richard?"

"I told him that if you asked, I'd go in a heartbeat."

"Wonderful," she said with a smile, "but did he tell you the whole story?"

"About the missing ship and the possibility that we might be facing a serious new threat?"

"That's part of it."

"What else is there?"

"The GA Council intends to move the entire Senate to Quesann."

"Oh, that. They've been talking and arguing about that ever since you defeated the Milori."

"It's more than just after-dinner conversation now."

"What have they said?"

"It's apparently a done deal. They're developing construction plans for building and housing complexes."

"When is all this supposed to happen?"

"Not for a while yet. It will take some time to build a secure complex for the Senate and another for Space Command Supreme Headquarters. We'll need new quarters for dignitaries and Space command personnel, and an area for the— press corps. Of course there will be a need for restaurants, visitor lodging, and business complexes, plus residences for the usual lobbyists and other political hacks."

Holt made a face that caused Jenetta to chuckle.

"I agree," Jenetta said. "I've spent my career trying to stay away from that situation, and now I've been thrust smack into the middle of it. I suppose I'll just have to make the best of it."

"So on the bright side, we'll obviously have to build a complete city. That could take years."

"The longer the better. Does that mean you'll come?"

"I can't think of any job I'd like more. I've done everything I could to avoid going back to Earth for my final years in Space Command, and I've secretly wished I could find an excuse to travel to Region Two and perhaps even finish my career out there at one of your new space stations. Things have gotten a bit boring here at Higgins, and establishing a new station in a new territory could really enliven my remaining years in the service."

"You do know they're planning to extend the retirement age again, don't you?"

"No. That's apparently something Richard forgot to mention."

"If the senate passes the measure, and I'm confident they will, the new mandatory retirement age will be one hundred twenty-five."

"That's wonderful news. I've been wondering how I was going to spend the four decades after retirement. With any luck, they'll extend it again in the future."

"We'll have to see. I know my father would agree with you."

"So when do we leave?"

"There's a bit more to tell you. I want you to go into this with your eyes wide open. I cut short my vacation time by almost a week because I received a Priority-One message from Augustus. Another scout-destroyer is overdue and not responding to messages."

"Which one?"

"The *Salado.*"

"Wasn't that just launched recently?"

"About eight months ago. He was on his first patrol."

"Who's his captain?"

"Commander Judith Deneau. SHSA class of '71."

"I've never met her."

"She was promoted off the *Portland.*"

"That's Gregory's destroyer, isn't it?"

"Yes. He told me she's good and deserves the promotion. I only met her once when the *Salado* reported for assignment to my fleet."

"Any ideas on what happened to the ship?"

"They reported spotting several ships on their DeTect system and were going to investigate. Nothing after that."

"That's ominous. Isn't that the same situation as the *Yenisei?*"

"Yes. That's why I cut my vacation short. Something serious is going on in Region Two and I need to be out there and find out what it is."

"Then we'd better get going."

"You can leave now?"

"I've already received orders to proceed to Quesann to assume the new post of Deputy Military Governor of Regions Two and Three with a promotion to Vice-Admiral."

Jenetta smiled and said, "Congratulations, Admiral."

"Thank you. Admiral. I'm delighted to be assigned to your command. I've already said all my goodbyes here and attended a goodbye party thrown by my officers last evening. My bags are packed and can be brought to the ship immediately. Do you have an empty hold?"

"An entire hold for your luggage?"

"You collect a lot of things over the years when you're not moving around." After punctuating that with a smile, he added, "Just kidding. I can't leave Project Springboard here. You know why I can't brief anyone on the specifics of the project, and we can't risk having it fall into someone's hands if proper security isn't maintained by a commanding officer who doesn't understand the reason for such security. The only solution is to bring it with us."

"I agree. I wasn't thinking about Springboard being part of your personal possessions."

"And on top of everything else, it's best that Springboard be in the most secure place imaginable. To my mind, that would be Quesann, the Space Command HQ for Regions Two and Three, and the future home of Supreme Head-quarters and the GA Senate. And a place where *both* of us can ensure it's not abused."

"Yes, Quesann is probably the safest long-term storage location."

"Good. Although my staff doesn't know the contents of the containers, they're ready to supervise the move as soon as Larry can arrange for space aboard the *Ares*."

Tapping her Space Command ring to initiate a carrier, Jenetta asked Captain Gavin to come to her office.

Four hours later the *Ares* backed away from the station's docking ring and set course for Region Two. Admiral Holt had personally verified that all containers were received aboard the ship and that all seals were intact. When all of the components for Project Springboard were securely nestled in a large hold, a security team of Marines was assigned to see that no one entered the hold unless either Admiral Carver or Admiral Holt was present.

* * *

"Come in, Larry," Jenetta said as the door to her office opened to reveal Captain Gavin waiting for admittance. "Fix yourself a beverage and join us."

Gavin prepared a cup of coffee at the beverage machine and then walked to where Jenetta and Admiral Holt were seated in her informal seating area. He chose to sit on the sofa so he'd have a table on which to set his cup.

"Brian and I were just discussing the trip ahead," Jenetta said.

"Any changes planned?" Gavin asked

"No, we'll stop at Stewart as planned, then proceed to Flordarya."

"I thought you were anxious to get back, Jen."

"We're going to pick up Captain Barbara DeWitt, the head of the Weapons Research and Development section there, and most of her team. As soon as I heard that a second DS ship was missing, I sent a request to the Admiralty Board that she be posted to Region Two HQ to head up *our* new Weapons Research section. We don't know who or what we're facing yet, but they must be formidable if they were able to take down two DS ships before our people could get a message off. Barbara's team worked on the development of the Phalanx system and kept at it until it was almost ninety-five percent effective. I want her at Quesann when we learn what we're facing, and the Admiralty Board approved my request. I know that Brian knows her because she headed up the small Weapons Research section at Higgins before being sent to Stewart."

"I've met her, but I don't know her well," Gavin said.

"She's incredibly gifted," Holt said. "I was sorry to lose her, but Jen needed her more than I did at the time, and the move included a promotion once Jen was moved up to Admiral."

"Knowing the almost total indestructibility of Dakinium," Gavin said, "I wonder if we'll be able to stop an enemy that's been able to defeat those two ships. Perhaps you should delay the diplomatic trip to Flordarya and head straight to Quesann."

"We still have no information regarding their disappearance," Jenetta said, "so there's nothing we can do at Quesann right now, and the Admiralty Board wants the representatives delivered promptly to begin GA membership talks and trade negotiations. Augustus will notify us immediately if he learns anything."

"Has an ambassador been assigned to Flordarya?" Holt asked.

"We're delivering an envoy to begin the discussions that could lead to Flordarya becoming a member of the GA. The planned talks will determine if the Flordaryns are acceptable candidates and ready to become a member planet. If they are, the envoy will remain on as the new ambassador."

"How do things look?" Gavin asked.

"It all appears pretty standard so far. The Flordaryns are adapting well to having their planet and their freedom back. The Tsgardi may have subjugated them for decades, but they never lost their indomitable spirit. That's one of the reasons for the upcoming trade talks. They apparently continued numerous research projects right under the noses of the Tsgardi and supposedly made great advances. They never shared any of the new technology with the Tsgardi and the Tsgardi were too ignorant to notice. Now they want to become a full trading partner with advanced civilizations in the GA and are offering a sharing of technical knowledge."

"It's amazing that the Tsgardi never picked up on the subterfuge," Holt said.

"Many people believe that the Tsgardi are not even sentient," Jenetta said, "and I won't argue that the assessment is very far off the mark. They'd never have made it into space if they hadn't enslaved peaceful Flordaryn travelers."

"It's a good thing their military is restricted to their own solar system now," Holt said. "I don't doubt that once they fully understand exactly what the loss of Flordaryn expertise means to them, they might try to roll back the clock."

"I think I adequately impressed upon them what would happen if they ever tried anything like that."

"Let's hope they remember. As you said, they're barely sentient."

* * *

Sixteen days after leaving Higgins, The *Ares* arrived at Stewart Space Command base. Jenetta preferred not to go through any welcoming ceremonies, so she invited Admiral Thaddeus Vroman to visit her aboard the ship. He was waiting on the docking pier as the vessel completed its dock-and-lock procedure and was instantly welcomed aboard by the OD who had a Lt.(jg) escort Admiral Vroman to Admiral Carver's office.

"This is a damn impressive ship, Jen," Vroman said as he entered the imposing office.

"Yes, it is Thad. And you haven't seen anything yet. Would you like the full tour?"

"If you have the time, I'd love one."

"We'll make the time. But first, you know Brian Holt and Larry Gavin, don't you?"

Turning to the other officers, Vroman said, "Of course. Hello, Brian. Hi, Larry. Congratulations on the promotion, Brian. And I just heard you'll be the Deputy Military Governor in Regions Two and Three."

"Yes, I'm looking forward to the position and delighted to be working with Jen again."

Turning towards Jenetta, Admiral Vroman said, "I understand you're having some trouble in Region Two."

"That's why I wanted Barbara and her team. We don't yet know what we're facing. Let's take the tour and we can talk along the way."

They wrapped up the tour back at the Admiral's bridge and Jenetta delighted in showing Vroman the Sim technology that made the walls seem to melt away. He took it pretty well but got a bit nervous when the deck almost completely disappeared. Jenetta signaled the tac officer to restore the deck after Vroman reached for one of the command chairs and hung on.

"That's something I wouldn't use very often," Admiral Vroman said. "I felt like I was going to fall right through those thin grid lines."

Jenetta smiled slightly and said, "It does take a bit of getting used to, but we were never in any danger."

"On some level I knew that, but on a different level all logic fled."

"Gavin, out," the captain said. Then turning towards Jenetta, he said, "I just received a message via my CT. Captain DeWitt and her people are aboard, and the equipment they're bringing has all been stowed."

"Excellent." To Admiral Vroman, she said, "Guess it's time to go, Thad. Thanks for your hospitality. I hope to see you again soon."

"You're always welcome, Jen. I hope you locate the two missing ships and that everyone is alive."

"Thanks, Thad. That's our hope as well."

Chapter Seven
~ April 28th, 2286 ~

"General quarters— general quarters — all hands proceed to your assigned battle locations," suddenly blared from the overhead speaker in Jenetta's quarters in the middle of the night. At the same instant, an identical message began to reverberate in her head thanks to her CT. The strobe mounted on the overhead was flashing alternating colors of red and white as she sat up in bed and gave the order for the room to illuminate. She was trying to rub the sleep from her eyes while she slid to the edge of her bed when the com chimed. She stopped what she was doing and leaned over to raise the cover. The face of Captain Gavin immediately filled the screen. Her screen was on blackout so Gavin was only seeing a previously recorded image.

"Jen, we're approaching Flordarya. It's surrounded by what appears to be warships."

"Surrounded?"

"There're at least five, all about the same size from what we can see from here, spread out in roughly geosynchronous orbit around the planet. It appears they've taken up positions over the major cities. I've cancelled our FTL envelope and we're sitting at almost maximum DeTect range, so the data is still sketchy. The ships could be innocent transports or even small single-hulled freighters, but my tac officer says the return signals suggest otherwise. Given that two of our DS ships are missing, I decided to play it safe."

"Good call. I'll be on my bridge in five minutes. Carver out."

Jenetta leaped off the bed and yanked her clothes on. As she raced out of the bedroom, she discovered her steward standing in the sitting room with a steaming mug of coffee extended at arm's length. Jenetta took the cup and told her steward to get down to a Secure room immediately, then ran into the corridor. She didn't instruct the Marine security team to leave their posts because they wouldn't have gone willingly. Besides, on all new DS warships, destroyer and above, special four-point connection harnesses had been installed at all guard post positions. They were built into the bulkheads, and normally almost invisible. Like a seatbelt in a car, they were instantly ready for use, or could be released with a tug on a quick-release buckle. Once released, they would retract back into the bulkhead structure until needed again. They left a Marine's arms completely free so he or she was always ready for action. Located next to the harness area was a locker where the Marine stored the duffel containing his or her personal body armor when they reported to their post. They would probably never need it, but it was there if they did.

Jenetta raced onto the admiral's bridge and climbed into her command chair. The large monitor at the front of the bridge was displaying an image of the captain's bridge. Gavin was in his command chair reading a report from a monitor mounted to the chair near his right hand. Jenetta stabbed lightly at a contact point on her left-hand monitor that would allow an image of the admiral's bridge to be seen on the captain's bridge.

"Any change in status, Larry?" Jenetta asked.

Gavin looked up and said, "No change, Admiral."

A tac officer was always on duty on the admiral's bridge, ready with answers in an instant. He had a direct connection to the lead tac officer on the captain's bridge to allow them to coordinate all functions. As Gavin and Jenetta talked, the other crewmembers assigned to the admiral's bridge entered and manned their consoles.

"Okay," Jenetta said as she buckled her seat belt, "once most crewmen are at their posts, let's move in to a hundred thousand kilometers."

Gavin checked a monitor and said, "We're at ninety-eight-point-two percent of full readiness and climbing fast."

"Okay, let's go see what the situation is."

* * *

"Admiral," the booming voice of a Tsgardi tactical officer announced excitedly through the ceiling speaker, "our DeTect systems have just reported the approach of a large ship."

Admiral Kelakmius of the Tsgardi Defense Command was just sitting down to have dinner in his cabin. He stood back up and pushed his chair back, then hurried over to the intercom control on the bulkhead. "What kind of ship?" he said calmly.

"It's still too distant to be sure, but it's coming on fast and appears to be a warship. We'll have better data shortly as it gets closer."

"A warship? What makes you think it's a warship?"

"It's too large to be a single-hulled freighter and too fast for either a freighter or passenger liner. If it's a warship, it's almost certainly Space Command. The Territorial Guard warships don't venture this far outside the original Milori Empire."

"Space Command? What would they be doing here?"

"We'll get better data as they move closer."

"Sound general quarters— no— wait. Do *not* sound general quarters. If they are Space Command, we must not put them on alert."

"What action *should* we take, sir?"

"I'll be on the bridge in a couple of minutes. Just standby until then." Kelakmius glanced over at the table where his fresh zeepaza was wiggling and squirming over bright yellow relliso leaves. By the time he returned, the zeepaza would probably be dead and the relliso would be wilted and tasteless. Damn all Spaccs. Why did they have to show up now, of all times?

* * *

"Tac, any change in status?" Jenetta asked of her tac officer as they approached the planet.

"The ships are still in geo orbit, Admiral. We're starting to get a little better data now that we're closer. All five ships appear to be exactly the same size." After a short pause, he added, "Admiral, the ships appear to be Tsgardi destroyers."

"Tsgardi?"

"Based on the return data, that's what the ship identification system is reporting, although it's only showing a seventy-eight percent accuracy at this time. Wait, the accuracy indicator just jumped to ninety-two percent."

"Could they be new ships the Flordaryns are building for home system defense?"

"The configuration is one that was discontinued some forty years ago."

"That would indicate that they're Tsgardi System Defense ships because that's all they had left after the war. Have they gone on alert?"

"There's no indication of activity."

"Perhaps they haven't noticed us. Com, are you picking up any local chatter on the frequencies the Tsgardi use?"

"Negative, Admiral. Everything seems peaceful on all military channels."

"Get me the Planetary Council Headquarters."

"Aye, Admiral. Working on it."

* * *

"The ship is almost definitely Space Command, Admiral. It looks like a *Prometheus*-class battleship, but there are some slight discrepancies. It might be a new class."

"Great. We're sitting here in these old rust buckets while Space Command's newest class of battleship bears down on us. Those little scout ships took out most of our fleet while never losing a single ship. How could we ever stand up to a new battleship?"

* * *

Twenty seconds later, the com chief on the admiral's bridge aboard the *Ares* said, "I have the Council President, Admiral."

"Put him on my left-hand monitor."

"Aye, Admiral. He's there."

Jenetta looked at the image of the Flordaryn. He didn't appear distressed at all. "Mr. President, there appears to be five Tsgardi destroyers in orbit around your planet."

"Yes, Admiral Carver, we know," Jenetta heard through her CT. "They've come looking for help."

"Help? Help with what?"

"Their ships are breaking down and they have no one to fix them. While we were being held as slaves, they tried to have us train some of their people to be engineers, but few could even master the use of a screwdriver."

"Those ships are never supposed to leave their solar system. That was in the terms of their surrender."

"They've brought them to us here because we refused to go there. This is the only way we'd agree to fix them."

"You've put me in a very delicate position, Mr. President. I had told them that if any Tsgardi warships ever left their home system, we'd destroy them on sight."

"They claim they need the ships in good working order if they're to protect their home system and had no other alternative."

"We're going to approach the planet, but no closer than twenty-five thousand kilometers to any Tsgardi warship. Tell them that if they make the slightest provocative move, we'll blast them to space dust."

"If they do move, it won't be very far or very fast, Admiral. Their FTL drives and Sub-Light engine systems are all off-line. All they have available is their deuterium thrusters."

"How long have they been here?"

"Several GST weeks."

"And their claims of needing service are genuine?"

"More than genuine. I'm amazed they even reached us. If we were more than eight light-years distant, they probably wouldn't have even tried to make the trip. These ships are the oldest they had. They were unfit for real combat, so they kept them home as a basic security force. You have little to fear from these ships."

"It's not the ships I fear; it's their torpedoes. Even the oldest ships can fire the newest torpedoes."

"They arrived with just five torpedoes apiece, and we required them to offload the missiles to a storage barge before we'd begin work. We also disabled their laser arrays. I don't think they know that yet."

"That was a very prudent measure."

"We didn't want there to be any *accidents* while they were here that could be used to cover up kidnappings with claims that the missing people had been vaporized in a laser array accident or torpedo explosion."

"How much longer will it take to complete the repairs?"

"My chief engineers say that a proper overhaul would take several GST years but they estimate we can make the ships reliably space worthy again in nine to ten more GST months."

"I can't assign any of my ships to stay in orbit that long to ensure your safety."

"I think we're safe enough, Admiral. They have no offensive weapons, and if they do anything to harm any of our people, they know we'll never work on their ships again. Since we're the only ones who would even consider working on their ships, they have to comply with our demands."

"Tsgardi don't necessarily think very far ahead. Their leaders do, but the average Tsgardi warrior doesn't correlate the current situation with something that might happen as far away as dinnertime."

"We know the culture all too well, Admiral, and we thank you for your concern, but if the Tsgardi ever try to enslave our people again, they'll learn we're not as trusting as we once were, or as defenseless."

"I'm glad to hear that, Mr. President."

"We look forward to welcoming you and the delegation you're escorting. When can we expect you?"

"The delegation leader will be responsible for making all arrangements, so she will no doubt be in touch very soon. At present, she and the other delegates are in a Secure room. We took every precaution for their safety when we spotted the warships in orbit around your planet."

"As you can see, the situation is not as bad as one might expect."

"Are there any Tsgardi on the planet?"

"No, we refused to let them land. The population might react badly after so many years of slavery and the loss of so many family members. Fully half our engineering people refused to work on their ships."

"I understand. It will take many generations for the memories to dim."

"If ever. Many people have written books about their years in captivity. Some of the tales are quite graphic and even stir the blood of people who were least affected during the occupation."

"I suppose that's why I was so surprised to hear you had agreed to repair their ships."

"Truth be told, I was afraid to refuse them. They are quick to anger and might have attacked us before Space Command could arrive to assist."

"If you'd like to terminate your agreement, I could ensure this group would never bother you again."

"Tempting, Admiral, but we've always prided ourselves on meeting our commitments, and we did commit to doing this work."

"May I ask how the Tsgardi intend to pay for your services?"

"They have already paid us. The form is precious metals and stones. As you know, most Tsgardi have strong backs and weak minds, so mining is a very suitable occupation and they are quite good at it. We, uh, doubled what we would have charged anyone else to make up for past treatment we endured at their— paws."

"Very well, Mr. President. I'll be contacting them myself very soon. Now that I know the situation, I'm better positioned to deal with them. The leader of the trade delegation will be making arrangements with your office for the trade discussions. Thank you for your time."

"Of course, Admiral. And may I extend the thanks of all my people to you for freeing us from Tsgardi rule. We look forward to becoming an active and voting member of the Galactic Alliance. Good day."

Jenetta leaned back into her chair and thought about the situation. She wasn't so sure she could have so soon entered into a working relationship with a race that had subjugated hers for so long. The Flordaryns were a truly unique people. Or perhaps they had an unseen agenda. Jenetta shook her head to clear her thoughts. Perhaps she was just becoming paranoid, but the President of the Flordaryn planet was a politician, and she didn't have very much respect for politicians. These days, they always seemed to be embroiled in bribery, corruption, or sex scandals. Of course, she knew it had always been that way with the ruling classes. It had just gotten worse down through the centuries as people won the right to vote, while governments had grown larger and power had become centralized. During their careers, politicians seemed to slip deeper and deeper into the wallets of big business until they all but lost sight of their constituents—until it was time to seek reelection. And now the GA Senate wanted to establish a new center for operations on Quesann—her Quesann. What had she ever done to deserve that?

* * *

"I'm Admiral Jenetta Carver," she said when communications had finally been established with the senior Tsgardi officer aboard the destroyer *Vekezemos*.

"I know who you are, Terran. You destroyed the Kingdom's fleet and murdered our military forces."

"Yes, well— that sometimes happens when a would-be conqueror attacks a peaceful nation in the belief they can steal that nation's territory. You chose to chew on something that could bite back and had much sharper teeth. I gave the

Tsgardi fleet the opportunity to surrender peacefully. They foolishly made a decision to fight. Once that occurred, the outcome was inevitable."

"Every Tsgardi warrior carries your picture, Terran."

Jenetta quickly formulated a strategy for dealing with this latest obnoxious commander who was all bluff and bluster. She knew she had to knock him down a peg or two without it actually coming to blows, so messing with his head a little might throw him off balance from the start. Smiling sweetly, she said in a totally girly voice, "Oh, that's so sweet. Are they hoping to get my autograph?"

"What?" the Tsgardi asked with a confused look. He was expecting death threats.

"Are they carrying my picture around so I can autograph it for them if we ever happen to meet?"

The Tsgardi sneered and said, "They carry it so they can study it every night and burn your image into their mind. They will recognize you instantly should you meet, and they will exact revenge for our dead comrades."

"Oh, I guess it's not so sweet then." Jenetta had known exactly why Tsgardi warriors carried the images. It was reported that they never fell asleep at night until they had studied each image of their enemies for at least five minutes. "Tell you what, let's you and me duke it out right here."

"What's this 'duke it out' mean?"

"It means fight," Jenetta said as she pressed a spot on her left monitor. "There, I just gave the order to ready five torpedoes. That's one for each of your ships."

"Wait, we're unarmed. You can't fire on us."

"Oh, but I can. You see, when the Tsgardi War Council surrendered unconditionally, they were told that no Tsgardi warship could ever leave your solar system without permission. You did not request permission from Quesann and yet here you are in a different solar system. Legally, I can reduce you to space dust and no one can say a word against my action."

"But we're unarmed."

"I think we both know that doesn't really matter. You wouldn't stand a chance even if you were armed. So we might as well just finish this right here and now and have it over with. Are you ready?" Jenetta poised her finger over a contact spot on the monitor.

"You can't do this," Admiral Kelakmius screamed. "You're a Space Command officer. This is murder."

"Why shouldn't I do it? You believe me to be a murderer anyway."

"But that wasn't cold-blooded murder. It was murder during battle."

"Oh, murder during battle, was it? Well, we'll call this a battle and then it will be alright, okay?"

"We're defenseless. You can't murder us like this."

Jenetta had tired of the game so she said, "Oh, I just remembered something. I promised the Flordaryn Council President that I wouldn't destroy your ships until after they finish their work. So I guess I can't destroy you just yet."

Kelakmius seemed to breathe a sigh of relief before saying, "We're no match for a Space Command battleship."

"That's probably the first thing you've said that I agree with. I'll tell you what—when your repairs are finished, you contact Space Command at Quesann and request an escort back to your home solar system. We'll send someone to see that no one destroys you on the way home. And in the future, I expect you to request an escort should you ever again need to leave your solar system. This is your final warning. If any warship ever again leaves your solar system without permission, we will destroy it without further word when we spot it. Is that understood?"

Kelakmius was bristling, but he was smart enough to simply say, "Understood."

"Good. *Never* forget it."

Jenetta waited until after the connection was severed before allowing herself to smile. She hoped she had finally put the fear of Space Command into Kelakmius. He had to understand that the Tsgardi warships may not leave their home solar system without permission and without an escort. He was understandably having difficulty coping with the loss of their kingdom, but if he left his planet's system again, she would have to take more drastic action than a mind game and simple tongue lashing.

* * *

In the weeks that followed, the delegation from the GA conducted numerous sessions with government scientists and engineers. Jenetta sat in on some of the higher-level meetings, and of course engaged in many closed-door meetings with senior military, intelligence, and political figures on the planet. At the end of the meeting schedule, she was more convinced than ever that the planet's leaders had some hidden agenda, but it was like that on every world. They would only tell the GA, and Jenetta as the GA's official representative, so much of what they were doing or planning for their people. That was their right and perfectly acceptable because what they did on their own planet was entirely their own business. The GA would only get involved if matters moved off-planet. And even then involvement was only required if the planet violated Galactic Alliance laws.

Jenetta was tiring of the endless meetings that should be handled by the GA Diplomatic Corps, and would be once Flordarya became a member of the GA, when she received a message from Admiral Augustus Poole.

"Hello, Jen. I have the sad duty to report that we've found the *Yenisei*. According to the report from the captain of the *Thames*, the hull is so riddled with holes that it resembles a brick of Swiss cheese. The crew never had a chance. All hands are accounted for. Following my report in early March, I dispatched one of the new ship transporters to the last reported location of the *Yenisei*. I certainly wasn't expecting the news that we've just received, but I expected that the ship, when found, might be disabled. The *Winston* should reach the location within a few days and return here by about June 26th.

"In the meantime, all of the *Yenisei's* logs will be downloaded to the *Thames* and then transmitted to Intelligence here at Quesann. The captain of the *Thames* will send his complete report within twenty-four hours. I'll forward a copy to you as soon as we receive it. We're continuing the search for the *Salado* with every ship we can get to their last reported location, and there's even more urgency now that we've learned the fate of the *Yenisei*.

"Augustus Poole, Rear Admiral, Upper Half, Base Commander, Quesann SCB, message complete."

Jenetta immediately cancelled her participation in all further meetings and scheduled the *Ares* to depart the following day. The delegation would remain on the planet to conclude their business, then request that a ship pick them up.

The *Ares* left on schedule the following morning. Jenetta was actually glad to have a reason to go, but not for the reason she was leaving. DS warships were considered almost indestructible. That an unknown enemy was so able to riddle a ship with holes that it resembled Swiss cheese was the worst of all possible news. Until now it had been hoped that the GA was entering a period of peace where a little smuggling would be the worst they would have to face. The appearance of an enemy more dangerous than any Space Command had faced would create many sleepless nights among senior military personnel for some time to come.

Chapter Eight

~ May 10th, 2286 ~

"Any word yet, Jen?" Admiral Holt asked as he entered her office off the admiral's bridge and joined her in the informal seating area. He selected a comfortable chair that could recline almost horizontally if the occupant wished, but he didn't use the control to move it from its regular format. The padded, soft brown leather and gentle recline was enough.

"Nothing yet, Brian. I'm just as anxious to receive the *Thames'* report. I keep going over and over the basic report we received from Augustus. When the archeological scientists on Dakistee discovered that first underground bunker, they used every cutting tool available to them and yet couldn't even mar the surface. They even used a plasma torch without effect. So how could someone have riddled the *Yenisei's* hull with holes?"

"But the material we call Dakinium isn't the same as that material you found on Dakistee. As I recall, it's as close as they could come to reproducing it at the time."

"True. And the new material does allow us to create the resonance that builds the double-envelope, where the original material doesn't, so the designers went with the newer material for shipbuilding. I don't know if the scientists ever continued their research, but I've never heard of them finding a weapon that could damage the Dakinium sheathing in the manner described by Augustus. Dakinium absorbs energy like a sponge absorbs water, and that energy only serves to make it stronger. When a torpedo from a Tsgardi ship flew into one of our sub-light engines on the *Colorado*, it destroyed the internal workings but never harmed the Dakinium nacelle cover. I can't image what sort of weapon could cause the damage the *Yenisei* suffered. And just as important at this point is finding out who is responsible."

"It has to be either the Ruwalchu or the Uthlaro."

"It seems logical that it would be one or the other, but I just don't know. We seriously crippled the Uthlaro government, and I wouldn't expect them to try something *this* overt so soon after suffering the loss of their entire military force, not to mention their territory. If they are behind it, it's not an act of war; it's an act of sedition. I warned them that the penalties are far more severe for sedition than for a nation that declares war on another. Region Three is now part of the GA, and I'll come down hard on the Uthlaro if I find they're responsible."

"What about the Ruwalchu?"

"I just don't know. From all accounts, they're a peaceful race who only want to be left alone, and we've never bothered them. We've never entered their space and never even had diplomatic contact. It wouldn't make sense that they would attack us."

"Perhaps they're looking to expand their territory?"

"My Hudeerac contact once said that the Ruwalchu were more powerful than the Milori, which was why Maxxiloth never antagonized them. If they craved more territory, they should have been able to take over the Milori Empire decades ago."

"Perhaps they weren't looking back then but are now. Have you maintained your contact with the Hudeerac?"

"I haven't corresponded with him recently, but there hasn't been a falling out. Are you suggesting I send a message and ask?"

"Are you on the kind of terms where he would answer honestly?"

"I believe so— at least as honestly as any government would ever be with another. We managed to reestablish our intelligence arrangement after the Hudeerac Order withdrew from the THUG pact."

"Well, it can't hurt to ask. Maybe they'll be able to provide some answers to this problem, or at least clear one of the suspect nations."

"Okay, I'll send a query to my contact. As you say, it can't hurt to ask. At worst, we'll be indebted if we learn something."

*   *   *

Since completion of the palace shuttle pad, Jenetta had been able to leave and return without using the base's space-port. This meant that the welcoming ceremonies for her returns to the base were mostly a thing of the past. They still greeted visiting planetary officials that way, but that was de rigueur throughout the GA.

"Welcome back, Jen," Augustus Poole said as he greeted the two admirals at the palace shuttle pad. "I can't tell you how delighted we all were to hear that your sister recovered from her wounds and has returned to active duty."

"Thank you, Augustus. And I'm glad to be back."

"And welcome, Brian," he said to Admiral Holt. "Congratulations on your promotion and your new posting here at Quesann."

"Thank you, Augustus. I've envied all of you for some time so I'm happy to be out here at last."

"Let's go inside," Jen said, "and you can brief us on the situation here."

"The Region Two Headquarters Staff is assembling in the HQ Building. I thought it better that we make it an official briefing session. I have two vehicles waiting."

"Okay, let's head over there."

Ten minutes later, in her capacity as Military Governor of Region Two, Jenetta called the Region Two HQ Board to order in emergency session. Also in attendance were Admirals Brian Holt, the new Deputy Military Governor of Regions Two and Three, Keith Kanes, Intelligence Director for Regions Two and Three, Augustus Poole, the commanding officer of Quesann Space Command Base, and Benjamin Buckner, Director of Supply & Logistics for Regions Two and Three. A plethora of aides sat dutifully behind their Admirals, but clerks were limited to those with the highest security ratings.

"It's nice to be back at Quesann," Jenetta said, "but I wish our business here today wasn't so distressing. As I'm sure you all know by now, one of our missing ships has been found. All hands are deceased. When I first learned that the *Yenisei* was missing, I hoped against hope that it was merely a technical problem such as the one I experienced with the first Dakinium-sheathed ship, the *Colorado*. But the lockout system developed at the Mars shipyard that prevents a Light-9790 ship from engaging double-envelope travel while a single-envelope is in place has to date been completely effective, so there have been no more catastrophic energy failures aboard any DS ship. The condition of the *Yenisei's* hull makes it almost a certainty that we are facing a new enemy threat— one that is unlike any we've faced before, because this enemy appears to have a weapon capable of destroying what we believed was almost indestructible. This news doesn't bode well for the fate of the *Salado,* which is still missing. I've read the report sent by Commander Nydia Romonova, captain of the *Thames,* until I know it by heart, but I still don't have a clue to the identity of the attackers. I've transmitted a request for information to my contact in the Hudeerac Order asking if they have any knowledge of a new enemy or an old enemy who might be making a fresh assault. But owing to the distance, I haven't yet received a reply.

"Keith, have you received the *Yenisei's* log information yet?"

"No, not yet, Jen, but we're expecting it at any time. I'll notify your office as soon as we receive it."

"Thank you. So then here's all we have so far," Jen said as she nodded to Lt. Commander Ashraf.

An image of the *Yenisei's* hull, sent by Commander Romonova, appeared on large monitors mounted on the walls around the room.

"As you can see, the ship looks like a piece of space junk. No wonder it was so difficult to locate. Before this, I wouldn't have believed that a DS ship could suffer this kind of damage.

And the damage is not limited to the outer skin. It extends for up to thirty meters into the ship, which means that most of the atmo was evacuated in minutes. What hasn't been explained is why the entire crew died. A weapon that penetrates thirty meters into a ship would be able to breach most areas of a scout-destroyer, but there should have been at least a few small areas that remained airtight. We probably won't have more insight into the deaths until the *Thames'* doctor completes his report, or info about air-tight areas until we receive the *Yenisei's* logs.

"That's all I have. Any thoughts?"

"If this enemy's weapons can penetrate thirty meters beyond the Dakinium hull," Admiral Kanes said, "our cruisers and battleships will have to spearhead any actions. Personnel aboard lesser-sized ships must wear Marine body armor or EVA suits during any engagements."

"It appears that way," Admiral Buckner said. "Unfortunately we have neither sufficient Marine armor supplies to outfit all Space Command personnel nor enough of the bulky EVA suits."

"How many ships do we have looking for the *Salado*, Augustus?" Admiral Holt asked.

"Every ship we could spare. As of today, fifty-one ships are involved in the search, in groups of three. I'll send you a roster later. For now, all I can say is that most are scout-destroyers and that they all have orders to be acutely cautious when approaching unidentified ships. Each group leader has been ordered to transmit location information every sixty seconds when investigating anything unusual."

"So we have seventeen groups sweeping that area of space," Jenetta said. "It's not nearly enough."

"It's the best we can do."

"I know. It's just that a complete search by seventeen teams in an area a thousand light-years by a thousand light-years, covering a thousand light-years ante-median and a thousand light-years post-median, could take thousands of years *if* we don't have to stop to investigate every anomaly."

"That's only if we don't locate them reasonably close to their last reported position," Admiral Kanes said.

"How close was the *Yenisei* to its last reported position?"

"Roughly eight light-years."

"And it took months to find it."

"It wasn't emitting a power signature," Kanes said as he shrugged his shoulders.

"Exactly. And I'll bet that neither will the *Salado*, if the same fate befell him. So we'll have to stop to investigate every anomaly."

"I'm open to a better solution," Admiral Poole said, "if you have one."

"I don't have one," Jenetta replied. "I know of no way to speed up a search like this. It's even possible that we could miss spotting the *Salado* since our search vessels will be traveling at Light-9790. If we don't find the *Salado* within twelve light-years of their last reported position, I suggest we search the same area again. Twelve light-years represents almost half a day of travel for a Light-9790 vessel. I really doubt they would have traveled further than that without reporting their position."

"I have to agree," Admiral Poole said. "In fact, we should even consider *three* passes of the primary area before moving further afield. A worst-case scenario would have the *Salado* being taken by surprise and not having a chance to report in, but the captain would have filed her daily report at ten hundred hours if he was able."

"Discounting the time required to investigate all anomalies," Jenetta said, "the seventeen groups can cover the primary area in just under five days at maximum speed. That's a lot more workable."

"Have the search groups reported seeing anything unusual?" Admiral Holt asked of Admiral Poole.

"Unusual in what way?"

"Anything out of the ordinary that might point to who is behind these attacks."

"No other ships were spotted by the original searchers. But you have to remember that most of the searching for the *Yenisei* was done by just two ships that happened to be within two hundred light-years when the ship went missing. It's taken time for the others to reach the search area. Region Two is enormous, and we're really spread out here. I don't have to tell this board that we have less than ten percent of the ships we need to patrol properly."

"We're still getting most of the new ships coming out of the Mars facility," Jenetta said, "but it will take time for the Second Fleet to reach approved ship strength. One of the items we have to discuss today is the creation of a ship-building facility here in Region Two. And that's just one of the many issues. There's little more we can do on the subject of the *Yenisei* and *Salado* until we have more information, so let's move on to regular business. Augustus, after you brief us on what's happened since I left, I'll brief the HQ Board on important matters being discussed at the Admiralty Board."

*   *   *

"What the devil..." the image of Commander Kevin Bemming said in the bridge log being viewed by the Region Two HQ Board in their meeting hall several days later. Bemming moved forward in his command chair and stared at the image on the front monitor before asking no one in particular, "Are those ships?"

Another monitor in the HQ Board hall was showing the image that Bemming was staring at.

"Freeze image," Jenetta said. "Look at those objects."

"They appear more like the froth on a glass of ale than spaceships," Admiral Poole said.

The HQ Board had been viewing the logs from the *Yenisei* for more than an hour before reaching this point. The small ship had pursued a cluster of three ships for over seven hours, attempting to close the distance without using Light-9790, but was unable to overtake the vessels using its maximum single-envelope speed. In the end, Commander Bemming had given the order to jump ahead of the unidentified ships and wait for them.

When the three ships discovered the *Yenisei* sitting in front of them, they slowed to sub-light speeds and slowly closed the distance between the vessels. Jenetta had ordered the replay to be fast-forwarded until the unknown ships slowed to sub-light speeds after Admiral Kanes informed the board that nothing noteworthy had happened after the *Yenisei* had begun pursuit until it confronted the three ships.

"The design is certainly unique," Admiral Holt said. "I've never seen anything even remotely like it before. I have to wonder about the hull construction. It looks so fragile."

"Continue playing the log," Jenetta said.

As the vid started again, the unidentified ships moved slowly closer to the *Yenisei*.

"Com, attempt to contact those ships again," Commander Bemming said.

"Aye, Captain," the com chief said, then could be heard saying, "Unidentified ships, this is the GSC ship *Yenisei*. You have entered Galactic Alliance Space. You must identify yourselves immediately." The com chief repeated the message two more times when the ships failed to respond.

The ships continued to move closer without any response. Suddenly, the tac officer aboard the *Yenisei* shouted, "Multiple weapons launched. Ninety-two seconds to first contact."

"All laser gunners fire at will," Commander Bemming announced over the ship-wide system. "Knock those birds down and target the alien ships." Looking toward the helmsman he said, "Helm, evade."

"Aye, Captain," the helmsman said and the ship began to move. "We canceled our envelope so we're limited to sub-light speeds."

"Should I target the alien ships with torpedoes, sir?" the tac officer asked.

"Not yet. They can't hurt us with their weapons and I want a chance to talk to them before we use torpedoes. Com, try to contact them again. Tell them to stop firing on us or we'll be forced to destroy them."

"There are too many torpedoes coming in, Captain," the tac officer said. "I'm seeing over ten thousand."

"What? Over ten thousand torpedoes? From three ships? That's not possible."

"They're small, sir. Tiny. Nothing like ours."

"That's a relief. Tiny torpedoes can't harm our Dakinium hull. But let's shoot down as many as possible just to be sure."

Laser pulses stretched out from the *Yenisei*, searching for targets, and small explosions dotted space between the two ships.

"The Phalanx system is taking control of all guns but the torpedoes are small and moving fast," the tac officer said. "It's having trouble tracking them."

"It's still better than a human gunner. Don't override the control."

The admirals and their aides watched the log in safety but, knowing the outcome, felt anxiety for the *Yenisei* crew, coupled with sadness and regret that they couldn't warn them.

Expectedly, torpedoes began to penetrate the umbrella of fire from the overwhelmed Phalanx system and impacted against the hull. On the bridge, no buffeting was felt, but alarms soon began to sound at the tac station.

"Tac, what's going on?" Bemming barked over the alarms.

"I don't know, Captain. The missiles are tiny and causing no apparent damage, yet we're getting warnings that the hull has been breached in multiple locations. Large areas of the ship are opening to space. We're losing atmo at a far faster rate than should be possible."

"How can their tiny missiles be responsible for that?"

"I don't know, sir. They seem more like annoying stings than powerful weapons."

"So what's causing the hull damage?"

"Unknown, sir. Perhaps Engineering can investigate."

In response to new explosions that suddenly began rocking the ship, alarms suddenly began shrieking on the bridge.

"Multiple bulkheads have been breached in this frame section," the tac officer yelled. "Evacuate the bridge."

Crew people on the bridge began jumping from their chairs. Most ran towards the corridor doors, while a few headed for emergency air supplies. None were able to save themselves. The evacuation of atmosphere suddenly turned into a tsunami of wind as a new explosion ripped away a huge section of a bridge bulkhead. The surge of air towards the hole was enough that most crewmembers lost their footing. By then, the corridor was also breached, so no safety would be found there. The ones who tried to reach the emergency supplies were already in the grip of hypoxia and just didn't have enough time or strength left to open the emergency cabinets, pull out the equipment, and activate the tanks. They collapsed to the deck and never moved again.

"How could that have happened?" Admiral Buckner asked aloud. "How could that bulkhead have burst like that?"

"It can't," Admiral Kanes said. "At least not normally. Small missiles with minimal explosive power should not have been able to do that. They should not even have been able to perforate the outer Dakinium hull."

"Obviously, the warhead on these missiles is the key," Admiral Holt said. "They don't achieve the damage through explosive force but rather with some sort of particle manipulation or molecular disintegration. Plus, the sheer volume of devices fired at the *Yenisei* overwhelmed its Phalanx system. I doubt that even a battleship could have survived that onslaught of missiles."

"The report by the captain of the *Thames* that accompanied the logs states that the metal immediately around the hull penetrations crumbles like papier-mâché," Admiral Poole said.

"We have to face the fact that this enemy might be in league with the Raiders," Jenetta said.

"The Raiders?" Admiral Buckner echoed. "What leads you to that assessment?"

"We know for a fact that the Raiders managed to get a sample of Dakinium a few years ago. By now, they'll have put it through every metallurgical test their scientists know. And they may have shared their findings with whoever it is that attacked our ship. Even if the attackers can't manufacture Dakinium, they might have been able to use the information to develop that weapon."

"I'm not sure the Raiders have the kind of resources necessary to do that," Admiral Holt said, "but I can think of one enemy who is intelligent enough to develop something like that, and has the resources."

"Don't keep us in suspense, Brian," Admiral Poole said. "Who?"

"The Uthlaro."

"But Jenetta knocked their heads against the bulkhead and wiped out their entire military force."

"But we didn't level the planet's surface, so they still have all their scientific resources and industrial complexes in place."

Silence in the room was complete as everyone considered Holt's statement.

Finally, Jenetta broke the silence. "Our first priority must be to find a defense, and until the *Yenisei* is returned to Quesann where our metallurgical experts and chemical analysis people can study it, we can't begin to know how we'll combat this threat. We'll worry about finding out who is ultimately responsible once we're able to meet these ships on our terms. Augustus, alert all captains, both SC and Territorial Guard, that they must avoid contact with any ships whose appearance is similar to the ones we observed in the vid logs. I don't want any additional confrontations until we have a way to mount a decent defense."

"You want me to tell them to run away?"

"No Space Command captain likes to run from a fight, but it's better than losing our ships and people needlessly. From what I just saw, we don't stand a chance against those weapons."

"Should we continue to search for the *Salado*?"

"Yes. There may be crew members still alive in airtight compartments. At the very least, we'll have additional information from the logs and additional samples of the damage if we need it. But I don't want any new contact with the enemy until we have a plan of attack that gives us a fighting chance. Keith, we need to know everything possible about those three ships. Have your people magnify the images from the logs, enhance them, and examine them under an electron microscope if necessary. We saw a sample of their firepower. It's prodigious— but was that the full extent of it? What's their reload time, or is it a one-shot weapons system? How large are the ships and what's the estimated crew size? Plus anything else you can discern or estimate."

"My people are already working on it, but I wanted to show the logs to the Board members as soon as possible."

"Good. Any answers would be appreciated. I haven't felt this helpless since I found myself in a Raider jail cell."

Chapter Nine
~ May 14ᵗʰ, 2286 ~

"Captain, contact off the larboard quarter," the tac officer aboard the scout-destroyer *Gambia* announced loudly."

"Helm, all stop. Leave the envelope intact."

"Aye, Captain," the helmsman said. "We're stopped. Our envelope in still active."

"Tac, how far is that contact?"

"Two million, seven hundred forty-two thousand, eight hundred six kilometers, sir."

"Is it under power?"

"Negative, sir. I'm not reading a power signature."

"Size?"

"About the size of a scout-destroyer."

"Tac, send the coordinates to the helm and com. Com, notify the *Vistula* and *Yukon* that we're going to investigate, and feed them the location."

"Aye, Captain," both said.

"Tac, sound GQ. Helm, cancel the envelope and take us to the location of the contact at Sub-Light-100. Hold us at twenty-five thousand kilometers."

"Aye, Captain."

Commander Wilson Teffler leaned back in his command chair and buckled his seat belt just as the sub-light engines kicked in. The inertial compensators absorbed most of the sudden acceleration, and the lurch was barely noticeable. The seat belt was for when the ship started to slow, just in case the inertial compensators failed.

At one hundred thousand kilometers per second, the *Gambia* closed with the target in less than half a minute.

Unlike traveling at FTL speeds where a temporal envelope was used, sub-light travel didn't just end when the engines were disengaged. After achieving Sub-Light-100, the helmsman canceled the thrust and swung the rotating engine nacelles around to face backwards. At the appropriate point, he began applying power to slow and stop the ship.

"Twenty-five thousand kilometers, sir," the Helmsman said.

"Tac, put the image of the target up on the front monitor."

"Aye, sir."

A second later, a close-up image of the *Salado* appeared on the full bulkhead monitor at the front of the bridge. The image was enough to elicit a gasp from everyone who saw it. If compared to nineteenth-century vessels that had fought a battle at sea and lost, the ship could be said to look like one that had been sunk and then raised after fifty years on the bottom of the sea. It was that terrible.

"Any signs of life, tac?" Commander Teffler asked.

"Negative, sir. Nothing showing on the board. It's possible that someone could be alive in a stasis chamber or escape pod."

"Helm, take us in to one thousand kilometers." On ship-wide announcement, Teffler said, "Attention crew, this is the captain. We've found what looks like the *Salado*. We'll be sending teams over to look for survivors. Remain at your GQ posts unless you receive orders to the contrary."

To his XO, sitting in the chair next to his, Teffler said, "Deploy the teams, XO. I want every inch of the *Salado* checked for signs of life. Have the Marines go in first and check for rigged explosives before the engineers move in to recover the system logs."

"Aye, Captain," the XO said as he called up the duty lists and began to assemble the teams.

"Captain, the captains of the *Vistula* and *Yukon* are asking to speak with you," the com chief said.

"Put them on my left-hand monitor, Chief."

A second later, the monitor was showing a split screen image with Commander Ashlyn Flanery of the *Vistula* on the left and Commander Shawn Fischer of the *Yukon* on the right.

"Is it confirmed, Wilson?" Flanery asked immediately. "Is it the *Salado*?"

"It's confirmed, although I wish it wasn't."

"Like the *Yenisei*?" Fischer asked tersely.

"Yeah, it looks as bad as the images of the *Yenisei* that we saw, if not worse. We're preparing to go aboard and search for survivors, but there're no signs of life at this point. I think we're going to need a lot of body bags."

"How can we assist?" Flanery asked.

"Your people could start the external examination, Ashlyn. I'm sure that HQ is going to want the images as soon as possible. Shawn, it would great if you could perform picket duty. Whoever did this might still be lurking around."

"Sure thing, Wilson. We'll circle the area three billion kilometers out."

"Thanks, Shawn. Well guys, let's get to work."

In the *Gambia's* shuttle bay, a pilot was performing a walk-around with the head mechanic while Marines in EVA suits lined up before boarding. Normally, the Marines would wear the new body armor when boarding another ship, but the *Salado* was open to space and they would need the extra protection of an EVA suit. An engineer, also suited-up in an EVA, would ride over in the airlock. When the shuttle reached the *Salado*, the engineer would leave the ship and attempt to use the *Salado's* outside control panel to open the shuttle bay door. The engineer carried a small auxiliary battery pack to provide power if the *Salado's* power cells were completely drained.

Twenty minutes later, the Marines were beginning a careful search of the *Salado*. The monitor on the *Gambia's* bridge was a patchwork of small images from the helmet cams. The sights were gruesome. As on the *Yenisei*, the crew had died almost instantly as the atmosphere was evacuated through numerous holes in the hull and bulkheads.

Meanwhile, the *Vistula's* engineers were taking images of the exterior damage and collecting samples of the crumbling hull material. Knowing the normal strength of the material, they couldn't believe that weapons fire had been able to degrade Dakinium this way.

The *Yukon* was on its eighth pass at Light-9790 speed three billion kilometers from the *Salado*, when the tac officer said loudly, "Captain, I have a contact at maximum DeTect Range."

"Sound GQ. How many ships, Tac?"

"The contact is still too distant for detailed data, sir."

"How much time do we have before they can be in range of the *Salado*?"

"About fifty-two seconds at its present speed."

"Damn. Com, get me the *Gambia* and the *Vistula*."

"They're on, Captain."

Fischer looked down at the monitor by his left hand. The other two captains were looking at him apprehensively.

"There's an unidentified contact heading this way. I'm assuming it's one or more enemy ships. Start building your envelopes. We have fifty seconds before they reach us at present speed."

"We don't see it," Flanery of the *Vistula* said. "It's not on our DeTect monitors yet."

"Nor ours," Teffler said.

"I can't possibly recover my people in less than ten minutes," Flanery said.

"I need about thirty minutes," Teffler said.

"We don't have even one. Tell your people to get inside the *Salado* and find undamaged life pods. Then have them use the stasis beds. We'll return when we can. Tell them not to respond to your message and to maintain strict radio silence."

"I won't leave my people," Flanery said flatly.

"Nor will I," Teffler said. "We'll have to fight."

"Open your eyes and look at the *Salado*. We have no defense against whatever weapons did that. For that reason, Standing Orders are to avoid contact. If we stay here, we lose our ships and our entire crews. Think of the hundreds of other lives you hold in your hands, not just the teams aboard the *Salado*."

"Dammit, dammit, dammit," Teffler grumbled through clenched teeth, then shouted excitedly, "Helm, build our envelope."

"Helm, build our envelope," Flanery said to her helmsman. A second later, she said to Teffler and Fischer, "Our shuttle bay door is still open. We're closing it so we can build the envelope."

"My envelope is already built," Fischer said, "so I'll try to distract the enemy ship to give you a little time."

"You're not going to engage, are you?" Flanery asked.

"No. And I won't drop my envelope to fire torpedoes. I'll just stop a second and fire my lasers to see if I can stop him or pull him off course by faking an attack. If he fires on us, I'll be gone before his missiles can clear the tubes."

"I hope it works," Flanery said. "Uh— thanks, Shawn."

"Good luck, Shawn," Teffler said. His face still showed the frustration he was feeling, but Fischer knew it wasn't directed at him.

"Good luck to all of us," Fischer said.

*   *   *

Nicole Ravenau stepped lightly into the shuttle and walked to her seat, trying not to evince the pain she felt. Her spine was on fire, and every step today had been torture. The pain she experienced as she eased herself down into her seat was almost unbearable. She had done everything she could to mask the beauty of her face and body and was now trying to suppress contortion of her features because she didn't want to draw attention to herself through sympathy or concern for her health. But inside she was screaming in agony.

Over the past few weeks, Ravenau had toiled to move her agenda forward. She had first worked to secure an incontestable copy of Strauss's fingerprints. A janitor had supplied a water glass from Strauss's office, a busboy had pocketed a dessert dish from the restaurant in Strauss's apartment building as he cleared the table following Strauss's meal, and a Raider clerk had supplied a fingerprints image and DNA record from the corporate files. After Ravenau had cross-matched the fingerprints and verified that she had a correct set, she paid off the people who had supplied the data. A hired assassin would ensure the janitor, busboy, and clerk never told anyone about their activity once Ravenau was away from the planet. Each death would appear to be an accident.

Before Strauss could integrate Ravenau's lab with the Raider Central Lab, Ravenau worked with her scientists to create a new body for her. She dreaded the thought of under-going another year of almost constant pain, but she had decided to return to a male form. She had completed the Age Regression procedure, and having undergone the Age Prolon-gation procedure long ago, she could now probably depend on having five thousand years to perfect a full immortality procedure. The sex change should guarantee that her sexual frustration problems were behind her. A side benefit of the procedure was that with the Carvers looking for a woman, she would once again be invisible to them.

Just before Ravenau left to catch her shuttle flight to the passenger liner in space, she had set the timer on explosive charges hidden in the lab. When her people met for the scheduled meeting later that day, the entire building would disappear in a blast that might even destroy the surrounding buildings as well. It would be assumed that had Ravenau died with the rest. She hoped it would be enough to convince Strauss. In any event, she intended to disappear until her body changes were complete. No one outside of a few lab person-nel knew what her new appearance would be, and they would all be dead before morning, along with the destruction of all the records.

* * *

The assassin didn't know who had hired him, or why, and didn't care. He usually worked for the Raider Corporation, but he took jobs on the side as well. He had a reputation for being one of the best at dispatching people who had a full security force protecting them, so offing a few nobodies would be a cakewalk. Since starting down a slippery slope by outlawing all guns, restrictions had progressed until private citizens were prohibited from even carrying metal keys, paperweights, or a sock full of coins. But anyone who wished could still get a free whistle from their local police department. Still not satisfied, politicians used the argument that the hands of a martial arts expert were deadly weapons and made martial arts study and practice by private citizens illegal. Every thief, rapist, or murderer knew that as long as he didn't target an off-duty cop, security person, or former Marine, he would have little trouble doing whatever he planned to a law-abiding citizen.

The assassin had already checked the complete background of each of the three targets using the planet's 'Open and Transparent Society' database. The janitor had been suspended from school for two weeks when he was seven for making a threatening gesture towards a fellow male student— he'd pointed an index finger at another small boy. The woman had slapped another six-year-old who ratted her out while she was trying to shoplift a candy bar from a sweets shop. The busboy had kicked another child in pre-school when the other youth took one of the toy farm animals he was playing with. These violent and antisocial episodes were responsible for the three never having been able to get a decent job, but in the mind of the assassin, the three targets were milquetoast. The payment of a hundred-credit fee to the government's Citizen History Department had bought him the same hundred-page biography that was available to all prospective employers. Another five credits bought him a file history from Boogel.com of every product each target had ever purchased or looked up on their computer. A quick scan revealed no purchase of dangerous self-defense weaponry, such as pocketknives, or attempts to acquire knowledge regarding the manufacture of explosives from ordinary household or gardening chemicals. Having the full details of a target's life was always a justifiable expense in his business.

In three days' time the three targets would be dead. One would die horribly in an elevator accident, another in an apartment fire, and the third by a drug prescription error for a common sleeping aid. Then the assassin would be off to his vacation lodge for a month of rest and relaxation.

* * *

Nicole Ravenau was so ill that she never came out of her suite after boarding the passenger liner. Her body needed food to fuel the changes being made, so she forced herself to eat the six meals delivered to her cabin each day. Immediately after eating, she generally took a pill so she could sleep until it was mealtime again.

The news had confirmed the *accidental* demise of the three people whose deaths Ravenau had arranged, as well as the explosion at her former lab. Her name was on the list of people who had died that day. She had used yet another identity when buying the tickets for the cruise, so no one should make a connection even if she showed her face outside her suite. When she did reveal herself next, she would look radically different than when she had boarded. She already had another cover identity that matched her expected appearance.

The passenger liner would be underway for months, stopping briefly at six planets before reaching Ravenau's destination: Pelomious. As Mikel Arneu, she had once purchased a ranch there under a cover name and constructed a deluxe underground bunker using funds siphoned from the Age Prolongation project. The sparsely populated agrarian planet would be her home until it was time for her to surface again and carry out the rest of her plan.

* * *

"This is *very* disturbing news," Arthur Strauss, the chairman of the Raider Lower Council said to longtime councilmember Bentley Blosworth at a regularly scheduled meeting. "You're saying that after we gave a complete laboratory analysis of Dakinium to the Uthlaro, *free of charge*, in order for them to duplicate and manufacture the material for us, they're *selling* the formula to everyone who can meet their price?"

"Not a formula to produce Dakinium," Blosworth said calmly, "just the laboratory analysis we sent. It appears that they've been unable to reproduce Dakinium and are hoping that one of the purchasers of the analysis will develop a formula and then share it with the Uthlaro, at which time the Uthlaro will return the fifty trillion credits paid for the analysis."

"It doesn't matter that it's not the actual formula," Strauss snapped. "We gave them that analysis and now they're profiting from it. We could have sold the laboratory report ourselves. We didn't need them for that. And you've said that they've also offered to sell the formula, once it's developed, to any interested parties for a hundred trillion credits."

"Yes, that's perhaps the most disturbing part. It's one thing to seek help with the development but another to sell something that results from what we sent as part of our deal."

"Our deal required them to manufacture Dakinium exclusively for us."

"And they say they will honor those terms. But they also say that the agreement doesn't specifically preclude them from selling the *formula* to others so Dakinium can be manufactured by other parties who are not operating under the manufacturing exclusivity agreement. And we can't exactly take them to court to prove our case."

"Damn all Uthlaro businessmen. You can't trust any of them." Strauss leaned back in his chair and appeared to be studying the ceiling as he thought. Suddenly he sat back up and said to no one in particular, "What do you think Admiral Carver would do if she learned that the Uthlaro were selling an analysis of Dakinium to all interested parties?"

"She'd probably do what she should have done initially—" Councilmember Erika Overgaard said, "return to Uthlarigasset and blast them back to their stone age, as she almost did to the Milori home world."

"Yes," Strauss said. "What a delightful thought."

"But what about the warships the Uthlaro are building for us?" Councilmember Frederick Kelleher asked. "We're depending on getting those ships by the promised delivery dates. We need them to continue our efforts against the Aguspod."

"Those ships are being built a thousand light-years from Uthlarigasset, just outside GA Space in unclaimed territory. Space Command won't venture there and I doubt they have any idea what's going on out there anyway. The foundry and shipyard will continue production regardless of what happens on Uthlarigasset. Besides, once their home world is destroyed, the shipyard will be all the workers have, and they'll blame the destruction on Carver. The question now is: how do we alert Carver in a way that she'll believe the information is credible and take action? If Ravenau were still alive, I'd have her send a vidMail. Carver would have believed her in an instant."

*   *   *

The subject in the message that appeared in Jenetta's message queue was simply marked 'Vertap.' The sender name and date was scrambled. Jenetta walked to her safe and removed the box of data rings she kept there. Pushing the rings around with her finger until she found the silver one with the delicate filigree décoration, she lifted it out, then returned the box to the safe and closed the door. Once back at her desk, she touched the ring to the small, flexible spindle on the keyboard, then leaned in towards the monitor to provide the required retinal scan. When the sender name and date unscrambled, she took her seat and pressed the play button.

"Greetings, Admiral Carver," the image of the Hudeerac Minister of Intelligence said. "It was so nice to hear from you again. Thank you for inquiring after my king's health. I'm delighted to inform you that all is well here. In fact, it's better than it has been in decades. The leadership King Jamolendre has displayed since the Milori first attacked the GA has fostered greater support from the nobility than any king has enjoyed in thousands of annuals. The nobles who tried to usurp his throne by pushing us into war during that terrible time are in such disgrace that they fear to show their faces in the capital. We've worked to restore the structure of government on the planets the Milori had occupied, and the kingdom is once again united. We owe you much and are happy to share any intelligence data we have for our mutual benefit.

"With regard to your questions, I can offer only a small amount. We know the Ruwalchu adopted an extremely aggressive posture approximately an annual ago. They have been building new warships and expanding their military at an unprecedented rate, but we haven't been able to ascertain their future intentions.

"It's confusing because they've always been a benign neighbor who, by our evaluation, only wished to live in peace. Their technology was advanced enough to ensure that Maxxiloth, aware that he probably couldn't win a war, didn't attack them as he revived his grandfather's delusions of manifest destiny. At best, a conflict might have ended in a draw, so Maxxiloth was wise enough to wait until he was stronger before deciding if he should attack them.

"To learn recently that the Ruwalchu seem to be on a war footing has been distressing. There's speculation that they may fear a neighbor, but we know little of neighbors who might border their territory on the side away from the one we share with them.

"The Uthlaro are quite another story. After you defeated them and annexed their territory, they became much more secretive within their top ranks. Our contacts have not been able to penetrate the new inner circles. The story we hear is that they so fear your promises of punishment for sedition that information regarding their future plans is limited to a select few.

"We do know that the planetary government has recruited tens of thousands of workers and sent them somewhere, but we haven't been able to find out where. The talk is that they've been sent off-world to a place where they could build a base that would allow them to prepare for a future war with the GA. We assume that means it's outside GA space since more than half the space bordering your Region Three is still unclaimed. They can work there, free from worry that you'll happen across them. Even if you do, you have no authority to stop them or even question them. They might even establish a new nation and claim the territory. That would give them very real sovereign rights under Galactic Alliance law. You would not be able to enter their territory without permission unless you first declared war, and you would have no justification for making such a declaration. I'm tempted to state that it's an interesting dilemma, but I don't wish to minimize the danger in any way. It's a situation you must both be aware of and prepared for.

"Finally, there's speculation that the Ruwalchu and Uthlaro are working together. We know that the Uthlaro Intelligence Service has been in close contact with the Ruwalchu Intelligence Service since you defeated the Uthlaro, but we haven't been able to examine any of their communications. Some of my people even believe that Ruwalchu is making preparations to go to war with the Galactic Alliance.

"I would welcome any updated information you secure, and I wish you well."

"Minister Vertap Aloyandro, end of message."

Jenetta leaned back in her chair to stare at the ceiling while she thought. The SC databases contained no images of Ruwalchu warships and just a basic description of the nation's primary population. Until Transverse Wave Travel was discovered, speeds beyond Light-450 were considered impossible with current technology, and no one ever really expected the GA to have contact with such a distant neighbor. But now that the GA bordered directly on Ruwalchu space, the Confederacy might be fearful that the GA was casting jealous eyes on their territory. Since the GA knew nothing about the Ruwalchu, it made sense that the Ruwalchu knew nothing about the GA. If their only information about the GA was coming from the Uthlaro, that information was sure to be tainted. Jenetta wished she'd originally asked Vertap for images of Ruwalchu warship designs.

"Well, that's easily correctable," she said aloud, and she leaned forward to prepare a new message. "Too bad it takes a minimum of six weeks to hear back."

Chapter Ten

~ June 12th, 2286 ~

"I've got news," Admiral Poole said to Jenetta via the vid call to her office in the palace. "Little of it good."

Jenetta sighed lightly. She'd had too much bad news lately. She could use some good news for a change, but it was in short supply these days. "I've never known bad news to improve with age. Tell me, Augustus."

"We've found the *Salado*. Its condition is similar to the *Yenisei*. All aboard were killed in the conflict. Worse, we lost crewmembers aboard the *Gambia* and *Vistula* when the unknown enemy showed up."

"What? How could that happen? We issued orders *not* to engage."

"The captain of the *Yukon* reports that their search group found the *Salado*. SC Engineers and Marines from the *Gambia* went aboard to search the interior for survivors and to download the ship's logs while engineers from the *Vistula* were investigating the exterior so they could produce a report about the hull damage. The *Yukon* then took up a circling picket defense three billion kilometers out.

"When the enemy showed up, there wasn't time for the *Gambia* and *Vistula* to get their people back aboard, so their captains ordered them to occupy undamaged life pods in the *Salado*, use the stasis beds, and maintain radio silence.

"Even without recovering their people, the *Gambia* and *Vistula* didn't have enough time to build their envelopes, so the *Yukon* tried to distract the enemy ships to give the others a little more time. It had to keep an adequate distance from the enemy ships and never dropped its envelope to fire torpedoes, but it came to a halt and fired its laser arrays. The ruse worked and delayed the enemy's approach enough that the other two ships were able to complete their envelopes before the enemy ships got within range to fire their missiles. So we've only lost the people who ducked into the *Salado*, or were there already. If they all made it to intact life pods, and if the enemy didn't return to further destroy the ship, they may be able to recover them. We don't know. The captain of the *Yukon* reports that they would have stayed and fought if Standing Orders hadn't called for them to evacuate the area immediately."

"I'm glad they didn't try to be heroic and sacrifice their ships and crews needlessly."

"I get the impression they were incredibly upset about leaving comrades to die, and that's completely understand-able. I sent a message applauding their adherence to orders and tried to make them feel better by congratulating them for taking exactly the right action to save their ships and the rest of their crews. It probably won't make them feel any better right now, but eventually they'll understand it was absolutely necessary."

"I think we all understand how they feel, but as you say, they took the correct action. What's the good news?"

"The *Yukon* was able to get high-resolution images of the enemy ships when they faked their attack and the enemy ships came to a stop, dropped their envelopes, and fired their missiles. The *Yukon* was also receiving a copy of the *Salado's* log as it was being downloaded to the *Gambia*, as well as all of the images being sent by the *Gambia* and *Vistula* Marines and Engineers. The information burst is still coming in, and then Keith will get his people working on it. A full report should be ready for the Board's session tomorrow."

"Wonderful. I look forward to that session. Thanks, Augustus."

"See you tomorrow, Jen."

* * *

"Keith tells me that his people have spent all night working on the data stream from the *Yukon*," Jenetta said after opening the Board meeting the next morning, "so let's jump right in. Show us what you have, Keith."

"The battle between the *Salado* and the enemy ships went pretty much like the battle between the *Yenisei* and the enemy, so let's move directly to the high-resolution images taken by the *Yukon* during its brief skirmish." Admiral Keith Kanes nodded to the clerk at the console and an image of the enemy ship appeared on the full wall monitor behind Jenetta.

Everyone in the room turned their chairs to face the image as Kanes walked to the wall.

"Computer, Kanes presentation fourteen, first stage."

An arrow pointing to a part of the enemy ship lit up on the image.

"As you can see, those bubbles we saw previously are actually segmented protective domes that cover missile-launching platforms mounted around all exterior surfaces of the ships. When retracted, the launchers are exposed and the enemy can fire hundreds of missiles at the same instant from each platform. Computer, next stage."

A new image appeared that showed a missile platform with the dome cover retracted.

"We're estimating that each ship can fire up to a hundred missiles from each platform before they have to close the dome to rearm, and there are a total of about two hundred of these small platforms located around the full circumference of each ship from bow to stern."

"Good Lord," Admiral Poole said. "Each ship can fire twenty thousand of those small missiles without reloading?"

"That's what we're estimating," Kanes said as he returned to his chair.

"Is there anything else, Keith?" Jenetta asked.

"We have the logs of the battle, and the reports and images from the people who boarded the *Salado*, but there wasn't anything new so I didn't think you'd want to go over it here. It's available through the computer system to anyone with the proper clearance, or authorized personnel can view it in the holo-theater downstairs."

"I'll view it later in my office unless anyone on the Board wants to view it now."

Jenetta looked around the table at the other admirals. One by one they all shook their heads.

"The high-res images were enlightening," Jenetta said. "I'm surer than ever that we must avoid a confrontation with these attackers until we have a plan for defeating them."

"How can we defend against an enemy that can assault us with sixty thousand missiles before they have to reload," Admiral Poole said, "and where their tiny missiles can destroy Dakinium?"

"I don't know, Augustus," Jenetta said. "The *Winston* should arrive here in two weeks with the *Yenisei* in her hold. Our weapons research people and engineers are waiting anxiously to begin examining him. Perhaps they'll find something or figure out something that will give us an edge, or at least a fighting chance. Okay, let's proceed with regular business."

* * *

The *Winston* arrived at Quesann right on schedule. Since the base had no shipbuilding facilities or enclosed repair docks, the enormous transport would serve as the dock for the people performing the investigation and analysis work. It meant that the workers wouldn't have to wear EVA suits or even carry oxygen, and the lack of gravity in the hold facilitated movement. Visitor's quarters aboard ship would make commuting to the base or another ship unnecessary.

Jenetta and the other admirals were the first to view the damaged *Yenisei* when the *Winston* arrived. The transport had barely established orbit around the planet before a shuttle carrying the R2HQ Board members entered one of its shuttle bays. As soon as the greeting formalities were completed, the prestigious party was escorted to the hold.

Bodies of the *Yenisei* crewmembers had been collected at the battle site and stored in refrigerated compartments in the *Winston*. Medical personnel would perform an autopsy on every cadaver to verify the cause of death.

Outside the entrance to the hold, each of the admirals was provided with a radiation suit, a small propulsion backpack, and magnetic boots. Then the *Winston's* captain took the party on an inspection tour of the hull damage. It seemed even more horrific than the transmitted images had indicated. The hull had the look of a derelict ship hundreds of years old, despite having been built less than a year before the attack. All of the officers had seen blast damage from explosive weapons and laser arrays, but the damage to the *Yenisei* seemed to have been caused by heat. The edges of the holes were smooth like melted plastic rather than jagged metal. This evidence confirmed what had already been suspected. Tiny warheads on the enemy missiles could not be responsible for the damage to the ship. So just what had evacuated the atmosphere, destroyed bulkheads and decks, and killed the crew?

* * *

Two weeks later, the admirals met not in the R2HQ Admiralty Hall but in a conference room in the Governor's Palace. The only officers not of flag rank were Captain Barbara DeWitt and each admiral's senior aide.

"You said you have a preliminary report, Barbara?" Jenetta asked.

"Yes, Admiral. I'm sure you've surmised much of what we've learned from your own observations, but I wanted to announce what we've confirmed. The holes in the hull are not owed to explosive force. Prior to our examination of the hull material, and relying solely on the transmitted images, we thought the loss of the ship might be due to some sort of small nuclear device. We still believe that."

"Nuclear weapons can't penetrate Dakinium," Jenetta said. "That's been proven through extensive testing."

"Yes, Admiral, nuclear weapons cannot damage Dakinium, but once the Dakinium layer was breached, the interior damage can be attributed to nuclear fission. There are excessively high levels of radiation at every blast point, and although the crew died of hypoxia, their bodies also have lethal concentrations of radiation. My staff and I believe that upon reaching their target the missiles attach themselves to the hull in some manner. The warhead then disperses some sort of chemical that begins to melt the Dakinium. Once a hole of sufficient size is achieved, a tiny nuclear charge takes care of the rest. The enemy fires thousands of missiles and depends on at least a few hundred getting through. I don't have to tell you the effectiveness of the attack."

"So you're saying that the enemy missiles are like a slow-acting limpet mine?"

"Uh— essentially. I'd liken it more to the 'sticky bombs' developed by the British during World War II on Earth."

"Sticky bombs?" Admiral Poole said.

"In 1940," Captain DeWitt said, "following the Dunkirk withdrawal, the British government believed that an invasion by Germany was likely. Of great concern was possible attacks by Germany's formidable tank corps. The Brits had left eighty-five percent of the military's anti-tank guns behind in France during their hasty retreat. One solution to their lack of weapons, albeit a desperate one, was the 'sticky bomb.' Essentially, it was designed as a hand grenade for use against tanks. A core of nitroglycerine was surrounded by a viscous mass with the properties of a petroleum jelly, which was then in turn surrounded by a two-piece light metal case. When the pin was pulled, the outer casing fell away, exposing the inner viscous-covered mass while initiating a five-second fuse in the nitro. If the sticky bomb landed in a vulnerable spot where it could stick to the surface, such as near the tank's treads, it could potentially incapacitate the vehicle.

"We believe the enemy's missiles are somewhat like those sticky bombs. The head of the warhead breaks open on contact, spreading a chemical that makes the missile stick to the hull while it eats away at the Dakinium. Then something triggers a tiny nuclear fission device, possibly the outflow of atmo, or perhaps just a timed fuse, which directs the force into the ship. Bulkheads are blown open, and the evacuation of atmo is almost instantaneous while the area is flooded with deadly radiation. Even if the survivors in other areas can access the damaged frame sections and seal the hull, the radiation must be dealt with before the area can be used safely. Essentially, the ship is incapacitated even if the crew-members are not all killed."

"What kind of chemical can open holes in Dakinium?" Admiral Buckner asked.

"At this time, ships in space cannot repair damage to Dakinium as we once did with tritanium plating. Fortunately, we haven't had to. But if damaged, the ship would have to cover the hole with a temporary Dakinium patch and then travel back to Mars for a proper repair. Mars would perform a repair with chemical processes that have been developed for cutting and welding Dakinium. The reason that only Mars can perform the repair is that SHQ wants the chemical process to remain completely secret. We know the Raiders managed to secure a sample of Dakinium, and it now appears possible that someone might have sold the chemical formulas to the enemy that's attacking us."

"You're saying we have a traitor at the most secret and secure manufacturing facility in the galaxy?" Jenetta said.

"Well, that seems the most likely scenario. I don't have to remind *you* that we've had traitors at the very top in Space Command before this. Of course, it's possible that an enemy nation developed the formula on their own after getting their hands on a piece of Dakinium. It's also possible that this is a standard weapon of theirs which just happens to work well against Dakinium. But I tend not to believe such things are mere coincidences."

"Well, this certainly makes my morning," Admiral Holt said.

"So we're talking about a two-stage warhead," Jenetta said, "that doesn't detonate until it makes contact. What about missiles that don't hit their targets, Barbara? Do they self-denote as our torpedoes do to prevent hazards to other traffic?"

"We were unable to see any detonations in the ship's log that were not owed to strikes by our laser arrays."

"So there could be hundreds or even thousands of these small missiles floating around out there?"

"Unless the enemy ships have a way of detonating them later or some way of collecting them, that's a distinct possibility. With the 'sticky bombs' I mentioned earlier, there were reports of the devices getting stuck to soldiers' clothing as they were attempting to throw them. They only had five seconds to get it free. Perhaps the enemy's own hull is impervious to the chemical in the warhead."

"And the nuclear charge?" Admiral Poole asked.

"Our ships are normally impervious to the nuclear charge and so might the ships we're facing."

"I wonder what the chances are of finding an intact missile," Jenetta mused.

"That would enable us to nail down the detonation premise and also perform an analysis of the chemical being used in the warhead."

"It'd be like finding a needle in a haystack," Admiral Poole said. "We might not even be able to locate the exact spot where the *Yenisei* was attacked now that the battle site has been cleaned up."

"True," Jenetta said, "but we still have a ship out there that must be retrieved. There are dozens of crewmembers from the *Gambia* and *Vistula* missing and we're hoping they were able to get to stasis beds in the *Salado*. We've been waiting until the enemy ships got tired of hanging around the battle site before returning to get our people. And while we're recovering our people, we could perform a search for one of those missiles."

"Those missiles might still be armed and dangerous," Admiral Buckner said. "One mistake and the nuclear charge could detonate inside the ship recovering the device."

"So far all we've been doing is guessing. I think it's imperative we make an effort to recover one of the weapons. It might provide a lot of answers, including the identity of the attackers."

"We still can't defend against that kind of missile attack," Admiral Holt said. "Our Phalanx systems can't hope to knock down tens of thousands of tiny missiles."

"That's true," Jenetta said, "but every piece of information about an enemy, no matter how small or seemingly insignificant, might be just the piece we need to turn the tide. I think it's worth the risk but only on a volunteer basis."

"How do you get an entire ship's crew to volunteer for such a dangerous task?" Admiral Buckner asked.

"One way could be to have the search conducted by one or more shuttles," Admiral Holt said. "If an intact missile were to be located, a demolitions expert in an EVA suit could exit through the airlock, retrieve the device, and bring it back inside where it would be defused before the shuttle reentered its ship."

"How about simply defusing it robotically outside the shuttle?" Admiral Buckner asked.

"We don't know exactly what we're dealing with," Admiral Holt said. "We believe the missiles are nuclear weapons, but a robot isn't an acceptable substitute for a demolitions expert in that kind of situation. Once we've observed the construction of the missile, unlocked its secrets, and documented the disassembly, robots will be able to take over if and when others are found."

"It seems to me that if we're ever to have a chance against these invaders," Admiral Buckner said, "it's now, when we have an enormous presence in that area because of the search effort."

"So far, all we've done is provide these attackers with a lot of targets," Jenetta said. "We now believe that a three-ship task force of enemy vessels can fire sixty thousand missiles in one barrage before they have to reload. What if we were to encounter a hundred-ship enemy fleet?"

"How about doing what you advocated at Higgins?" Admiral Holt said. "Present them with an irresistible target of opportunity, then duck under the incoming missile barrage and attack them from the rear?"

"Unfortunately, all of my previous tactics have been so widely publicized and discussed that none would come as a surprise."

"That didn't come into play when the Uthlaro armada attacked Quesann," Admiral Buckner said.

"Actually, it did. Admiral Krakosso was familiar with my bluff of the Milori at our second encounter and he believed the ships his tac officers were seeing on their DeTect monitors were unarmed civilian vessels. I used that to have him lower his guard slightly and initially make him an easier target for our ships."

"I'm sure you have something in mind for the new invaders," Admiral Holt said with a chuckle.

"I have the barest kernel of an idea, but it's so outlandish that I'm not willing to discuss it just yet. I want to think about it a bit more. And I could sure use more information about our enemy. I guess it's like that old saying: 'I need more information about my enemy in order to defeat him, but it seems I can't get the information I need until after I defeat him.'"

"There has to be someone who knows where these enemy ships have come from," Admiral Poole said.

"Yes, someone knows," Jenetta agreed. "But who?

* * *

Jenetta estimated that Vertap must have recorded his response to her most recent message within two days of having received it. The investigations were still underway and to date they had little new information, so she anxiously retrieved the decryption ring from her safe and dropped it on the small data spindle that was part of her computer keyboard. She leaned in to provide the retinal identification when required and then sat back as the image of the Hudeerac Minister of Intelligence formed on the monitor.

"Good day, Admiral Carver. I'm happy to share the intelligence data we've gathered with a peaceful neighbor, but I'm afraid that in this case our knowledge is quite limited.

We've had no contact with any species having ships employing the configuration you describe."

Jenetta's face immediately reflected her unhappiness. She had been counting on getting some small piece of information from Vertap. She knew of nowhere else to turn and sighed as Vertap continued.

"But I *can* offer you some *unconfirmed* data we've secured from a trader with whom we've had contact. I must stress again that none of this is confirmed, but your description seems to match configuration information provided by the trader about a species known as the Denubbewa. Their home system, known as the Denubbew Dominancy, is twelve thousand light-years beyond the Ruwalchu Confederacy. According to the trader, the Denubbewa have roaming colonies where the inhabitants spend their entire lives aboard immense mother ships, but he mentioned he had never heard of a Denubbewa ship coming within five thousand light-years of the Hudeerac border. However, I suppose it's possible that the Denubbewa may have expanded their influence, much as the Milora were attempting to do.

"I'm appending the full report regarding the Denubbewa that was prepared from conversations with the trader an annual ago. I hope it helps resolve your contact with the unknown species that is attacking your ships.

"Minister Vertap Aloyandro, end of message."

Jenetta opened the attachment and read all reports covering the conversations with the trader, then leaned back in her chair to think about this new information. It was the first lead to a possible identity of the attackers, but how credible was it if the species had never been spotted within five thousand light-years of the outer borders?

* * *

"Admiral," Lt. Commander Ashraf's voice announced through Jenetta's com, "Admiral Kanes is here."

"Send him in, Lori."

A few seconds later, the office door opened and Admiral Keith Kanes entered her large office in the HQ Admiralty building.

"Good morning, Jen," Kanes said. "What's so urgent that you wanted me to hurry over before I even had my first cup of coffee?"

"I thought that would make you understand how important this is. Fix yourself a cup at my beverage synthesizer and come have a seat."

Kanes prepared a cup of coffee using the special blend recipe Jenetta had uploaded to her synthesizer just for him, then joined her in her informal area.

"The urgency is owed to learning who might be attacking our ships." Jenetta gave Kanes a brief summary of the information provided by the Hudeerac.

"So this Denubbew Dominancy might be looking to expand their territory by taking space from us?"

"The motivation behind the attacks is unknown. So far all I have is a possible match based on the ship configuration. But if the Hudeerac information is correct, it gives us a starting place. And even though the Hudeerac stress that the information wasn't confirmed, I don't think they would have even mentioned it if they weren't somewhat confident that their source was being truthful."

"I have no recollection of ever having heard of these Denubbewa."

"That's not surprising, given the distance to their home system. Their appearance must be startling, if the report is correct. Their progeny are an artificially conceived organic life form. Once the infant reaches three years of age, its brain and other vital organs are placed into a bionic skeleton. They can reportedly be anywhere from one meter to nine meters in height."

"Nine meters?" Kanes said. "Seriously?"

That's what the report states.

"Do the organ transplants include a heart?"

"The file doesn't mention one. I assume you're asking if they are merciless?"

"Yes."

"From the viciousness of the attacks, i.e. without warning, I'd have to say that mercy and fair play are not included in their lexicons."

"Do they breathe air?"

"Not the oxygen/nitrogen mix we require. The report states that it's a methane mixture."

"Why the discrepancies in height?"

"Those destined for work in tight places are placed into small skeletons, while those who will perform heavy work receive the largest and most powerful skeletons. I imagine they come in all sizes and shapes to fit the role of the worker."

"Sounds like it's sort of an anthill where they breed workers and soldiers to perform different tasks."

"Yes, exactly."

"So where do we go from here?"

"I performed a search of the Space Command database for the names Denubbew and Denubbewa, or any close phonetic equivalents, hoping to uncover any information about them that we might already have. Nothing turned up. Now, I'd like you to send a query out to every agent in your section asking if anyone has ever heard of them. If this is the face of the enemy killing our people, we need to know anything and everything we can learn about them."

"That still may not tell us the motivation behind the attacks."

"No, but we have to start somewhere, and this seems like a good starting place. Um— how many agents do you have on Uthlarigasset?"

"One hundred sixty-two."

"Wonderful. I didn't realize we had that many there."

"We learned during the war just how duplicitous and tenacious they are, so we want to be prepared. We know it's just a matter of time before they take seditious action against the GA, so my people have orders to watch for any signs that they've crossed over the boundary into illegality."

"Right now, we don't know if the Denubbewa, if that's the face on the enemy attacking us, are acting on their own or in concert with the Ruwalchu, the Uthlaro, or someone else. I know you've been unable to infiltrate the Ruwalchu, so I'm glad you're concentrating on the Uthlaro."

"We not only have been unable to infiltrate the Ruwalchu, we haven't even been able to enter their space. They forbid entry by any species whose home system is located in GA space, and to most other species, such as the Gondusans, as well."

"I know. They've even refused to permit diplomatic contact. They say they just want to be left alone, but the Hudeerac have told us the Ruwalchu are apparently preparing for war in a major way. Their statements of wanting to be left alone don't ring true with their behind-the-scenes actions." Jenetta sighed before saying, "It's maddening knowing a war is coming, and may already have been launched, and not even knowing who's on the other side of the weapons being aimed at you."

Chapter Eleven

~ July 28th, 2286 ~

"The Upper Council has reached consensus on distribution of the DNA Manipulation and Aging formulas," Lower Council Chairman Strauss said. "First, the Age Prolongation will *only* be made available to Upper and Lower Council members, our brothel slaves, and select others to be named by the Upper Council. The reason is simple— they don't wish to establish a general population group with exceptional longevity. However, the DNA Manipulation process will be available to anyone who can pay the established price. Additionally, the Age Regression process will be available on a continuing basis to any female who has purchased the DNA Manipulation process. Males who have endured DNA Manipulation to change gender in order to avail themselves of the Age Regression process will be offered an opportunity to return to a male body within a reasonable time-frame at no additional charge."

"And the price to us?" Councilwoman Erika Overgaard asked.

"It's free to any council member in good standing."

"Good standing?"

"Alive."

"As a councilmember in good standing," Councilman Bentley Blosworth said with a chuckle, "I request that I receive the full treatment."

"You'll have to wait until after the Upper Council has com-pleted their transformations. Their advanced ages necessitate they go first, and we can't have both councils affected by mass absenteeism for long periods of time."

"How long an absenteeism period are we talking about?"

"Since eight of the twelve members on the Upper Council are male, the Council will be without a quorum for a minimum of six months. Although the gender swap process takes a full year to complete the basic body-shape changes, I've been told that a person has full motor control restoration after six months. Of course, the process hasn't been performed on subjects as aged as the Upper Council members, so we're treading on new ground here."

"I can wait," Blosworth said. "The formulas have been fully tested, I assume, if the Upper Council is ready to undergo the transformations."

"After subjecting herself to the treatments, Nicole Ravenau, a.k.a. Mikel Arneu, was as healthy as a human could ever expect to be. It's unfortunate that we lost her in that explosion because having a living lab specimen would have been invaluable. However, the Central Labs have assured me that their testing has revealed nothing that disagrees with the reports produced from decades of testing."

"I'd feel more comfortable if we had a larger sample of successful transformations. One successful test is hardly proof positive that the process is safe for all humans. Ravenau was subjected to the original DNA formula, and that gave her body certain recuperative powers. Suppose the new formulas have flaws that her body was able to overcome only because of the previous treatments?"

"The Upper Council doesn't feel they can wait any longer. Several of the members might pass away before testing proves the process is safe. They're willing to take the chance."

"I suppose they have a point. Better to take a minor risk on life than face certain death."

* * *

"My Lady," the image of Chamberlain Yaghutol said, "before I begin my monthly financial report, I must inform you of an— issue— we're currently facing here on Gavistee. I'm afraid it's rather delicate, and I hesitate to bring it up, but I must. My Lady, the Azula Mum may be guilty of sedition."

Upon hearing the word 'sedition,' Jenetta's eyes opened wide, she sat straight up in her chair, and she practically spit up the mouthful of coffee she had just taken from her mug. It was a heck of the way to start the morning.

"Since you left, months ago, the Azula Mum has been traveling around Gavistee, talking to your tenants. She's concerned with their welfare, and that's admirable, but she almost seems to be inciting them to demonstrate in protest against the present poor living conditions on the planet.

"My Lady, if word of this gets back to the crown, the king and queen will be most upset, and I fear what action they might take. I hope you will speak with her about tempering her— maternalistic— public speaking.

"Here are the monthly figures for your estate…"

Jenetta sat back in her chair without really hearing the rest of the message. She'd had so much on her mind that she hadn't really listened closely to the weekly messages from her mom. She knew her mother was traveling around the country-side, talking to the tenants and trying to make their lives easier, but she had no inkling that the activity could be construed as seditious. There was a new message from her mom in her personal mail queue, and although she normally only listened to personal mail after returning to her quarters each evening, she made an exception on this occasion.

"Hello, dear," the smiling face of her mother said as the message opened. "I have the most exciting news. There's to be a large harvest celebration in September and I've been invited by the Glinesku town council to speak. I'm told that it's always the largest celebration on the estate, probably because Glinesku is the largest town on the estate. Marisa has been helping me write my speech. I'm going to tell the farmers that they need to organize and demand that the king reduce the percentage of their crop that he takes as tribute every year."

If Jenetta hadn't stopped drinking her coffee after seeing the vidMail from her chamberlain, she probably would have spilled it all over herself with this announcement.

"Can you believe," her mother continued, "that he takes half their crop every year? It barely leaves them enough to live on. I don't know how they do it. They struggle all year to produce a crop and then he swoops in here and takes half of it. It's criminal.

"Marisa sends her love, as do I. Call soon, dear, and be careful out there.

"Annette Carver, Palace of the Family Carver, Gavistee Peninsula, Obotymot, message complete."

Jenetta was aghast but took several minutes to calm down before she recorded her response.

"Computer, new message. To Annette Carver, Palace of the Family Carver, Gavistee Peninsula, Obotymot.

"Mama, I appreciate your desire to help our people live a better life, but you have to remember that you're on Obotymot, not Earth. On Earth, specifically in the United States, the federal government now collects a flat fee income tax of fifteen percent from all those citizens who earn between the officially established poverty level and ten times the poverty level. It's understandable that some people think of that as the total tax rate for everyone because that's what politicians want you to think, but that's only a small part of the tax collection system. Almost every state has an income tax, many with rates as high as the federal rate. Then there're property taxes, school taxes, sales taxes, use taxes, health care taxes, retirement taxes, fuel taxes, travel taxes, hotel taxes, luxury taxes, alcohol taxes, food taxes, and on and on and on. Many of the taxes are taxes on things already taxed many times already, so the price of products and services are already much higher because of all the previous layers of taxes, and much is done to hide taxes to avoid taxpayer revolts. Directly and indirectly, the average middle class citizen pays approximately eighty percent of all their income to one government bureaucracy or another for taxes every year, and wealthy citizens pay up to ninety percent. Your income is taxed before you even see any of it, and when you try to spend the remainder, it's taxed again and again.

"Obotymot citizens pay just fifty percent of their crops if they're farmers or of their income if they're a merchant or tradesman. There is only *one* collection system and no other taxes. Having just one collection point means that the colossal costs of administering thousands of redundant tax collection programs like those in the United States are avoided. So fewer taxes need to be collected, and the taxes that are collected can be better utilized. Our people on Obotymot receive free health care, free education, and an untaxed retirement income. The tenants are not paying tribute to the crown; they are paying a tax for all the services they receive. In addition to the services I mentioned, money from the crops fully support the church, pay for military and police protection, and assist families who are certifiably unable to till the land or provide for themselves.

"So you see, our people aren't suffering. The planet sustained a devastating natural disaster when the meteor struck. The crown and the nobles have picked up the *entire* cost of cleansing the atmosphere and rebuilding the agrarian society on Obotymot while continuing to provide food, care, and shelter to all citizens. Yes, times were difficult, but the system works and the planet is on its way to a full recovery. As crop yields improve, the tenants will have more disposable income and a better life than they've had over the past two decades. If anyone is suffering, they're still eligible for assistance. The system isn't at fault for the suffering and every effort has been made to reduce it. Prior to the meteor strike, the people on Obotymot were happy and prosperous. They will be again.

"I love that you have embraced our people and want to help them achieve a more productive and enjoyable life, but I ask that you do it within the system rather than trying to change it. Please remember that when you speak, you are a part of the nobility. You are the Azula Mum. Your words carry a weight you may not yet fully appreciate. You must support the government, not denigrate it.

"My love to you and Marisa and I'm glad you're enjoying your time on the estate.

"Jenetta Carver, Admiral, Commander of the Second Fleet and Military Governor of Regions Two and Three, Palace of the Governor, Quesann, message complete."

Jenetta took a deep breath and leaned back into her chair. She hoped the message reached her mother before the harvest festival so the speech could be altered. She had so much to worry about already and wished that one more problem hadn't just been added to her burden.

Before she returned to Space Command business, she sent a message to Chamberlain Yaghutol explaining that she had sent a message to the Azula Mum in which she attempted to curb any behavior inconsistent with her elevated position on the estate.

* * *

"Any sign of enemy ships?" Commander Shawn Fischer asked as the three ships of his search group established a three-way conference.

The search group, as per orders from Captain Zakir Singh of the DS destroyer *Duluth*, senior officer among the ships tasked with finding the *Salado*, had waited weeks to give time for the enemy ships to leave the vicinity of the destroyed ship so the SC ships could return to retrieve the crewmembers they had been forced to leave behind. The three small ships had just rendezvoused after completing a full Light-9790 search of space within a hundred billion kilometers in every direction.

"Nothing showed up on *our* screens," Commander Ashlyn Flanery of the *Vistula* said. The image on Fischer's office monitor showed her to be sitting in her office with her XO.

"Ditto," Commander Wilson Teffler of the *Gambia* said from his office. "We didn't see so much as a rogue asteroid. There was nothing out of place in our search area."

"Same here," Fisher said. "I think we should contact the *Sebastian* and inform them that it appears to be safe for them to come in."

"You're senior here," Flanery said, "so it's your call. But for the record, I concur."

"Ditto," Teffler said. "But I suggest we add that they shouldn't drop their envelope once they arrive next to the *Salado* until we can each place our Distant DeTect satellites and establish a safe zone of twenty-four billion kilometers. Once the *Sebastian* opens her hull to take the *Salado* inside, she'll be a sitting duck if the enemy shows up. Twenty-four billion kilometers will give her a safety margin of three minutes. It's a small margin to be sure if her hull is still open, but if the enemy ships do show up, maybe we can distract them long enough for her to seal her hull and build an envelope as you did for us when we needed the time."

"Okay, good idea, Wilson. Let's do it, guys."

It took several hours for the three small ships to seed the area with Distant DeTect Grid satellites, activate them, and fully test the system. Once the grid was online, the *Sebastian* was given a green light to approach the *Salado* and take her inside.

With everyone working as quickly as possible, the destroyed ship was soon secure inside the *Sebastian* and the hull resealed. Once the ship transporter had rebuilt her envelope, everyone breathed a little easier. Only then did engineers enter the *Salado* with hopes of finding the *Gambia* and *Vistula* crewmembers. If the enemy ships showed up on the DDG, the ships could easily be gone before the enemy arrived.

Guarding against the possibility that the enemy might have left explosive devices aboard the ship after they were foiled in their attempt to catch the *Gambia*, *Vistula*, and *Yukon*, Marines first performed a complete sweep of the ship. Once it was determined to be clear of any such devices, engineers began examining all of the onboard stasis chambers. Since the hull of the *Sebastian* was Dakinium-sheathed and Dakinium blocked all transmission signals, the enemy could never detonate a planted charge from outside. In fact, if the enemy had planted a locator beacon, they wouldn't even know that the *Salado* had been moved, just that the beacon had stopped transmitting.

After retrieving their DDG satellites, the three scout-destroyers rejoined the other search ships at the RP while the *Sebastian* headed for Quesann at Light-9790.

In a conference call with all ships, Captain Zakir Singh asked Commander Fischer for a full status report.

"As previously reported in our official mission report," Fischer said, "the SC transporter ship *Sebastian* is currently on its way to Quesann with the *Salado* in its hull. The enemy ships never put in an appearance, so all remained quiet at the battle site. Following a search for explosive devices aboard the *Salado*, the engineers searched the stasis beds in all life pods. None were occupied and never had been, but many were missing. The number missing exactly equals the number of crewmembers we were forced to leave behind at the earlier confrontation. We did find all three of the shuttles that were sent over initially, two from the *Gambia* and one from the *Vistula*. The conclusion would have to be that the enemy seized the stasis beds containing our people."

"Was there any indication of why they chose to take prisoners now and not earlier?"

"We know of no reason for their action."

"Very well. Thank you, Commanders Fisher, Flanery, and Teffler. This concludes your ship's role in the incident that occurred while investigating the attack on the *Salado*. We can only hope that we will one day recover our missing crewmen and that they will be healthy.

"Normally, we would likely receive orders to resume the patrol routes we were following when the call went out for search ships, but Region Two HQ has new orders for all of us. We're to begin a new search. This time we'll be hunting for the enemy ships that have attacked us, and in so doing declared war against the Galactic Alliance.

"R2HQ believes that a race known as the Denubbewa are responsible for the attacks on the *Yenisei* and *Salado*.

Reportedly, whole colonies of these aliens spend their entire lives aboard enormous mother ships. R2HQ believes that one or more of these mother ships might have entered GA space and is acting as a staging platform for upcoming attacks. They believe that the two attacks were only to test our ships and weapons. The coming storm will probably see them attempt to purge our forces, much as the THUG pact tried to do. We must locate their forces, and especially their mother ships if we're to have a chance of defeating them.

"All searchers will use Light-9790 speed and never drop their envelopes. At that speed, we need not fear the enemy ships. It's true that we cannot engage them at that speed, but it's also true that they cannot harm us. Our task is to locate every enemy ship in GA space. Since we expect that all will have an obvious power signature, we won't stop to investigate dormant anomalies."

"Will reports require verification by other ships?" one of the scout-destroyer captains asked.

"No. Our search fleet is too small. Just report the sighting and send the recorded data for the contact."

"It could take thousands of years to search all of Region Two space with just fifty-two search ships."

"Then we should get started. Any other questions?" When no one spoke up, Captain Singh said, "Okay. The navigator on each ship will shortly receive the coordinates of the ship's search territory. If you have any questions at that time, contact me. Otherwise, deploy whenever you're ready. Dismissed."

* * *

Vyx entered the flight deck of the *Scorpion* in response to an audible alert in the living quarters and saw the reason for the signal immediately. A light on the flight console, indicating an incoming message, was winking on and off. He plopped down into the pilot's seat, lightly stabbed at a button on the console, and watched a small monitor as a vid message played for several minutes. At the conclusion of the message, he erased all record of the communication and returned to the living quarters. The flight deck was unattended because the ship had been parked for several months at a spaceport at Humalerret on the planet Uthlarigasset. Living aboard the ship meant that Vyx's team of Intelligence agents could talk freely without fear that anyone might be eavesdropping or recording their conversations.

"We have new orders," Vyx said to his associates as he returned to the dining room where Byers had begun serving dinner in his absence.

"What's up?" Brenda asked. "I was just getting into the swing of the old assignment. We *have* to stop the slave trade in this region."

"It's big," Vyx said as he sat down in his regular seat next to Brenda. "Real big. Bigger than Admiral Carver's goal of eliminating the slave trade. A new enemy has appeared in Region Two."

"New?" Nelligen said, "As in someone we haven't fought before? I had begun to think we'd run out of new enemies and could just concentrate on the old familiar ones, like the Uthlaro and Raiders."

"They might be involved. That's why we're being called into the act."

"So who is this new enemy?" Kathryn asked.

"R2HQ doesn't know for sure. All we know is that they've destroyed two of our scout-destroyers in Region Two near the Hudeerac/Ruwalchu border and their ship configuration resembles ships of a race called the Denubbewa."

"Denubbewa?" Byers said. "Never heard of them."

"Neither have I. But that's what R2HQ is saying. They're not locals. Apparently their home system is twelve thousand light-years beyond our border."

"Are they kidding?" Nelligen said. "Why did they have to come *here* to pick a fight?"

"That's one of the things R2HQ would like to know."

"As much as I love this ship, if these Denubbewa could destroy two Dakinium-sheathed ships, the *Scorpion* is certainly no match for them," Brenda said. "What's our role in this?"

"The Quesann Intelligence Section has received information that the Uthlaro have been recruiting workers and sending them off-world. Nobody knows where they've gone, but R2HQ thinks they're being sent outside GA space. HQ wants to know what they're doing, for whom, and why they're doing it outside GA space."

"Space Command doesn't have any authority outside GA space," Kathryn said.

"Actually, we do. We're not supposed to enter another nation without orders or permission, but open space is— well— open. In any event, we have orders to track the workers and find out what's going on. HQ also wants to know if the Uthlaro are involved with the Denubbewa and if the two things are related."

"The Uthlaro have always tolerated Terrans here because of their association with the Raiders," Brenda said, "but since the war they certainly don't trust any of us. How are we supposed to get one to open up and tell us where the workers have gone?"

"I don't know. I guess they expect us to use the superlative talents that got us into this wonderful line of work in the first place."

"I don't like this assignment already," Byers said. "I don't have any superlative talents except for cooking."

"You don't like anything," Nelligen said.

"Not true. I'm very partial to my new Crème Brulee dessert recipe."

"It's too sweet."

"Just sprinkle it with red and black pepper like you do everything else and you'll love it too."

"I'm not crazy about this new assignment myself," Vyx said, interrupting the verbal repartee and returning attention to the business at hand, "but orders are orders. Someone pass the mashed sweet potatoes and turkey platter, please."

Chapter Twelve
~ September 25th, 2286 ~

"If the new GA Senate complex isn't located on this island, it will be more difficult to defend, Admiral," Captain Graham Daltas, the architect heading the design effort, said. "And the weather on this island is perfect for year-round government operations. It's ideal for the Senate Complex."

"Captain," Jenetta said, "there are thousands of islands suitable for the GA Senate on this planet. Many enjoy the same temperate weather we have here, and I know the Senators will love whichever one we choose. When I laid claim to this planet on behalf of Space Command, I established a zone of exclusion that covers the entire solar system. Anyone who tries to enter the solar system without an invitation will learn that when we say, 'Stay away,' we mean it. Defense of the facilities is not a major consideration since it's unlikely that an enemy ship will ever get close to the planet. Select another."

"But Admiral, locating the complexes here will mean less travel time to the new Supreme Headquarters complex, which SHQ requires be located immediately next to the GAS."

"I don't think we should refer to the Galactic Alliance Senate as 'the GAS,'" Admiral Holt said with a chuckle. "I appreciate that it might be entirely appropriate at times, but I don't believe the senators will appreciate it."

"Yes, Captain," Jenetta said, "don't refer to the Senate as the GAS. I understand and appreciate your concern for my inconvenience, but newsies must have access to the Senate's complex, and I won't have them running around on this island, which is devoted solely to military operations and therefore limited to military personnel and civilians with a military clearance of top-secret or higher."

"Yes, ma'am."

"I do like the basic designs created by you and your staff, Captain. I especially like the amount of free space you've left near the complexes for future expansion. A one-hundred-kilometer-square space should be ample for the government bureaucracy as we expand our presence in Regions Two and Three. Planetary representatives will naturally seek to have their embassies located as close as possible to the senate complex, but we must reserve that inner zone of space exclusively for governmental operations. The high-speed travel system facilities you've designed will make everyone's commute a swift one. Locating sufficient shuttle pads in the government's space will allow Senators and their staffs to travel to and from the senate complex in minutes. The newsies and political hacks will no doubt object to their housing being two hundred kilometers away, but that's too bad."

"Thank you, ma'am. My people have worked hard to accommodate everyone's requirements."

"The island selected for the senate should be distant enough that our air traffic controllers can ensure that only authorized shuttles get within a thousand kilometers of this base."

"A thousand kilometers, Ma'am?"

"Yes. A thousand kilometers, Captain."

"Yes, ma'am."

"Continue your work, Captain, and report back when you have suggestions for which island we'll use."

"Yes, ma'am."

"Is there any new business for the Board today?" Jenetta asked the assembled members."

"Just before we convened, I was notified that the Flordaryns have sent an urgent message for assistance," Admiral Poole said. "I ordered the *Hephaestus* to Flordarya to look into the issue."

"What was the reported problem?"

"They claim that the Tsgardi are demanding their torpedoes be returned to them immediately rather than waiting until their ships are ready to depart."

Jenetta sighed. "The Tsgardi again! Why do they want their torpedoes back before their ship repairs are complete?"

"The Flordaryns say the Tsgardi have learned we've lost two of our ships, and they claim to be fearful that there might be someone who can defeat us. They want to be able to protect themselves if the aggressor shows up at Flordarya."

"That's Tsgardi logic for you. They know we could destroy them in an instant, and there's nothing they could do to stop us. Now they want their torpedoes back to help them against an enemy they believe might be even more powerful than us." Jenetta shook her head sadly before saying, "And the Flordaryns refused their request, I assume?"

"Yes, and the Tsgardi threatened to attack the planet with their laser arrays if the torpedoes were not immediately returned, at which point the Flordaryns informed them that their laser arrays had been disabled the first day the Flordaryns had access to their ships."

"I bet that wasn't greeted warmly."

"No, it wasn't. Then the Tsgardi refused to allow the technicians working aboard their ships to leave until the laser capability was restored *and* their torpedoes returned."

"Then?"

"The Flordaryns flatly refused. That's where things stood when the Flordaryns sent their appeal for help."

"Wonderful. I felt sure those Tsgardi were going to be a problem when they traveled outside their home system without permission. I should have had them towed home in their disabled condition."

"How stern do you want to be?"

Jenetta thought for a minute while everyone in the room looked on. "We don't want to risk the lives of the Flordaryn workers, but I won't continue to play games with these Tsgardi. They now have two strikes against them. One more and we'll toss them out of the game, permanently."

"You mean…?"

"Yes, I mean exactly that. If they harm even one Flordaryn worker, the kid gloves come off. We'll destroy those tissue paper ships of theirs and drop any survivors off on their home world as a lesson to the rest of the race. They've been warned repeatedly, and they seem incapable of understanding. Perhaps we need to destroy *all* their ships and leave them completely isolated on their world. The galaxy will be the better for it."

"They are sentient beings, Jen." Admiral Buckner said.

"That has often been a subject for heated debate. If they can't coexist peacefully with their neighbors, we'll see that they are unable to annoy or threaten them."

"Have you considered that the Tsgardi might be in league with the Denubbewa?" Admiral Holt asked.

Jenetta turned to look at him. "You think they might be?"

"Oh, not as a senior partner or even an equal partner. I was thinking that the Denubbewa might be using them as the Milori and Uthlaro used them. You know how revenge-minded the Tsgardi are. They'd love to see you— uh…"

"Yes, I know. Their senior officer at Flordarya, Admiral Kelakmius, as much as told me that when we were there. Do you really think they'd allow themselves to become the pawn of another race so soon after their last debacle?"

"I know that their current troublemaking would seem to be perfectly timed to function as a diversion."

"I admit I don't personally like the species, but I have trouble believing even they could be that dumb."

"Never overestimate the intelligence of an enemy. That assumption could help support a claim of innocence if they deny any involvement while evidence points to the contrary."

"This is beginning to look like the THUG pact."

"How so?" Holt asked.

"We have the Denubbewa, Ruwalchu, Uthlaro, and now the Tsgardi. Is it possible they're all involved?"

"It's not *im*possible."

"No, that's true. This is all so frustrating. I much prefer an enemy that announces their intentions and then comes straight at you."

"Yes," Holt said with a chuckle, "but I'm afraid that went out of style in the twentieth century when nations grew so powerful that aggressors didn't dare attack openly, or at least didn't announce their intentions before they commenced their attacks."

*   *   *

"Good morning, Admiral," Captain Barbara DeWitt said as she entered Jenetta's office in the Governor's Palace the next day.

"Good morning, Barbara. Fix yourself a beverage and join me in my informal area."

When both women were seated in comfortable chairs, Jenetta said, "Barbara, we need a new weapon. As you know, our Phalanx system is unable to defend our ships against the enemy missile barrage. Right now, all we can do is run away if we see them coming."

"Yes, Admiral. My staff has been brainstorming ideas, but every suggestion has the same weakness. We just can't get close enough to ensure delivery and survive the encounter. Unless we find a ship full of volunteers willing to die to complete the mission, we don't have a chance of success. Even if we did find those volunteers, there's no guarantee we'd succeed. We don't know the weaknesses of the enemy ships, so we may not cause enough damage to even slow them down."

"I realize that, so I've been trying to work out the details of a weapon that could allow us to bypass all their defenses without putting our people in harm's way, doesn't give them time to build an envelope and escape, can attack them even if they're traveling FTL, and is capable of destroying any ship we attack. I know this will sound crazy and impossible when you hear it, but I've given it a lot of thought and believe it's feasible. Of course, we may not know that until we build and test it."

"It sounds like the ideal weapon. We've always sought a weapon that can be used in FTL since lasers and torpedoes are useless. Can you give me the details?"

"This has to remain most secret. I'll relate all the details at the appropriate time."

"Of course, Admiral. I trust all of my people implicitly. Most have been with me for years, and there's never been a hint that anyone has passed secrets."

"I'm sure, but we can't risk an outside person even getting a suggestion of how the weapon will work. It has to be treated like the Manhattan Project during World War II. The people working on the weapon will be sequestered somewhere far from all other military and civilian personnel until after we make the first use of the weapon. That means no vidMail to loved ones and no contact with anyone outside of the project team."

"Where did you have in mind?"

"There's a small Marine base designated as a weapons-testing area but has never been used for that purpose. We'll use that for the duration of this project. There's a hangar where the weapon planning and construction can take place, a barracks, and a kitchen."

"When do we leave?"

"As soon as you can organize your people. Have them notify loved ones that they'll be out of contact for a while but not to worry. I'll give you forty-eight hours to prepare. Don't even tell them that they're going to the Marine base. Make sure they bring nothing that will allow anyone to track their movements or location."

"Yes, ma'am."

Once you're settled in at the base, I'll fly in and brief you and your team. You'll probably think my idea is nuts, but I've been mulling the problem over for months and this is all I've been able to come up with that doesn't require a suicide mission."

"That sounds encouraging. My people would give their lives for the good of the service, but they're not anxious to die."

* * *

Jenetta logged the flight as practice time and climbed into the cockpit of the Marine fighter reserved for her exclusive use after completing her walk-around. She had already briefed her protection detail regarding her destination and forbidden them to come within ten kilometers of the now off-limits Marine base. They would set their ships down just outside the perimeter and wait until she was ready to return to the SC base. The base had been restricted to all unauthorized flights, including flyovers.

It may have been a business trip, but Jenetta enjoyed it as much as any practice flight she had taken over the years. As usual, she took her ship down to the deck and stayed there until she approached the island that was her destination. When she received clearance to land, she wiped the grin from her face and began to prepare herself mentally for the briefing.

Captain DeWitt, upon learning that Admiral Carver had requested clearance to land at the base, immediately jumped into a driverless oh-gee vehicle and went to the flight line to greet her.

"Good morning, Barbara," Jenetta said as she climbed down from the cockpit. "All settled in?"

"My people are already getting antsy to start this new project, Admiral. They know that if you're directly involved, it's big."

"The biggest. Okay, let's head over to the hangar."

A few minutes later, Jenetta entered the hangar to a loud, "Admiral on deck." Everyone inside came to attention and held it until Jenetta said, "As you were."

"Okay, people, take your seats," a commander said, referring to the chairs arranged before a podium in the center of the hangar.

As everyone grabbed a chair, Jenetta strode to the platform and dropped a data ring over a small data spindle on the lectern.

"Good morning," Jenetta said, "Welcome to Project Gazebo. Don't look for any significance in the name; it was simply chosen at random. Our goal here is to develop a weapon capable of destroying the enemy ships that have been killing our people in this unannounced war. Most of you have seen the *Yenisei*, so you know what we're up against. The enemy has developed a weapon that can penetrate the Dakinium hull, then detonate a small nuclear device. The nuclear charge might be tiny, but without the protection afforded by the Dakinium, it's devastating. Furthermore, each enemy vessel appears able to fire approximately twenty thousand small missiles before having to pause to reload. All missiles can be fired simultaneously, so the Phalanx system is quickly overwhelmed and unable to provide adequate protection. As a result, we can't win in a shooting contest.

"So we have to devise a way to attack them in which their missile barrages are rendered immaterial. We can't depend upon finding them in a relaxed mode as we did with the Uthlaro armada. Right now, our DS ships are scouring the region at Light-9790, searching for the enemy ships. Once we locate them, we'll need a weapon that will forever end their attacks on ships in GA space. This next fight will not depend on who has the biggest gun or the most missiles, but who can deliver the first swift, killing blows.

"Here're my thoughts for the weapon. I'm hoping you can make it a reality. This is, of course, a rough drawing composed by my computer from verbal instructions. You are the first to see it, other than myself. Computer, Carver Gazebo One."

An image appeared on the large monitor behind her and Jenetta stepped to the side so everyone could see. There was silence for several minutes as the knowledgeable audience studied the diagrams.

Finally, Captain DeWitt said, "Admiral, I don't see a delivery system. It appears to simply be a bomb."

"Yes, Captain, that's correct. It's a simple bomb. At the front is a hemispherical piece of Dakinium. Behind that is a nuclear device in a cylindrical casing. The rearmost part of the cylinder contains the delivery mechanism."

"It hardly seems like a challenging weapon to manufacture. The Dakinium face will be the only component that may present some difficulties. How powerful a weapon are you proposing?"

"Large enough to destroy the enemy ships you've seen in the high-resolution images provided by the *Yukon*. Building the bomb is not the challenge here. The delivery is the challenge. The bomb is simple because passing through a ship's temporal envelope would destroy any electronic information. Once deployed, the bomb must detonate using strictly mechanical means."

"You intend to simply drop the bomb like a wet navy ship would drop depth charges on submarines and underwater installations?"

"Essentially, yes. But it's far more complicated than that. I want a weapon we can plant inside an enemy ship using Transverse Wave technology."

The hangar was so silent that one could hear the proverbial pin drop.

"With all due respect, Admiral," Captain DeWitt said, finally breaking the silence, "that's impossible."

"Why? It's been amply proven that when traveling at Light-9790, our ships pass through any solid matter. The bomb cylinder will be secure inside a Dakinium cradle until released. When that happens, air pressure jets in the rearmost bomb cylinder will push the bomb away from our ship. We simply eject the bomb while we're inside the enemy ship. As soon as the separation distance is enough, the envelope surrounding the bomb dissipates and the bomb is back in normal space. The bomb cradle inside the SC ship will be surfaced with Dakinium, so the envelope will instantly re-form and remain intact once the bomb is released."

"There's nothing simple about it, Admiral. At that speed, you can't determine where the bomb will wind up. You could be a billion kilometers away by the time the envelope around the bomb dissipates."

"That's what makes this project a challenge. Anyone can build this bomb. Placement is where your section's expertise will come into play. If you need additional expertise, just tell me who or what skills are needed, and I'll assign them to you for the length of the project if they're available."

Captain DeWitt stepped closer to the image and studied it again. "We can't shape Dakinium. That level of manipulation can only be accomplished at the Jupiter foundry."

"The cap need not be hemispherical. I only drew it that way because it would allow visual confirmation that the bomb had released if we mount vid devices near the bomb placement area. We only need to provide an almost unbroken Dakinium surface so the ship can build the double envelope. But it does require that the cradle be surfaced with Dakinium.

"This hangar is yours for as long as you require it. When you're ready to modify a ship, the *Winston* will provide you with concealed workspace where no one can see what you intend. The ship to be used for this project is the scout-destroyer *Tigris*.

"Once the basic work on the bomb and ship is complete, we can begin testing to see if this is feasible or not. We'll use dummy bombs and cargo containers for the tests."

"The chances of placing a bomb exactly where we want it are probably about one in ten trillion," Captain DeWitt said.

"Back in World War I on earth, pilots dropped hand grenades over the side of the cockpit walls because they hadn't developed bombs yet. It took time, but by the next war, twenty-five years later, they had precision bombsights that used the aircraft's ground speed, direction, and altitude when computing the drop point. With the computers and instrumentation we have these days, we should be able to cut that time down by a wide measure."

"Admiral, at Light-9790, actually Light-9793.48, the ship will be traveling at almost three billion kilometers per *second*. The chances of depositing a bomb inside the enemy ship are about the same as dropping a pebble from fifty kilometers above the earth and expecting it to land in Admiral Moore's coffee cup on his desk in the Admiralty Board Hall."

"If you could calculate drift from all wind currents, and there's a hole in the ABH roof, even that's possible. Here, we don't even have to consider wind drifts. It's all a matter of timing. I have confidence in you and your team, Barbara. The people that gave us a ninety-five percent kill rate with the Phalanx system can do almost anything."

"Okay, Admiral," Captain DeWitt said in seeming resignation. "We'll make it work, somehow."

"Wonderful." Picking up her data ring, Jenetta added, "It's time for me to go. Let me know if you need *anything*. You have top priority for all available SC resources."

When Jenetta turned towards the hangar door, someone shouted, "Attention on deck," and everyone in the hangar jumped to their feet.

As Jenetta walked towards the entrance, Captain DeWitt watched her admiral's back and shook her head almost imperceptibly as she muttered, "One of us is definitely certifiable— and I'm really afraid it's me for saying I could do this."

As the fighter climbed to minimum altitude, Jenetta smiled. She had alerted her protection detail and was now planning her course back to the SC base. She would definitely take the long way around.

Once clear of land and oh-gee traffic, she dropped down to the deck and skimmed across the ocean's surface. Her instruments showed no other aircraft or watercraft ahead, so she punched the throttle and wave-hopped all the way back to the base.

* * *

"We picked up some chatter in a bar about a ship headed out 'to the black' in a few days," Nelligen said as the team of agents sat down to dinner aboard the *Scorpion*.

"What's the cargo?" Vyx asked.

"Mainly food, from what we gathered."

"That can be significant or insignificant."

"We've listened to hundreds of conversations between Uthlaro freight haulers, and they always mention a specific destination— either a planet or a base. This is the first time I've heard one use the term 'to the black.'"

"It *is* unusual for a freight hauler to say it like that. Anything else?"

"No, that was the only interesting tidbit we heard all day in the bar."

"It's more than we got," Byers said. "Vyx and I spent the day in what I believe to be the foulest-smelling bar on the planet and got nothing but nauseated."

"The question is," Brenda asked, "do we spend months and months tracking a freighter simply because someone used the term 'to the black?'"

"He might have simply been referring to traveling in space," Kathryn said.

"Perhaps," Vyx agreed, "but space is where they spend most of their lives and spacers don't usually refer to it like that. That's a sod-lubber term."

"Do you want to make the decision," Nelligen asked of Vyx, "or do you want us to vote on it?"

"Uh— let's vote. All in favor of following a freighter hauler 'to the black,' raise your hand." A second later he said, "Okay, we're heading 'to the black.'"

* * *

"My Lady," the image of Chamberlain Yaghutol said, "I'm pleased to announce that the Azula Mum's speech at the Harvest Festival was very well received. She talked about the great strides we've made in restoring the quality of life on the planet and encouraged everyone to work harder so that all might enjoy a better life. I'm glad you were able to redirect her— spirit— along a more traditional path.

"Here is my monthly financial report…"

As Chamberlain Yaghutol rambled on with facts and figures, Jenetta leaned back in her chair and smiled. "One potential disaster averted," she said, "just a thousand more to go."

Chapter Thirteen

~ October 12th, 2286 ~

"We could be out here for years, Captain," Lt. Commander Jasson Lister said to Commander Marc Hodenfield during their morning briefing session aboard the scout-destroyer *Rio Grande*.

"Yeah, we could, but let's hope not. If the enemy ships have left GA space, we'll still have to search every cubic light-year, but I dread finding them more than not finding them after reading the damage reports about the *Yenisei* and the *Salado*."

"Admiral Carver will find us an edge."

"I love your optimism, but this problem might be beyond even her incredible talents. Before the *Yenisei* incident, I believed nothing could damage Dakinium. It goes to show you that there's no such thing as an impregnable hull. I can't help but wonder if the *Yenisei* and *Salado* went down because their crews put too much faith in their ship's ability to survive any attack."

"If anyone was arrogant or overconfident before, you can be sure they aren't any more."

"I guess…"

Hodenfield stopped when his com sounded an emergency signal from the third officer who had the bridge whenever Hodenfield wasn't there during first watch.

"What's the emergency, Third?" Hodenfield said.

"Captain, we just passed something off our larboard side."

"What was it?"

"Unknown, sir. It was at our maximum Detect range and only on the screen for a second."

"It's not in the celestial database or the navigation hazard database?"

"They show nothing located in that area, sir."

"Is the *Mekong* still in the search lane off our larboard side?"

"At last report, sir."

"Ask them if they ID'd the contact."

"Yes, sir."

Several minutes later, Lt. Sardani, the third officer, comm'd with his report. "Sir, the *Mekong* didn't see it. They believe the contact was just outside their max range. They want to know if we'll investigate or if you'd prefer them to do it."

"Tell them we'll take a look. Have the com return to the location. But— pass it at three billion kilometers and Light-9790. If it has an energy signature, we'll know right away and still have a decent amount of information without alerting them to our presence."

"Aye, sir."

As Hodenfield clicked off the com, his XO said, "Three billion kilometers probably won't enable us to determine if it's one of the enemy ships we're searching for or simply a small freighter."

"Perhaps not, but I want to take it one step at a time. I intend to treat the aliens with all the care and respect for their weapons ordered by R2HQ. First let's determine if it's a ship or a rogue asteroid. After that we'll make a decision as to how close we go."

"Captain," Lt. Sardani said via the com, "you should see this."

"What is it, Third?"

"I don't know, sir. That's why you should see it. It's— it's— massive."

Commander Hodenfield immediately activated the bulk-head monitor in his office. His eyes opened wide at the size of the object on the DeTect channel. "I'm coming out, Third."

Seconds later, Hodenfield and XO Lister emerged from the captain's office. The Captain relieved Lt. Sardani and took his seat in the command chair while Lister sat in his First Officer's chair.

"Tac," Hodenfield said as he stared at the DeTect image on the front monitor, "is that accurate?"

"That's what the DeTect monitor is reporting, sir."

"And it's emitting a power signature?"

"Yes, sir. Off the scale."

"How large is it?"

"The longitudinal dimension of the object appears to span one hundred twenty-six kilometers with a breadth of eighteen kilometers and a depth of seven kilometers."

"Good Lord. Is it stationary?"

"Yes, sir."

"Could it be a natural celestial object with spacecraft on the surface?"

"Possible, but unlikely from the power readings, sir."

"We'll have to take a closer look, sir," Lister said. "We can't determine its composition and construction from three billion kilometers away."

Hodenfield released a breath, but didn't actually sigh. "Com, notify the *Mekong* that we've spotted an oblong object one hundred twenty-six kilometers in length with a beam of eighteen kilometers and a depth of seven kilometers. The shape is smooth rather than rough and does not appear to be natural in formation. It's emitting a sustained power signature. Inform them that a first pass didn't provide the detail we need to make an assessment of its origins, so we're making another, much closer pass. Helm, take us past the unidentified object again. A distance of one million kilometers should be adequate. Tac, at Light-9790 we should appear as just a momentary blip on their systems, but I don't want to have to do this again, so check your equipment before we start the run."

"Aye, sir," all three crewmembers said.

A minute later the helmsman said, "We've completed a one-hundred-eighty-degree turn and are ready to begin our run, Captain."

"Tac?"

"All equipment verified fully operational and active. At one million kilometers, we should get sufficient detail to clearly identify the target."

"Commence the run, helm."

"Aye, Captain, commencing the run."

A few minutes later as the image of the unknown object jumped into clarity on the front monitor, someone uttered, "Oh my God."

If the *Rio Grande* hadn't already been traveling at Light-9790, Commander Hodenfield would have ordered it.

* * *

"Admiral Kelakmius," the image of the Space Command officer on the bridge monitor said, "I'm Captain Steven Powers of the GSC Battleship *Hephaestus*. The Flordaryn president has accused you of holding some of his people aboard your ships. You will release them immediately or suffer the consequences."

"I am an admiral, Captain. I do not take orders from lesser ranked officers."

"My authorization comes directly from Admirals Carver and Poole. Admiral Carver says she warned you about starting trouble here and says that if you don't release the Flordaryns immediately, you will never see the Tsgardi home system again."

Kelakmius bristled at the threat. "We will not return the Flordaryn workers until the Flordaryns return our torpedoes. They've left us defenseless up here. We must have our torpedoes back and our laser arrays functioning again before we release the workers."

"Admiral, you have one hour to comply with my directive. After that we will take action and reduce your ship to scrap."

"You wouldn't do that. You would kill the Flordaryns, as well as us."

"Never underestimate the power of Space Command, Admiral. We can reduce your ship to scrap without killing anyone. We'll start with your sub-light engines and when we're done, they'll never be of use to anyone again. One hour, Admiral. After that it will be too late."

* * *

"Come in, Barbara," Jenetta said from behind her desk as the computer opened the door to her office.

Captain Barbara DeWitt entered and gestured towards the beverage dispenser. Jenetta immediately nodded.

"How about you, Admiral?" DeWitt asked as her mug was filling with coffee.

"I'm fine," Jenetta said, looking up from her com screen. "I just prepared a fresh mug a few minutes ago."

DeWitt took her coffee and sat down in one of the chairs facing a desk large enough to host a small conference. Like everything in the Governor's Palace, it was meant to impress visitors.

Jenetta finished reading a report from Admiral Poole and looked up. "How's it going at South Island?"

"Everyone's tired, but we feel a real sense of accomplishment. We've completed the design of the bomb and we're ready to push ahead as soon as we can get the materials we need." Standing, she leaned over the desk and handed Jenetta a data ring. "Call up file BC01P."

Jenetta placed the ring on her keyboard's data spindle and accessed the file. She activated the room's large wall monitor and it filled with small images.

DeWitt stood, walked to the monitor, and touched one of the small images. It immediately expanded to fill the monitor. "This is the bomb. As you can see, the end is the necessary cap made from Dakinium that will allow the ship to build an envelope. We've designed it as you suggested, with a convex extension at the fore. The principal reason is, as you request-ed, for visual confirmation of firings and remaining weapons using sensors mounted on the hull. For the weapon itself, we've actually designed three different bomb strengths. They range from the power of a WOLaR torpedo down to one-tenth of one percent of standard nuclear torpedo strength. If you merely want to get their attention, you could use the lowest strength. If that doesn't give them pause, then you have the two full-strength weapons available. All three bombs are identical in size so they will fit into the same size cradle in the hull of the ship."

Touching the image again shrank it back to a tiny size. DeWitt touched another and the new image filled the monitor. "Here's the cradle we designed for the ship. It will be fitted into the hull to secure the bomb until release. It's made of Dakinium so the ship won't lose its envelope when a bomb is released. The bomb locks into position inside the cradle and cannot be released until the locking mechanism for that unit is retracted. Two tiny contact points activate the ejection jets in the bomb and the bomb becomes functional once it complete-ly clears the cradle. Precision ejection jets are necessary so we can precisely time how long it takes for the envelope around the bomb to dissipate. From the time the bomb clears the cradle, there are four seconds before detonation. The bomb absolutely cannot detonate while in the cradle."

A touch on the monitor collapsed the image again and DeWitt returned to her seat.

"How soon can you go into production?" Jenetta asked.

"As soon as we can get the Dakinium components from the Jupiter foundry and the bomb components from whoever is selected to produce them. All the specs are on the data ring. In the meantime, we can begin cutting holes in the ship to accept the cradles and adapting the weapons computer so the bombs can be released on command from the bridge, and only when the ship is traveling at Light-9790."

"Did you say *holes*?"

"Yes, Admiral. We've decided that the ship should not be limited to just one bomb. It should be able to release as many as one hundred bombs before halting for reloading."

"That's a considerable number of holes."

"My team has agreed that one hundred is the optimum number."

"Why so many?"

"Mainly because the first pass may not do it. The ship will be traveling so fast that numerous misses are expected, despite our best efforts. I'm sure you understand just how small and insignificant a spaceship will seem when traveling at almost three billion kilometers per second. Second, the bomb cradles will have to be reloaded from outside the ship. An internal self-loading mechanism will have to be integral to the construction of the vessel and is something ship designers can plan for in the future if this armament system proves practical, but it's beyond our capabilities out here at present. Then there's the possibility that there may be dozens, perhaps hundreds, of enemy ships out there. We know of three, but what if there is a full fleet waiting to attack? Lastly, you may want to carry bombs of different strengths— a light-weight one, simply to get their attention, a mid-sized with a normal nuclear payload for small ships, and a very large one with a WOLaR payload for larger ships.

"To allow for testing, possible defects, and the actual units required for construction, we'll need a minimum of one hundred twenty Dakinium cradles— and I recommend one thousand bombs."

Jenetta nodded. "That's reasonable. What else will you need to move this project forward, besides the Dakinium components?"

"We'll need one hundred of the best ordnance engineers in the Second Fleet and a first-class machine shop."

"I can get you the one hundred best ordnance engineers posted on Quesann or aboard the ships in orbit. I can't prom- ise they're the best in the Fleet because we have so many on ships out on patrol and other engineers that are posted to space stations in the region."

"I'm sure that will be fine. We'll evaluate their abilities as they work and assign the best of the group to assemble the most critical components."

"Anything else you'll need?"

"Fissionable material. We can either use fresh supplies from Region One stocks, or we can salvage material from our inventory of torpedo warheads. We'll also need a place to handle the material safely so no one is exposed to radiation."

"I'll arrange for the material from Region One rather than destroying usable torpedoes. We'll have to wait for the Dakinium cradles and bomb components anyway, so the time delay isn't a consideration. I'll find out if the nuclear ordnance center can be used for your purposes. If not, I'll get construction engineers working on a materials handling location remote enough that it won't endanger anyone else. I'll also attempt to have as much of the bomb assembly work completed in Region One as possible to take advantage of their greater production capability. That it?"

"Only that we're going to do our best, but I still have my doubts about being able to drop a bomb into a cargo container while traveling at Light-9790."

Jenetta smiled. "I know you always strive to do your best, and you've always delivered it."

* * *

Five months into her gender transformation, Nicole Ravenau had suffered through the most difficult stages. There had been weeks when the pain was so bad she'd wished she would just die. At times, even the sleep medication hadn't been powerful enough to let her lapse into unconsciousness, but the scientists had warned that stronger doses could have serious long-term consequences, so she had suffered and tried to lose herself in daydreams about the days to come.

When the ship arrived at Pelomious in two months' time, she should be able to walk without aids. There would still be pain, but it would be bearable. And over the following months it would lessen a little more each day. The thing that kept her going was keeping her eye on the prize. Within a year, she should have everything she had ever dreamed of.

* * *

"I'm bored already," Byers said as the five-member team sat down to dinner. "Do you have any idea where we're headed yet?"

"Nope," Vyx, who had just returned from the bridge, said pithily. "Our present course will take us close to dozens of systems. Our destination could be any of them or none of them."

"I wish that damn freighter was faster," Nelligen said. "Sitting in bars all day trying to overhear conversations isn't exactly stimulating, but it beats sitting around here all day."

"Funny you should mention that. The DeTect alarm that called me to the bridge was because the freighter suddenly sped up to Light-450."

"Light-450? That's as fast as their fastest warships used to be."

"Yeah, it looks like they're using the warship FTL drives in their new freighters since they're forbidden to make warships now."

"Can the link sections take the additional strain?" Brenda asked.

"They can if they're using tritanium now instead of titanium. I'm sure they considered that when they decided to use the FTL drive."

"We might as well turn around now," Byers said. "We can't hope to keep up with them."

"No?" Vyx said. "Remember that engine repair we had at Stewart just before we headed for Region Two?"

"Yeah. What about it?"

"We didn't need an engine repair. Our FTL drive was upgraded to the same system used in the newest scout-destroyers."

"So we can achieve Light-450 now?"

"Light-487 actually. The original SD's were limited to Light-450 with a single envelope. The newest ones can travel at Light-487 with a single envelope, just like all of the recently modified warships in Space Command. Eventually, all of the ships will have that as their top single-envelope speed. The oldest ships in the fleet still can't be upgraded because their drive systems are too different from what we use now, but they'll probably be phased out in another decade."

"So our speed is even greater than the freighter we're following?"

"As far as I know. If they suddenly speed up beyond Light-487, we'll have to turn around, but I don't expect that to happen."

"That's great," Nelligen said, "but I'm still bored."

"Try reading a book," Brenda suggested. "That's what we do and the time seems to pass at FTL speed."

"Come on, nobody here believes that all you two do is read all day," Byers said.

"It is all we do all *day*," Vyx countered, "but it's certainly not what we do all *night*." He grunted as Brenda poked him in the ribs.

"I feel like a fifth wheel," Kathryn said. "I wish I had someone to read with all day and do other things with all night."

"You have your puppy as a companion," Brenda said.

"It's not a puppy. It's a Lyoxma wimlot."

"It looks like a puppy."

"It's cute, but it's not as cuddly and lovable. It's kind of finicky and aloof, like a cat, and jumps around like a monkey. I should have shelled out for a real puppy, or even a kitten, from Earth, but they were so expensive and lots of people were buying these."

"They probably would have been buying Earth puppies if they had been familiar with the species the way we are," Brenda said.

"That makes me feel better," Kathryn said sardonically.

Brenda giggled. "I'm sorry. I meant that they were buying what they were familiar with while you were buying because you thought they were knowledgeable pet owners and had a preference for the— Lyoxma wimlot over the Earth puppies."

"Okay. Point taken. I was too hasty."

"Nooo, that's not what I meant."

"Look," Vyx said. "If you haven't developed an attachment for the wimlot by the time we get back, sell it and buy an Earth puppy. I prefer Golden retrievers myself, but everyone's different."

"I like Beagles," Brenda said.

"I like Labs," Nelligen chimed in.

"I'm partial to Boxers," Byers said.

"Well, I like German shepherds," Kathryn said.

"Yeah," Byers said, "but what kind of *dog* do you like?"

Kathryn looked at him strangely for a second, then grinned and threw a dinner roll at him, hitting him in the forehead.

"No need to get violent," Byers said with a grin. "I was only curious."

"I think we're getting cabin fever," Vyx said. "I wonder what it's going to be like after we've been trailing this freighter for a year. Maybe we should have stayed in a hotel while we were on Uthlarigasset."

"And leave our love nest?" Brenda said. "No way."

"What makes you think we'll still be following this freighter a year from now?" Nelligen asked.

"Just an unshakable feeling."

* * *

"Good morning, Jen," Admiral Augustus Poole said as he entered Jenetta's office in the Region Two HQ Admiralty building."

"Good morning, Gus. What's up?"

"I just got a message from Steve Powers at Flordarya. The situation with the Tsgardi is resolved— at least for now.

Steve put on his war face and threatened to blast the Tsgardi ships out of the sky if they didn't immediately release all the Flordaryn workers they were holding hostage aboard the five destroyers. The Tsgardi admiral blustered a bit, but in the end he had no choice. The Flordaryns were wise to offload their torpedoes and disable their laser arrays before they started repair efforts on the Tsgardi warships. It left the Tsgardi without a decent card in their hands when it came time to put up or shut up."

"Are the Flordaryn workers all okay?"

"Yep. The Tsgardis simply assigned them quarters and forbade them to move about the ship. They didn't even know they were being used as a bargaining chip to get the torpedoes back."

"The question is, why? Why did the Tsgardi pull this harebrained stunt? I don't imagine the Flordaryns are going to do any more work for them."

"Not true. All repairs had already been paid for in advance, but the Tsgardi action voided the previous contract. The Flordaryns will continue the work, but only for double the amount of the previous contract, which was already double what they would have charged anyone else. And it must be paid in advance."

"And?"

"And the Tsgardi say that it will take time to have the precious metals and gemstones sent from their home world by freighter."

Jenetta chuckled. "I can imagine the look on Admiral Kelakmius' face when he had to agree to the new price."

"Yes. Their irrational kidnapping of Flordaryn workers got them nowhere."

Turning serious, Jenetta said, "But was it irrational?"

"What do you mean? Of course it was irrational. They had no weapons to back up their bluster."

"That's what I mean. They were defenseless, so most people would know that we wouldn't fire on them until all other avenues had been explored. What if some puppet master is pulling their strings and ordered them to do this?"

"Who?"

"I don't know. It could be the Raiders, or perhaps the Denubbewa."

"What possible motive could they have?"

"I don't know. Perhaps I'm grasping at straws. Perhaps the Tsgardis acted alone using their traditional absurd rationale." Jenetta sighed loudly. "Oh, don't mind me, Gus. I'm just sick of not knowing what's going on. Who is attacking us and why? Are there multiple nations involved in this war? And most of all, where are the Denubbewa hiding?"

Chapter Fourteen
~ October 29th, 2286 ~

"Thank you all for coming on such short notice," Jenetta said. "This emergency session of the R2HQ Admiralty Board is now in session. As you all know by now, one hour ago we received a message from the DS scout-destroyer *Rio Grande*. The *Rio Grande* was part of the fifty-one-ship task force that originally searched for the *Salado*. After finding him, the task force was given new orders to search for any sign of the aliens that attacked our ships.

"You know how frustrated we've all been, not being able to identify the attackers. Although we had a lead to their possible identity, we were unsure if we were on the right track. It now appears that we were. We still don't know if other parties or nations are involved, but we're confident that we know who attacked our ships. Computer, project *Rio Grande* 01."

The three large monitors on the walls surrounding the horseshoe-shaped table showed the image first seen by the bridge crew of the *Rio Grande*. It had the same impact on most of the room's occupants. Admirals Carver, Holt, Poole, and Kanes had all seen it soon after it came in. Of the five permanent members of the Board, only Admiral Buckner hadn't seen it, and his eyes opened wide as he realized the enormity of the ship he was seeing.

"At the Battle for Higgins," Jenetta said, "we were startled when we saw a Raider battleship that was three kilometers in length. Our newest battleships, the *Ares* class, are just a little over two kilometers."

"How big is this enemy ship?" Buckner asked.

"The *Rio Grande* estimates it's about one hundred twenty-six kilometers."

"Sixty-three times the size of the *Ares*?"

"Sixty-three times the length. In total mass, it's probably a thousand times larger. It makes the *Ares* look like a lifepod, as it does all of the Denubbewa warships alongside it in the next image. Computer, project *Rio Grande* 02."

"Good God," Admiral Buckner said. "Are those tiny warships the same size as the ones that attacked the *Gambia*, *Yukon*, and *Vistula* while they were trying to salvage the *Salado*?"

"We believe so."

Shaking his head slightly, Buckner said, "As you said, they look like lifepods when compared to that monster ship."

"On the one hand I'm a little relieved that we at last have an enemy we can see. On the other hand, I'm as much in awe of their ship capabilities and the size of this mother ship as everyone else. This is a close-up of the mother ship, and if you look closely you can see a dozen warships on its perimeter. You can also see what appears to be a major entranceway into the ship, so it might have a hollow interior like the Dixon and Stewart Space Command bases. There's no way of knowing how many ships are inside or the speed capability of that ship. I'm assuming it wouldn't even be here if it didn't have FTL speeds, but how fast is it? It seems that I have more questions now than before. All we really know for sure is that the mother ship is four times the size of Stewart SCB."

"But is this ship from the Denubbew Dominancy?" Admiral Buckner asked.

"We can't state categorically that it is, but we're close to certain that the mother ship isn't a Raider, Uthlaro, or Ruwalchu vessel, so unless we were wrong when we identified the Denubbewa as possible aggressors, it stands to reason that this ship belongs to them. At this point it doesn't really matter who the ship belongs to. We've got to find a way to destroy it."

"How?" Buckner asked. "We can't even get within firing range of their warships unless we perform a suicide run, and if that thing is filled with their warships, we'll never get close to that either. They'll come flying out of there and send a hundred thousand of those small missiles at our ships."

"Well, we're working on a project that might allow us to take on that mother ship, but I can't discuss it here."

"You're talking about Project Gazebo?"

Jenetta looked at Buckner in silence for a second. "Yes, but never again repeat that name aloud or in writing until the project is completed." Raising her voice, Jenetta said, "No one in this room will repeat that name under any circumstances, and they will report anyone who does. That project, and even the goals of that project, are not to be discussed. Period."

"Now that we know where the ship is, how long will it be before we're ready to take some sort of action against it?" Poole asked.

"That's still unknown."

"Then finding it was a useless effort since it might move light-years from its present position by the time we're ready to do something about it."

"It wasn't a useless effort because it provides valuable information regarding their resources. I've ordered most of the search forces to continue their efforts. We want to know if there are any more of these things out there.

"We also want keep an eye on any movements of the ships we've found. As far as we know, the warships of the race that attacked us are limited to about Light-450. Scout-destroyers have been assigned to watch the enemy in the same way that we kept tabs on the Uthlaro armada just before we attacked them at their RP. Our ships, operating at Light-9790, will perform flybys at near maximum DeTect range to watch for movement. If any of the warships move, we'll attempt to monitor their travel in the same way. There will always be at least one scout-destroyer devoted to keeping tabs on the mother ship. We'll know if it goes anywhere and where it's gone when we're ready to take them on."

"Do we have *any* idea when that will be?" Admiral Poole asked.

"All I can say is that we have a plan, and we're working towards a definite goal. When there's something else to report, you'll be among the very first to hear."

* * *

"Good morning," Admiral Moore said. "Welcome to this emergency session of the Board. Only Board members and their chief aides have been invited to this session. We'll suspend all normal formalities and jump immediately to the issue at hand."

Moore nodded to his aide, who activated the monitors around the room. When the image of the enemy ship first appeared, everyone's eyes opened wider, but no one commented. A head-and-shoulders image of Admiral Carver appeared and proceeded to reiterate the key facts about the alien ship as presented in the R2HQ Board session.

"That's the situation," Admiral Moore said when the message ended. "Comments?"

"Have we confirmed the size estimate of the mother ship as provided by the *Rio Grande*?" Admiral Platt asked.

"No, we received this message just an hour ago. I'm sure Admiral Carver confirmed the information to the greatest extent possible, but our analysts here will also be reviewing the images and reporting their findings. I see no reason to doubt it at this time."

"So we now know we're facing a mother ship that would seem to be at least sixty times the size of any of our warships," Admiral Bradlee said, "and which might be filled with hundreds or even thousands of the same class of warships that destroyed the *Yenisei* and *Salado*. Further, each of these warships is capable of simultaneously firing tens of thousands of small, deadly missiles that overwhelm our Phalanx systems and which therefore make it impossible for us to survive an attack. Are we considering admitting defeat? Because if we are, my recommendation is to attack regardless of the consequences in an attempt to destroy as many of the warships as we can, and possibly the mother ship. If we can't stop them, let's sting them so bad they leave to find easier targets."

"I don't believe anyone is considering giving up at this point, Roger. Kamikaze tactics didn't work for the Japanese in World War II, so that's definitely an option reserved for a time when you admit that you cannot hope to beat an enemy without it. For decades we've enjoyed a definite edge over our enemies because of our superior ships and weapons. Now we're faced with an enemy who appears to have the edge in both areas. However, we have one weapon left in our arsenal."

"Which weapon, Richard?" Admiral Platt asked with furrowed brow.

"Our people, Evelyn. If we do ask for kamikaze volunteers, I have no doubt that we'd have more than we need. And while we've believed for some time that Dakinium was virtually indestructible, the material discovered on Dakistee was even more so. We've continued to use our composite material because of its unique ability to establish a second temporal envelope around the first. But if the enemy is using the original material, or something even stronger, our ships might collapse against their hulls like eggs thrown at a bulkhead."

"But we don't know that," Admiral Woo said. "Their hull material might be simple tritanium. Or even titanium. They might rely on their weapons to ensure that no enemy gets close enough to damage them."

"Yes, Lon, that's true. And I hope we never have to find out how the strength of our hulls will compare to theirs."

"What choice do we have?" Admiral Bradlee asked.

"We have another vid to view that might answer that question to some degree. The second message is also from Admiral Carver. It was sent using the most secret and secure encryption code we have, which indicates how sensitive this data is. The people in this room are the only people who will see and hear this message for the foreseeable future. It will not even be shared with the GA Council, as allowed under the GA laws regarding military preparedness. Everyone in this room is bound by that same law. Anyone even repeating the code name for the project you're about to learn about could be subject to prosecution."

Looking towards his aide, Admiral Moore nodded. An image of Admiral Carver again filled the screens around the room. Her presentation explained Project Gazebo in full detail. She wrapped up the message by requesting the immediate support she required of the Jupiter foundry."

"Admiral Carver's brilliant battle strategies have always impressed me," Admiral Plimley said, "but as the Director of Weapons Research and Development for Space Command, I have to say— she's totally missed the mark here. Which is something that will happen if we buy into this idea and try to plant bombs inside enemy ships."

"I think it sounds ingenious, Loretta." Admiral Hillaire said. "We pass right through the enemy ships using Transverse Wave technology and leave a little present behind each time. The missiles and lasers of the enemy can't hurt us, and we risk no injury to our personnel because our ship is out of phase with the enemy ships. It's brilliant."

"Arnold, at Light-9793.48, the ship is traveling at almost three *billion* kilometers per *second*. At that speed, it's impossible to drop a bomb within a million kilometers of a target, much less inside a ship. If it happens, it'll be pure— dumb— luck."

"Does anyone have any better suggestions?" Admiral Moore asked.

When no one answered after a minute, Moore said, "Then since no else has any idea how to fight this enemy, I propose we give Admiral Carver everything she's requested for this project. Once it reaches the testing phase, we'll know whether or not it has a chance of succeeding. All in favor?"

The vote was unanimous.

"Now that everyone understands the situation, I'm sure you'll give serious thought to alternative tactics for fighting this new enemy, but in the meantime, the Jupiter foundry will begin work on the Project Gazebo components."

"Richard," Admiral Platt said, "I support the proposal fully, but if Loretta is right, a lot more passes may be necessary than Admiral Carver seems to be considering. I'd like to propose that we alter the Dakinium cradle quantity from one hundred twenty to one thousand twenty. That will allow us to arm ten ships with this weapon if testing is effective. Also, I propose that we alter the requested bomb quantities. I would eliminate the low-yield devices completely because I don't think we need to get their attention. I would increase the number of requested bombs with a standard nuclear payload to ten thousand devices and increase the number of bombs with a WOLaR payload to five thousand devices. Once we take on this enemy, we can't stop and wait six months to get additional devices prepared if the first batch is insufficient."

"That sounds sensible to me, Evelyn. All in favor?"

Again, the vote was unanimous.

"I guess that covers the matter for now," Moore said. "I remind everyone not to mention this project outside this hall."

* * *

"Come," the commanding officer of the Jupiter foundry said. The doors opened, permitting his chief engineer to enter the office. "What's up, Sal?"

"Sir, I was just reviewing this new parts requisition from SHQ. What is this thing?"

"The specs just call it a cap."

"A cap for what, sir?"

"I don't know, Sal, but the specs look complete. Is there a problem with producing it?"

"No, sir. We can make it alright, but it might help if I knew its purpose. I'd hate to make fifteen thousand of these things and then learn that someone down the line had gotten the specs wrong."

"I don't know much more than what was contained in the work order you received, but the production order I received was approved by the AB. How soon can you deliver them?"

"It'll probably take about a month to set up the process and jigs, and then we'll have to see where we can work it into the production schedule."

"This has top priority, Sal."

"Ahead of production for ship hull components, sir?"

"Ahead of *everything*, Sal. My orders were marked, 'Most Urgent.'"

"Then we really should confirm the design specs, sir. I'd hate to waste a couple of months if they need this thing so badly— whatever it is."

"Sal, I'm not going to the Admiralty Board and suggest that they don't know what they're doing."

"Uh— I didn't mean that, sir."

"I can't imagine that asking for confirmation of specs they provided could be viewed any other way, unless you've found a discrepancy in the specs."

"The only thing that doesn't make sense is why they need something like this. It doesn't seem to fit in with anything else we manufacture. And why do they need such a great quantity?"

"How do you know it doesn't fit with something else we produce?"

"I had the design computer try to find any possible link to our manufactured items. The results were zero. I also asked our system to check the SHQ Central Design Systems database on Earth to see who might have created the specs. The results there were also zero."

"You went outside our facility with this without permission?"

"Uh— yes sir. There's no confidentiality statement on the specs."

"That's because it's so top secret they didn't want to include a statement that would draw more attention to it."

"I'm sorry, sir."

"My fault, Sal. I should have communicated that information to you verbally. We'll just have hope it doesn't come back to bite us on the arse. Well, all I can say is that the AB ordered us to make it, provided the specs, and gave us the quantity they need. So let's do what they order with all possible speed, and if there's a problem with the specs, we're in the clear."

"Yes, sir. I hope so."

* * *

"New orders, Jasson," Commander Marc Hodenfield, Captain of the *Rio Grande* said when his XO, Lt. Commander Jasson Lister, arrived for their morning briefing.

"About time, sir. We're all getting a little jumpy sitting out here without an envelope built. I keep expecting to hear the GQ message when I'm not on the bridge because some of those nasty buggers have located us."

"Well, if being twenty-five light-years from their last reported position hasn't made you feel safer, the new orders certainly won't."

Lister scrunched up his face and said, "I don't much like the sound of that, sir."

Hodenfield actually smiled a little. "Relax, XO. Even though we're headed back to their location, we should be safe enough from those missile barrages of theirs. We're to start keeping an eye on them, effective immediately."

"How close an eye, sir?"

"The new orders assign the *Rio Grande* and the *Mekong* to perform Light- 9790 flybys every four hours on an alternating schedule at the most distant DeTect range possible. It's simply to verify their continued presence at the location. If they move, we're to report their new location every thirty minutes."

"Is something up, sir? I mean, the Standing Orders were to avoid them at all costs, and now they're sending us in to keep an eye on them."

"All I know is what I've just told you. But there must be a reason why they want to keep an eye on that mother ship. Maybe HQ has developed a plan of attack."

"As long as it doesn't involve us performing a suicide run against that mother ship, I'm all for it."

"Don't worry, Jasson. If Admiral Carver orders the *Rio Grande* to undertake a suicide mission, I'll give everyone on board an opportunity to transfer to the *Mekong* or another ship not involved in the attack before we go in."

"Are you serious, sir? You'd take the ship on a suicide run?"

"If Admiral Carver orders us in, I go. I know she wouldn't order it unless it was necessary. She'd never throw us to the wolves without damn good reason."

"Well, if *she* orders it, sir, I volunteer. For the same reasons."

"Let's just hope it's never necessary. Okay, let's head back to the last position of that alien ship."

* * *

"Commander," the technician at one of the thirty-six scanning consoles in the Approach and Departure Center said, "I just spotted that anomaly again."

This was the heart of the base station. Fully manned every minute of every day, the technicians watched for anything that might represent danger to *Exovadan*.

Commander Blithallo, who spent his shift roaming around and looking over the shoulders of his staff, moved behind the technician reporting the anomaly again and stared at the screen.

"I don't see anything unusual."

"It only appears for a second and then disappears again."

"What's its direction and speed?"

"I'm not even sure it's moving, Commander. It's just there and then it's not there. It's not there long enough to change position."

"It has to be this alien technology we've begun using. When we were given this DeTect system, we were told it was the most sophisticated distant warning equipment available."

"It has quadrupled the distance we've been able to monitor, sir. And we've verified that it's the same exact equipment Space Command is using in their newest warships."

"That doesn't mean it's the best possible system. I'm sure that, in time, our scientists will be able to improve on it."

"Yes, sir. Our scientists are the best in the universe."

"That they are. I'm only surprised that these disgusting Terrans managed to come up with something before we did."

"I'm sure it was purely by accident, sir."

"No doubt. Have you performed a self-test on this console?"

"Yes, sir. Twice. I discovered no malfunction."

"Interesting that it seems to be isolated to this one console. That might mean there's a problem with this unit, or it might mean that the contact isn't moving and only appears occasionally due to the distance. In any event, I'll notify the city fathers and let them decide what action should be taken. Good work. Keep watching and recording all incidences."

Chapter Fifteen
~ February 6th, 2287 ~

Nicole Ravenau was ten months into her transformation. The pain had subsided sufficiently that the medication was now able to suppress it for much of the day. She was also able to sleep through the night now unless a dream or nightmare caused her to move suddenly.

The underground complex had all of the amenities of a five-star hotel, but Ravenau was bored, and she spent her days planning her return to the Raider Corporation and plotting her revenge against Strauss for having forced her into this exile and isolation.

It was doubtful that anyone in the district even knew Ravenau was on the planet. Pelomious was still sparsely populated, and the complex had been completed and then sealed more than a decade ago. Crop dusting oh-gee vehicles probably overflew the ten thousand hectare tract, but the only structure they'd see was a small dilapidated shack designed to draw attention away from the real access point. When approaching the home, a large, camouflaged plasticrete pad could raise up to reveal the entrance to the underground domicile. After the oh-gee vehicle had disappeared below ground, the plasticrete pad settled back into place and all trace of the entrance was gone.

The underground complex included fifteen thousand square feet of living space and another fifteen thousand square feet for garage space, power generation, and storage. Ravenau had always enjoyed wide open spaces and would have felt claustrophobic in anything smaller.

There was enough food cryo'd in the storage areas to feed an army for a lifetime, and the power plant would sustain the complex for a thousand lifetimes, which might be necessary now that Ravenau would live for five thousand years at a minimum.

Simage panels covered every wall throughout the complex and gave the impression of being above ground. Unlike Strauss, who preferred to look down on the 'little' people from great heights, Ravenau's images were from a third floor level so she could almost 'feel' the people around her. Throughout Ravenau's career, she had always been closely surrounded by the people whose lives she controlled, so most of the Simages were from casino towns where the action never stopped. She had a few scenes of unpopulated panoramic vistas, but it was very rare that she played any of them. The crowds in the Simages made her feel that she was still connected to the galactic experience.

Robot cleaners kept the home immaculate whether occupied or unoccupied, and Nicole had her choice of a dozen master bedrooms. Moving around helped reduce the feeling of sameness and isolation. The home received thousands of news and entertainment channels, and it would take a lifetime to read and view all of the books and movies in the residence's computer system.

Still, Ravenau was bored. The complex might be grand, but to someone used to always being on the go, it was almost like a prison. It wouldn't be so for much longer. Ravenau had made all the arrangements, and she would leave in another day. She had progressed far enough along on her transform-ation to be accepted as a male and would use the new ID prepared for just this trip. Some basic cosmetic alteration would ensure that no one aboard the passenger liner would ever recognize her after the trip ended.

She would probably spend the next two months in her cabin, but after that she would be able to socialize with the other travelers and enjoy the casinos and other features aboard ship.

* * *

"Helm, all stop," Lieutenant Kay Poulin said.

"All stop," the helmsman said as he stopped the creation of new envelopes but didn't cancel the current envelope.

"What is it tac?" Commander Marsh Osborne asked.

"Another possible hit, Captain."

"How many does this make?"

"The log indicates that this is number three hundred forty-six."

"Three hundred forty-five mini asteroids plus one more."

"This seems to have a more defined shape than any of the others I've seen, sir. But we won't know until we get closer."

"Well, let us hope it's the real thing. Helm, take us to ten kilometers. Tac, alert the chief engineer and notify the next shuttle pilot in the rotation."

"Aye, sir."

Five minutes later the helmsman announced, "Holding at ten kilometers from the target, Captain," as the scout-destroyer *Tagus* eased up on the contact and came to a stop.

"Tac, anything on the DeTect?"

"The screens are clear, sir."

"Helm, cancel the envelope. Tac, clear the shuttle for launch."

"Aye, sir," both said as they complied.

In the shuttle bay, Lieutenant Remus completed the walk-around and entered the small ship. The engineering personnel were already aboard and preparing their equipment. By the time the shuttle was ready to launch, CPO Caine was suited up in his EVA suit.

As the shuttle approached the three-meter-long contact, Caine cycled the airlock and was ready to disembark when Remus halted the small ship five hundred meters away.

Using suit jets, Caine maneuvered to within five meters. He took a deep breath as he activated the suit's cameras and then circled the device slowly, visually examining every square millimeter. There was no doubt whatsoever that this was one of the objects they had been seeking for months.

"*Tagus*, we've found one. Are you receiving the images?"

"Affirmative. Proceed."

"Roger."

As Caine moved to within arm's length of the unit, he aimed a small sensory device. Panning the device up and down slowly, he again circled the contact slowly. When he had completed the task, he had detailed images of the construction and an analysis of radiation emissions. Using his suit helmet's playback capabilities to view the images just recorded by the sensory device, Caine again visually examined every millimeter of the rocket.

"Specialist Stevens," Caine said to his man aboard the shuttle, "are you receiving this data?"

"Aye, Chief. I'm seeing everything you do."

"I spotted two tiny holes in the casing. They might be integral to the disassembly, but it's also possible that the warhead screws off."

"I concur, Chief."

"I'm going to attempt to loosen the warhead by unscrewing it in a clockwise direction."

Caine gripped the warhead tightly with his right hand and the body of the missile with his left, just below the point where he believed the warhead would separate. He took a deep breath and tried to twist with all his might.

"No joy," Caine said finally. "I'll try to twist it counter-clockwise."

After straining without success, Caine let go of the missile.

"No joy," Caine said again, as he thought about the problem. "I'm going to assume that the two holes in the casing are part of the release mechanism. I'll try inserting a ceramic probe into the top hole.

Caine took the tool from his kit and stretched out his left hand to hold the missile steady. He then extended his right hand towards the hole closest to the warhead and aligned the tip of the ceramic probe with the hole but didn't insert it more than a millimeter. It was possible that inserting the probe would cause the warhead to explode, so before he committed himself, he reviewed everything in his mind. Unscrewing the warhead might still be the proper disassembly step. It's possible the freezing temperatures of space might be responsible for preventing the warhead from unscrewing from the missile. He wondered if he should try unscrewing the warhead again using a power device he had brought with him that could exert far more force than he could manually.

Caine was sweating inside the spacesuit despite it being a temperature-controlled environment. Terran armaments pretty much followed a general construction form, but this was alien technology, and Caine had no idea how they thought. After reviewing it again for a third time, he made a decision to proceed. He steeled his nerves and prepared to push the probe into the hole.

"What's going on, Chief?" suddenly shattered the silence inside his helmet.

Caine's arms immediately tensed and he froze as he was. After a couple of seconds, he retracted the probe and said, "Lieutenant Remus, sir. With all due respect, never interrupt a demolitions engineer when he's trying to disassemble an unknown device. If there's anything to report, I'll report it."

"Uh— sorry, Chief. Carry on."

"Yes, sir."

Caine steeled himself again and placed the tip of the probe at the hole. He took a deep breath and said, "Inserting the probe into the casing hole."

He pressed it very slowly into the hole, ready to retract it immediately. As it slid into the hole without resistance, Caine could only wonder if there was some other reason for the hole. Then he felt the probe encounter something. He stopped and said, "I've reached the end of the unobstructed travel. The probe cannot go further unless I add force. Adding force."

Caine pushed slightly and felt something give. The probe slid forward a few more millimeters.

"Something gave inside the casing. It's possible I've depressed an activation switch. If the missile doesn't explode, I'll see if the warhead is loose."

Caine breathed in controlled breaths for ten seconds before reaching out and taking hold of the warhead with his right hand. He still held the shaft with his left. As he gently pulled, it separated from the missile.

"The warhead is off," he said.

Examining the warhead and missile body, he saw how the warhead was intended to be attached.

"It's a simple and effective attachment system. A munitions worker can swap warheads in seconds if necessary. The warhead isn't giving off any radiation, so the fissionable material must be limited to the second section. I'll try to separate the second section from the missile. Inserting probe."

Caine took a couple of deep breaths and slowly pushed the probe into the casing. Just because it worked with the warhead didn't mean that the second section would detach the same way, but the money would be on the systems being the same.

When Caine felt resistance, he paused. "I've met resistance in the second hole. Increasing pressure."

He took a deep breath and held it. Again, Caine felt something give and the probe traveled a few more millimeters. When the missile didn't explode, he released the breath he had been holding and relaxed.

"Attempting to remove the second section."

The piece separated and floated free.

"The second section is off, and the sensors tell me that it contains the fissionable material. The third section is giving off only mild radiation, no doubt from having been in close proximity to the second section. *Tagus*, how do you wish to proceed?"

"Proceed according to plan, Chief," Commander Osborne said.

"Aye, Captain. Stevens?"

"Here, Chief."

"Bring me the bomb disposal containers."

"On my way, Chief."

Within an hour, the warhead had been secured in one container, the nuclear weapon stage in a second, and the delivery rocket portion in a third. It was expected that the delivery rocket had exhausted its fuel and posed no threat but better safe than sorry. The Dakinium locker housing the nuclear section was fully lined and no radiation would leak through. It was also expected that if the nuclear weapon were to detonate, the Dakinium would absorb the energy fully. The only question was the warhead. If it contained a substance that could destroy Dakinium, it might pose a danger. But the size of the warhead was small, and the explosive force was probably minor and only sufficient to spread the substance upon impact with the hull of the target since a larger explosion would most likely destroy the second stage nuclear weapon before it could be detonated. It was only the unknown aspects of the substance in the first-stage warhead that caused any real misgivings about taking the missile into the shuttle and then the *Tagus*.

"Good morning, sir," the *Tagus* XO said to Commander Osborne a week later when he reported for the daily briefing.

"Good morning, Jerry. I just received new orders. We're to take the missile we recovered to Quesann ASAP."

"Then they're calling off the search effort?"

"No, the search will continue for weapons that might have gone ballistic and not exploded after failing to hit a target. We're the only ship pulled out of the search effort. HQ wants this thing fast. Since we found it, we get to ferry it back."

"Well, I can't say I'll be sorry to see Quesann's pristine sandy beaches again. I wonder if they've cleared the sea for swimming yet."

"I don't know. And I don't know if we'll have time for R&R. We'll probably deliver the missile and then be sent right back out again."

"Without even a liberty weekend?"

"We'll have to see. With enemy ships destroying ours without even a fight, I don't imagine much shore leave is being approved these days."

*   *   *

"Let me see if I understand this," Director Wpleshoi said to Commander Blithallo, the senior officer at the Approach and Departure Center, "You want this Board of Directors to authorize moving the city because a single console in the Center is intermittently displaying a single dot for only an instant a few times during each shift, then is fine again."

"Yes, ma'am. The equipment has been tested and retested and we can find nothing wrong with it, which would indicate that the contact is very real."

"And you feel that this intermittent problem represents a threat to the city?" Another Board member asked.

"Uh— not necessarily a threat, sir. It's more of a mystery that must be solved if we're to continue to have trust in our equipment and know that it is reporting the situation correctly. There might be a danger that we're unaware of."

"Our generals have reported that the most powerful military in this part of space poses no threat to us. In two confrontations, we've destroyed their ships easily. In successive encounters, they've run away before we've had a chance to engage them. We've reported our success to the Denubbew Dominancy High Council and expect to hear soon about plans to assimilate this part of space. When other cities join us here, we expect to move through this part of space, destroying all sentient beings and terraforming the surfaces for colonization of our species on every viable planet. Why should we care that a single piece of electronic equipment is malfunctioning?"

"That's just it, Director. Repeated testing of the equipment has proven beyond any doubt that the equipment is not malfunctioning. I believe there's something out there and that we need to know what it is so we're prepared to handle it when the time comes."

"I'll approve sending out a ship to investigate."

"I've already done that."

"How? You don't have the authority to dispatch a ship."

"True, but I do have the authority to reroute returning and outbound ships, advising them to be on the lookout for unidentified objects as they pass a certain point."

"Very clever, Commander. And has anyone reported seeing anything suspicious at the specified coordinates?"

"Uh— no, ma'am."

"And yet you still want to move the city to that area."

"Yes, ma'am."

"We'll take it under advisement. Dismissed, Commander."

"Yes, ma'am."

As the door to the chamber closed behind the departing Commander, the head director said to the others, "Any thoughts? Should we give any credence to this reported console reading that can't be substantiated by visual sightings from spaceships?"

"If there was something out there," one of the board members said, "one of the rerouted ships would have seen it. It has to be a malfunction in the console despite what the technicians have said."

"I agree," said another. "The DeTect system was a valuable addition to our defenses, and it has proven itself reliable in the past, but it simply might be seeing something just large enough to record a hit, such as a micrometeorite, but not large enough to register visually. In any event, something that tiny can't represent a threat to this city."

"Let's take a vote," the head director said. "All in favor of moving the city, signify now. All in favor of not moving the city, signify now. The vote is unanimous. We stay where we are. Is there any new business to discuss?"

* * *

"Where are we?" Marine corporal Beth Rondara said to the PFC who was on his knees, bent over her as she lay on a deck without benefit of blankets, mattress pads, or even oh-gee shielding. Some light slaps to her face had awakened her.

"I think we're in an enemy ship," PFC Vincent Kilburn said, straightening up. "This appears to be some kind of laboratory."

Rondara struggled to sit up, her mind still slightly clouded from stasis sleep. The room was completely empty. "What makes you think that?"

"It's not a brig, and you can see all sorts of equipment through that window over there," Kilburn said, pointing to a window at one end of the small room.

Rondara looked down, only then realizing she was naked, as was Kilburn. She recalled stripping down and slipping into a standard, formfitting stasis suit before climbing into a chamber in a lifepod aboard the *Salado*. But the deck here wasn't cold, so clothing wasn't a necessity, and modesty was one of the last things they needed to be concerned about right then.

Kilburn stood up and extended a hand towards Rondara. She took it and he helped her stand, then held her arm until she was steady on her feet. It was a couple of minutes before the room and her brain were in complete sync. As she let go of Kilburn's arm, she walked to the only window. She could see a room full of equipment, the purpose of which was unclear, and two stasis beds in the background. The door to the room where they were being held had no mechanism for opening it from their side.

"Think they intend to do a little testing?" she asked Kilburn.

"Wouldn't we? I suppose all that matters is whether we'll survive intact."

"Yeah, but that's not all that matters. They're going to try to learn everything they can about SC and the Corps. And they may want to know how we're put together first."

"Put together? You mean…"

"Yeah," Rondara said. "Exactly. And even if they put us back together, the experience of being taken apart isn't something we should look forward to."

"So, we try and escape then?"

"And go where?"

"I don't know. Hey, maybe we can sabotage this ship."

"And kill ourselves and the others that were with us aboard the *Salado*?"

"I don't really think we're getting out of this intact, Corporal. They didn't hesitate to kill everyone aboard the *Yenisei* and the *Salado*."

"Never give up, Kilburn. We still have something they will never have."

"What's that?"

"Admiral Carver."

"No offense, Corporal, but the Admiral can't help us here. We don't even know where we are, so how can she?"

"I don't know, but she's been in tough scrapes and never given up hope, and neither will we."

A noise at the window drew their attention. Something was moving around in the lab.

"What the heck is *that* thing?" Kilburn said.

"Looks kinda like a robot— or maybe a cyborg."

"Cyborg? You mean like half human?"

"Well, a creature whose body has been replaced in part by electromechanical devices to improve functionality, such as mobility, strength, or dexterity. It may not even be animal-based life. It might be aquatic or plantlike in its natural form. Look at that small window in its chest. That looks like it's filled with a clear fluid."

"Yeah, but how does that indicate it's not animal based?"

"It doesn't— not completely. But of all the sentient beings we've encountered in GA space, all evolved from animal life, and none live in fluid."

"It looks sort of like a human skeleton. Why does it look so much like us?"

"Well, it might be a coincidence, but…"

"But what?"

"It's basically a machine. They might have constructed it to appear like us on purpose."

"Why?"

"Maybe they expect that we'll adapt better to a form we know."

"It's a machine. They can't expect us to cozy up to that."

"I didn't mean it like that. I meant they might want to turn us into cyborgs, and perhaps think our coordination will be better if the body shape conforms to what we were born with."

"What? Are you kidding?"

"No. They might put the brains of captives into those kinds of bodies and make them work as slaves. In fact, that might be one of our fellow Marines or an SC engineer. For all we know, we're the last to be awakened."

"No way. If that was one of our guys, he'd be freeing us right now."

"The aliens would probably wipe the mind of a captive when they put it into a new body. I agree that if it *was* still one of us, it would be freeing us. So whatever or whoever it might have been, it's one of them now."

"Oh, yeah? Well if it's one of them, I wonder how well its head would hold up to a home run hit with a meter-long piece of steel pipe?"

"We may never know. They didn't leave us anything in here that we could use as a weapon. In fact they didn't leave us anything. I wish they'd at least left us our stasis suits."

"If we ever get out of here, I'm going to find out if I can knock it over the outfield fence."

"No attacks until I give the order. Understood, PFC?"

Kilburn sighed lightly. "Aye, Corporal."

"Now let's concentrate on memorizing the position of everything in the laboratory so we can find our way around in pitch black."

"Do you have a plan?"

"Not yet. I just want to be prepared if an opportunity presents itself."

"Do you think that thing breathes air?"

"I would say that it probably doesn't breathe. That fluid in its chest might be some sort of fuel. But still, the stasis beds are out there, and we're in here. They never would have gotten them through the narrow door into this room, so we must have been removed in the lab and carried in here. That might mean there's oxygen out there."

"But what if the oxygen ends at the door from that room?"

"A very good question, PFC. And one that I don't have an answer to."

* * *

Vertap Aloyandro of the Hudeerac Order leaned in towards the monitor's retinal images recording sensors so the encrypted message would play. When the system was satisfied with his identity, the scrambled image on the monitor immediately resolved itself into a clear image of Admiral Jenetta Carver. After a few seconds, the message began to play.

"Hello Minister. As part of our continuing commitment to share intelligence information with our peaceful galactic partners, I offer this data. The logs of the two Space Command ships attacked and destroyed by an unknown enemy yielded only fuzzy images. At first, it appeared that the ships resembled a handful of foam bubbles. We later learned that the bubbles were shields to protect missile platforms mounted on the ships. The segmented covers are retracted to expose the platform and allow the ship to fire thousands of small missiles— all at once, if desired.

"As we conducted a recovery operation of one ship, the attackers returned. During their attack run, one of our ships involved in the recovery operation was able to get high-resolution images of the attacking ships from several angles. I'm including all images with this transmission.

"We haven't yet been able to verify the identity of the attackers, so we continue to use the information you provided and refer to them as the Denubbewa.

"When we have additional information regarding this new enemy, I shall forward it to you. If you should learn anything new, especially regarding their weaknesses, I hope you will forward it with all haste.

"Jenetta Carver, Admiral, Region Two HQ at Quesann, message complete, attachments."

Vertap leaned back in his seat and looked at the frozen image of Admiral Carver on his monitor. He didn't like to repeat unconfirmed information, especially when the information came from a distant source with no real allegiance to the Hudeerac Order. Paid informants were notoriously unreliable, especially when the information was alleged to have been overhead in a bar. But the situation seemed so dangerous that every shred of information must be considered.

Vertap leaned back in towards the scanner, engaged the device to record his retinal information, then began to record a new message.

"To Jenetta Carver, Admiral, Space Command Region Two Headquarters on Quesann, begin message."

"Good day, Admiral. I hesitate to pass on information which may have no foundation in truth and ask that you treat it with all due skepticism. A paid informant in the territory controlled by the Denubbew Dominancy has recently reported that the Denubbewa sent a mother ship in our direction to investigate possible territorial expansion. Our territory is small, so the ship might have continued right past us and into GA space. All reports suggest that their mother ships are far beyond anything that one might think of when hearing the word 'ship.' In a new communication received just one solar ago, the informant states that the mother ship reported an easy time with local forces and asked that a full contingent of mother ships join them to help establish control over their new territory. As yet, we have no information regarding a deployment of mother ships. I shall certainly inform you if and when I have more information.

"Vertap Aloyandro, Director of Intelligence for the Hudeerac Order, from the Royal Palace on Hudeera, end of message."

Aloyandro wondered how Admiral Carver would treat the information. Were he in her place, no scrap of intelligence, regardless of its credibility, would be ignored until disproven.

Chapter Sixteen

~ April 14th, 2287 ~

"The two ships assigned to track the Denubbewa mother ship continue to perform their flybys at the maximum DeTect range each day," Jenetta said to the R2HQ Board at the regularly scheduled meeting. "So far, the mother ship has remained stationary, although the number of smaller ships outside the mother ship changes frequently. We believe the ships are kept on patrol at distances far enough from the mother ship to give adequate time to prepare should Space Command commence an attack. That would mean they perform like the Distant DeTect Grids we establish at all our bases."

"Can they DeTect the scout-destroyers performing the monitoring activities?" Admiral Buckner asked.

"If a vessel passes within four billion kilometers, they will see a reflection on their screens," Admiral Holt said, "but unless they know what's causing it, they will probably dismiss it as a momentary anomaly. Since the scout-destroyers are encapsulated in a transverse-wave envelope during their flybys, the DeTect image is more like a momentary shadow than the solid image you'd see with vessels traveling at slower FTL or sub-light speeds."

"If they move, our ships will follow them wherever they go," Jenetta said. "We'll always know where they are when we're ready to take them on."

"I like your confidence, Jen," Admiral Poole said. "So far, they've been the ones doing the ass-kicking."

"They caught us cold, twice, with their still undeclared war. But we've been able to learn a little about them, and we do have at least one major advantage."

"Major advantage?" Admiral Buckner said.

"Our Light-9790 speed. As far as we know, their top speed is about Light-450."

"We can't know that's their top speed. All we know is that they haven't been observed exceeding that speed."

"True, but our Intelligence people have been examining the high-resolution images of their ships and are confident that the ships are not sheathed with Dakinium. So unless they've discovered another way to create a double envelope, Light-450 may be their top speed. Scientists still insist that the theoretical absolute limit for single envelope travel is Light-862, so if they haven't mastered Transverse Wave travel, our ships are at least eleven times faster and most likely about twenty-one times faster."

"Have our Intelligence people discovered any new information about the invaders?" Admiral Buckner asked, looking towards Admiral Kanes.

"Admiral Carver provided some new information just this morning," Kanes said. "She has a direct contact that has been providing her with solid intelligence data for years. The AB knows the identity of the source, as do I, and we fully support the sharing of information vital to the protection of both nations. According to the source, the Denubbewa mother ship in our space has reported that the Galactic Alliance territory is ripe for takeover. It's requested that a full contingent of mother ships join them here to assist in completing the takeover of our space."

The R2HQ Board Hall fell into complete silence as everyone's thoughts turned to further possible invasion by alien forces.

"How long do we have to prepare?" Admiral Holt asked.

"Unknown," Kanes said. "We don't know if the Denubbew Dominancy has dispatched the requested ships or if they intend to do so in the near future. We don't know how far they would have to travel or how long that journey would take. We don't even know how many ships are considered a contingent. Is it five ships or five hundred? We have no idea how large their population is, but since they appear to have expansionist intentions, it would be prudent to assume that they will come at some point. However, without further intelligence inform-ation, we have no idea when that might be."

"Good God," Admiral Buckner said. "If they come with five hundred of those mother ships, there's no way we can stop them."

"Our best bet would be to destroy the mother ship already in our space as soon as possible," Jenetta said. "That will send a powerful message because they've essentially said we're powerless to stop their takeover. When their leaders back home learn of the destruction, or at least when they fail to get any response to their messages, they might rethink their position."

"Have we made any progress on your plan?" Admiral Poole asked.

"Since this meeting isn't as private as it would have to be to discuss details, all I can say is that things are progressing. Certain components are scheduled to leave production facili-ties in Region One any day now. In two months' time, we should be able to begin assembly of test components. Once the test components are constructed, we'll be ready to test the delivery system. I can't say how long that phase will take, but given the task, it could be considerable."

"I'm sure we all appreciate the precision required for that phase," Admiral Holt said. "But if your plan works as outlined, we'll have a weapon that will forever shift the bal-ance of power back to Space Command."

"I'm not ready to make *that* strong a pronouncement," Jenetta said. "I thought we would be the most powerful force in this part of space for decades to come when we began to use Dakinium sheathing on our ships, but even Dakinium didn't stop this new enemy from destroying our two scout-destroyers with ease. But perhaps the new weapon will give us an edge again— for a while."

* * *

Nicole Ravenau examined her face in the mirror and then smiled. After a year of almost constant pain, her gender transformation was almost complete. She was a man again.

She— He hadn't enjoyed sex since surrendering his sex in exchange for youth and now yearned for female companionship, but he would be patient. His goal was within sight and he wasn't going to do anything to jeopardize that just to enjoy a few minutes of sexual pleasure. There would be plenty of time for that later, after he was ensconced back in the Raider family. With his handsome new face, women would be fawning over him now. His old face, the one before he became Nicole, hadn't been ugly. In fact, he'd always thought of it as ruggedly attractive. But this new face, one crafted by the top scientists in genetic research, would turn the heads of most females, especially the attractive ones for whom a handsome face and muscular body was the ticket to their boudoir. And best of all, he would enjoy that access for thousands of years. By then, he believed, he would have found the secret to eternal life. The accomplishments of his scientists to date was all the proof he needed that anything was possible through the manipulation of the human genome.

It was a shame that he'd felt it necessary to murder all his people and destroy the lab, but he'd believed it was the only way to escape the wrath of Strauss for the attack on Christa Carver. Of course, a full copy of all research data since the beginning of the projects was safely hidden away in several of his secret locations.

The genetic makeup of his new body eliminated the need to ever shave his face again, so after bathing and getting dressed, he prepared for a night in the casino. He slipped his new ID into the inside pocket of his sports coat and pulled the door to the corridor closed behind him. It would be the first appearance of Gregory Foster since he had come aboard the passenger liner at Pelomious.

* * *

"A transport carrying the requested materials left for Quesann today, Richard," Admiral Ahmed said in response to Admiral Moore's query in a regular session of the AB.

"Was the entire order filled, Raihana?" Admiral Moore asked.

"Everything Admiral Carver requested, plus the additional quantities we felt were justified. All devices are fully assembled and ready to be deployed once the safeties are removed."

"The six new scout-destroyers that recently completed their space trials were held at the Mars shipyard until the transport was ready to depart," Admiral Platt said. "They'll function as escorts for the transport, even though it's not subject to attack since it will be traveling at Light-9790."

"It's good to have the extra protection available in case the transport suffers a drive problem," Admiral Bradlee said. "The load is too important to be left unguarded."

"In a pinch, part of the load could even be offloaded to one of the small ships and sent on ahead so Quesann can begin preparing for their testing phase," Admiral Plimley said.

"Yes," Admiral Hillaire said, "I'm sure that holding the scout-destroyers for an extra two weeks didn't present a problem for Admiral Carver's Second Fleet."

"Now the difficult part for us begins," Admiral Moore said. "We must wait to see if the weapon will meet expectations. I'm beginning to feel as anxious as when we began to mount our defense against the THUG pact."

* * *

"We've been on long cruises before," Nelligen said, "But at least we've always had a destination and some idea of when we'd get there. Following a freighter without knowing where we're heading is getting on my nerves."

"It's getting to all of us," Byers said. "Vyx, I don't know how you stay so calm about this."

"I'm treating it like a vacation. The DeTect system will alert us if the freighter changes course or speed, so let's just sit back and enjoy the ride."

"How can we enjoy the ride when we know we're going to run out of beer in three more months?" Nelligen said. "We should have stocked more."

"Any chance of slipping away and restocking the supplies?" Byers asked. "The freighter hasn't changed course since we left Uthlarigasset, and you said we have much greater speed. We could angle off four billion kilometers to avoid their DeTect, zip around them, stop at an inhabited world ahead, and pick up their trail again after getting supplies."

"We have enough food to last five years, so we're in no danger of starving before we get back. You'll just have to stretch your beer supply out as long as possible because there are no decently sized colonies on this course between here and the border with open space."

"If there are no decently sized colonies ahead, then where the heck is that freighter going?"

"The guy in the tavern said 'to the black.' I guess he meant outside of GA space."

"But we're at least two years from the GA Border."

"Yes, it's going to be a long voyage."

"I'm suddenly getting a very bad feeling about this," Byers said.

"The only difference between space in the GA and unclaimed space beyond our border is an imaginary line."

"Yeah, but we received that alert about the Denubbewa," Nelligen said. "What if that freighter is headed for a rendezvous with them and one of their mother ships? The Uthlaro might be supplying them with food and stuff in exchange for them attacking our ships."

"Then we turn around and hightail it back to GA space as fast as we can. And we hope that none of them can travel faster than Light-487."

"If we have two more years before we get to our destination, that means two more years for the return voyage as well— assuming there is a return voyage."

"Yes, I've been thinking about that. Once we ascertain what's going on, we can call for a Light-9790 vessel to pick us up."

"That'll save us the return trip," Byers said, "but what about the outgoing trip? If there are no more decently sized colonies ahead, why don't we call for a Light-9790 ship now and zip ahead until we figure out where that freighter is headed? We could save years of travel time."

"Yes, I admit I've considered that. I guess I've been enjoying the vacation a bit."

"We're running out of beer," Nelligen said, "so it's time to call for that ship now. Even with the ride, we'll be lucky to get back before we run out."

Vyx smiled and expelled a phony sigh. "Okay, I'll call for a ship large enough to carry us. I suppose it'll have to be a battleship or ship transporter. The old *Scorpion* could squeeze into the maintenance bay of a destroyer, but this ship wouldn't even get halfway inside."

* * *

"I've just received notification from the Admiralty Board," Jenetta said to the R2HQ Board during their morning session, "that the *special* materials we requested from them have been shipped. Deducting the eighteen days it took for the communication to reach Quesann from the roughly fifty-two days' travel time means that the transport should arrive here in thirty-four days."

"Has the entire request been filled?" Admiral Holt asked.

"And then some. The AB increased the quantities I ordered by a considerable measure. I kept the order small because I knew we'd be interrupting production of other needed materials. I didn't want there to be any substantial delays owed to previous scheduling. However, the AB gave it top priority at every production facility, so the time required to produce the additional materials and assemblies was negligible once the facilities were geared up for manufacture of the items. We'll be able to outfit ten ships for the delivery of the weapon and have a decent stockpile for rearming."

"How long are we talking about for ship preparation?" Admiral Poole asked.

"One ship has already been prepared to accept the special devices. Once fully outfitted, we'll begin testing to see if the idea is practicable. If it is, we'll begin outfitting nine more."

"Why don't we begin outfitting the additional nine now?" Admiral Buckner asked."

"The practicality of my idea has been questioned at the highest levels of Weapons Research and Development at SHQ. Perhaps they're right and I'm wrong. Perhaps it will never work. But so far no one in WRD at SHQ has come up with an idea that doesn't involve suicide runs against those enemy ships. I've wracked my brain and been unable to come up with a better solution than the one I've put into development. If my idea is impractical, we can't have nine ships out of action while they're prepared for a useless system and then repaired when acceptable results cannot be achieved. And if that's the case, I don't know where we go from here."

* * *

Come in, Barbara," Jenetta said to Captain DeWitt when she arrived at Jenetta's office.

"Good morning, Admiral."

"Help yourself to a beverage and then join me at my desk."

A minute later, Captain DeWitt sat in one of the comfortable oh-gee chairs across the desk from Jenetta. She looked exhausted and her uniform was a bit rumpled. Jenetta had never seen her when her appearance was less than impeccable.

"You look terrible, Barbara. When was the last time you slept?"

"Not since the ordnance arrived from Region One. I guess it's been about three days. I'm sorry about my appearance, Admiral, but your message said to come immediately."

Jenetta nodded. "After we're done here, I want you to return to your quarters and get some rest. That goes for your people as well. You can't do your best work if you're too tired to think clearly. We can't afford even the smallest of errors with the installation."

"Aye, Admiral."

"What's the current situation?"

"Our twelve most senior engineers have installed the first three bomb cradles in the ship. While we were waiting for the Dakinium cradles to arrive, we practiced repeatedly with the mockup tritanium units our engineers constructed, so the installation work with the Dakinium units went smoothly. We've tested the connections with the weapons computer and everything went perfectly. Each of the twelve senior engineers will now head up an installation team as we install the other ninety-seven cradles in the ship. After we all get some rest, that is."

"Estimated time before we can begin test runs?"

"If everything continues to go well, we could be ready in three weeks. But even with the best of plans, something usually goes askew. So to be safe, I'd allow five weeks."

"Okay. Five weeks is the plan then. The test area has been placed off-limits to all vessels, and the cargo containers are ready to be delivered there. Have the dummy bombs been prepared?"

"Aye, Admiral. The mass of each dummy load is identical to the real ordnance down to the microgram. As the dummy passes out of the ship, and beyond the TW envelope, a simple mechanical switch activates a homing signal so we can track our bombing accuracy and recover the dummy."

"Has anyone established a pool for how close the first release will be?" Jenetta asked with a smile.

"I'm sure there is, Admiral," DeWitt said, returning the smile, "but I haven't been asked to participate. We've crunched numbers for weeks trying to establish a formula for the bomb release timing, but until we drop the first dummy, we can't begin to refine the process. I'm just hoping we're within a billion kilometers for the first drop."

"I know how hard you've worked on this project, Barbara, and I appreciate all your efforts. I have every confidence in you and your team. If anybody can do this, it's you. Okay, go get some rest, and tell your people to get some. I'm pleased with the progress you've made so far and I want everyone rested and healthy. Dismissed."

After Captain DeWitt had gone, Jenetta leaned back in her chair to think about the upcoming targeting phase. Jenetta knew that DeWitt wouldn't pad an estimate and the project was too important to press, possibly forcing someone to take shortcuts. The Denubbewa mother ship was still at the previously reported location according to the latest reports from the ships assigned to watch it. It was probably waiting for the requested reinforcements before it began a push through Region Two space.

* * *

"Sir," the tac officer aboard the *Mekong* said with some urgency, "the target is gone."

Lt. Kyle Gleason, the second officer and watch commander sat up a bit straighter. "Gone? No sign on the DeTect?"

"Negative, sir. The board is clear."

Gleason looked up at the chronometer. It was 0315. He bit his lower lip lightly, then said, "Com, notify the Captain that the Denubbewa mother ship has moved and is not in DeTect range. No—, never mind. I'd better do it."

Captain Cody Morrow scowled at the chronometer after wiping the sleep from his eyes. He reached over, tapped the com on the nightstand, and said, "Captain."

"Uh, sorry to wake you at this hour, Captain. I needed to inform you that the target has moved. It's not within DeTect range."

Morrow cursed under his breath, then said, "The *Rio Grande* certainly would have notified us if the mother ship wasn't there four hours ago. Notify them of this situation, then initiate a search using the pattern we've prepared for this possibility. If that ship is limited to single-envelope travel, as we believe, it can't have gone more than three-point-five trillion kilometers in four hours, and more likely only about two trillion kilometers if it didn't leave immediately after the *Rio Grande* made its last flyby."

"Aye, sir."

"I'll be on the bridge in fifteen minutes, but don't wait on my arrival to begin the search."

"Aye, sir."

Morrow pushed the com screen down and yawned. The months of performing flybys to verify the mother ship hadn't moved had become routine and even a bit boring, but he preferred that to searching. The tac officer would certainly know that the *Mekong* hadn't passed the mother ship on their way to perform their flyby, so that was one direction they didn't have to search. That left just forty-six million, six hundred fifty-five thousand, nine hundred ninety-nine other vectors the mother ship could have taken when leaving the area. Well, at least the *Mekong* only had to search half of those. The *Rio Grande* would handle the other half.

Morrow got out of bed, stretched, and headed for the bathroom, hoping that a brisk shower would wake him up. His only real task right now was to notify R2HQ that the mother ship was missing and that they were initiating a search, but he wanted to look awake and alert when he prepared that message.

* * *

"Sorry to wake you, Captain," Lt. Janet Spears said when Commander Marc Hodenfield raised the screen on his com unit. "We've just received a message from the *Mekong*. The target is no longer at the location we've been monitoring. They're initiating Search Pattern Zulu-Six and taking the Alpha role. They request that we commence the search in the Beta role."

"Understood, Lieutenant. Confirm to them that the *Rio Grande* is immediately commencing the search in the Beta role."

"Aye, sir. I'll notify the *Mekong* and initiate the search pattern."

"Keep me advised if anything changes."

"Aye, sir. Out."

"Out."

Chapter Seventeen

~ June 26th, 2287 ~

Captain Barbara DeWitt sat back in her chair in the Weapons Control computer room aboard the *Tigris* and said through her com link, "Okay, that's the entire checklist. Everything seems go. Everyone agree?"

From half a dozen locations in the ship, voices acknowledged their agreement that everything was go.

"Affirmative. All stations standby, I'm alerting the bridge that we're go."

* * *

Gregory Foster, a.k.a. Nicole Ravenau, a.k.a. Mikel Arneu, stepped through the shuttle hatchway and walked to his seat for the short flight down to the surface. He had been eagerly anticipating this day since leaving more than a year ago. The stage makeup he'd applied to his face as he prepared to disembark altered his appearance so dramatically that even the people with whom he'd been playing cards every night for the past several weeks wouldn't recognize him.

The customs agent at the spaceport slipped the ID into the computer slot and looked at the image that appeared on the monitor. It correctly matched Foster's current appearance, so he handed back the ID and waved Foster through.

Smiling pleasantly, Foster picked up his briefcase and continued on towards the building exit. His luggage would be delivered to his hotel suite in a few hours. As he stepped outside, he breathed deeply and thought the air decidedly more polluted here than the air on Pelomious, but it would be difficult to find a planet where that wasn't the case. Anywhere there are people, there will be at least a modicum of pollution despite the best efforts to purify the air.

Foster checked into his hotel and removed the stage makeup, then relaxed in a tub of warm water for an hour. He'd always been a shower person as a male, but as Nicole he'd developed a fondness for baths and had no intention of ending that just because he had switched genders again. Since he wasn't going out tonight, he'd ordered a bottle of Sebastian Colony semi-dry Maulon wine and placed it into the wine chiller basket. Once it achieved the recommended consumption temperature, he'd pulled the cork and poured his first glass.

As Foster swirled the first sip around in his mouth, allowing his taste buds to appraise the vintage, he thought about the formulas he had turned over to the Director at the Raider Central Labs a year ago. The package contained mounds of research detailing decades of work and results. No one would ever know from the submitted data that one of the *proven* formulas actually represented a failed process where the adverse effects didn't manifest until after a full year had passed, and by then it would be too late to stop the mutation effects on internal organs that eventually took the subject down a very painful path to sure death.

Foster smiled as he thought about the members of the Upper Council celebrating their metamorphosis— at least temporarily. Once they began to experience health issues, they would learn that they had just months to live. Perhaps they would take out their anger on Strauss. Foster grinned. That would teach him a lesson. Too bad Foster wasn't in a position to observe the severe chastisement he expected Strauss to receive and fully enjoy the experience. The thought had occurred to Foster before he set this plan in motion that Strauss might be removed from his position as Lower Council Chairman or even made to vanish without a trace. Foster hoped not, as that would impact his future plans for rejoining the Raider Corporation.

So far, his plan had worked perfectly. Now that Foster was close to reemerging from his self-imposed isolation, he had to ensure that the rest of his plan went just as well.

* * *

"Here are the results of the first tests, Admiral," Captain DeWitt said as she held out a data ring to Jenetta.

"You don't appear very happy or excited," Jenetta said as she accepted the ring and dropped it over the small spindle on her keyboard.

"That would be very hard, given the results. I never really expected to have the first bomb land within a billion kilometers of the shipping container, but I wasn't prepared for the actual results."

"That sounds pretty ominous," Jenetta said as she tapped the keyboard to download the report. A second later it appeared on her monitor. "Eight *billion* kilometers?" Jenetta exclaimed.

"I'm afraid so, Admiral. But that *was* the first attempt. And it had the worst result. After the test, we modified the calculation algorithm and made another run."

Looking at the monitor, Jenetta said, "But you improved with each run. Your closest drop was four billion kilometers from the target."

"Yes, ma'am that was the best on our first day."

"But you can continue tweaking the targeting algorithm, can't you?"

"We'll continue working on the problem, but I haven't scheduled any more tests at this time. You see, the problem is that by the time our system can even see the target, we're almost on top of it. We're traveling at roughly two-point-nine-three-six billion kilometers per second, and the DeTect station can only see four billion kilometers ahead of the ship. This means that we have one-point-three-six seconds from the time the DeTect system identifies the target until we pass it by. Now, that lends itself fine to monitoring the presence of an enemy ship because it's okay if the information isn't accessible until after we've passed the target, but we need the targeting information before we reach the target. If we can get the precise information we need three-point-four seconds before we reach the target, I think we can put the bomb inside the shipping container every time."

"But you were able to cut the drop distance down to four billion kilometers?"

"Only after we stopped trying to place the bomb using currently available data. We started using the data from previous runs, but that's 'by guess and by golly' targeting."

"I'll accept that, if you can hit the target in one of ten attempts."

"That's just it. We can't guarantee that we'll ever get closer than four billion kilometers. Everything in space is moving, even when it seems to be standing still. Moons are circling planets, planets— other than rogue planets— are circling stars, stars are moving within galaxies, and galaxies are constantly moving with respect to other galaxies. You're an astrophysicist, so I know I'm not telling you anything you don't already know very well. Normally, I can discount all those things. We can hit a ship with a torpedo because once the ship is targeted, the torpedo can handle the targeting task on its own and continue to make corrections even if we're not riding herd on it. And when both the target and the source are moving at sub-light speeds, the weapons control systems provide advance correction data. Laser beams travel at the speed of light, so once you fire, the beam is usually going to hit whatever you aimed at. But with our current bombing problem at FTL speeds, we can't see the quarry in time to fire by other than an intuitive sense, and that's just not accurate enough. We must have a little over three seconds for targeting and deployment of the bomb, and all we have is one second."

Jenetta nodded. "I understand the problem, and I admit I've been concerned about it since the idea first entered my head, but I was hoping someone would suggest a way we might make it work. Well, we now have bombs and a delivery system that almost guarantees our ships and people will be safe. All we need is a foolproof targeting system that allows enough time to deploy the bombs."

"With all due respect, Admiral, that's like Galileo saying, 'I can see the moon, and I know how it moves, so now all I need is a way to get there.'"

Jenetta smiled. "And now, six centuries later, traveling to the moon takes minutes. I just hope it doesn't take six centuries to solve this problem."

"If it does, I won't be around to see it," DeWitt said with a smile.

But I might, Jenetta thought, although she'd never say it aloud. She had still never told anyone outside the family of her, Christa, and Eliza's projected longevity. "We don't have that long, anyway, Barbara. If we can't defeat this enemy, it may be the end of Space Command and the GA. It's a challenge, but we must find a way."

"It's useless, Admiral. Current technology doesn't allow us to see further than four billion kilometers with the DeTect system. That's less than one-point-three seconds when traveling at Light-9793.48, and it takes three seconds to locate the target and deploy the bomb. It's not a challenge; it's impossible."

"Impossible or not, we must do it. Barbara, assemble your brightest people and start brainstorming the problem. Don't dismiss any idea until it's proved unworkable. There has to be a way, so let's find it. And if it requires that we develop a new DeTect system, so be it."

"The present DeTect system took decades to develop, Admiral."

"And that was almost a century ago, so surely someone's proposed a new system by now. Let's find that person or persons and investigate his/her/their ideas. Four billion kilometers has been satisfactory until now, so there's been no urgency to reinvent the wheel. Well, now we have that urgency. We need to reinvent the wheel. We need twelve billion kilometers for our new weapon. That will give us four seconds. We've accomplished the Manhattan Project phase. We have the bomb. Now we need to enter the Norden Bombsight development phase."

"The original goal of the Norden Bombsight was to place a bomb within a seventy-five foot circle. In reality, they never succeeded beyond a one-thousand, two-hundred-foot radius most of the time."

"I'll take twelve hundred feet."

"And so would I, but it's unlikely in the extreme." DeWitt took a deep breath, looked at Jenetta intently, and then released the breath slowly. "Very well, Admiral. We'll see if we can improve on the DeTect system. If the current technology isn't adequate, I suppose it's time to develop new technology."

"Thank you, Barbara. I know the team that developed the Phalanx targeting system will find a way."

* * *

"Good morning, Jen," Admiral Holt said as the doors opened to admit him and he strode into the office.

"Good morning, Brian."

"Am I disturbing you?"

"No, not at all," she said with a sad smile. "I was disturbed long before you arrived. I'm sitting here pulling my hair out over our problems with the Denubbewa."

"New problems?"

"Yes."

"I'm sorry to hear that. I'm also sorry I haven't spent more time working with you on that issue. I've been so wrapped up with development of the new GA Senate complex and SHQ base that I've paid little attention to the problems with the Denubbewa. I believed you had a handle on it with Project Gazebo and were progressing towards a final solution."

"Brian, I can't tell you how much I appreciate your taking on that development project. By turning it over to you completely, I've been able to concentrate on the other major issues facing us here, not to mention the minor issues at home. If development of the new complexes was waiting on me for attention, they'd still just be at the drawing-board stage."

"What's the problem at home? I thought everything was great with your mom. Aren't your sisters, brothers, and father all on deployment?" Holt lowered his frame in a chair in front of Jenetta's desk and said with a smile, "Now tell Uncle Brian all about it."

Jenetta smiled widely for the first time in weeks. "Okay, *Uncle* Brian. I've told you that my mom is at the estate on Obotymot and that my sister-in-law Marisa was with her. Well, recently, my other sister-in-law Regina joined them. Billy's ship is still assigned to Stewart and he hasn't been home for a while, so Mom invited Regina to come to the estate. It's become sort of like an SC deployment widows convention for the Carver family. Anyway, my chamberlain is having fits. He's had the run of the place since the peninsula was turned over to the Family Carver, and he feels that mom and the girls are interfering with his running of the estate."

"Are they?"

"A little— but not in bad way. I almost fainted a few months ago when mom began traveling down a road that would have had her criticizing the monarchy on Nordakia. I managed to stop her in time by explaining how the residents of Obotymot are actually taxed far less than the citizens of most planets, including Earth."

"Are they?"

"Of course. They turn over fifty percent of their crop or, if a merchant, income to their landlord and pay no other taxes or fees except fines if they violate the law. Paying one tax means that government agencies at all levels aren't involved in tax collection efforts or dreaming up new ways to tax its people. Compare that with some countries on Earth where people pay up to ninety percent when all taxes are factored in, and half of all civilian government worker time is consumed with tax collection or *fee* collection efforts. A tax by any other name is still a tax."

"So what are your mother and in-laws doing that your chamberlain finds so invasive or disruptive?"

"According to Chamberlain Yaghutol, mom has been traveling around the estate trying to help farmers improve their crops by putting them in touch with the proper experts."

"How is that bad?"

"I never said it was bad. It's Chamberlain Yaghutol who resents her involvement. I've tried to make him understand that she just wants to be helpful and that he should look upon it as being useful if the crops are improved."

"But he doesn't buy that?"

"He might, but he's just so caught up with not having any control over her or the girls."

"Ah, I see. It's a matter of pride. He wants to get all the credit for any improvements in the crop production."

"Perhaps. Or it might be that he sees it as an intrusion into his empire. Either way, he'll have to get used to it. I'm glad mom, Marisa, and Regina are there and getting involved. I just have to keep an eye on things to make sure we don't have any more issues where they're intruding into governmental affairs. Anything else can be handled."

Admiral Holt chuckled. "I imagine it's frustrating to be so far away."

"Yes, the distance makes timely communications imposs-ible. That's something *I'll* just have to get used to."

"So, tell me what I can do to help with the Denubbewa issue."

"I wish I knew. Let me bring you up to date." After Jenetta had filled him in on the problem with the bombing tests and the fact that the Denubbewa mother ship was missing, she said, "If you have any suggestions, I'd love to hear them."

"I don't have anything off the top of my head. You say the mother ship has evaded our scout-destroyers?"

"That might be an exaggeration. My last communication was that the two ships had begun a search of the surrounding space but so far turned up no trace of it."

"Not good."

"Tell me about it. We had believed they were limited to single-envelope FTL, but perhaps they've found a way that doesn't require Dakinium-sheathing. We've always known it takes a very specific hull to establish the proper resonance and Dakinium is the only material we've found that can do that, but that doesn't mean it's the only material."

"There's another possibility."

"I'm listening," Jenetta said.

"They might have found a way of shielding themselves."

"You mean like an invisibility cloak?"

"Nothing so grandiose. I'm referring to a way to shield themselves from the DeTect detection like the skin cover we once used on our tritanium-sheathed warships to make their DeTect signature so tiny that it confused our enemies. But perhaps they can achieve one hundred percent DeTect invisibility."

"If that's the case, we have a real problem. Right now, our search pattern depends on being able to consider each six-billion-kilometer-wide pass as being accurate if the DeTect monitor remains clear. If we need visual proof for confirmation of their presence, it will take us a thousand times longer to find them."

"And if we have to narrow each pass by that much, they might have time to escape completely."

"I thought you were here to make me feel better, *Uncle* Brian."

Admiral Holt chuckled. "You've never needed to be shielded from either the facts or speculation."

Jenetta grinned. "And I'm not now. I was joking. I always want people to openly tell me what they know, what they think might be possible, or what they think might be impossible."

"I think that's why we get along so well. I'm the same way. So— what do we do about the Denubbewa?"

"First we have to find them. But in the meantime we're not going to stop working on a way to combat them. I asked Captain DeWitt to develop a new DeTect system that can see twelve billion kilometers."

Holt chuckled again. "You don't ask for much from your people, do you?"

"If you establish a bar height that's high but not totally absurd, the best and brightest will sometimes surprise even themselves."

"What are the chances that we *can* achieve twelve billion kilometers with a new DeTect system?"

"That's for the engineers to answer. I do recall reading, long ago, that the people working on the DeTect system were able to greatly extend the range, but the results were unreliable. As the distance increased, a proportionally greater percentage of false positives were recorded. In the end, they decided to sacrifice distance for accuracy. At four billion kilometers, accuracy was ninety-nine percent. I don't know how far they tried to extend the range or what the percentage of false positives was at greater distances, but it's worth investigating. We must make an effort to see if improved technology can improve the reliability of data at a greater distance. Even if we only manage to improve it by ten percent, it will be well worth the effort, although it won't solve our present problem."

"A ten percent improvement would have significant advantages for base security also. As ship speeds have increased, warning time has decreased, making our bases more susceptible to attack without a proper defense net in place. Even with our Distant DeTect Grid at Higgins, I was always concerned about possible attack after the Raiders tried to destroy us. If we hadn't had advanced intel about that attack, they would have rolled over us with the first wave."

"I had a great advantage at Dixon and Stewart. Being inside an asteroid severely reduces concerns about a surprise attack, but it's become a great concern here. And with the GA Senate and SHQ taking up residence here, I'll have to commit a greater portion of our fleet to Quesann's defense. When you factor in the forces I'll have to commit to safeguarding the new shipyard and foundry, it's going to further weaken our ability to patrol the regions and respond to problems. Given the new threat from the Denubbewa, I wish the Senate and SHQ would reevaluate their decision to move here. I tried to tell the AB how dangerous it still is out here, but they said the GA Senate has decided to move and that's that."

"They trust that Admiral Carver will protect them from any harm."

"I wish Admiral Carver was as confident as they are. And I admit to having felt a lot more confident before the Denubbewa showed up."

Speaking of the Denubbewa, I haven't heard anything about that missile the *Tagus* found."

"We believe the missile was one used during the attack on the *Yenisei*, which as you know occurred at the furthest sectors of Region Two. It's taken months for the *Tagus*, traveling at Light-9790 to bring it here for laboratory analysis. The engineers aboard the *Tagus* had orders to only dismantle it sufficiently to ensure it didn't pose an imminent threat to the ship, so we only know a little bit about it at this point. What we do know has confirmed our hypotheses developed from examinations of the *Yenisei* and *Salado*. We now know for certain that there are three sections consisting of a small warhead at the fore end, a small nuclear payload behind that, and then the delivery section. The fuel in the delivery section was completely exhausted. That's about all we know for sure right now, but we hope to have more information very soon."

Chapter Eighteen
~ July 12th, 2287 ~

"Lieutenant," the com chief said, "we've just received a message on the SC General Broadcast frequency."

"From R2HQ, Chief?" Lt. Kyle Gleason, the third watch commander aboard the *Mekong,* asked from the bridge command chair.

"No, sir. It's from a Region Two Territorial Guard ship."

"In the clear?"

"No, sir. The message is encrypted, and it's one of the new encryption codes put into use following the *Yenisei* and *Salado* incidents."

"Put it on the front monitor, Chief."

"Aye, sir."

A second later, the head-and-shoulders image of a Milora wearing a Territorial Guard officer uniform appeared on the large screen. After a two-second pause, the Milora began to speak.

"This is Captain Bdillaaq of the SC Territorial Guard destroyer *Mnesppretul* on routine patrol in the sectors around Ruwaler Space Command Base. Minutes ago, we were startled to encounter a mother ship like the one described in reports about the Denubbewa. We established its size as being roughly one hundred twenty-six kilometers, and it was covered in those bubbles that the alert named as missile platforms. In compliance with Standing Orders to avoid all contact with the Denubbewa, we immediately altered course. The mother ship was under power and we were able to determine its course using DeTect information as we put distance between us. My navigator and tac officers will append their data to this report.

"Uriqollor Bdillaaq, SC Territorial Guard, Captain of the *Mnesppretul*, near the Ruwaler base, end of message."

"Chief, put the reports of the navigator and tac officer on my right monitor."

"Aye, sir."

Gleason viewed each of the reports carefully. The images of the ship showed it to be nearly identical to the one the *Mekong* and *Rio Grande* had been watching until it disappeared. Audio from monitors mounted on the command chair was automatically routed through the chair occupant's CT. After listening to the reports and scanning the graphed data, Gleason touched his SC ring to establish a carrier. His eyes darted to a chronometer reading on another monitor and he closed his eyes for a second before taking a deep breath and releasing it slowly. "Captain's quarters," he said.

Commander Cody Morrow, Captain of the *Mekong*, scowled at the dim numbers on his bulkhead chronometer after waking to the chime of the com unit on his nightstand. It seemed like he'd just gone to bed, but the chronometer indicated that it was 0408.

"Captain," was all he said as he raised the com lid.

"Sir, we just received a broadcast that reports the position of a Denubbewa mother ship."

"A broadcast?" Morrow said sleepily.

"Yes, sir. It was an encrypted message from the captain of the Territorial Guard destroyer *Mnesppretul*. It puts the Denubbewa ship eighty-six light-years from the Ruwaler base."

"Ruwaler?" Morrow said with obvious incredulity as he came fully awake. "That can't be *our* missing ship. There's no way it could have gotten all the way up there since it disappeared."

"No, sir. That's why I felt the information was important enough to disturb your sleep."

"Was the ship stationary?"

"No, it was under power."

"Where's it headed?"

"Uh— this way, sir."

"Towards us?"

"Yes, sir. Not directly, of course, but in this general direction. It's reported course will take it directly towards the location of the mother ship we had been observing."

"Hmm, sounds like they intended to rendezvous," Morrow said almost absentmindedly.

"Yes, sir. It does sound that way. I thought they still might."

"Are we near the course *our* mother ship would follow if there is an intended rendezvous?"

"No, sir. The search plan we're following has that area assigned to the *Rio Grande*."

"Very well. Contact the *Rio Grande* and tell them of our suspicions. Commander Hodenfield will have to decide whether or not to alter his search to investigate the search area where we suspect the mother ship might be. Uh— ask them to keep us advised. I'm going back to sleep. Out."

"Yes, sir. Out."

As Morrow laid back down, he thought about the situation. If Hodenfield decided not to break off his search and follow the vector the mother ship might have taken if a rendezvous was planned, he would take it upon himself to do so. But he knew Marc Hodenfield pretty well and couldn't really imagine him not following up on this lead.

* * *

"A message for you just arrived from the *Mekong*, Captain," the com chief said early in the first watch.

"Put it on my right-hand monitor, Chief."

"Aye, sir. After tapping a point on his console, he said, "It's there, sir."

Morrow scanned the queue and selected the message.

"Hi, Cody," Morrow heard in his CT as the image of Commander Marc Hodenfield appeared on the monitor. "We've located the missing mother ship along the vector you suggested. My compliments to your third watch bridge crew. We received the Territorial Guard broadcast, but my third watch commander decided not to wake me and just put the message in my queue. However, when your message came in, he decided I should hear it right away. I had him immediately alter course and we've just located the Denubbewa ship.

"Since we've just confirmed the presence of the ship, you're up next in four hours. My navigator will send you the position, course, and the exact time we plotted it so you can plot the next location for your flyby. The ship is traveling at Light-462.

"Assuming that our mother ship is on its way to rendezvous with the one reported by the Territorial Guard ship, and that both are traveling at only Light-462, my navigator estimates they won't meet up for months. So I suppose the question is whether or not there are others also headed to the rendezvous location in preparation for making a concerted push through Region Two. But I guess that's something for R2HQ to think about. We'll just keep following our orders.

"Marc Hodenfield, Commander, Captain of the *Rio Grande* GSC-SDD063 in Region Two, message complete."

* * *

"The laboratory analysis of the missile is complete, Admiral," Captain DeWitt said.

"Tell me you have good news," Jenetta said.

"I have— news."

"Okay, tell me anyway."

"The warhead is as we expected. A substance is contained in a glass globule which is protected by a composite metal shield that shatters on contact with a target. The substance in the globule is a thick viscous matter rather than a liquid, so it doesn't spurt out. We envision it as spreading from the force of the strike but never separating. Upon contact with the hull, a chemical process is initiated that eats away at the Dakinium. The missile shaft remains firmly rooted in the goo while the chemical process takes place. The tip of the missile beneath the glass globe contains a fuse and the goo also eats away at that while eating away at the ship's hull. When it eats through to the fuse, the nuclear charge is detonated. By that time, the hull where the goo spread out is ready to flake apart, so the small nuclear charge blasts through, destroying bulkheads and flooding the interior of the ship with radiation. Following the explosion, the atmo is evacuated. It's a simple device, much like our bomb, but highly effective."

"Yes, we've seen the evidence of that. Now for the big question. Do you think the goo was developed from the chemical formula we use to cut and mold Dakinium?"

"No. We believe it was just a coincidence. The goo has destroyed everything we've tested it on. It's just a sort of all-purpose hull penetration chemical."

"So you're saying they just got lucky?"

"I can't say that. Perhaps an enemy they've encountered in the past had a material like Dakinium, and they had to develop a chemical that would destroy it as well as anything else. We know that the Dakistians had a Dakinium-like material hundreds of centuries ago."

"So much for our vaunted invincibility," Jenetta said.

"If it makes you feel any better, the Denubbewa goo also eats through tritanium in seconds."

"It doesn't. It means that our older ships and the Territorial Guard ships will be just as vulnerable as the DS ships. We still have to find a way to defeat this race. Any luck with the DeTect issue?"

"Not yet. My people are studying everything ever written about the development work, but we're only partway through the hundreds of thousands of pages of research notes."

"Okay, Barbara. Thank you. Good work on the missile analysis. Is there anything else?"

"No. That was all, Admiral. I wanted to get this report to you right away."

* * *

"As all of you know," Arthur Strauss, Chairman of the Lower Council said to the other council members, "the eight male members of the Upper Council unanimously opted to undergo the DNA Manipulation process and change their gender so they could undergo the Age Regression process which, as you also know, only works on females. The four female members of the Upper Council elected to undergo the Age Regression and Age Prolongation process immediately since their gender was already suited to the processes. Once the DNA Manipulation process was complete for the males, they also immediately opted to begin the Age Regression and Age Prolongation processes. Last night I was informed that the four members of the Upper Council who first partook of the Age Regression process are now terminally ill. Inexplicably, their internal organs have begun mutating. They are not expected to live beyond the end of this year. The other eight show no sign of the mutations— as yet, but will be closely monitored for any such changes."

"Mutating into what?" Councilmember Erika Overgaard asked.

"Not mutating *into* anything. They're simply changing form, composition, and function. To repeat what a doctor said to me: What happens when your heart no longer performs like a heart? If it was just one organ, it could be replaced, but their entire internal physiology structure seems to be changing. The doctors don't know any more than that at this time.

"All four patients are under twenty-four-hour observation and are highly medicated to ease their pain. The eight former males are also under round-the-clock observation because the doctors expect they'll suffer from the same mutating effects. The only successful application of the Age Regression process was Nicole Ravenau, a.k.a. Mikel Arneu, and all medical records of her regression were lost when her laboratory was destroyed. If she hadn't been killed, the doctors could examine her and possibly get some insight into the problem."

"Since Ravenau had been a male originally," Overgaard said, "perhaps the eight members of the Upper Council who had been males will not suffer the mutations."

"That's our hope at this point. It's possible that the recuperative powers of the DNA Manipulation process made the males immune to the mutation effects."

"So where does that leave us?" Councilmember Frederick Kelleher asked.

"The Upper Council is the guiding force of the corporation, but this council conducts the day-to-day operations, so business will continue as always. Once we know more about the long-term medical situation of the Upper Council members, decisions will be made regarding a possible restructuring of both councils."

* * *

"Commander," the technician in the Approach and Departure Center said, "That anomaly has returned."

Commander Blithallo moved behind the technician reporting the anomaly again and stared at the DeTect screen.

"It's gone already, sir. It only appears for an instant and only twice each shift."

"We're under power now. It doesn't make sense that we would see it out here."

"Yes, sir, I know, but it keeps showing up nevertheless."

"The city directors must be correct. Despite assertions by the repair technicians that the equipment is working properly, it has to be a mechanical problem."

"Yes, sir. I should ignore it then?"

"I had a dozen different ships visually check that area of our perimeter when we were stationary, and they never saw anything out there. We're under power now, so if there was something, we should have left it far behind us. It has to be a problem with the equipment. Yes, just ignore it."

"Yes, sir."

* * *

"Increase the power, slowly," Captain DeWitt said.

The hangar was as quiet as a tomb as the forty-three engineers, scientists, and technicians stared in silence at the several monitors located around the work area. All were displaying an image of the new Extended Range DeTect screen being used for the test.

As the power increased slowly from zero, blips representing ships in orbit around Quesann popped onto the screen. Ten shuttles had been positioned in billion-kilometer intervals beginning at a distance of five billion kilometers from the base and extending out to fourteen billion. When a blip representing the first shuttle appeared, scattered noise was also visible, but a cheer went up in the hangar.

"Quiet down," Captain DeWitt said. "You can cheer when we see the shuttle sitting at fourteen billion kilometers."

The technician continued to increase the power, and more of the deployed shuttles appeared, but white background noise began to appear just beyond the four billion kilometer range and began to increase rapidly as the distance was increased. When blips representing the shuttle at the seven-billion-kilometer range should have made an appearance, it was impossible to discern anything on a screen that appeared as a solid image of white noise.

"Shut it down," Captain DeWitt finally said to the technician at the console. "Okay, people," she said to the others in the hangar, "just as there was no reason for cheering before, there's no reason for long faces now. All we were attempting to do here today was duplicate the results of the last test by the original creative team who gave us the DeTect system. The white noise we've seen today is exactly what they were getting so long ago. When they couldn't make any further improvements, they locked the system in at four billion kilometers and that's where it's remained until now. At that distance there's no background noise in the image.

"We've collected all the data we need, so now it's time to get to work. Let's analyze the data in the computers and develop some theories about making improvements to the system. You all know what to do, so let's start doing it."

To the com chief, Captain DeWitt said, "Recall the deployed shuttles, Chief. Have them report back to their ships."

"Aye, Captain."

* * *

The audible signal in the living quarters area sent Vyx scrambling to the bridge. A light on the com was flashing so Vyx flicked a switch on the console and listened to the incoming message.

"Attention Desert Denizen. Respond using encryption code 19AR94HW463D."

Vyx called up the specified encryption code from the computer and activated it. "This is the *Scorpion*," was all he said as he keyed the mic.

"*Scorpion*, this is the SC Transport Ship *Edison*. Transmit your current location."

Vyx deftly keyed an instruction into the navigation computer and verified the information that popped up on the screen. "Transmitting," Vyx said as he tapped the send key on the navigation computer.

"Data received, *Scorpion*. Standby."

"Roger."

Less than a minute later, Vyx heard, "*Scorpion*, cancel your envelope. We will arrive at your vicinity in ninety-two seconds."

"Roger. *Scorpion* cancelling envelope." As Vyx tapped a contact point on the helm console, the *Scorpion* came to a complete stop and its envelope dissolved. Vyx leaned back in his chair and waited for the *Edison* to arrive.

*   *   *

As the *Edison* neared the coordinates provided by the *Scorpion*, the helmsman canceled the double envelope and engaged the sub-light engines. Over the next sixty seconds, the transport closed with the small ship.

"The *Scorpion* is just ahead, Captain," the *Edison* tac officer said.

"Helm, take us to five kilometers from the ship," Commander Garth Ginsburg said.

"All stop," the Helmsman said a few seconds later.

An image of the *Scorpion* filled the full bulkhead monitor at the front of the bridge.

"Com, inform the *Scorpion* that we're preparing to take her aboard."

"Aye, Captain."

"Tac, open the bow and send out the tugs."

"Aye, sir."

Ten minutes later, tugs were visible on the front monitor as they approached the *Scorpion*. The process of guiding the small ship into the enormous transport took the better part of an hour, but as the *Edison's* bow began to close, the *Scorpion* was being secured in place.

"The captain of the *Scorpion* is here," the computer advised Captain Ginsburg as he sat at his desk in his office next to the bridge.

"Come," Ginsburg said, and the doors parted to allow Vyx to enter.

"Welcome aboard, Trader," Ginsburg said as Vyx strode into the office.

"Thank you, Captain," Vyx said as he looked around. Compared to the offices of captains on most warships, Vyx would have to describe Ginsburg's office as austere. The walls seemed to be covered in some sort of fabric applied directly to metal surfaces, and the furniture was covered in a kind of plastic or vinyl material rather than the real leather found in the offices of warship commanders. Vyx reminded himself that command officers aboard support vessels came from the group who never made the cut for warship command and so never attended the Warship Command Institute in Australia. It was rare when they risked their lives during their careers, so they didn't get all the perks of the people for whom such risk could be a daily occurrence.

"Have a seat," Ginsburg said, gesturing to the chairs facing his desk.

Vyx dropped into the nearest chair and crossed his legs. "We appreciate your giving us a lift, Captain. We didn't particularly relish the idea of spending the next four years traveling to our destination and back."

"My orders are a little vague, Trader. Perhaps you can enlighten me. Where do you need a ride to? And why have we been ordered to transport a civilian spacecraft?"

"I wish I could tell you where we're going, but I can't. It's not because I wouldn't like to, but simply because I don't know. I can give you a course but not a specific destination. As to why you're transporting a civilian spacecraft— you're not. We both work for the same boss on Quesann."

"You're SCI?"

"Yes, Captain. We've been tailing a freighter of interest for months. We've come to believe that it's headed to a destination outside GA space. At their present speed of Light-450, they won't reach the border for two years, and then we don't know how far outside GA space they intend to travel. We don't wish to spend the next six years tailing them to where they're going and then traveling back to Uthlarigasset. This ship can reach the border in a few months and have us back to Uthlarigasset in six."

"You've been following them at Light-450? In that small ship?"

"That small ship can keep up with any non-DS ship in the First or Second Fleets. We had no trouble following the freighter at Light-450, but without Light-9790 we'll be following along for possibly years and then have to return the same way."

"We can take you to the border, but we're not permitted to cross out of GA space. We're not a warship."

"What are your orders for this mission in exact terms?"

"To pick you up and take you wherever you wish to go."

"So there's your authorization to cross the border. The responsibility is on my head. If you still feel hesitant to do as I ask, I can send a message to Admiral Carver and ask her to clarify the orders for you."

"Carver? Not Kanes?"

"Kanes isn't in your chain of command. I want you to feel comfortable that Standing Orders about crossing the border are suspended on this occasion."

Ginsburg thought for a few seconds before saying, "My orders do say to take you wherever you wish to go, so I can't be faulted for following orders."

"Exactly. I'll provide you with the course the freighter was following. Then I'd like you to move five billion kilometers away and follow a parallel course until we're sure we've passed the freighter without their knowledge. Then we can return to the course and keep on traveling until we see something."

"What is it you expect to see?"

"A rendezvous area, although exactly who might be rendezvousing I don't know. It could be Uthlaro, Raiders, Denubbewa, or someone else."

"Denubbewa?"

"Possibly."

"We have Standing Orders to avoid them."

"I'm not asking you take them on. I don't want to mess with them either. We just want to learn what's going on out here."

"Okay, Trader. I'll play along. I just hope you know what you're doing."

"As do I, Captain. And I must remind you not to repeat anything I've told you. Your crew must not know we're SCI. They might surmise it, but you mustn't confirm it. They also should not know the speed capability of my ship. If you have to tell them something, tell them we can only travel at Light-150."

"I'll have to tell my XO. He's in charge should anything happen to me."

"Okay, but no one else."

Chapter Nineteen

~ October 2nd, 2287 ~

"The doctors say that the four Upper Council members have little time left," Chairman Strauss announced at the Lower Council meeting. "The mutating organs have not responded to any attempted treatments and bodily functions are failing."

"What of the other members?" Council member Kelleher asked.

"So far, they seem perfectly healthy."

"So if the female members had taken the DNA Manipulation process first, they might be okay?" Council member Overgaard said. "Even if they didn't use it to change their gender?"

"Yes, perhaps if they only used it to alter their appearance slightly, the recuperative powers the process offers might have saved them," council member Blosworth offered.

"That's strictly speculation," Strauss said. "We don't know if that's the reason the eight members are still healthy. We'll have to perform a lot more testing before we allow anyone else to use the processes. Nicole Ravenau warned me that more testing should be done, and I passed that warning on to the Upper Council, but they felt they couldn't wait. No one is at fault here. It's just been a tragic turn of events."

"So it may be a considerable time before we can avail ourselves of the processes?" Council member Ahil Fazid asked.

"If you value your life, Ahil, I'd suggest waiting. However, if you'd like to sign up as a test subject, I'm sure we can squeeze you in as one of the early experimentations. "

"Uh— no, that's quite alright. I'll wait."

"I thought you might, Ahil," Strauss said with a grin.

*   *   *

"Come in, Trader," Ginsburg said as the doors of his office opened to admit Vyx.

"Good morning, sir," Vyx said. "You wanted to see me?

"Yes, I did. We crossed the border from GA space into unclaimed territory about four days ago and are presently ninety-eight light-years 'into the black' as you've called it. I'm working on my daily report and wondering how much longer you intend to keep going. We haven't seen a sign of another ship for almost a month. There's nothing of value out here. That's why no nation has ever claimed it."

"My team and I were discussing that yesterday. We feel that if someone wanted to establish a rendezvous area outside GA Space where it was unlikely that Space Command would ever happen across it, it would be located in an area such as this with no habitable planets and a hundred parsecs from the border."

"Why a hundred parsecs?"

"It's a nice round number. It's enough to be outside the area that a Space Command patrol vessel might travel on a whim after crossing the border and yet not too far for vessels that are trying to avoid contact with Space Command."

"Trader, I'm beginning to think that you and your companions have been out here too long."

Vyx smiled. "Perhaps, Captain, but playing hunches has always worked well for us. Sometimes it plays out and sometimes it doesn't. So let's keep going for another ten days. We'll turn back at a hundred parsecs if we don't spot anything."

"Okay, Trader, it's your call. Another ten days it is. But if we don't spot anything, we turn around, right?"

"Right, Captain. We turn around at a hundred parsecs and head back to GA space."

*   *   *

Jenetta trudged wearily to her suite on the top floor of the military governor's palace after another long, hard day. The days seemed to be getting longer and longer, but that might be because good news had been so scarce lately. The weapons research people were still attempting to expand the DeTect range, but they hadn't yet achieved any decent measure of success. Work on the one scout-destroyer converted for dropping a bomb on an as yet unidentified enemy had been completed long ago, but without a way to place a bomb where it would be effective, the conversion work had been a wasted effort. For that reason, Jenetta had not authorized conversion work on other ships. Construction work on the Senate and SHQ complexes was progressing rapidly under Brian Holt, and each step forward was a reminder that her dream of being captain of a warship was slipping away. She imagined that once the complexes were finished, she would be pulled more and more into the political bureaucracy. She didn't object to losing the governorship of Regions Two and Three. Those jobs were better placed with the civilian GA Council. But having to take a seat on the AB would forever anchor her dirt-side. She'd be lucky to even slip away for a quick wave-hopping flight around Quesann. The day she dreaded was coming closer with each sunset.

As the doors to her suite opened before her, Cayla and Tayna bounded into the room. They loved coming home at night because it usually meant playtime. They sat quietly in one of her offices all day and looked forward with great eagerness to their play at night. Jenetta knew she had to give them some time, so even feeling as tired as she did, she rolled around on the floor with them for a while, then spent some time brushing their fur while they mewled lightly and gently nuzzled her legs. When she felt consciousness slipping away, she got up off the floor and slid into bed. She was fast asleep in minutes.

Jenetta awoke at the usual time, but she felt just as tired as she had when she climbed into bed. She recognized the signs of depression immediately, so she called her office and told them she would be late. Then she called the hangar where her plane was stored and told them to prepare it for use. When she completed the calls, she felt more invigorated than she had in days. A quick shower lifted her spirits even more and she almost had a spring in her step when she left her suite to start her day.

The first order of business was an hour of flight time. Her cats would wait patiently in an office at the hangar until she returned. Her protection detail would see that she came to no harm from external enemies. Of course, they couldn't protect her from herself, and they just hoped that today wasn't the day a slight lapse in flying judgment or attention would prove fatal.

It wasn't. Her flight ended as they always did, with her landing safely back at the base and feeling more alive than she had in days.

* * *

"Sir," the tac officer aboard the *Rio Grande* said, "the target is not at the expected location."

Lt. Cmdr. Jasson Lister cursed silently and mumbled, "Not again," under his breath before saying, "Helm, swing us around and retrace the course the enemy ship would have followed since having its presence confirmed by the *Mekong* four hours ago to see if it halted somewhere. Com, notify the *Mekong* that we've turned to search for the enemy mother ship."

As the ship turned, Lister contacted the Captain, who happened to be working in his office.

"The mother ship is missing, sir," Lister said when Commander Marc Hodenfield raised the cover on his desk's com unit. "I've ordered a reverse search of their expected course since the last confirmed sighting."

"I'll be right out, Jasson."

"Aye, sir."

Commander Hodenfield pushed the com unit's cover down and sighed. He was working on tomorrow's daily report and would now have to rewrite it from the beginning where he had stated that they continued to monitor the travel of the enemy mother ship and that nothing had changed.

Hodenfield emerged from his office and walked to the command chair. As he settled into the comfortable seat, he grimaced at Lister and said, "I hope this doesn't lead to a full-scale search. I wonder if the two mother ships changed their plans to rendezvous."

Lister hadn't uttered even word one of his intended response when the tac officer said, "Contact ahead."

A second later, the scout-destroyer *Rio Grande* passed a halted mother ship at Light-9790. Then they passed another.

"Good Lord!" Hodenfield said. "How did that get here so quickly? We estimated that they couldn't meet up for months."

"Unless…" Lister said.

"Unless what?" Hodenfield asked.

"Unless that isn't the second ship we've been expecting."

Hodenfield stared at him for several seconds before responding. "I hope you're wrong, Jasson— but it's a possibility."

"So what do we do, Captain?"

Turning to the com chief, Hodenfield said, "Get me Commander Morrow aboard the *Mekong*."

"Aye, sir," the com chief said.

"The *Mekong*, sir?" Lister questioned.

"There's only one way to find out the situation here. Either there are more of these ships in GA space than we thought just yesterday, or they have substantially greater speed than we thought. At this point I don't know which would be worse."

"Commander Morrow is responding, sir," the com chief announced.

"Put him on my left monitor, chief."

"Aye, sir."

A second later the image of Commander Cody Morrow appeared on the screen and Hodenfield's CT chimed to indicate it was active.

"Cody, we have a problem. A big problem." It took just thirty seconds to bring Morrow up to speed. "So one of us has to go looking for the ship reported by the Territorial Guard ship. If you'll take over here and perform the four-hour checks, we'll continue on and see if we can locate a third ship."

"Wow, Marc, you're just full of good news today aren't you."

"I wish it was otherwise."

"Yeah, me too. If R2HQ was right about the maximum speed of these mother ships, then I agree that there must be a third, or even more. In any event, we need to know. We'll take over responsibility for the four-hour checks while you go learn what you can. Stay safe."

"Roger that. We'll message you as soon as we learn what's what and then hightail it back here as soon as we're able. *Rio Grande* out."

"*Mekong* out."

* * *

"Hello, sweetheart," the image of her mom said as Jenetta tapped the play button on the new vidMail message. "My news is so big that I couldn't wait until tomorrow to vidMail you. Regina is pregnant."

Jenetta's jaw dropped. She had originally been concerned because the message had arrived a day earlier than normal for the weekly messages from Obotymot, but now she was concerned because Regina hadn't seen her husband, Jenetta's brother Billy, in over two years.

"Billy and Regina had decided to wait, but since it doesn't appear that Billy is going to make it home any time soon, they decided to use the cryo'd sperm Billy deposited in a sperm bank just after their marriage. Regina was impregnated just before coming to Obotymot. It was a big secret, but now that she's starting to show, she told Marisa and me. And get this— her sisters and parents are going to come *here* for the birth. Isn't that wonderful? Regina and Billy's baby is going to be the first member of the Family Carver to be born on Obotymot.

"And now that Regina and Billy are going to have a baby, Marisa wants to have a baby. She just sent a message to Richie telling him to cryo some sperm and send it here so *she* can be impregnated.

"This is all too wonderful for words. I'm finally going to be a grandmother. It's funny, but I always thought you would be the first one to have children. Of course, that was back when you were just going to be a science officer. I thought you'd meet a nice man at whatever base you were assigned to and decide to become a mommy. Well, I know it will happen in time.

"I hope you can come home for a visit when Regina is near the end of her term. By then, Marisa might have begun to show also. Oh, I'm so excited. I've sent a message to your father, and now I'm going to send messages to your sisters and brothers. Of course, Billy and Richie know already. Well, it doesn't matter. I'll congratulate Billy again and tell Richie that I hope he'll send the sperm for Marisa. There's the timer, so I have go. I love you.

"Annette Carver, Palace of the Family Carver, Gavistee Peninsula, Obotymot, message complete."

There were two other messages waiting, one from Marisa and one from Regina, but Jenetta wanted to think about the changing situation before she listened to them. She had been sitting on the edge of the bed watching the message on the nightstand com unit and now flopped back onto her bed and stared up at the ceiling. Naturally, she was excited and happy for her sisters-in-law and her brothers, but it had caught her totally by surprise. Another thing that caught her by surprise was her mother talking about her coming home for a visit. It was the first time her mom had referred to the palace on Obotymot as home. That was significant. Annette and Marisa had now been on Obotymot for seven months and showed no indications that they were leaving, or were even thinking about leaving. To the contrary, they seemed to be putting down roots. That pleased Jenetta no end. She had always regretted that the palace was empty, and it was wonderful to see it being used by family members.

Jenetta didn't know how the upcoming confrontation with the Denubbewa was going to end, but if Space Command and the Marines were able to defeat them, or at least end their efforts to arrogate GA space, it might be time to take an extended leave from the service. So far, she was only sure about one thing— she didn't want to become a permanent member of the AB and be forever tied to a chair in the AB Hall. Keith Kanes had once suggested that as the older members of the Board retired from the service, Jenetta might be pushed to accept the position of Admiral of the Fleet. The post had never interested her and didn't interest her now in the slightest.

* * *

"Contact off starboard, Captain," the tac officer aboard the *Rio Grande* said.

"Is it the enemy mother ship?" Commander Marc Hodenfield asked.

"It's right at the limit of our DeTect capability, so I can't say for sure, but it's under power and appears to have the right mass. I would say yes."

"Is it on course for the expected rendezvous point?"

"I'll need another pass to determine course and speed."

"Helm, swing us around for another look. Keep us at the edge of the DeTect range. We don't want to spook them."

"Aye, sir. Beginning our turn now."

"The ship is exactly on course for the rendezvous point, Captain," the tac officer said as they performed another flyby of the mother ship. "Speed is Light-462."

"That's good enough for me," Hodenfield said. "She's exactly where we expected her to be and headed on a course that would have her rendezvous with the other ship we were following. So now we know that we have three mother ships to deal with. Com, send a message to the *Mekong* that we've identified the enemy mother ship at the expected location and that we're headed back. Helm, take us back."

"Aye, sir," both the com chief and helmsman said.

* * *

Marine corporal Beth Rondara awoke just as a Denubbewa technician lifted her right arm off the surgical table and carried it away. She was mortified as she looked to where the arm had been. It seemed to have been efficiently severed at the shoulder. Strangely, she felt no pain. She wondered if her body was simply in shock right now and that waves of pain would soon drive her mad.

She twisted her head the other way and saw that her left arm was missing as well. She should have been hyperventilating by this point, but she couldn't seem to get excited. Even when she raised her head and looked down to where both legs had been the last time she was awake, her respiration didn't increase.

The Denubbewa technician returned to the table and applied some kind of a surgical dressing to the newly opened wound. Within seconds the dressing, which looked simply like a piece of cloth, had shrunk and self-sealed around the shoulder. Lastly, a garment of some sort was slid up what was now her lower extremity. Like the surgical dressing, it instantly shrank for a tight fit and fluid seal.

PFC Vincent Kilburn, on a table in a different operating room, was likewise being dissected piece by piece while awake and witness to the process. As with Rondara, he felt no pain or exhibited any agitation over the surgical process.

When Kilburn's surgical wounds were sealed and a tiny garment fitted over his lower torso, he was picked up by a very large cyborg and brought to a recovery room where Rondara, sans arms and legs, was already lying on a table.

Rondara watched as the cyborg gently set Kilburn down and strapped him to the table. As the large creature left the room, Rondara tried to talk. She believed that her lips were moving, but she didn't hear anything or feel any vibration in her throat that might suggest she was making a sound. She was surprised when she heard a response from Kilburn in her head.

"They cut off my arms and legs also," Kilburn said. "But I didn't feel any pain."

"You can hear me?" Rondara said.

"Uh— yeah. But you sound funny."

"Funny how?"

"It doesn't sound like your voice."

"Whose voice does it sound like?"

"Uh— it doesn't really sound like a voice at all. I'm hearing words but they're not like real sounds."

Rondara stopped moving her lips and just thought about what she wanted to say. To her surprise, Kilburn answered her.

"What do you mean that they might have removed our vocal chords? I heard everything you just said."

"I didn't say anything. I just thought it. Try it."

"Okay, here's me trying to talk without talking. Can you hear me?"

"Every word. This is weird. Your lips didn't move."

"Holy God. What have they done to us, Corporal?"

"They must have done something to our brains so we can communicate telepathically."

"You mean like supernatural, alien stuff?"

"There doesn't seem to be anything supernatural about it. We've been watching them since they captured us and I've never heard them say anything. So they must use telepathy."

"Why didn't I feel any pain when they chopped me up? Do they care if we're in pain?"

"It's more likely they want to reduce the trauma to the body."

"Why are they doing this? Do you think they're trying to turn us into one of them? Are they going to put us inside one of those cyborg bodies?"

"Maybe parts of us."

"Parts of us?"

"They've already removed our arms and legs. They might be dismantling us to determine what they need to include in new bodies. Or…"

"Or what."

"They might be preparing us to act as baby-making machines."

"Baby making?"

"Yeah, we wouldn't need arms or legs to procreate. We just need a male and female."

"Not even," Kilburn said.

"No?"

"All they'd have to do is harvest your eggs and pump me for my sperm."

"Human babies are reportedly much healthier when they get breast milk for the first year after birth. The mother passes on a lot of antibodies. And males can continue to produce spermatozoa until old age."

"So they need us alive, even if we can't move around?"

"It's possible. And not being able to move on our own would make us easier to control."

"I don't want to live like that. Just being part of a baby factory partnership is no way to live."

"That's the way it was for all women until the twentieth century. Many women died in childbirth or before reaching forty-five."

"Long before our time, Corporal. But we males didn't have it so good either. Back then you were lucky to reach thirty-five."

"Whatever. Anyway, like this, without arms and legs, there's nothing we can do to fight back. We can't even end our own lives."

"We're screwed, Corporal."

"Royally."

Chapter Twenty
~ October 11th, 2287 ~

"Come in, Trader," Commander Ginsburg said as the doors of his office opened.

"Good morning, sir," Vyx said. "I got your message."

"I have something to show you. Take a seat."

When Vyx was settled into one of the reasonably comfortable chairs covered in imitation leather, Ginsburg tapped a button on his computer keyboard. The large monitor mounted on a side bulkhead illuminated with an image that had been recorded overnight.

"Here's what set our warning system off initially," Ginsburg said as a freighter with a ten-kilometer load came into view and was passed in the blink of an eye. "I'll stop the vid so you can see what we passed next." As Ginsburg pressed a button, the image stabilized on a view of ship docks that extended far into the distance.

Vyx whistled. "Wow. How many docks do you think are out here?"

"We counted five hundred ten open docks and three hundred fifteen enclosed docks. Most of the open docks have warship hulls already laid. As you can see, there are dock workers everywhere. Either this is the busiest hour of the day, or they are pushing hard to get these ships built. We've identified three older warships guarding the place, all of Uthlaro design."

"Eight hundred twenty-five docks," Vyx repeated. "Now we know what the leaders on Uthlarigasset have been up to. You're sure the hulls are for warships?"

"They're too big to be single-hull freighters and too small to be passenger liners. Their shape agrees with that of the

Uthlaro destroyers we fought in the last war, so we're pretty sure they're warship hulls. It looks like they're trying to rebuild their entire military fleet in two years." Ginsburg looked over at Vyx. "This doesn't really catch you by surprise, does it, Trader? You're the one responsible for us finding this shipyard. Did you know what they were up to out here?"

"We suspected they were doing something out here that they wanted to hide, but this is quite a bit more than I was expecting."

"What do you want us to do now?"

"Did they see us when we passed the yard?"

"Possibly. We weren't anticipating it and passed it by at only about five kilometers. But we were at Light-9790, and we only made the one pass. It's possible they saw something on their DeTect screens but didn't know what it was, so they chalked it up as just a temporary anomaly. They wouldn't have had more than a second's notice before we were past the base, and in another second we were long gone. Aboard an SC ship, the tac officer wouldn't even have time to sound GQ before we were just a distant memory. Even so, our sensors automatically activate the cameras, so we got some great high-res images."

"Now that we have the proof of what they're doing, let's head back to Region Two," Vyx said. "I'll prepare a message for SCI on Quesann. I doubt they'll want us to hang around out here. My ship is armed, as is yours, but neither of them is a warship, so we're not in a position to take any offensive action with the three destroyers protecting their yard."

"Okay, I'll have the helmsman turn us around."

"Yeah, and uh— I'm sure I don't have to tell you that we should cut a wide track on the way back."

"I already figured that much, Trader."

"Yeah. Sorry."

* * *

"So that's the story," Vyx said as he finished briefing his team.

"A new warship fleet?" Nelligen said. "They're going to come at us again? They didn't get enough pain last time around?"

Vyx just shrugged. "People who occupy powerful political positions are usually there because they are consumed— first with attaining power and second with holding onto that power. If they lose it, once they've had a taste of it, a void opens up in their lives that's just not tolerable, and they will do anything to get the power back. The Uthlaro gambled everything in order to double the size of their territory, and they lost not just the new territory they'd hoped to add but their existing empire as well. Admiral Carver should have reduced their world to ruins as she did with the Milori. It would have given the Uthlaro something to occupy their energies while they came to grips with the fact that they had lost. Instead, they were able to immediately begin working on a plan to take back their empire."

"So what do you think Admiral Carver will do now?" Brenda asked.

"I know what I'd do, but I can never predict what Admiral Carver would do. She always seems to have the perfect solution."

"What would you do?" Byers asked.

"I'd assemble a taskforce to reduce those shipdocks and partially completed ships to scrap like she did to the yards at Milor and again at the three shipyards where the Uthlaro were building ships in Region Three."

"Even though they're in open, unclaimed space?"

"The Uthlaro, whether they want to admit it or not, are now citizens of the Galactic Alliance. The planet doesn't have to participate as a member world in trade, but everything they do in space above the sensible atmosphere of their world is governed by GA law. By most definitions, building a warship fleet to fight Space Command and take back their territory is sedition. Sedition has always been defined under the law as 'an illegal action inciting resistance to lawful authority and tending to cause the disruption or overthrow of the government.' It doesn't matter if the illegal action is a direct attack on soldiers on a military base or planting a couple of bombs at a sporting event. If the goal is to disrupt the government, it's sedition. Just the very act of building those ships is enough to warrant the death penalty. That the ships are located in open space makes the decision to destroy them easier because there're no other nations involved. We can go in there and clean house, and then we should go to Uthlarigasset and finally clean house."

"I don't think she could spare the ships right now," Kathleen said. "She has to keep her fleet ready to fight the Denubbewa."

"The yards out here aren't going anywhere," Vyx said, "and they probably don't have any ships even remotely close to being ready to launch. After the Admiral takes care of the new threat, she can send a task force out here and destroy the yards. And I hope she sends them to Uthlarigasset afterwards to teach them a lesson they won't forget this time."

* * *

"Welcome back, Marc," Commander Cody Morrow aboard the *Mekong* said to Commander Marc Hodenfield aboard the *Rio Grande* when the scout-destroyer arrived at its established jump-off point for the flybys of the two mother ships. It was First Watch and both officers were in their offices off the bridge.

"Thanks, Cody. Everything quiet?"

"Yeah, so far. It's anybody's guess what's going to happen when that third mother ship gets here. Are they going to stand down for a while or immediately begin an offensive? Are they going to proceed together or head off for different objectives?"

"Good questions all."

"Yeah. Well, at least we won't be out here alone."

"What do you mean?"

"I received a message a little while ago that the DS destroyer *Duluth* and scout-destroyers *Yukon*, *Gambia*, and *Nile* are proceeding here with all haste."

"Is something up?"

"Nothing I've been informed about. I suppose they just want a greater presence in the area in case more of those mother ships show up. If they deploy, we'll need at least one ship tailing each of them."

"Yeah. At some point somebody's going to start shooting. I expected the Admiral to come up with a plan by now."

"Maybe she has, and it's just taking time to move assets into place or something. I'm sure she hasn't forgotten about these mother ships. Or us."

"Yeah. I guess I'm just tired of this 'watching from afar' duty."

"I suspect that when things start to happen, the action will come fast and furious."

* * *

"That's everything we needed to discuss today, Admiral," Lt. Commander Ashraf said. "Your schedule is pretty full for this afternoon, but you can relax and work on other things until 1330 hours."

"Thank you, Lori. As always I appreciate your dedication and hard work." Standing up, Jenetta said loudly, "The room shall come to attention."

Lt. Commander Ashraf was the only other one in the room, and she was taken completely unawares, but she stood up and came to attention.

"Lieutenant Commander Lori Elaine Ashraf, by special order from Region Two Space Command Headquarters, you are immediately advanced to the rank of Commander." Coming out from behind her desk, Jenetta took an insignia from a small box and replaced the rank insignia on Commander Ashraf's right shoulder, then took a step backward and saluted Space Command's newest O-5 officer as she said, "Congratulations, Commander."

Commander Ashraf returned the salute, then relaxed as Jenetta dropped her hand.

"Thank you, Admiral. This is a bit unexpected."

"Your name appears on the new Promotions Board List for Commander, so I temporarily bypassed a little of the red tape because I wanted to surprise you. The paperwork is all filled out in my computer and stored in a private file. I'll send that to you so you can forward it to the proper departments for recording the promotion."

"Yes, ma'am."

"Oh, here's the insignia for your other shoulder," Jenetta said, holding out a small box.

"Thank you, Admiral."

"That's all, Lori."

Jenetta moved the paperwork to Commander Ashraf's queue and then walked to her window to stare out at the blue sky. The day was gorgeous and perfect for an hour of flight time, but she had a lot on her mind and couldn't afford the time even though she had nothing scheduled for hours.

Jenetta was still at the window ten minutes later when Cmdr. Ashraf comm'd her with a message that Admiral Kanes was asking to see her.

"Send him in, Lori," Jenetta said as she returned to her desk.

"Good morning, Jen," Kanes said as he entered. "Hope I'm not disturbing you."

"I've always got time for you, Keith. What's up?"

"We received a message overnight from one of our teams in Region Three. I believe you know them. It's Trader Vyx and four other agents."

"Yes, I know Vyx and the others very well. They've done great work for Space Command and the GA."

"They do have a unique working relationship. We run most of our people as single agents because they prefer it that way, but this group has worked together for some time and delivered so well as a group that we've kept them together."

"So what was in the message?"

"A few weeks ago, Vyx requested that his ship be picked up by a DS ship. He had been following an Uthlaro freighter capable of Light-450 but wanted to speed ahead to find out where it was headed. He suspected the ship was headed out of Region Three space and needed Light-9790 speed to avoid spending four or five years round trip travel time. His team believed the Uthlaro were engaged in illegal activities outside of GA space where patrols don't travel. I arranged with Augustus to send a transport ship to rendezvous and take the *Scorpion* wherever Vyx wanted to go. In his latest message, he says the trip paid off. He claims that he's located a base outside GA space where the Uthlaro are building a fleet of warships. The base is about a hundred parsecs beyond the Region Three border. He's sent the coordinates. "

"How large a base?'

"Here's a vid created by the transporter ship during a flyby," Kanes said as he extended a data ring.

Jenetta placed the ring over the spindle on her keyboard and activated the large wall monitor. When she selected the file marked 'shipyard,' the vid began to play. She paused the vid several times to see still images.

"That's quite a shipyard," Jenetta said as the vid ended. "It reminds me of the shipyard Maxxiloth had built near Milor."

"Vyx says the shipyard appears to contain eight hundred twenty-five docks. We've viewed the vid and confirm that count."

Jenetta took a deep breath and then released it slowly. "Eight hundred twenty-five docks. I've suspected the Uthlaro were in league with the Denubbewa, but this news almost makes that seem impossible."

"Why? It could be a pact to arrogate the two regions, like the THUG pact. The Uthlaro get their territory back and the Denubbewa get to keep Region Two."

"No, the Uthlaro wouldn't share the territory, and the Denubbewa seem too strong for the Uthlaro to overcome. I could see a working relationship between the two, but not a deal to take over the territory and then split it. With the Tsgardi, Hudeerac, and Gondusans, there's little doubt that the Uthlaro intended to defeat them after we were driven out. The Uthlaro would then have absorbed all of the territory. In this case, I think it would be the Denubbewa absorbing the entire territory."

"So what do we do now?" Kanes asked. "Head out there and destroy their docks and then teach the Uthlaro politicians on Uthlarigasset a lesson they won't soon forget?"

"It's tempting, but not yet. The ships in the open dock aren't much more than keels, and I doubt there's anything in the enclosed docks because they haven't had time to make much progress. Even if they'd started working on this plan within hours of learning their armada had been defeated, they haven't had time to complete any ships. First they had to organize their materials shipments and workers and get every-thing to the site. They don't have Light-9790, so the travel time alone is about two years from Uthlarigasset at Light-450. Having converted the FTL drives on their freighters to military grade is the only reason they're not still trying to reach their planned shipbuilding location. They believe they've placed their base beyond our reach, but they've only made it easier for us take it out anytime we want. I don't wish to commit our resources to minor annoyances until after we deal with the Denubbewa. But we'll take care of this problem at the appropriate time. I take it our people are safe?"

"Yes, they're aboard the *Edison*. It performed the flyby at Light-9790 and then left the area so they never exposed themselves to attack."

"Good."

"What's happening with Project Gazebo?"

"We're still stuck in limbo. Captain DeWitt and her people are working day and night, but they haven't been able to expand our DeTect capability beyond that of the original development team. They're weapons scientists and technic-ians, and I've asked them to take on a task for which they're not really suited. What we probably need is a roomful of theoretical physicists, but I don't have anyone with that special knowledge and expertise."

"That's probably the one advantage in having SHQ move here. They'll bring all their research laboratories, physicists, and scientists with them."

"I'm not sure it's worth the price of having all those newsies, politicians, and political hacks all over the place."

"There must be another way to determine the optimal point for the drop."

"We have the finest minds in weapons research here and no one's come up with another idea. It's a little difficult to get past the problem of traveling almost three billion kilometers per second."

"How about this— if we make our presence known to the vessel we're about to attack, they'll probably start communicating with other vessels. Can we target the ship by homing in on their radio signals? The IDS Communications Band signals travel at 8.09 billion kilometers per second. That's almost three times faster than Light-9790."

Jenetta looked at Kanes for several seconds without speaking, then stood up and walked to her beverage dispenser to prepare a mug of fresh coffee. She turned as the coffee was pouring into the cup and looked at Kanes. "Coffee, Keith?"

"I could go for a cup."

When Jenetta returned from the dispenser, she placed Kanes' coffee in front of him and then returned to her chair behind the desk. She sipped at the hot coffee as she thought. Finally, she said, "That's an interesting idea. I can think of only one potential problem. The ship being targeted might not be transmitting or might cease transmitting at a critical juncture. How can we guarantee that they continue transmitting?"

"We could try to contact them and engage them in discussion, but we haven't been able to decode their transmissions. We don't even know what language they use, so it all sounds like gibberish."

"A problem the Japanese had in World War II on Earth when trying to crack the communications of the 'code talkers.'

"Ah, yes," Kanes said, "the Navajos who used their Native American language while functioning as radio operators in the Pacific theater of war. The Japanese never broke their code."

"I assume you've tried all of the universal language translation devices?"

"Of course. It still sounds like gibberish. Even the computers think it's gibberish."

"The Denubbewa have been able to take some of our people as prisoners," Jenetta said, "but we've never even seen one of them."

"For all we know they may not even have a spoken language. They might communicate with sign language, thought transference, or something else. We know they transmit radio signals on the IDS band, so all we have to do is figure a way to keep them transmitting while we attack."

"Yes, that's *all* we have to do," Jenetta said with a smile.

* * *

"Corporal, are you awake?" PFC Vincent Kilburn tried to project with his thoughts.

"I hear you," Corporal Beth Rondara replied in the thought-communication process they were still refining. Lately, she had been trying to figure out how to shield thoughts she didn't want to share with others. It hadn't worked so far. Every idea that popped into her head was heard by Kilburn.

"I can't take this anymore, Corporal. I want to die. All they do is keep stabbing us with needles to inject something and later take blood samples. We're just lab specimens to them."

"What choice do we have?"

"There must be a way to end our lives. You're smart. I've always been impressed by your intelligence. Since we became— linked— I've been even more impressed. You'll think of something."

"I don't know, Kilburn. We no longer have arms or legs, and we're strapped down on these tiny beds. It's been proven that a human can't hold his breath long enough to die because he simply passes out and his body resumes normal respiration when his conscious mind shuts down temporarily."

"Then you have been thinking about it?"

"Not really. I learned that years ago."

"There has to be a way. Will you at least think about it?"

"Okay, I'll think about it."

Chapter Twenty-One

~ November 24th, 2287 ~

"Good Morning," Captain Zakir Singh of the DS destroyer *Duluth* said to the faces appearing on the large monitor in his office. The faces belonged to the captains of the scout-destroyers *Gambia*, *Mekong*, *Nile*, *Rio Grande*, and *Yukon*. "Now that we're all on station, I've established a rotation list for the flybys. The *Nile* and *Yukon* will deploy almost immediately to begin performing flybys on the mother ship still headed in this direction. The rest of us will perform flybys of the two mother ships sitting at the rendezvous point."

"Sir," Commander Cody Morrow of the *Mekong* said, "is there any indication of what R2HQ might be planning to actually do about the enemy ships other than simply having us watch them?"

"I've received no briefings about their plans— which is not to say that there are no plans." Singh sighed. "Listen, I'm as frustrated as all of you with the tasks we've been assigned over the past six months. All we've been doing is searching and watching. Now we're assigned to keep vigil over an enemy which we had previously been told to avoid at all costs.

"We're all aching to do something to avenge our comrades aboard the *Yenisei* and *Salado*, but the facts indicate that the enemy is too strong— at this time. I've heard rumors that the scout-destroyer *Tigris* has remained enclosed in the ship transport *Winston* near Quesann for many months while modifications are being made to its hull. The speculation is that the engineers are testing materials that will make it impregnable to the weapons of the Denubbewa. I'm sure that the missile the *Tagus* found has been helpful in that regard. I know everyone involved in the search for an intact enemy missile was frustrated during months of searching for objects most of us believed must have self-destructed after the conflicts. But it's the small steps forward like that one that will help us defeat this enemy by preparing us for the giant leap forward.

"If I could tell you what was being developed at Quesann and when we would be ready to take on the monsters that have invaded our territory, I would. For now, all we can do is keep an eye on them so that when the Second Fleet is ready to send them to Hell, we'll know from where they'll begin their journey."

"That's good enough for me, sir," Morrow said. "I didn't mean to suggest that we were intentionally being kept in the dark. It's as you say; we're just frustrated with sitting around waiting."

"I believe you, Commander. And I'll tell you another thing I believe with absolute certainty. Every resource Admiral Carver has at her disposal is being directed to preparing the defenses of our ships and developing weapons capable of destroying the invaders."

* * *

"I'm sorry, Admiral," Captain DeWitt said as soon as she had taken a seat in Jenetta's office, "but it appears that extending the range of the DeTect system is beyond our present capabilities. We're not going to be able to use it to drop the bombs with any accuracy."

Jenetta breathed deeply and then released it before saying, "I'm disappointed, but I certainly don't blame you in any way, Barbara. I gave you what seemed to be an impossible task and can't be upset when we verify that it is truly impossible. When I asked you to take the job on, I knew you didn't have people trained in the discipline we required, but you took it on and made a remarkable attempt."

"Thank you, Admiral. I didn't want to let you down."

"You never have, Barbara."

"What now, Admiral? We seem to be back at square one."

"No, we're not back at square one. We're halfway to our goal. We have the bombs and the means of delivery. We simply need a way to put them on target— or rather *in* the target."

"But without that means, the development of the bombs and all the work of preparing the *Tigris* was wasted effort."

"Since the paths we've followed have led us to dead ends, it's simply time we take a different path."

"I get the impression you have an idea where that new path might begin," DeWitt said.

Jenetta smiled. "Well, I do have a kernel of an idea, but I'll need a lot of help to develop it. Any idea where I might find some weapons research people who might be willing to tackle a new project?"

"Just point us in the direction you want us to go, Admiral."

"Okay, here's the starting point. I was talking with Admiral Kanes yesterday and we discussed the problem with placing the bomb on the target. I told him you said we need three-point-four seconds of time for the targeting but that the four-billion-kilometer range of the DeTect system only gave us roughly one-point-three-six seconds before we had passed beyond the target.

"He suggested that if the target is transmitting a radio signal, then we might be able to target the mother ship using that since IDS signals travel at eight-point-zero-nine billion kilometers per second. I seem to recall that when the Japanese pilots attacked Pearl Harbor and pulled the U.S. into World War Two, they used their ADF navigation devices to follow the commercial radio signals being broadcast from different towers around the islands of Hawaii. The planes left their carriers when the ships were well over the horizon, so the Automatic Direction Finders allowed them to follow the signals directly to the broadcast source. Of course, our problem would be getting the enemy to transmit a constant signal so we could follow it to the mother ship. Are you with me so far?"

"Perfectly, Admiral. And I agree that if we could get the enemy to broadcast exactly when we wanted them to, we could use their IDS broadcast signal to target them. But if the signal is intermittent, it only provides a direction to a target, not the precise targeting signal we need. I can't imagine any way we can ensure we'll always have, or even occasionally have, an IDS signal to follow."

"I agree. There's no way we can depend on the enemy to broadcast exactly when we want. So I gave it some more thought and came up with a new idea, which was inspired by Admiral Kanes' idea. We use two DS ships to drop the bomb."

Captain DeWitt's attention was focused on every word Jenetta was saying, but she didn't grasp the idea immediately. "Two ships to drop one bomb?"

"Not literally. I was thinking that we have a targeting ship in the lead, with the bomber trailing. As soon as the lead ship passes through the target, it transmits the targeting data to the bomber. We'd probably want to keep the ships as close together as possible so the targeted ship doesn't have enough time to move or change course between the time the lead ship first gets a lock on it and the time the bomber can deposit its payload. You said you need three-point-four seconds for the drop, so I figure that the trailing ship should maintain an eight-billion-kilometer separation from the lead ship. With the four billion kilometers distance afforded by the DeTect system in the lead ship, the bomber will have four-point-one-one seconds before the drop."

"So you're suggesting a setup like the towed sonar arrays introduced by Earth's wet navies back in the twenty-first century but without the physical tether, and where the ROV is actually playing an offensive role?"

"Yes. What do you think?"

"I think that if we can make it work, it's brilliant."

"And what do you think the chances are that we can make it work?"

With a grin, DeWitt said, "Substantially greater than the chances of reinventing the DeTect system. I'll have to think on it for a bit, but it sounds entirely feasible. The trailing vessel in the partnership will have to temporarily give up control to the lead vessel during the bomb run. In that respect it will be sort of like bombing missions in the twentieth century where the bombardier briefly took control of the plane until the bombs were released. In this case, it will be the tactical officer in the lead vessel who actually sends the signal to drop the bomb."

"Now for the really difficult question. How long will it take to implement such a system?"

"I'll have to get back to you on that, Admiral. The Propulsion and Helm computer system in SC vessels is specifically designed to *prevent* anyone outside the ship from taking control. We'll have to reprogram that system in the bomber so the lead vessel can take control without leaving the system open to access by any other vessel or party."

"An encrypted code burned into circuit rods in both computers should solve that problem," Jenetta said.

"Yes, but we'll have to ensure that it's completely foolproof and can be interrupted in an instant by the crew aboard the bomber."

"Of course. What else will you need?"

"I need the scout-destroyer that will act as the lead vessel. We'll have to modify the tac station to take control of the second ship and drop the bombs at the precise instant required."

"I think the *Ohio* would be the best ship for the initial testing. I'll take care of that today. Anything else?"

"I think we should begin work on additional ships to function as bombers. We have sufficient Dakinium cradles to prepare ten scout-destroyers as bombers. I believe we should have at least five, given the size and capability of the ships we're facing."

"You believe in this new idea that much?"

"I do. I'm embarrassed that neither I nor any of my team thought of it."

"I'm sure you would have if you'd been searching for a solution instead of being totally absorbed in trying to make my Extended Range DeTect idea work."

"I promise we'll make *this* one work, Admiral."

"You have my full confidence, Barbara. Okay, let's get to work. The *Winston* is large enough to house a dozen scout-destroyers in its hold, so we'll have the engineers start the hull conversion work while you and your team work on the lead ship tactical station modifications and the reprogramming of the Propulsion Systems and Weapons Computer Systems aboard the trailing vessel."

*   *   *

Arthur Stephen Strauss, Deputy-Comptroller of MedZip Electronics, pressed his hand lightly against the palm plate and waited. A second later, the computer unlocked and opened the door to his penthouse suite. As he stepped inside, the lights remained at their dimmest setting instead of illuminating as programmed.

"Lights up," Strauss said loudly as the door closed behind him. When the lights continued to remain dim, Strauss said loudly, "Computer, why are the lights so dim?"

"The lights are illuminated according to their established setting, sir," he heard through small speakers discreetly disguised in the room.

"No, they're not. I want them at normal room illumination levels. Change them now."

"Please state your password, sir."

"Password? Computer. What's wrong with you? Perform a self test."

"Please state your password, sir."

"Computer, you're malfunctioning. Perform a self test."

"Please state your password, sir."

Strauss walked to a wall switch and manually raised the light level. As he did, he realized he wasn't alone in the room. Turning quickly, he focused on the intruder. It appeared to be a man, but he couldn't be sure because the person was wearing a heavy, fully buttoned, black winter coat. The black slacks visible below the coat's bottom edge, plus black leather loafers and a dark grey homburg with a wide brim were responsible for the gender assumption. A light grey scarf concealed all but the intruder's eye. "Who are you?" Strauss asked angrily.

The man, sitting in Strauss's favorite chair in the corner of the room, chuckled. "Just an old friend."

"Really?" Strauss said, with scorn in his voice. "And how did you get in here, *old friend*?"

"It was a simple matter. I just asked your computer politely to let me enter. It was very accommodating."

"Bullshit. My computer is keyed to my voice. It wouldn't have let you or anyone else into this apartment." Strauss had been drifting slowly towards the fireplace and rested his arm on the mantle as he said, "Computer, identify the stranger in this room."

"There is no stranger in the room."

"See, the computer knows me," the unidentified man said.

In one swift move, Strauss lifted the cover of a decorative box on the mantle and pulled out a small pistol. Aiming it at the visitor's face, he said, "Show me your face, *old friend*, or else."

The visitor chuckled. "Or else what?"

"I shall shoot it off."

The man chuckled again. "Go ahead."

"You *want* me to shoot?"

"No, I want you to try. You see, I removed the power cartridge from your little popgun earlier."

Strauss looked down at the gun in his hand and then at the unidentified visitor before squeezing the trigger. Nothing happened. In disgust, Strauss threw the pistol into the fireplace.

The visitor chuckled again. "You think I wouldn't have searched this place while I was waiting for you to arrive?"

Strauss's eyes flicked momentarily to his bedroom door.

"It's not there," the stranger said.

"What's not there?"

"The pistol in the nightstand drawer— or the one behind the hidden panel in the closet— whichever you were thinking about."

Strauss exhaled noisily through his nose. It wasn't quite a snort, but his exasperation was obvious.

The stranger raised his hand slightly, until then hidden by a fold in his coat. The hand was holding Strauss's nightstand pistol.

"That won't work for you," Strauss said. "It's keyed to my body."

"Really," the visitor said. Aiming the pistol at a small statuette on a shelf of a bookcase, he pulled the trigger. A beam shot out and melted a hole through the figurine. "It *seems* to be working."

The sneering look on Strauss's face had disappeared in a heartbeat and then turned to one of fear. He knew now that the intruder was armed. "That's impossible," he said, his voice not much more than a hoarse whisper.

"And yet it happened," the outsider said.

"How did you do that?"

"You saw. I simply aimed and pulled the trigger."

"The pistol was custom made especially for me. It couldn't be altered. The pistol grips are keyed to my body chemistry. "

"They just don't make things like they used to, I guess." Aiming the pistol at Strauss, the intruder said, "I can do it again if you'd like another demonstration."

"Who are you, dammit?" Strauss shouted.

"All in good time, Arthur."

"Computer, call my bodyguards," Strauss suddenly shouted in an effort to get the words out before the stranger could stop him.

The unknown visitor chuckled as the computer said, "Please state your password, sir."

"It's no use," the intruder said, "You can't summon your gorillas tonight. But they'll be in the building lobby waiting for you in the morning. When you don't show on time, they'll start trying to reach you and eventually come up here looking for you. When they're unable to contact you, they'll attempt to break in. It will take quite a bit to get in here, though. You've seen to that."

"How are you doing this?" Strauss screamed at the visitor. The room was so well soundproofed that his voice would never carry beyond the walls or the floor.

"Feeling a bit disconnected from your usual life-and-death power over almost everyone else on the planet?"

"What do you want? Is it money you're after?" With desperation clearly evident in his voice he said, "I have money."

The stranger chuckled and asked, "How much are you offering?"

"What am I buying?"

"Your life, perhaps."

"Perhaps?"

"I haven't heard an amount yet. What's your life worth to you, Arthur?"

"What's it worth to you?"

"How about— a trillion credits?"

"A trillion? You're mad."

The stranger chuckled. "The look on your face is priceless. It's been worth all the effort it took to set this up."

"Look, I can swing a million."

"A million? From the chairman of the Raider Lower Council?"

"Raider Lower Council? What's that? I'm just the Deputy-Comptroller of MedZip Electronics."

The visitor chuckled again. "Who do you think you're dealing with?"

"I don't know who I'm dealing with, but I have nothing to do with the Raiders."

"Have it your way, Arthur." As he aimed the pistol at Strauss's chest, the intruder said, "Any last words for posterity?"

"Wait a minute. Hold on. I can make it more."

"How much more?"

"Ten million. It's the best I can do."

"You probably steal that much every month from the Raider coffers."

"I tell you I have nothing to do with the Raiders. The ten million is my entire stock portfolio. It's all I've got. It's yours. Just let me live. Please."

"And how long would I live if I did? A day? Two days?"

"I don't even know who you are."

"True," the stranger said, reaching for the scarf that concealed his face. "But you should know who your executioner is."

"No wait." Strauss said. "I don't want to know. This way you won't have to kill me. I can get you the ten million and I'll never know who you are, so I can't seek revenge."

"Arthur, Arthur, Arthur. You must think me a fool. If I left without killing you, you'd have a dozen people waiting for me at a later rendezvous where you would ostensibly hand over the money."

"No, I swear. It will be just between you and me."

Well, I couldn't make a deal like that without you knowing who you were dealing with."

The intruder reached up and pulled down the scarf, revealing his features. Strauss's jaw nearly hit the floor.

"I don't understand," Strauss said. "You look like me."

"Wrong. I am you."

"What?"

"This has been almost as much fun as when I faced Christa Carver."

"Carver?"

"Yes, don't you remember? You threatened to kill me for doing that."

"Ravenau? But you're dead."

"Not quite. The body you found was an earlier experiment that used the same DNA Manipulation formula I later used. Of course, the process had been perfected by the time I used it on myself. I saved the body on a whim, and it came in handy when I had to disappear before you had me killed."

"I— I— wasn't going to have you killed. I decided that you could be useful."

"Nice try, but we both know better."

"No— No— I mean it. If I wanted you dead, I would have done it right after you turned over the formulas. I wasn't going to kill you."

"Oh, right. You were going to wipe my mind and ship me off to one of the *resorts*."

"No, I wasn't. I believed you were still important to us. You had brought us formulas worth hundreds of trillions of credits. I was going to find a new project for you."

"Nice try, but I don't believe you," Foster said.

"What did you hope to accomplish by making yourself look like me? Once I'm dead, all my IDs will be canceled and you'll never even get inside the building again."

"That's only if they *know* you're dead."

"So that's why you took my identity. You think you can just step into my spot? It won't work Ravenau."

"No? Why not?"

"You've been gone too long. You're out of the loop. You can't just step into my shoes without everyone with whom you'll have contact knowing something is wrong. You'll be discovered the first day. You should take the money I've offered you."

Foster pulled the trigger on the pistol and swept it across the area where Strauss's heart would be, if he had one. The pulse only lasted a second. Strauss clutched his chest and looked at Foster as if he couldn't believe Foster had fired. Or perhaps he simply couldn't believe he was going to die in a few seconds because his heart had stopped functioning. He fell to his knees first, and then fell flat on his face. The laser had cauterized the wound as it destroyed the heart, so there was no blood.

"Don't worry about me, Arthur. I'm a quick study. I'll pick up what I need to know and fake the rest."

Now that the deed was done, it was time to relax a little before cleaning up. Foster, who would now be known as Arthur Stephen Strauss, stepped over the corpse, walked to the wine closet, and selected a favorite vintage from among an impressive selection of chilled bottles. As he took a seat in the living room, he said, "Computer, cancel routine FOSTER637981." When the computer responded that the routine was canceled, he had the computer dim the lights in the room and open the draperies. As he enjoyed the spectacle of the city lights through the floor-to-ceiling glass windows, he sipped at his wine.

After draining the last drop of wine from the glass, the new Arthur Strauss walked to where the old Arthur Strauss was still lying and picked up the body to carry it to the bathroom. He was glad he had the strength of this new body because as Ravenau he never could have lifted Strauss.

Strauss dumped the body into the bathtub and was about to begin filling the tub with water but then remembered he hadn't gone through Strauss's pockets. He carefully removed the clothes from the body, then let the tub fill as he carried the personal items he'd found into the bedroom.

Five minutes later he returned to the bathroom and turned off the water. He took a step back from the tub and tossed in a small water-soluble packet. Turning, he exited the room and closed the door. In the morning, there would be little left of the corpse.

Chapter Twenty-Two

~ November 30th, 2287 ~

"Welcome to the new home of Space Command's Supreme Headquarters," Admiral Holt said to Jenetta as she stepped out of the shuttle and walked down the ramp. Her jumakas were at her sides as always when outside the palace or the R2HQ Admiralty Board Hall, except when in the fighter reserved for her personal use.

"Thank you, Brian." Looking around, she added, "There's not much to see."

"Not above ground— yet. Like the island where the Quesann Space Command base is built, this island has a core of incredibly dense rock. We've sunk shafts to a hundred meters and constructed a complete underground complex capable of protecting five thousand military and civilian personnel for three months in the event of an attack on the above-ground complex."

"That's barely enough for SHQ. What about the GA Senate?"

"We've sunk shafts for their own underground secure complex, but we're still in the process of excavating the areas below ground. Once the excavation is complete, the entire complex will be protected with pre-stressed plasticrete wall panels. I estimate two months before we'll be ready to begin construction of the above-ground complex there. Shall we tour the SHQ below-ground complex?"

"Let's go."

A couple of hours later as the two admirals rode the lift to the surface, Jenetta said, "You're doing an excellent job, Brian. I'm so grateful that you chose to join us here. With you in charge of this project, I haven't had to worry that it wasn't being managed properly."

"I'm doing my best. And I've been loving every minute of it. If I can lift part of the burden from your shoulders, I'm happy to do it."

"I *do* appreciate it. This region has known almost nothing except war since the day I first entered it. We've barely had time to breathe between new enemies seeking to kick us out. Sometimes it seems like they're lined up somewhere just waiting for their chance to take us down."

"I think you've pared that waiting list down to near zero."

"I wish that were true. I learned a few days ago that the Uthlaro are building a new fleet to take us on again."

"No! Where? Did one of our patrols find them?"

"We owe it to some good intelligence work on the part of SCI. The new shipyard is a hundred parsecs outside our Region Three border."

"That race is never going to accept the loss of their empire. I'm beginning to wonder if we're going to have to exercise the final solution."

"That's one of the decisions I've been wrestling with. It's not one that any person should ever have to make, but as the Military Governor in a lawless territory, I do have the author-ity to order it."

"You've given the Uthlaro every opportunity to become a peaceful member of the GA. If they won't stop coming at us, you'll have no choice. That was the reason for practically destroying the Milori home world. We knew Maxxiloth would never stop coming at us every time he was able to rebuild his forces. It was only when you made the decision to destroy the planet's infrastructure that the people finally brought down Maxxiloth in the interest of peace. When the Uthlaro people reach that same point, they'll do what has to be done and stop supporting their leaders."

"I'm not so sure. The Uthlaro military personnel were the most fanatical military we've fought. We learned that they would never give in while a single breath remained in their body, so we finally stopped trying to take prisoners. If the general populace is as fanatical, they won't stop supporting their political leaders while they live. We might have to decimate the population to get them to stop fighting us, but genocide is not an acceptable option. Isolating them on their planet would be a far better alternative if they refuse to cooperate and live in peace. Isolation means they will not be permitted to travel outside their planet's sensible atmosphere, and absolutely no trade with outside civilizations will be allowed. No one leaves and no one enters. This would not be like the arrangement we have with planets that don't wish to become a participating member of the GA. Those planets are barred from trading with GA member planets but are allowed freedom to leave their planet and trade with other non-member worlds as long as they obey the laws of the GA."

"Do you really think it'll come to that?"

"I hope not, but it's not looking good. That they began building this secret base in order to produce military ships so soon after they surrendered unconditionally doesn't bode well. Did they really think we wouldn't find out?"

"Perhaps they didn't think."

"How can business people who were able to build an empire the size of theirs be so obtuse?"

"Perhaps it was simply that fanatical loyalty and total lack of competition that allowed them to build that empire. When a person in power has no opposition to their programs or proposals, they can get reckless. They have never experienced failure before and so haven't learned the lessons that usually accompany that outcome."

"Yes, perhaps. Anyway, I'm not going to worry about it right now. Until the Denubbewa are either gone or defeated, almost all my attention is focused on them."

* * *

"We're ready to begin testing the new bombing procedure with the *Tigris* and the *Ohio*, Admiral," Captain DeWitt said as she and Jenetta walked the hull of the scout-destroyer *Purus*. The ship was one of the six newest vessels to arrive in

Region Two and was currently being fitted with one hundred Dakinium bomb cradles. Engineers were working around the clock to cut holes and install the devices in the hull.

Jenetta had decided to go all the way after Captain DeWitt had enthusiastically embraced the new bombing procedure. She had authorized installation work on nine additional scout-destroyers. That would exhaust most of the cradles authorized and supplied by SHQ. Only the devices intended as backups for defective or damaged cradles remained. So far, all install-ed cradles were found to have been machined perfectly, so none of the backup units had yet been used.

The *Purus* and the eight other newly designated bombing vessels were ensconced inside the transport ship *Winston* where the entire hold could be pressurized while maintaining a zero gravity environment safe from radiation and tempera-tures beyond that of human tolerances. Exterior work on the *Tigris* had been completed long ago, and it was not necessary to house it inside the large ship.

"Excellent, Barbara."

"My people are really excited about the testing phase. Our simulations have indicated that we have a good shot at accomplishing what most of them secretly believed was impossible after the dismal results with the DeTect work."

"When do you expect your first test to begin?"

"My people are aboard the two vessels already, completing the final calibration tests. We'll perform our first test run tomorrow at the start of the first watch. I want everyone rest-ed and alert, assuming they can sleep tonight. They know how important this effort is. A few are feeling nervous and all are very excited."

"I look forward to hearing your report after the test."

* * *

"Speak to me, Ernesto," Barbara DeWitt said to her second in command aboard the *Ohio*.

Commander Ernesto Villanova stopped what he was doing and turned towards the monitor. "We think we've narrowed down the problem a bit. The tactical console interface tests fine, but we're not getting a signal at the weapons computer, so it isn't sending a signal to the *Tigris* to release the dummy bomb. I've had people crawling through the access tunnels searching for the signal interruption problem, and I think we have the area identified. It's probably a break in a fiber optic wiring couple. It might be a cracked strand or perhaps just a loose fitting, either of which can be responsible for intermittent contact. Everything checked out when testing, so it should be just a matter of fixing this problem. The thing we have to worry about is thinking we've found the problem when the contact is suddenly restored from moving something, only to discover that the problem wasn't fixed. So we have to go slowly and make sure we really have found the real problem."

"How long?"

"I'm sorry, Captain, but I have no idea how long it will take to find the exact problem even though we know approximately where it's occurring. We could find it a minute from now, or it may not be found until tomorrow. It's like trying to find a flea on a collie. But at least it isn't moving around."

Captain DeWitt took a deep breath and exhaled it quickly, showing her exasperation. "Okay, Ernesto, keep at it."

Three hours and sixteen minutes later, Commander Villanova contacted Captain DeWitt. "We found a bad coupling connection in access tunnel 26LRV81P, and connection has been restored. We're hoping this is the only problem."

"Good work, Ernesto. Are you ready for another run at the target?"

"We're go from here, Captain."

"Okay, Ernesto. I'm going to contact the Captain."

"Aye, Captain. Villanova out."

"DeWitt out."

"We're ready to commence the run, Captain," Commander Katherine Jameson said to Captain DeWitt from her command chair.

"We're ready at tactical, Captain. We want to perform this test as if it's the real thing, so proceed whenever you and Captain Wilder decide to go."

Commander Jameson looked down at the monitor by her left hand where an image of Commander Dillon Wilder stared back at her. "We're ready here, Dillon. Our envelope is built."

"Roger, Katherine. Our envelope is built and telemetry is active. Take us for a ride."

Telemetry between the two ships would flow constantly as the helmsman aboard the *Ohio* dually provided all propulsion and course information for both the *Ohio* and the *Tigris*. Although the *Tigris* was functioning as a remotely operated vessel, either Commander Jameson or Commander Wilder could break the connection at any time and the *Tigris* would again regain full control over its movement.

Captain DeWitt sat in one of the tactical officer chairs outside the three-quarters-circular tactical console on the bridge of the *Ohio*. From there, she could see the same images that the lead tactical officer was seeing on his monitors inside the console ring as he prepared to drop the bomb.

The *Ohio* began its run when Captain Jameson looked towards the helmsman and said, "Attack." Since the envelope was already built, the ship was almost instantly at Light-9793.48, as was the *Tigris*. As the *Ohio* reached a point estimated to be fifteen seconds from the target, the tactical officer turned over firing control to the weapons computer. After that all he did was simply sit back and watch.

When the weapons system indicated that the bomb had been dropped by the trailing *Tigris*, Captain Jameson said, "All stop." To Captain DeWitt she said, "Should we maintain or cancel our envelope?"

"Maintain it, Captain, while I learn how the test went." Turning to the monitor in front of her where the image of Commander Villanova appeared, she said, "Speak to me, Ernesto. How did we do?"

"I can confirm that the bomb dropped, Captain. We're waiting now for the triangulation information to see how close we came. Ah, here it is now, Captain. The dummy bomb is sitting approximately fifty-two thousand, eight hundred fifty kilometers from the target."

"Before or after?"

"After. It dropped about eighteen nanoseconds late."

"Well, that won't get the job done, but it's a lot better than the last test we performed. Rather than run another test, let's get together and review all the telemetry data."

"Wouldn't it just be better to tweak the timing by eighteen nanoseconds and try again today, Captain?"

"No, I don't think so. We've run so many simulations that we should have done better than eighteen nanoseconds. There must be something we missed or miscalculated. I'll have Captain Wilder bring you here so we can work on this aboard the *Ohio*. DeWitt out."

"Villanova out."

"Captain, would you ask Captain Wilder to join us at this location and ferry my officers over to the *Ohio*? And we can cancel the envelope. We'll be working on our calculations for a while. Thank you."

While Commander Jameson relayed the instructions to the *Tigris*, Captain DeWitt headed to the conference room where her equipment was set up.

"We're still missing something," Captain DeWitt said to her senior staff after they had been at it for hours.

"We've covered everything, ma'am," Commander Villanova said. "Our calculations were perfect, and the timing of the drop was perfect. But the dummy bomb dropped almost fifty-three thousand kilometers from the target."

"If we had everything perfect, the bomb would be inside the target container. We're missing something."

"Why not just subtract eighteen nanoseconds and try the drop again."

"If we can't find the real problem we'll have to try that, but it sidesteps the calculations. I hate it when things disagree with the numbers."

"We can sit here for days and never find anything."

"We can't afford the time. The Admiral is depending on us. The entire GA is depending on us."

"It has to be a simple— a simple…"

"A simple what, Ernesto?"

"I just had a thought. I don't think it could be— no, that can't be it."

"Tell us."

"You'll all laugh."

"We could all use a good laugh about now." She smiled and added, "So give us all a good laugh at your expense."

Commander Villanova made a wry face before saying, "Okay, I was just thinking about the Dakinium cradle."

"What about it?"

"Well, we have a lot of measuring equipment inside the hull by the cradle, and that equipment generates a bit of heat. I wondered if maybe the heat affected the Dakinium. You know, like in expansion and contraction. When we timed the release of the bomb, we didn't have any of that equipment by the cradle. Aw, the idea is nuts because everyone knows that nothing affects Dakinium."

Instead of laughing, everyone at the table was looking around at everyone else as they thought.

"The manufacturing tolerances are in microns, and the cradles are intended for use in the cold of space," DeWitt said. "A slight variance could possibly distort the cradle a minute amount and slow the ejection by eighteen nano-seconds. If the bomb hadn't released at all, the cradle would have been one of the first places we looked. But since it only dropped eighteen nanoseconds late, we didn't look at that possibility. What does everyone think?"

"I think we should take a serious look at it," one of the technicians said, "but maybe we should get some sleep first. I've been awake for over forty-two hours, and I'm not sure I could perform a proper test right now, Captain."

Captain DeWitt chuckled. "I'm not sure I could do any better right now. Okay, everyone, let's call it a night, or a morning, or whatever it is. We start again in ten hours."

Twelve hours later, all of the measuring equipment had been removed from the test cradle, and the bulkhead entrance from the interior area of the ship to the hull was sealed to ensure the interior environment wouldn't have an effect on the cradle and thus the release of the bomb.

At 1100 hours, the two ships were positioned for another test. Captain DeWitt gave the go-ahead and the test was performed as before.

When DeWitt asked for the result, Villanova said, "The dummy bomb dropped, Captain, but the signal is garbled so we haven't identified its location yet."

"What do you mean the signal is garbled? Garbled how?"

"The signal is extremely weak and intermittent. Captain Wilder suggests we backtrack to see if we can locate it."

"Permission granted."

"Aye, Captain. We'll report back when we locate it."

About ninety minutes later, Villanova reported, "Uh— we've found it, Captain."

DeWitt and her entire team aboard the *Ohio* were crowded into the conference room they had been using for their work area.

"Where is it?" DeWitt asked. "How close are we to the target?"

"You're never going to believe this, ma'am. It's in the cargo container that we were targeting."

"In it?" DeWitt said excitedly with unrestrained delight. "You mean it landed inside the cargo container?"

"Uh— not exactly. You'll have to see this to believe it. I have an image ready to send. Here it is."

The image that appeared on the large bulkhead monitor showed just the front half of the dummy bomb. It appeared to be sitting on a metal deck.

"What happened to the rest of it?" DeWitt asked. "I can only see the front half. It appears to be sitting on a cargo bay deck."

"Uh— no ma'am. I'm in an EVA suit inside the cargo container. The dummy bomb is stuck in a sidewall. If I go outside the container, I can show you the back half."

Captain DeWitt chuckled, and then started to laugh out loud. It was infectious and her team was soon laughing as well.

"Commander," DeWitt said when she got her laughing under control, "I want you to have an engineer cut the dummy out of that sidewall, leaving half a meter of intact sidewall all around the dummy. Then patch the hole so we can perform another test run."

"Aye, Captain. I'll report back when we've finished and we're back aboard the *Tigris*."

"DeWitt, out."

"Villanova, out."

Six hours later, the two small ships were ready for the third test. Excitement was high to see if they could duplicate the incredible results of the second test. This time, the signal was loud and clear, but it wasn't coming from inside the container. Immediately after the test, the new dummy was discovered to be four hundred seventy-two kilometers from the container. The excitement they had felt after the second test evaporated as they learned the result.

"Okay, everyone," Captain DeWitt announced to her teams, "it's not close enough to declare it successful, but it's close enough to offer encouragement that we're still in the ballgame. We have seven more dummy bombs loaded into the *Tigris'* cradles. We're going to perform seven more bombing runs nonstop. Between runs we'll locate the dummy that was just dropped, but we're not going to retrieve the dummies until we've completed all seven tests. Then the engineering teams will evaluate each drop in the conference room aboard the *Ohio*. Okay, let's get set up for bombing run four."

The seven additional tests produced varying results. The worst was over ten thousand kilometers from the target, and the best of the seven was just six meters from the container. While the *Tigris* recovered the nine dummy bombs, the engineers assembled to review all the collected data from each run.

Chapter Twenty-Three
~ December 12th, 2287 ~

"I thought you might want to see the result of our second test, Admiral," Captain DeWitt said as Jenetta entered the hangar on South Island. The small base had been home to the Weapons Research and Development people for a number of months.

"I was impressed when I saw the numbers," Jenetta said as she stared at the dummy bomb that was still embedded in the section of cargo container removed from the target, "but seeing this is even more impressive."

"Unfortunately, it was just one of ten tests."

"But you also placed one just six meters from the container. Either of these two tests would have destroyed a targeted ship."

"Yes, but the results weren't consistent. We must do better than one in five."

"Still, it's impressive, Barbara. And with no other attack option open to us, it at least offers an opportunity to destroy enemy ships without sacrificing our people. Have you developed any ideas on how to improve the kill ratio?"

"We've studied the telemetry data until we can quote it in our sleep. It appears that everything works perfectly up to the point where the signal to release the bomb is sent. Having the first ship identify the target and send the release signal to a second ship appears to provide deadly accuracy, but the release is where the process seems to break down. With the first test, we were just eighteen nanoseconds off, and the bomb missed the target by fifty-two thousand, eight hundred fifty kilometers. We discovered the problem was the result of a minute expansion of the Dakinium cradle."

"Yes, that surprised me when I read the report. I'd always thought Dakinium was unaffected by heat or cold."

"Well, we *are* talking about just a micron of change. But it was enough to make a difference, and where you're talking nano-seconds, it doesn't take much. After reviewing the test data, we've decided that minute differences in bomb casing and cradles might be responsible. When we designed the bomb, we needed a way to eject it from the ship, so we used the principle of a ship's thruster to push it out. To ensure that the ship's Transverse Wave envelope was never in danger of failing due to a gap in Dakinium coverage, we built the thruster chamber into the bomb housing rather than into the cradle. The principal is sound, but the execution is imperfect. We're going to try increasing the air pressure in the thruster chamber to more forcibly eject the bomb. Rather than just pushing it out so it can pass beyond the Transverse Wave encapsulating the ship, we're going to *launch* it from the cradle in the hope that we can achieve a more consistent ejection release. We're also going to try using a special lubricating gel to create a better seal around the casing. We need to precisely control the pressure in the cradle to control the precise timing of the ejection."

"It sounds like a solid plan."

"We hope so. We're going out tomorrow to perform another series of tests."

"Barbara, as I look at this dummy bomb stuck inside a sidewall, I can't help but wonder how a real bomb will react to reintegration inside a deck or bulkhead once the Transverse Wave effect is lost."

"That's difficult to answer, Admiral, due to the many factors involved. We have discussed it at length since this test. We've been waiting anxiously to cut this dummy bomb apart to see how the casing material integrated with the composite material of the container's walls but have held off until you could view it. It seems to us that the physical prop-erties of the bomb material around the point where it merged with the container material could be altered sufficiently enough to render the bomb inert. But we may never know until we can actually test the bombs on real ships. But first we need to get to a point where we can place the bombs where they need to be placed."

Jenetta simply nodded. "Barbara, you've done an incredible job so far and I know that if anyone can solve the problems, it's you and your team. I'm grateful that we have such intelligent and dedicated people on our side in this conflict."

"Thank you. Admiral."

"Good luck. I look forward to hearing the results of your next tests."

* * *

By the time Foster had awakened on the morning after assuming Strauss's identity, the body of the real Strauss had been reduced to mere bones in a bubbling liquid of dissolved flesh and soft tissue. Foster had then tossed a second small packet of chemicals into the tub to neutralize the further effects of the first packet. As the color of the liquid changed, an indication that the acidity had been reduced to a safe level, Foster carefully flushed the tub and bones clean of any residual chemicals. The skull and bones then went into a small case he had brought for that very purpose and were locked in a closet where the cleaning staff would be unable to access the case.

It was an entire week before the new Strauss felt confident enough to carry the case out of the building and place it into a locker at a shuttleport. It would remain there until he could shake his security staff long enough to take the bones to where they would be ground up and mixed with the bones and byproducts of animals used as filler in the making of pet food.

Days later, when Strauss was finally able to dispose of the evidence, he took the case to the processing center and witnessed the entire procedure through to completion. It cost him a thousand credits, but it was well worth it.

Despite intensive efforts to surreptitiously learn Strauss's daily routines prior to confronting and killing the man, situations had arisen which could have raised suspicions that all was not right and proper, but Foster's long years as a senior Raider official helped immensely in carrying him through.

Foster's first session as the chairperson of the Lower Council had gone very smoothly. He had the minutes from the previous meeting and his office computer contained the names, photos, and histories of the other members, including private little notes Strauss had made regarding unusual personality traits and emotional preoccupations. But Strauss's duties and responsibilities in the Raider organization were wide and varied, and the daily interpersonal relationships were the most difficult because so much of that interaction took place behind closed doors. But Foster had prevailed, and by the end of the first month he was performing in the role as if he had been doing it for years.

"Today's meeting will come to order," Chairman Gladsworth said, pounding the decorative gravel once. The other members stopped talking among themselves and gave the chairman their full attention. "We have a visitor today who is not authorized to hear Upper Council business, so we shall dispense with the reading of the minutes. I again welcome the chairperson of the Lower Council, Arthur Stephen Strauss. You have the floor, Mr. Chairman."

Strauss rose to his feet and looked at the assembled members. It was hard to believe that these were the founders of the Raider organization. As he looked around the table, all he saw were eight of the most drop-dead-gorgeous females he'd ever seen assembled in one room. All were stylishly coiffed and wearing expensive fashions that showed off their new bodies to maximum advantage. Strauss had been through that phase and was aware of the internal conflicts each was feeling as they dealt with suddenly finding themselves incredibly desirable after enduring the gradual diminishment of sexual appeal that lasted for decades. Each appeared to be no more than twenty-five years of age, showing that they had availed themselves of the DNA Manipulation process and the

Age Regression process. He assumed they had also been administered the Age Prolongation process. The only real question was whether or not they wished to return to a male form. That was another dilemma Strauss had endured.

"Good morning. It's my unpleasant duty to report that the last of the four Upper Council members who suffered health problems related to their metamorphoses has passed away. Arrangements for funeral services are being made, and when complete, the UC secretary will notify each member should you wish to attend. On a more important note, the doctors continue to assure me that no sign of the problems suffered by the others has been observed in any of your physiologies.

"Thank you for allowing me to address you today."

* * *

"Today's tests will be conducted as if this were a real battle, Captains," Captain DeWitt said to Commanders Katherine Jameson and Dillon Wilder. Commander Jameson was in the conference room aboard the scout-destroyer *Ohio*, while Commander Wilder was participating via teleconference. "There will be ten drops of dummy bombs. We will run continuously, never stopping or dropping the envelopes. Once the *Ohio* helmsman assumes helm control of the *Tigris*, it should not be interrupted until the exercise is complete."

"I lose control of my ship until the entire test is complete?" Commander Wilder asked.

"Yes, because that's the way it will be in battle for the ships performing as bombers. The lead ship will maintain helm control until the action is over. I do understand your concern about losing control of your ship, but you are only losing helm control, and only for a short time. Most space battles last under an hour, and I believe the power of this weapon will shorten that considerably. Additionally, in the event that a problem does occur, such as a communication malfunction with the lead ship, the bomber can break the connection with the lead ship and assume full control over its helm at any time. For that matter, either captain can break the connection at any time."

"Will you be at the tactical station today?" Commander Jameson asked.

"No, I'll be down here, monitoring the information coming from the shuttles performing the triangulation duties. Your tactical people are well trained and know what has to be done now. The only difference today is that after dropping a dummy bomb, the *Ohio* helmsman will complete a wide three-sixty to return to the original starting position and then attack the shipping container again until all ten runs have been completed. At that time we'll begin a review of the bombing effort and retrieve the dummy bombs.

"Any other questions?"

Both Commander Jameson and Commander Wilder shook their heads.

"Fine. I'll alert you when the ordnance people and the shuttle crews are ready. Dismissed."

When the *Ohio's* Captain said, "Tac, prepare to commence the run," the tactical officer engaged the system that locked the helm of the *Ohio* to the helm of the *Tigris*. Both ships had already moved into position, built their Transverse Wave envelopes, and issued system commands that would permit their helms to be unified under the control of the lead ship.

"Helms unification active," the *Ohio* tac officer said as the computers confirmed readiness. "The *Tigris* confirms."

"Helm, commence the run," Commander Jameson said.

In the *Ohio* conference room, Captain DeWitt and her senior team members watched real-time images of both ship's bridges provided by the bridge log cameras. Development of the new weapon system had seemed to progress slowly, but it was actually advancing at breakneck speed compared to the development of other such weapon systems in the past. The urgency was owed to the fact that Space Command knew an invasion was imminent, in fact already having occurred although the invaders hadn't yet begun their push through

Region Two. Space Command needed this weapon system to be available and dependable before that happened.

"Attack run one commencing," Commander Ernesto Villanova said as the ships surged forward. Since they were moving FTL, there was no sensation of movement.

As the *Ohio* completed the run and began to turn for the second run, Commander Villanova received a message via his CT. "Villanova out," he said to cancel the carrier, then, "The first dummy dropped two meters before the target container."

"Two meters?" DeWitt said excitedly. "I'll take that every time."

Villanova smiled and said, "Let's not get too excited. It's just the first run. If the next one drops that close, then *I'll* get excited."

At the completion of the second run, Villanova announced, "The second dummy dropped twelve meters after the container."

"Twelve?" DeWitt echoed. "It's not two, but I consider anything within a radius of fifteen meters as a kill. Our destroyers have a beam of fifty-six meters, so a radius of fifteen would be sufficient to kill any of them. This small ship only has a beam of sixteen meters, but if you were to attack it longitudinally, a fifteen-meter radius would destroy it every time because its length is one hundred fifteen meters."

"From the estimates I've heard of the enemy ship sizes," Villanova said, "all we need is a drop radius of twenty meters to guarantee a kill when attacking from any direction."

"Yes, but let's keep to a higher standard for now. Fifteen meters should be our goal."

After the third run, the shuttles performing the triangulation reported that the dummy dropped just three meters from the target.

"I'm about ready to break out the champagne," DeWitt said.

"I'll drink to that," Villanova said.

"Not just yet, though. We still have seven more runs to perform."

The festive mood dropped into oblivion with the next run. The dummy bomb dropped over a thousand kilometers from the target.

"What happened?" DeWitt asked with unmistakable incredulity in her voice.

"It can't be the weapons system," Villanova said. "Either the tac officer failed to turn control over to the targeting computer in time, or it's a problem with either the dummy or the cradle. My money is on the dummy or cradle."

"I hope so. A defective dummy or cradle is acceptable. Both can easily be replaced."

The remaining six runs produced results like the first three. Only the one dummy bomb on run four dropped outside the fifteen-meter radius established by Captain DeWitt.

"Okay," DeWitt said as the dummy bombs were retrieved and the ships headed back to Quesann, "I'm going to break out the champagne when we get back."

"Even with the one bad run?" Villanova said.

"Even with one bad run. We know we've licked the main problems. We just have to tighten up production variables on the cradles and bombs. The important thing is that we can drop a bomb inside any of the enemy ships and they can't hurt us while we're doing it."

"As far as we know— ," Villanova said. "I'll hold off on the celebration until after we've successfully employed the weapons. We still don't know if the bombs will explode once they escape the Transverse Wave envelope if they reintegrate as part of a deck, bulkhead, or equipment."

"You're such a downer sometimes, Ernesto," DeWitt said. She looked serious, but Villanova had been with her for a long time and knew she was joking. "Okay, we'll hold off on the celebration party until after the bombs are used effectively."

* * *

"The tests went quite well, Admiral," Captain DeWitt said to Jenetta the following day. Only one dummy bomb fell outside the acceptable range."

"I read the report you submitted last evening," Jenetta said. "I'd have to agree that a thousand kilometers is outside the acceptable range, but I want to congratulate you on the success of the other nine. What went wrong with number four?"

"We've confirmed that the drop command was timed perfectly. The problem occurred after the release. Our original speculation was a defect with either the dummy or the cradle. The dummy checked out fine, so now we need to look at cradle Echo Four. In order to perform that inspection properly, we have to move the *Tigris* into the *Winston* again. We'd like to do that today, but we need you to issue that order."

"I'll have my aide take care of that as soon as we're done here."

"That's all I have, Admiral."

"Then we're done here."

* * *

Once the enormous pumps had reduced the pressure in the hold to zero, the forward hull doors of the *Winston* opened wide to accept the *Tigris*. The disparity in size between the ships could make one reminiscent of a guppy being swallowed by a large fish in an aquarium. Shipyard tugs then slowly and carefully pushed the *Tigris* into place inside the hull, where engineers in EVA suits secured it. The huge doors closed as soon the tugs returned to their parking docks inside the ship, but it would be an hour before the pressure and temperature returned to a level where workers didn't require special environmental suits to work in the hold.

To the naked eye, the Echo Four bomb cradle looked fine, but once the special measurement equipment was in place against the hull, the cradle was discovered to be misaligned with the hull opening. The misalignment was minute, but it was just enough to account for the release of the dummy bomb being delayed by a couple of nanoseconds.

Several hours later, the cradle had been removed and then reinstalled properly. During that time, engineers checked the alignment of the other ninety-nine cradles in the *Tigris* hull. They discovered three more cradles whose alignment didn't come up to spec, so each of the other cradles were removed and reinstalled.

A check of the installation records showed that the same engineering team had installed all four cradles. Their names were immediately removed from the work assignment roster and they were ordered confined to their quarters pending an investigation and possible preference of charges. If charged and found guilty of Failure to Follow Instructions and Directives, their pay could be docked, and they might have to work extra duty assignments. In addition to the four cradles in the *Tigris* hull, the team had installed sixteen cradles in the other ships being converted for use as bombers. All would have to be carefully checked to see if the sloppy work had persisted. Captain DeWitt, upset with learning that the poor workmanship involved more than the one cradle in the *Tigris*, issued orders that every cradle in every ship be checked for alignment after the work was declared complete and before the ship was released from the *Winston*.

While all ships and bridge crews were required to undergo training at the bomb drop test area before being certified ready for active duty with the new weapon system, Captain DeWitt further ordered that during the testing every single cradle had to meet the maximum radius drop requirement of fifteen meters. She immediately ordered her machinists to begin creating an additional one hundred dummy bombs for the new testing requirements.

"Four ships, the *Tigris*, *Zambezi*, *Purus*, and *Niagara,* are certified ready for bomber duty, Admiral. I expect to certify two more by the weekend, assuming they complete their testing by then. The other four could be ready as soon as ten days from now if all goes well."

"And each of the four ships that are certified now have all dropped their bombs in a fifteen-meter radius of the target, Barbara?"

"Yes, ma'am. That's the minimum I would accept after we proved the targeting system was capable of that performance level. All problems since then have been discovered to be with either the dummy bombs or owed to cradle misalignment, and all problems have been resolved and testing procedures put into practice to ensure those problems will not reoccur."

"And the issue of whether the weapons will explode if they reintegrate inside a bulkhead or deck?"

"For that, we'll just have to wait and see. We estimate that, statistically, a bomb will emerge in the clear at least twenty-five percent of the time. So at least one in four will detonate properly."

"One in four? Not very good odds."

"That's not to say that the bombs that reintegrate inside bulkheads and decks *won't* detonate. We just don't know."

"I'm sure you've heard of the mother ships being watched by our people out near the Hudeerac border, right?"

"Yes, ma'am."

"They're reported as being four times the size of Stewart SCB. With a target that size, our bombs should have no problems hitting their target, but I doubt that one bomb will do the job we need done. How difficult would it be to drop three bombs at once, like firing a three-round burst from an automatic weapon? The bombs should be spaced so that they drop roughly five to ten kilometers apart."

"It shouldn't be very difficult at all. It would only involve making a few changes to the weapons computer. The tac officer could have a choice of dropping a single bomb or a threesome."

"If you can accomplish that before all ten of the bombers are ready to deploy, I'd like to do it."

"Yes, ma'am. We'll get on it right away. It'll be ready before the bombers are ready to deploy."

"Thank you, Barbara. And extend my thanks to your entire department. I know how hard you've all worked to get us to this point. I'm sure your efforts will pay off when we meet the enemy. We're going to show them why they never should have entered our territory and attacked our ships. We'll teach the Denubbewa a lesson they won't live long enough to forget."

Chapter Twenty-Four

~ January 4th, 2288 ~

"Good God!" Captain Zakir Singh of the DS destroyer *Duluth* said after receiving a report about the latest flyby of the enemy mother ships. The mother ship they had been expecting for months had just reached the rendezvous point where the other two were waiting, but it didn't arrive alone. It was accompanied by yet another mother ship. "Now we know why it's a few hours late getting here. It met up with another ship on the way."

"It was alone when we located it and determined it was headed to this RP, sir," Commander Marc Hodenfield of the scout-destroyer *Rio Grande* said. "How many more of these things can there be in GA space?" he asked rhetorically.

"I don't know, but I know that four is four too many."

"The ship we've been watching was alone on the last flyby," Commander Fischer of the *Yukon* said. "They must have joined up in the last couple of hours. It's just a coincidence they arrived at about the same time."

"Coincidence or not, I'm not liking this situation," Captain Singh said.

"What do you think they'll do now, Captain?" Fischer asked.

"I wish I knew. If they feel they've reached adequate strength, or if all their assets are in place, they might begin their push into GA space. If they're waiting for additional reinforcements, they might just sit here until they arrive. Your guess is as good as mine."

*　*　*

"This will be the last meeting of the R2HQ Board that I chair for a while," Jenetta said after the formalities of opening the meeting had been satisfied. "Admiral Holt will be assuming my duties during my absence. A few hours from now, I'll be aboard the *Ares* when it deploys to join our assembled forces near the border with the Hudeerac nation. The scout-destroyers modified with the new bomb capability and the ten SD ships upgraded with the new targeting software will be accompanying the *Ares*. Our weapons people have done everything asked of them and more. I feel we have a weapon now that offers us a chance to defeat the enemy that has invaded our territory and murdered our people without issuing a formal declaration of war. I intend to make this attempt before any more of their mother ships arrive. We are currently tracking three, but there may be more on their way or already here. At our fastest speed, travel to the RP is about sixty days. Communications are twenty-four days each way, so the situation might already be different from our last reports. Based on current knowledge, our best chance to defeat this group is now while they're concentrated in one location. Once we use our new weapon for the first time, I expect them to retreat and attempt to adapt by formulating a new strategy or defense, just as we have done."

"The new weapon is proven, isn't it?" Admiral Buckner asked.

"In tests, it has performed up to the standards we've established, but the true effectiveness of a weapon is judged by how well it performs under battlefield conditions. It would be wonderful if development of this weapon was owed to military preparedness rather than response to an emergency condition, because much more testing would have answered some strong, lingering questions we have about its operational effectiveness, but the remaining questions will have to be answered in combat."

"What sort of operational effectiveness?" Buckner asked.

"Security concerns prevent me from discussing that aspect in this meeting, but I'll be happy to answer your question at a later time in a more secure environment."

Buckner nodded to show he understood. Although there was no gallery for this meeting, many of the clerks didn't have sufficient security clearance to hear specific facts about the new top-secret weapon.

"Welcome aboard, Admiral," Captain Lawrence Gavin said as Jenetta stepped from the shuttle with her two jumakas and her aide, Commander Ashraf.

"Thank you, Larry. I'm delighted to be aboard again." Jenetta paused and breathed deeply, then exhaled. "Ah, just as I remember it."

Gavin chuckled. "Feels like coming home, doesn't it?"

"It feels like years rather than just the eight months since we returned from Earth."

"Shall we go to your bridge office, Admiral?"

Jenetta nodded, and a few minutes later they were in a transport car zipping through the two-kilometer-long ship. Arriving at the frame section where the Admiral's bridge was located, they exited the car and entered a lift. When they stepped from the lift car, they were just a short walk from the corridor that led to the Admiral's bridge. Three Marine sentries were on duty there— one at the entrance to the corridor, one at the entrance to the Admiral's suite, and the third at the entrance to the bridge.

A tactical officer and com chief were the only personnel on duty on the Admiral's bridge when they entered, and both came to immediate attention.

"As you were," Jenetta said, then disappeared into her office with Captain Gavin right behind her. "Coffee, Larry?" she asked as she headed to the beverage dispenser. Her two jumakas headed to their favorite spots in the room.

"Thanks, Jen," he said. "I could go for a cup." He followed her over to the dispenser and accepted the mug when she held it out to him, then followed her to the informal seating area. Once both were settled, he said, "If I have to go into battle again, I'm glad you're leading the charge."

"This will be the first time we aren't on the front line. The missiles that the Denubbewa use mean we can't expose ourselves as we have in past wars. The scout-destroyers will take the lead, and even they won't be exposing themselves in a traditional sense. Let me explain the offensive strategy we'll be using."

Ten minutes later, Gavin said, "Whew. I'd heard the rumors about a new secret weapon, but this is above and beyond what I ever expected. So if I understand correctly, if the bomb reintegrates into an open area, it will detonate, but if it reintegrates inside a bulkhead or deck, it might not?"

"We don't know what the percentage of detonations would be under those circumstances. It's been speculated that if the bulkhead or deck intruded into the nuclear core, the reaction would be completely nullified, and that makes perfect sense because it wouldn't be able to reach critical mass. It would all depend on where the interruption occurs within the bomb."

"And if it fails to detonate?"

"The scout-destroyer will make another pass and try again. And again and again until we accomplish our goal, which is the complete destruction of the mother ship. My head of Weapons Research and Development, Captain DeWitt, estimates that as many as three out of four bombs could reintegrate inside a bulkhead or deck. But we'll keep at it until their ship looks twice as bad as the *Yenisei* and the *Salado*."

"Do we have enough ordnance for that?"

"The AB increased my modest ordnance request to fifteen thousand devices. I had no way of knowing if the idea was even workable, so I kept the original quantities low. Apparently, the AB had greater confidence in the idea and built enough for a protracted engagement. One thousand have already been loaded into the cradles of the ten bombers, and the other fourteen thousand are securely stored in a hold of the *Ferdinand*."

"I wondered why we were bringing a DS quartermaster transport with us."

"It had just delivered cargo to Quesann. I *appropriated* it temporarily for this campaign. I sent a vidMail to Admiral Ahmed, but since communication with Earth takes almost eighteen days, she hasn't received it yet. I doubt she'll object, given the gravity of the situation."

"I'm sure she won't. Are there really mother ships that are five times the size of the asteroid where Stewart SCB is located?"

"The mother ships are twice the length of the base but many times the width and depth. We have no idea how they're constructed inside, but they definitely have enough size to support hundreds of thousands of beings."

"And there are three of them?"

"That was the count in the last daily reports from the ships tasked to keep an eye on them. What we fear now is that more might be on the way. We have intelligence that says the ships here have reported back that this part of space is ripe for a takeover. They've requested a full contingent of ships to support their play. I assume that means an armada of those ships with tens of thousands of missiles."

Gavin nodded silently as he thought about the ramifications.

"That's the situation we're facing this time, Larry. Not a rosy picture. I'm betting everything we've got on this new weapon."

"That's good enough for me."

"I guess we should get going. We don't want to be late arriving at the party."

Gavin smiled, finished off his coffee and stood up. "Yes, ma'am, Admiral."

As he headed for the door, Jenetta said, "Come on back after we're underway. We have some catching up to do."

Gavin looked back, smiled again, and said, "Yes, ma'am, Admiral."

* * *

Stephen Strauss plopped into his office chair and sighed. He wasn't enjoying the job half as much as he'd expected. Life had become one long series of boring meetings. He'd always been the sort that enjoyed life on the front lines, and now he was just a button pusher. But it would all be worth it when he moved up to the Upper Council. They had four vacant positions to fill now that the four former members were gone. While the Lower Council members worked their tails off keeping the corporation running day to day, the Upper Council met just once a week to set policy and then disappeared back to their luxury existences as wealthy patrons of the arts or whatever.

Activating his computer, he checked his message queue. He was surprised to see one from the Upper Council Chairman. Perhaps this was what he'd been waiting for. He excitedly called the message and leaned in to provide a retinal scan. The DNA Manipulation process was complete for all soft tissues, so his retinal image and finger prints were identical to that of the real Strauss. Or at least identical to what had been the real Strauss before the flesh was melted from his bones and the rest became pet food.

Strauss smiled as the message began to play.

"Arthur," the image of the gorgeous Chairman said, "it's time to fill the vacancies on the Upper Council. We've long been impressed with your managerial capabilities and would love to have you join us— but we just don't have anyone who can fill your shoes. So we've decided to double your salary and expense accounts and have you remain where you are. We know the Lower Council will continue to perform at its extraordinary level under your guidance.

"But we still need to promote four top executives, so we've selected Erika Overgaard, Bentley Blosworth, Frederick Kelleher, and Ahil Fazid. It's not necessary that you notify them. We've already taken care of that. They'll join us at the next regularly scheduled meeting. In the meantime, you'll work with them to promote someone from each of their departments to the Lower Council. That's all."

Strauss barely heard the words after being told he wasn't being promoted to the Upper Council. That had been the reason for almost everything he'd done in the past year. It was the reason he became Strauss and stuck himself into this miserable job. And for what? Double pay? He could siphon off more than that every day. Strauss stood up and strode around the office until his anger started to wane. With the Age Regression and Age Prolongation formulas available to the Upper Council members, there would be little chance of positions opening in the near future from natural causes, or possibly at all. So his main task now was to arrange for a few openings on the Upper Council from *unnatural* causes, starting with the job of the current chairman.

* * *

"Hi, Larry," Jenetta said. "Come on in."

Jenetta was on the deck of her living room, combing the thick fur of Cayla as Gavin entered the room. Tayna was on her back next to Jenetta, squirming around on the carpet as if trying to relieve an itch. Jenetta had just finished sending her daily vid-Mails to family and friends, and it was now time to devote a little attention to her pets. It was playtime and grooming time, and the large cats were enjoying every minute of it.

"You wanted to see me, Jen?"

"Yes. I wanted to inform you that I've received a message from Captain Zakir Singh of the DS destroyer *Duluth*. He says that another mother ship has arrived at the RP. I want your tac officers to be on high alert for anything out of the ordinary. We have no idea how many of these things there are in GA space, but if we encounter any on the way to the RP, we'll stop and engage them. We can't afford to let any of them slip through our fingers."

"We're still forty-eight days from the RP. Do you think the four mother ships will still be there when we arrive?"

"I tasked five SD's, the *Gambia*, *Mekong*, *Nile*, *Rio Grande*, and *Yukon*, plus the DS destroyer *Duluth*, to keep an eye on them. If they leave the RP, our ships have orders to follow them. We'll know where they are at all times. It might be a little easier to take them on if they're still clustered, but we'll pursue and destroy if they're on the move. As far as we know, their top speed is Light-467, so they can't escape from us once we've found them."

"What if they do have Light-9790 capability?"

"One of the ships was first spotted by a Territorial Guard ship. The mother ship was under power and the TG ship correctly followed Standing Orders and avoided contact, but when they filed a report, we deployed two SD's to locate it and verify its reported course. Our ships then returned to the RP, but it took the mother ship months to arrive there. It doesn't make sense that they wouldn't have used Light-9790 if they had the capability."

"There is one possibility." Gavin stopped talking and stared at Jenetta.

"I'm listening."

"With their propulsion system, Light-9790 might consume much more energy than Light-450, and they were in no real hurry to get there since they knew when the mother ships were scheduled to begin their operation."

Jenetta was silent as she thought about the possibility that Gavin was right. They didn't know how the mother ship created its envelope, so it was possible. "You might have a point, Larry. We just won't know until they either use it or we get a chance to examine their ships."

"There's another thing that's been nagging at me since you explained the new weapons system." As before, Gavin stopped and waited for some indication that he should continue.

"I'm listening."

"What if the mother ship is traveling at Light-467 when you attack? Transverse Wave travel relies on having two DATFA envelopes with distinctly different resonances so they don't merge. What if one of the envelopes has the same resonance as the envelope of the mother ship? Will one of the SD envelopes merge with the mother ship envelope? Will the merge cause the collapse of the second envelope of the SD ship? Or might the mother ship develop a second envelope and suddenly be traveling at Light-9790 themselves?"

"Larry, stop, you're giving me a headache."

Gavin smiled. "Sorry. I got carried away. It's just that I haven't been able to stop thinking about these things since our last meeting."

"First, I don't know what will happen in all of those situations. They're some of the 'lingering questions we have about its operational effectiveness' that I mentioned when I described it to you.

"Second, the Transverse Wave dynamic moves the physical object out of phase with the normal three-dimensional dynamic, so it *should* be unaffected by passing through a ship enclosed in a single envelope. We believe that the envelopes won't merge and that the mother ships won't adopt any of the properties of the dual envelopes enclosing our ships.

"Of course, we won't know for sure without substantial testing. Your concerns were raised during preparation for this operation, and the scientists in Region One are supposed to be testing, or planning to test, the various situations to learn the answers. Since the Denubbewa may decide to become aggressive any day, we don't believe we can wait for testing to be completed."

"Okay, Jen. I guess we'll learn together what will happen."

"Larry, I wouldn't risk our people if I thought it was likely we'd lose them. There's a risk, but it's one we have to take. Once this enemy gets started, we might not be able to stop them from sweeping through GA space. We have no other viable defense against these aliens."

* * *

"We're coming up on your stop, Trader," Commander Garth Ginsburg of the *Edison* said when Vyx responded to the summons to come to the captain's office. "You'll be about a day from Uthlarigasset."

"Thanks for the ride, Captain," Vyx said.

"My pleasure. It was a nice break from the usual. Say, what do you think will happen now?"

"About what, Captain?"

"About that shipyard we saw?"

"I don't know, sir. We know it's an act of sedition by the Uthlaro, but it's so far outside the GA in unclaimed space that someone at the top will have to make a decision if we'll even take any action. We've done our part by identifying its location. Just between us, I suspect that Admiral Carver will take appropriate action, even if it's something we never hear about. Thank you for saving us more than four years of travel, Commander."

"My pleasure, Trader."

"And uh— you'll forget all about us now, right?"

"You were never here."

"Thanks again, Commander."

* * *

"Good morning," Captain Zakir Singh of the DS destroyer *Duluth* said to the faces of the five captains that appeared on the bulkhead monitor in his office. "I've just received notice that the Battleship *Ares*, a Quartermaster support ship named the *Ferdinand*, and a taskforce of ten SD's are headed to this location. Admiral Carver is aboard the *Ares*."

"The Admiral?" Commander Mojica of the *Nile* said in surprise.

"Yes."

"That has to mean we're finally going to get some payback for the *Yenisei*, the *Salado*, and the people we lost from the *Gambia* while trying to recover the *Salado*." Commander Teffler of the *Gambia* said.

"Perhaps," Captain Singh said.

"It has to be," Commander Fischer of the *Yukon* said. "There couldn't be any other reason for the Admiral to come here."

"Thank you for the benefit of your wisdom, Commander," Captain Singh said.

"Uh— sorry sir. It just seems so obvious. Whenever Jenetta Carver is near a dangerous situation, it ends in battle."

"Yes, well, we'll see about that when she gets here."

"Do we know when she expects to arrive, sir?" Commander Fischer of the *Yukon* asked.

"In thirty-two days."

*   *   *

"I want to die," PFC Kilburn lamented. "I just want to die. Why won't God let us die, Corporal?"

"God will choose when we die," Corporal Rondara said. "It's not up to us."

"I can't go on like this."

"We have no choice. They feed us through a tube, so we can't starve ourselves, and we have no limbs, so we can't fight back. We just have to pray that God takes us before much longer."

"What are they doing to us? We get a dozen injections a day and they take blood three times."

"I'm not a doc. I don't know what they're doing, but lately I've felt really funny in my belly. Does my belly look bigger to you?"

Kilburn looked at her abdomen. "Yeah, it does."

"Shit. I think they've impregnated me. And they didn't even buy me a nice dinner first."

Chapter Twenty-Five
~ February 7th, 2288 ~

"They're not there, Lieutenant," the tac officer on the bridge of the *Gambia* said.

"None of them?" Lt. Amanda Hess said.

"Not a one."

"Damn," she said under her breath. Tapping her Space Command ring, she said, "Captain."

Commander Wilson Teffler rolled over and tried to focus on the chronograph mounted on the bulkhead. He stopped, rubbed his eyes and looked again. It still said 0404. He reached over and lifted the cover of the com unit. "Captain."

"Captain, the mother ships are gone."

"All of them?"

"Aye, sir."

"Dammit, dammit, dammit. Of all times for this to happen. The Admiral is arriving *tomorrow*. No, she's arriving *today*."

"Should I notify the *Duluth*, sir?"

"Yes, we'll have to initiate a search right away, but it's Captain Singh's call. I'll be on the bridge in ten minutes, but start the ball rolling."

"Aye, sir. I'll take care of it right away."

"Teffler, out."

"Hess, out."

Commander Teffler arrived on the bridge nine minutes later.

"The *Duluth* has scheduled a senior officer's conference for 0500, sir," Lt. Hess said.

"Fine. Com, alert Lt. Commander Lawrence that he's to be in my office by 0459." Walking towards his office, he said, "I'm available until 0500 if you need me."

"Aye, sir," Lt. Hess said.

Teffler plopped into his chair and stared at the blank bulkhead monitor. He was still sitting there when the computer announced that Lt. Commander Lawrence was at the door. "Come," he said.

"Good morning, sir. I hear we have a problem."

"Yes, indeed. I was just sitting here wondering how they could possibly have known that Admiral Carver was coming today."

"That doesn't seem reasonable, sir."

"No, you're right. It isn't reasonable. I'm just frustrated that we've been sitting around here on our backsides for months, watching those mother ships do nothing, and they pick today to pack up and leave."

"I doubt they're leaving, sir."

"I meant leaving this RP, XO. They're not leaving GA space. They came here for a purpose. I suppose we're lucky it took them so long to assemble their forces. It gave our side some time to prepare. I have no idea what Admiral Carver has up her sleeve this time, but I can't wait to kick some Denubbewa butt. We lost a lot of good people over that *Salado* incident, and I've been itching to get some licks in ever since."

"We'll find them again, sir. Their FTL speed is limited."

"Yes, we will. But right now it's time for Captain Singh's conference broadcast."

Teffler activated the monitor and the screen filled with images broadcast from the captain's offices aboard the other ships. At exactly 0500, Singh looked up from what he was doing and said, "Good morning, though there's little good about it. By now you've probably heard that the four mother ships we've been tasked to watch have disappeared. At this time we don't know if they left singly or in a group. I've just spoken to the watch officer aboard the *Ares* and informed him that the mother ships have departed the RP. He'll notify Captain Gavin and Admiral Carver at the appropriate time. I informed him that we're commencing a search immediately. While we hoped we'd never need them, we do have search plans ready in case this happened. We've already sent assignments to each of your ship's tac officers and navigators. Each ship can depart this location as soon as you're ready. Any questions?"

When no one spoke up, Singh added, "Okay, let's go find those mother— ships. Singh, out."

* * *

"Loretta," Admiral Moore said, "You said you wished to make a comment for the record during this closed meeting?"

The Admiralty Board was meeting in closed session because of the topics being discussed. Only the admirals and their senior aides were present. Even clerks with top-secret clearance were denied access at this level.

"Yes, Richard. Thank you. My comment pertains to Project Gazebo. Many months ago, when we first learned of the new weapon being proposed by Admiral Carver, I stated that the weapon was unfeasible because it was impossible to drop a bomb with any accuracy while traveling at almost three billion kilometers a second. I firmly believed that the idea was foolhardy but couldn't offer an alternative at the time, so I didn't oppose Admiral Carver's ordnance request. Since that time it's been proven that Admiral Carver's idea was unworkable. The head of her Weapons Research and Development section, Captain DeWitt, and her team were unable to *drop* a bomb with accuracy greater than a million kilometers because targeting was impossible at Light-9790. The weapon was a complete failure— at that point.

"However, Admiral Carver came up with a new idea for targeting that uses two SD's working together. A lead ship performs the targeting and signals the release of the bomb being carried to the target by the second ship. The Weapons R&D people are to be congratulated because they have successfully established a consistent drop radius of just fifteen meters. That's no less than astounding and is almost beyond belief because we're talking about timing the event in nanoseconds. I applaud everyone involved with this project and I'm glad my initial opposition to this project did not prevent work from progressing on it.

"As a result of the success of this project, new questions have been raised regarding the potential hazards of ships traveling in Transverse Wave envelopes coming into contact with other ships. Testing conducted when Light-9790 was still in development proved that the ship would pass through any solid object without damage to either the ship or the object. Unfortunately, no tests were ever conducted where the double-envelope ship passed through an object with a single envelope in place or an object with a double envelope in place. That testing will take place as soon as it can be arranged.

"I can say that a panel of physicists who have recently examined the issue at length concur that if two ships, both of which had active double-envelopes in place, happened to collide, the effect would be the same as a collision between two ships where neither had a double-envelope in place. The panel was split as to what would happen if a ship with a double envelope attempted to pass through a ship with a single envelope. Half believe there would be no effect and half believe the results could be disastrous.

"You all remember what happened when Admiral Carver tried to take the *Colorado* to maximum speed during its space trials. The ship formed a second envelope a second before a massive short circuit fused all the circuits on the ship's main grid. They went flying through space out of control at Light-9793.48 for almost two weeks before the ship's Automatic Collision System shut the drive down.

"When we were attempting to make Light-9790 practical for everyday use, we discovered that we had to create both envelopes simultaneously. We've been trying ever since then to find a way to build the second envelope on top of the first but without success. Half of our physicists believe that if a ship with a double envelope flew through a ship with a single envelope, the envelope incongruity would short circuit the electrical system in both ships. It could even cause the envelopes to cancel, at which time the ship with the double envelope would reintegrate within the other."

"The ship would be merged with the ship it was passing through?" Admiral Hillaire said.

"This is all supposition and conjecture. Reintegrating within another ship is obviously the worst scenario. It's something that half of the physicists feel *might* happen, not what *will* happen."

"Then with ships that have managed to build their envelope, the bombs are as useless as torpedoes and laser arrays?" Admiral Bradlee asked.

"Loretta is only stating what the physicists have speculated might occur," Admiral Platt said. "It may happen, or it might all remain just textbook theory without any basis in fact."

"Still, I think we have to be very careful when employing this new technology until we know for sure what will happen or could happen," Admiral Woo said.

"Admiral Carver should be nearing the RP of the enemy mother ships as we speak. This information is just in and won't reach her for about forty days. She may know the true story long before she receives a copy of this report."

"Then I pray the conjecture about reintegration of our ship inside an enemy ship is erroneous," Admiral Moore said.

* * *

"Come," Jenetta said when the annunciator system responded to Captain Gavin's presence at the office door.

Gavin entered and walked to where Jenetta was sitting on a sofa in her informal area.

"You look depressed," Gavin said.

"I feel like we were invited to a party and the invitation contained the wrong date."

"I know how you feel. You prepare yourself for the confrontation and possible loss of life, then feel an emptiness when it doesn't happen. It's not a sadness that we don't have to kill today or see our people killed, it's just a disappointment that the event has been postponed and we'll again have to steel ourselves and brace for battle when we find the enemy. But find them we will."

"I know. To stay focused, I've been trying to think of all the possible reasons why they've left the RP now."

"And your decision?"

"No decision. Just a list of possibilities."

"Have you considered that they might have headed back towards unclaimed space?"

Jenetta looked up at Gavin solemnly. "Maybe I didn't think of *all* the possibilities."

"It is possible."

"Yes, it is. And if they did head back towards the border, it might take awhile to find them because the early search pattern areas are all inward towards the populated centers of Region Two. If the searchers fail to find them there, they'll search laterally. Searching back towards the border will be last. Have a seat, Larry."

After Gavin had taken a seat in a comfortable chair facing the sofa, he said, "What will you do if we find them heading back towards the border?"

"You have to ask?"

"Just wondering if I'm right."

"I'll do the same thing I'd do if we find them heading *into* Region Two."

"You won't just let them leave?"

"No. They destroyed two of our ships and murdered their crews. I don't think for a moment that if we find them heading towards open space it's because they're leaving forever. If anything, they're simply falling back until reinforcements arrive. I don't intend to let them leave and then wait for them to attack again. We tried that with Maxxiloth, and I have no doubt the consequence would be the same here. If we locate them, I intend to prosecute this undeclared war to its fullest extent. When the legions back home, wherever that is, fail to make contact with the ships they sent, they'll understand that the GA is not the pushover they're expecting. That message must resonate loud and clear."

"Then we offer no quarter?"

"No more than they offered us. I once told someone that it's an immutable fact of war that you must be just as brutal as the enemy if you're ever to see an end to a conflict. We didn't invite the Denubbewa here and certainly did nothing to precipitate their attack. So we'll give them as good as we've gotten, if not better, and keep on giving it to them until they beg for mercy or they're dead. And I sort of hope they don't beg for mercy."

* * *

"Something's different," PFC Vincent Kilburn said.

"Different how?" Corporal Beth Rondara asked.

"They haven't been in to take any blood today. They've only injected stuff into us."

"Yeah. I hadn't noticed. My tummy is really upset today."

"You're getting big."

"It's too fast for a normal pregnancy."

"I wonder who the father is?"

"I assumed it was you."

"Me? I've never touched you."

"Not you directly. I assumed they— milked you— somehow."

"I don't remember anything like that happening."

"They had to get the sperm from somewhere."

"Maybe it's from their species."

"Oh, God. I hope not. It's bad enough they've cut off our arms and legs, cut out our vocal cords, and implanted something into us that makes us telepathic. A half-breed baby would be the final straw. It would be like those experiments the Nazis did during World War II on Earth."

"I don't know anything about them. What did they do?"

"During the trials for war criminals following the war, it was learned that the Nazis experimented on Jewish concentration camp prisoners for a number of things, including injecting them with deadly diseases to later test possible vaccines and experiments that examined ethnicity."

"So you think they're injecting us with deadly diseases to see if we're immune?"

"They might be looking for something they can release on all planets to kill the human population but which is harmless to their race if they later decide to colonize that planet."

"Bastards."

"Literally."

"What?"

"They probably don't know who their parents are."

"That's not what I meant. I mean, it is, but it isn't."

"I know."

"So, you think you're having a half-breed baby and I've been injected with deadly diseases?"

"It all fits, but I could be totally wrong. Perhaps the father of the baby is one of the other Marine or Space Command males that were aboard the *Salado* with us. And perhaps the injections and blood work are to understand our physiology."

"Or perhaps they're trying to determine what it would take to make us like them?"

"That's also a possibility."

"I'm going to assume that whatever they're doing, it's not something we'd like."

"I agree with that."

"So the best thing that could happen to us is to die peacefully or die quickly."

"I agree with that also."

*   *   *

"Captain," the tac officer aboard the *Yukon* said. "We've passed beyond the furthest point any of the mother ships could have traveled at Light-467."

"Helm, move us to the next vector and head back towards the RP."

"Aye, Captain."

"Captain," the tac officer said, "if the mother ships traveled a distance from the RP and then changed course, we might miss them searching like this. We're assuming they traveled in a straight line from the RP."

"That's true, Lieutenant. But it's the most logical search pattern based on their past history of movement and the expected objectives of an enemy fleet that has invaded our space with intentions to conquer."

"Yes, sir— if they were human."

* * *

"What the hell is *that*?" Captain Gwilloquak of the Milori freighter *Detrizoqan* said when the security station crewman put the image up on the monitor at the front of the bridge.

"It appears to be a ship, sir."

"I know it's a ship, you fool. Where did it come from? Is it Gondusan? What are they doing in GA space? Is it going to intersect our course?"

"It's not Gondusan. According to the ship identification database, it resembles a Ruwalchu warship. Their course is almost parallel with ours, so there's no danger if neither of us alters direction."

"Can't be Ruwalchu. We're at least ten light-years from the Ruwalchu border. Their ships never travel outside their own space."

"I can only tell you what the database reports. The hull shape and weaponry mounted on the ship is consistent with what's been reported for Ruwalchu warships in the past."

"Com, report this encounter to the Territorial Guard."

"Aye, Captain."

"Should I maintain course, Captain?" the helmsman asked.

"Security, has the Ruwalchu vessel changed course or speed?"

"No change, Captain. She's had to have seen us by now."

"Of course she's seen us. We're maxed out with ten kilometers of cargo. She could see us even without DeTect capability. Helm, maintain course and speed."

"Aye, Captain."

"I reported the sighting on the Territorial Guard channel, Captain," the com chief said. "No response yet."

"There probably aren't any ships nearby. Well, we've done our duty. If the Ruwalchu ship doesn't attempt interdiction, we'll simply continue on to our destination."

* * *

Strauss sat in his beautiful penthouse suite, tossing down glass after glass of wine and cursing the DNA Manipulation process that had altered his physiology so that alcohol had virtually no effect. He desperately wanted to get so drunk he would pass out, but his body wouldn't allow it. He could enjoy the taste of wine, but it had little more effect than drinking water. He would switch to hard liquor if that would have more effect, but it would be the same, and he preferred the taste of wine.

So far, none of the eight senior members of the Upper Council had decided to become male again. They actually seemed to be enjoying their new gender. It had been so long since any of them had enjoyed sex that they probably hadn't discovered how unsatisfying it was for a former male. His unfettered access to every division in the Raider corporation had enabled him to substitute a deadly formula for the correct DNA Manipulation formula, but he couldn't force the Upper Council members to begin the process. They would have to initiate that themselves.

It had been weeks since he'd substituted the formulas and the longer it was before they started the change, the more likely it was that someone might discover the menace of the current formula.

Strauss finished off a bottle and opened another. It just wasn't fair. He'd worked so hard to get to the Upper Council and had been deprived of his rightful place. And to heap injury on top of injury, four of Strauss's subordinates had been promoted over him. Not just one but four. Strauss downed the entire liter before lowering the bottle. At that moment, he would have paid almost any price for the ability to get falling-down drunk.

Chapter Twenty-Six
~ February 15th, 2288 ~

Captain Gavin was having supper with Jenetta when he heard a soft chime in his ear and a message that the watch commander was trying to contact him. He touched a finger to the face of his Space Command ring and heard the voice of his XO.

"Captain, we've just intercepted a message on the Territorial Guard Reporting channel. A Milori freighter claims to have spotted a Ruwalchu warship ten light-years inside our border. They gave the location, speed, and heading of the ship. Our navigator confirms that the location cited is eleven-point-two-six-eight light-years inside the border we share with the Ruwalchu. I thought you should know right away in case you wish to take action."

"Thank you, Commander. No action at present. Gavin, out."

"Interesting," was all Gavin said after the contact ended.

"Don't rouse my interest and then go silent," Jenetta said, and punctuated it with a smile.

"Oh, sorry. We just intercepted a message from a Milori freighter to the Territorial Guard. The freighter claims to have spotted a Ruwalchu warship in our space, eleven light-years this side of the border."

"Not just a Ruwalchu ship, but a Ruwalchu *war*ship?"

"That's how the report read," Gavin said.

"Interesting," Jenetta said, also in an enigmatic manner.

"Have you ever heard of a Ruwalchu warship, or any Ruwalchu ship, entering GA space?"

"No. They've never entered our space as far as I know."

"So why now?"

"Ever since we learned of the Denubbewa ships, I've wondered if there was a connection to any of our former foes. Unusual events involving the Tsgardi and Uthlaro have occurred since I returned from Region One. Now we have a neighbor with whom we've never had a problem entering our space with a warship. The question is: Are *any* of these events related to the situation with the Denubbewa?"

"Perhaps the thing to do is confront the Ruwalchu ship."

"How far are we from their location?"

"Off hand, I'd have to say about nine to ten days at Light-9790."

"It could take weeks to find the Denubbewa ships again," Jenetta said. "Rather than sitting around here, let's see if we can find the Ruwalchu warship that's in our territory. Have the *Ferdinand* remain here, along with eight of the bombers and eight of the targeting ships. We'll take the other two bombers and targeting ships with us."

Gavin nodded and then touched his ring to activate a carrier signal. He relayed Jenetta's instructions to his XO, then closed the carrier with a "Gavin, out." Picking up his fork, he said, "Everything is in the works. We should be on our way to the estimated location of the Ruwalchu ship within the hour. ETA is roughly nine days, eighteen hours. We'll have an exact time once we're under way."

* * *

The Ruwalchu ship wasn't at the estimated location when the *Ares* and its small battle group arrived, but no one really expected it to be. It would have been beyond luck to find it exactly where they estimated it might be after almost ten days of travel.

The five ships that comprised the battle group then divided up and began a search of the sector. One of the SD's located the ship after just two days of searching. The rest of the ships joined it at an established RP an hour from the last reported location of the vessel. When the group was whole again, they moved to intercept the ship. After passing it at Light-9790, the task group returned to position themselves in the path of the Ruwalchu ship, dropped their double envelopes, and established a single envelope.

The Ruwalchu ship DeTect'd the battle group ahead of it and came to a halt a million kilometers from the SC ships. It had been crisscrossing this part of space for many months expecting to find a Space Command vessel on patrol, but its captain had never expected to come face to face with an entire battle group.

Jenetta was on the Admiral's bridge and had her com chief attempt to make contact. It took several minutes, but the Ruwalchu ship finally responded. Jenetta was able to get her first real-time look at a Ruwalchite. The creature that stared back at her looked oddly disproportionate by human standards. It had a thick body, almost massively thick, and two spindly arms that each ended in eight fingers. It didn't have shoulders exactly. The top part of its body just narrowed into a wide head. There was no visible nose, but it had a mouth and two eyes.

"I'm Admiral Jenetta Carver, the Military Governor of this part of space. I welcome you to Region Two. How may we assist you? Do you need help finding your way back to the Ruwalchu Confederacy border?"

The Ruwalchite military officer simply stared at her. He knew he was outgunned by a contingent of military vessels whose weapons were every bit as powerful as those of his own ship.

Jenetta had delivered her little speech, so it was up to the Ruwalchu to either respond or take some action. She sat patiently, as if she had all the time in the world.

The Ruwalchite finally responded. "How dare you block our passage."

"You're in Galactic Alliance space. You have no right of passage here."

"We are the Ruwalchu Military. We go where we please, when we please."

"That's fine, when you're inside your own nation. But right now you're in our nation, and we decide where you may go and when."

"I've heard of you. Your arrogance is legendary."

"Is it? You haven't told me your name yet."

"I am Captain Debillisa of the *Vormeddo*, a ship of the Ruwalchu Confederacy Space Society, Advanced Fleet Services, Section Two, Division Four."

"Thank you. And can you tell me why you've invaded our space?"

"We go where we please, when we please."

"You've said that once already. Are you saying you don't respect a neighbor's borders?"

"We go where we please, when we please."

Jenetta sat and stared at the Ruwalchite. He was definitely in the wrong, but as far as she knew, he hadn't attacked any ships or settlements and hadn't broken any laws other than trespassing. She wasn't about to start a shooting war simply because he had trespassed in GA space. She also believed she wasn't going to get anywhere talking with him. He almost seemed to be daring her to attack.

Jenetta touched a point on her left-hand monitor from among a row of contact points just below the image of Captain Gavin. An instant later, the communication between the *Ares* and the *Vormeddo* ended. At the same instant all five ships engaged their FTL drive at maximum. They passed the Ruwalchu ship, still sitting where it had stopped, at almost one hundred thirty-five million kilometers per second. If the Ruwalchu ship had fired torpedoes, they never would have even cleared the tubes before the SC ships were a distant memory.

The Ruwalchu captain had expected an attack as a result of his displayed attitude. General Ardlessel had been quite specific on what Debillisa's responses should be when the *Vormeddo* encountered a patrol ship, and despite the fact that they had encountered not one but five ships, he had played the part as spelled out by Advanced Fleet Services Command.

When the communication ended and Jenetta's image disappeared from the monitor at the front of the bridge, Debillisa yelled, "Tactical, prepare to fire torpedoes, but *they* must fire first."

"But they're gone, sir."

"What?"

"They're gone. They're almost a billion kilometers away right now."

"Gone?"

"Yes, sir. They left the instant the communication ended."

Debillisa sat back in his command chair, stunned. This was as unexpected as encountering five ships on patrol. This certainly didn't fit the image of the enemy identified in his mission briefing.

Once beyond the four-billion-kilometer range of the DeTect system, the five ships stopped, canceled their single envelopes and built Transverse Wave envelopes. In just over two minutes they were underway again, but this time they were traveling at Light-9790.

Captain Gavin left third officer Lt. Commander Eliza Carver in command of the bridge while he went to the Admiral's bridge to talk with Jenetta.

"That went well," Gavin said facetiously.

"Think so?" Jenetta said, in the same spirit. "I think I would have liked a more congenial first contact."

"What now?"

"Now, we give them a taste of their own."

"I don't understand."

"That was an obvious confrontation. They wanted us to react badly. Now we allow them the same opportunity. Let's head for Ruwalch."

"You intend to invade the Ruwalchu Confederacy?"

Mimicking the voice of Captain Debillisa, she said, "We go where we please, when we please."

Gavin chuckled. "I hope you know what you're doing."

"It was obvious we weren't going to get any answers from Debillisa. When we reach Ruwalch, make sure that none of the ships drop their TW envelopes. We're not going to fire torpedoes or lasers despite any provocation. This is a talking mission."

"I'll make sure all ship captains understand that."

"Do you have a rough idea of the travel time required to reach their planet?"

"I'll have to check with my navigator, but I'd say between twenty to thirty days if we go around the Hudeerac nation. If we take a shortcut through their space, we could save probably five to seven days."

"Five days would be a nice saving. I'll contact them and ask for permission to cross through their space, going and returning."

"I hope we'll be returning."

"No problem. If we never drop our TW envelope, they can't touch us."

"Never underestimate an enemy. A year ago we thought no one could harm a Dakinium-sheathed ship."

"You're right. I have to remember not to depend too much on the technological wonders we've created or discovered."

* * *

Hudeerac Intelligence Minister Vertap Aloyandro's eyes opened wide as he listened to the message from Admiral Carver. As it finished, he immediately contacted the king's secretary and asked for a meeting as soon as possible. The secretary said the king had completed his last appointment early and didn't have another scheduled for thirty minutes, so if Aloyandro was brief, he could come right away. Aloyandro was on his way out the door of his office a few seconds later.

"My King," Aloyandro said with utmost respect, "I've just received a communication from Admiral Carver."

"Is there a problem?"

"Uh— not a problem, Your Highness. It's a request. She asks for permission to cross our space into Ruwalchu space."

"She's attacking the Ruwalchu? And she wants to involve us? The Ruwalchu will accuse us of being complicit."

"She states categorically that she is not planning to engage the Ruwalchu in anything more than dialog. She says she confronted a Ruwalchu warship, the *Vormeddo*, eleven light-years inside their border, and the captain responded most belligerently when asked why he was there."

"Did she destroy the ship?"

"She says she simply broke off contact and decided to take up the issue with the Ruwalchu Gilesset directly. She seeks only friendly dialog."

"And you believe her?"

"To the best of my knowledge, she has never lied to us and has always acted most honorably. Yes, I trust her word."

The king stood and walked around his large office twice as he thought.

"I would like to meet this human. Ask her to stop here."

"Going or coming, sire?"

"Which would you suggest?"

"I imagine she feels some sense of urgency in contacting the Ruwalchu and would be distracted before. I suggest requesting a meeting on her return visit."

"Fine. Give her permission to cross our space and request a meeting on her return trip."

"Yes, Your Majesty. It shall be done."

* * *

"The Hudeerac approved our request," Jenetta said to Gavin, "so plot a course through their nation that will get us to the Ruwalchu Confederacy as quickly as possible."

"We've already plotted the optimal course. We were only waiting for permission. I'll have my helmsman change course immediately."

"Very good. Would you join me for supper tonight?"

"It would be my pleasure."

"Good, I'll see you then."

* * *

Seventeen days after the confrontation with the *Vormeddo*, the five-ship task force approached the solar system where the Ruwalchu had evolved and which still functioned as its capital system. Patrols along the borders shared with the GA had been increased substantially in recent years, but patrols along the border with the Hudeerac were light and the task force never spotted a single military ship until they neared the main system.

"General," an aide whispered desperately to General Ardlessel as he sat in on a planning session, "we've had contact with the Terrans."

"Yes, I read the report from Captain Debillisa days ago," the general whispered back. With a smile he added, "The Terrans ran away."

"Not away, General. They headed here."

"What?" Ardlessel said loudly, interrupting the present speaker at the podium. "What did you say?"

"They've come here, General. They're asking to speak with the Gilesset."

"What do you mean, they've come here? They couldn't have gotten here without being spotted."

"Nevertheless, they're here."

"What do you mean by 'here?'"

"Close enough for almost instantaneous communications."

"Impossible."

The aide simply shrugged.

"Where are they?"

"Just outside our solar system."

Without explaining himself, Ardlessel jumped up and headed to the communications center at a run while the speaker at the podium just stared in stunned silence.

"Let me talk to this Terran!" Ardlessel shouted as he entered the communications center. He walked directly into a secure conference room and closed the door. A few seconds later, the image of Jenetta popped up on the conference monitor.

"I'm Admiral Jenetta Carver," she said as she became aware of the open line. The distance meant that there would be a slight delay, but it would be minor since IDS communications traveled at 8.09 billion kilometers per second.

"I know who you are, Terran. What do you want?"

"I wish to address the Gilesset."

"You can address your comments to me."

"Do you speak for the government? Are your words binding?"

"I'm the senior military officer for all of the Ruwalchu people."

"But you don't speak for the government?"

"I'm empowered to communicate with aliens."

"But you don't speak for the government. You can't commit the government to any policy."

"It doesn't matter. Whatever you have to say can be said to me."

"Thank you, General, and no disrespect, but I'll wait until the policy-makers can be addressed. Contact us on this frequency when that's possible."

With that, the signal from the *Ares* ended.

Ardlessel jumped up, screaming at the blank monitor. His aide, who had followed him into the secure room, said, "She can't hear you, sir. The connection has ended."

"I know that!" he shouted. "Notify the War Council that an emergency meeting has been called. We'll meet in the War Conference Center in two hours."

"But she requested an audience with the Gilesset, sir."

"I don't care *what* she requested. I'm calling an emergency session of the War Council. Now *do* it."

"Immediately, sir."

Two hours later, the Prime Minister called the meeting to order. Member and aides were still scurrying to take their seats.

"What's the emergency, General?" Prime Minister Pemillisa asked as soon as the room quieted down.

"We were just contacted by Admiral Carver, the Terran in command of the former Milori territory."

"Contacted? In response to your forays into their space? Did they engage your ship?"

"No, Prime Minister. They confronted it and then left. When I got the report, I thought they had run away."

"But they didn't?"

"No, Prime Minister. They're here."

"What do you mean by that?"

"Carver and a small task force are outside our system. I spoke with her two hours ago."

"You spoke to her. Via a direct communication?"

"Yes, Mr. Prime Minister."

"Great Protector," the chair of the Space Services committee said. "How did they get here? Are all your ships on the border taking a holiday?"

Turning to face the SS committee chairman, Ardlessel said, "I don't know how they did it, Mr. Chairman. We'll look to solving that riddle later. Right now I'm trying to move assets into place to fight them once they attack."

"Once they attack?" the Prime Minister asked. "If they intended to attack, why haven't they started already?"

"I don't know, Mr. Prime Minister."

"They didn't give the Milori or the Uthlaro advance warning before they attacked their shipyards. Why would she give us an advance warning?"

"I don't know, Mr. Chairman."

"Well, what exactly did she say?" the Prime Minister asked.

"She said she wanted to address the Gilesset. She wouldn't speak with me because I can't set policy for the government."

"Then we should be discussing this in the Gilesset chambers."

"I wouldn't do that, Mr. Prime Minister."

"Why not?"

"I believe it's a ploy to get all the council members together so she can kill them all at once."

"As I recall, she addressed the Uthlaro Council of Ministers directly from just outside their solar system and didn't attack them."

"I don't trust her, Mr. Prime Minister. Our Uthlaro contacts have consistently told us how merciless and untrustworthy she is."

"I think it's worth the risk. She has already evaded all your protections. If she wanted to rain down destruction on us, she could have begun hours ago without giving us warning."

"If you do this, Mr. Prime Minister, we'll all regret it."

"We shall see, General."

Chapter Twenty-Seven

~ March 8th, 2288 ~

Jenetta was working in her office when she received a message from the Admiral's Bridge com chief that an incoming call, purportedly from the Ruwalchu Gilesset, was holding.

"Thank you, Chief," she said as she activated the large monitor on the bulkhead. "Put it through."

The monitor illuminated with a view of the Gilesset chambers. The room was packed and everyone was wearing headphones in preparation for hearing the translation.

"Good morning," Jenetta said.

"Good morning, Admiral," a Ruwalchite said as the camera turned to frame one individual. "I'm Prime Minister Pemillisa. The presence of your small task force in our space surprises us."

"No more, I'm sure, than the presence of one of your warships in our space surprised us."

"I understand we've been receiving daily reports from that ship. We were led to believe you would attack it on sight."

"Then you've been misled, Mr. Prime Minister. As far as I know, and still believe, your warship has not attacked any shipping or planetary settlements. We ask that warships from visiting nations contact us for permission before entering our space, but we never attack first and question later. I tried to determine why your warship was in our space, but the captain was most uncooperative. I decided it was time to open discussions with your government, but we've only been treated with hostility until now."

"Our information has been that you intend to absorb our nation into the Galactic Alliance."

"As I've said, you've been misled. We do not absorb the territory of other nations without due cause. Three large nations, each of them with severe internal problems, exist on the other side of Region One. One is on the verge of full civil war. But as long as they make no effort to absorb our territory, we will not make such an effort towards theirs. We are certainly strong enough to absorb any of them, or all of them at once, but we haven't. Throughout the entire history of the Galactic Alliance, we have only claimed open space, except in those situations where we were first attacked by hostile nations who had designs on our territory. The Milori attacked us, and after we defeated their invasion fleet, we made them leave our territory. Then they came at us again with a larger fleet. We were forced to destroy their entire second invasion force. We knew then that the Milori would never stop attacking us while Maxxiloth was in power, so it became necessary to bring the war he started directly to their planet. We only claimed the territory after their unconditional surrender and as a means to ensure they never attacked us again. The Milori people are now an important part of the GA and are enjoying peace for the first time in many decades.

"We had a similar situation with the Tsgardi. They entered our territory with three hundred warships and intentions of absorbing Region Two in concert with the Uthlaro. I ordered them to leave our space and they attacked us. We knew they would never live in peace with their neighbors, so we destroyed their entire invasion force and absorbed their territory so we might restrict them to just their home system. The planets the Tsgardi enslaved after acquiring space travel capability are now free of any outside rule and beginning to prosper.

"The Uthlaro are yet another example of a nation that attacked us first, and which we knew would never stop attacking us. We were forced to destroy their entire military armada and absorb their territory to keep them from waging war when they again felt strong enough. Even now, after the loss of their territory, they continue to plot against us, and they're actively trying to poison minds against us."

"What you say sounds credible."

"We seek only peace with nations that seek peace in return. We'd like to have friendly relations with the Ruwalchu people, but if you simply want to be left alone, we will leave and never return. All we ask is that you practice what you preach. If you don't want open relations and accessible markets for goods and services, then don't send ships into our territory. Regardless of what you decide regarding trade, we require that you ask permission before sending any *war*ships into our territory."

"And yet you came here with five warships."

"After you sent at least one warship into our territory *first*. And that warship seemed to be deliberately hostile, as if they wanted us to attack them."

"Yes— well, that was a decision by one of our military people. He didn't consult with this body before taking that action."

"Then you'll see that the ship is recalled?"

"I will."

"Thank you. And is it your desire that diplomatic relations be established between our nations, or do you prefer isolationism?"

"We shall have to discuss these issues. I admit that you've opened our eyes a bit."

"Very well. For our part, we prefer to enjoy peaceful diplomatic relations and open trade with our neighbors. With such interaction, they see for themselves where the truth lies rather than relying solely on intelligence from a single source with a private agenda of subversive activity. Should you reach a decision favoring diplomatic relations, you can send a message to the Region Two Headquarters at Quesann and we will send envoys to draft a formal agreement. Our envoys always travel by military vessel, but we are careful to ensure that the nation knows they are coming before we enter their space."

"That raises a question, Admiral. Why is Region Two still under military rule?"

"A great deal of lawlessness still exists in both Region Two and Region Three, although we've made great advances towards establishing the rule of law in Region Two. We're currently building governmental complexes on Quesann, from which the elected civilian government of the Galactic Alliance that currently presides over Region One from their complex on Earth will preside over Regions One and Two, and eventually Region Three.

"Beyond that, military rule must continue until outside nations cease their efforts to arrogate our territory. The Denubbewa Dominancy recently sent a massive war fleet into Region Two. The reason for my presence in this part of space is to confront the invaders with my taskforce. I'm not talking about the small group that has accompanied me here today. When I learned of the presence of your warship in our space, I came here to determine if you are in league with the Denubbewa before we destroy them. I certainly hope your nation isn't involved. Are you involved, Mr. Prime Minister?"

"We are not. We were not even aware of an invasion and have no contact with the Denubbewa."

"I'm glad to hear that."

"I think you've made your case well, Admiral."

"Thank you, Mr. Prime Minister."

"I shall instruct our military not to attack you on your way out of our space."

"That's not necessary, Mr. Prime Minister. Your weapons can't harm us, and your ships will never even see us leave."

"You sound very confident of that, Admiral."

"Yes. Thank you for your time today and the opportunity to introduce myself to the Ruwalchu Gilesset and present my nation's hope for a peaceful coexistence with your nation. Good day."

* * *

Jenetta hadn't felt she could refuse the king's request that she visit the Hudeerac home world upon her return from the Ruwalchu home world. He had, after all, graciously granted permission for the taskforce to cross their space, saving days of travel time. A state visit to a valuable ally seemed a small price, despite her eagerness to return to the sector where the search for the Denubbewa mother ships was still being conducted.

"Admiral Carver, we meet at last," Vertap Aloyandro said as Jenetta stepped out of the shuttle with her two pets at her side and four protection detail people behind. Planetary Airborne Control had directed her small ship to the shuttle pad on the palace grounds.

Jenetta knew from the protocol database that the Hudeerac didn't shake hands, so she didn't extends hers. Instead she bowed slightly and then said, "Minister, I feel very honored to finally meet you in person on this fine morning."

"This is an honor for me as well. When I first made contact with you while you were still the base commander at Stewart SCB, I never expected that we would meet one day. The distance between our nations seemed so great. And now here we are, neighbors."

"Our relationship has certainly had its ups and downs over the years. I'm pleased we seem to have found a mutual ground that allows us to work together for the benefit of both our nations."

"As am I. May I inquire about your visit with the Ruwalchu? Was it successful?"

"We shall see. They had apparently believed we were about to invade their space and absorb them into the Galactic Alliance. I did my best to disabuse them of that idea. Time will tell if I was successful."

"Wherever did they get the idea that you intended to invade their nation?"

"I couldn't deny, and didn't try, that we have expanded our borders substantially during the past decade by defeating the Milori, Tsgardi, and Uthlaro. The Ruwalchu believed they were next."

"I would be most happy to provide an excellent character reference, but alas, the Ruwalchu have no love for us."

"What have *you* done to threaten them?"

"Nothing to threaten them, but I'm afraid we did alienate them by asking for help when Maxxiloth was doing his best to absorb our small nation. They refused, claiming they didn't want to get involved in the disputes of other nations. My king was most upset and told them that if they didn't do something to stop Maxxiloth, it was only a matter of time before he felt powerful enough to crush them and take their territory. Fortunately for them and us, Maxxiloth turned his attention to the Galactic Alliance next. I suppose he felt you were the easier target. I'm happy to say it was his undoing."

"The information you provided about Maxxiloth's clandestine operations in GA space and the estimated date of his second invasion effort was invaluable. We were most grateful you shared that information. That gratitude made it easier to reestablish our former relations after the Uthlaro were defeated."

"I shall always be most embarrassed about our part in the Uthlaro pact, but I suppose things like that will happen in a society where a few short-sighted but powerful political leaders can sway opinions or strong-arm the less powerful into supporting poor choices made for personal gain."

"Yes, such people will always be present in any society."

"I would love to stand here for hours but my sovereign awaits in his chambers. So if you will follow me, Admiral Carver, I'll take you to him." As they moved towards the palace, the Intelligence Minister said, "Uh, your pets are beautiful, Admiral, but palace security will not allow them inside the king's chambers."

"My pets are very well behaved. I assure you they will not be a problem."

"I doubt they will accept that. We have a similar animal in the royal zoo, and over the years it has damaged several zookeepers. One died."

"Jumakas can be dangerous, but usually only to people who either threaten them, their owners, or the owner's property. Is your animal a pure-bred Taurentlus-Thur Jumaka?"

"I only know that it looks like your pets except for the coloration of its fur and eyes."

"I'd like to see it, if possible."

"Of course. I shall arrange for a tour of the zoo following your meeting with the king."

The palace of the king was like so many palaces all over the known galaxy in that it had been constructed to last for hundreds, if not thousands, of years by using the sturdiest building materials available on the planet. On the Hudeerac home world, this meant the building was predominantly made of stone.

Since the Hudeerac people had seemed to evolve from cold-blooded reptiles, it made sense that they would enjoy the warmth of the sun. The palace was designed to offer as many windows as possible and yet still maintain structural integrity. The hallways were lined with rich tapestries and statuary. The decorations reflected the history of the planet and the dominant species.

When the party arrived at the king's chambers, the security guards there insisted that Cayla, Tayna, and Jenetta's armed protection detail remain outside. Jenetta insisted just as strongly that the security detail could wait outside but that her pets went where she went. When the security people refused to bend, Jenetta turned towards Vertap, bowed, and said, "Minister, thank you for inviting me to meet your sovereign. I regret that I won't have that honor on this occasion. If I ever happen to be in this part of space again, I shall inquire if your security forces have relaxed their requirements regarding pets. I can find my own way back to the shuttle pad if you have other commitments on your time."

"Admiral, please, you've come such a long way. Don't leave now without meeting my sovereign."

"That decision is not mine, Minister. Your palace security has decided the issue."

"Please, would you give me a moment?"

Jenetta nodded and Vertap turned and entered the king's chambers. A minute later he reemerged and looked at the head of security, then nodded his head towards the door. The security chief hurried inside. A minute later, the security chief emerged and whispered something in Vertap's ear opening.

"Good news, Admiral. The security chief has decided to make an exception for your visit. You may take your pets into the king's chambers."

"Wonderful. Shall we go in?"

As they entered the chamber, the king stepped forward and extended his hand. The Hudeera had three fingers on each hand— two very wide fingers and an opposing digit that acted like a thumb. Jenetta was surprised by the action but took the proffered appendage and shook it as if they were in a Terran setting.

"Welcome, Admiral Carver. A curious custom, this shaking of hands. How did it come about?"

"Thank you for welcoming me to your planet and your chambers, Your Majesty. The custom of greeting by shaking hands is said to be as old as our civilization. As we've seen everywhere we've traveled in this galaxy, most life forms are very territorial and zealously guard their land. As intelligence increased and trade developed, people stopped killing intruders first and questioning afterward. When meeting, people would shake hands to show they weren't concealing any weapons in their hands or up their sleeves."

"Ah, I see." Turning to Minister Aloyandro, the king said, "That will be all for now, Vertap."

"Yes, My King," Vertap said as he bowed and then backed out of the room.

Turning back to Jenetta, the king said, "I understand that the Family Carver is part of the nobility on Obotymot and that you hold the title of Azula in the Nordakian system?"

"Yes, Your Majesty."

"Excellent." Gesturing towards the comfortable seating area where he often entertained the nobles of his planet, he said, "May I invite you to have a seat in my lounge area? By long tradition, only nobles may sit there."

"Thank you, Your Majesty."

While all of the chairs looked comfortable, one chair in the area stood out for its majestic appearance. Jenetta assumed that was the king's chair and so selected a seat facing it from two meters away. The king smiled and sat in his chair.

"I refer to this as my Seat of Power," he said with a grin as he wiggled slightly to get his short, reptilian tail properly positioned in the cutout at the back of the seat. "The nobles of my planet and I often sit in here and work out our problems. I imagine you have a similar seating arrangement."

"Yes, I have an area in each of my offices where problems and issues can be discussed in comfort. Setting aside even token formality, such as conversing with someone from across a desk, can often open the way for more meaningful discussions of important issues."

"Exactly, Azula Carver."

"Your Majesty, how are things on your planet?"

"At the moment, quiet. Thanks to you and the GA, we've entered a period of peace and prosperity unlike any we've known since before Maxxiloth's grandfather ascended to power."

"I'm glad. I wish we could say the same."

"Ah, yes. Minister Aloyandro has told me of this race called the Denubbewa. They are new to this part of the galaxy."

"And quite powerful, from what we've observed. They destroyed two of our ships before we were aware of their presence in Region Two."

"And none since?"

"All ships were ordered to avoid contact until we had a chance to prepare our defenses."

"And have you?'

"We believe we have a chance now. We've been searching for them."

"Perhaps they've returned to their own part of space."

"No, I don't think so. They believe they're here to stay."

"How can you know that?"

"Would-be conquerors all show a similar pattern of aggression. The Denubbewa haven't left, and we *will* track them down and destroy them."

"I wish we could help."

"Minister Aloyandro has been very helpful, and we appreciate it. It was he who first identified the species we're facing."

"Let us all hope you can eliminate this newest threat and enjoy a time of peace yourselves."

"That is always our wish."

Jenetta spent several hours with the king and then was invited to lunch in the palace dining room. While the king enjoyed the usual delicacy of his planet, live Sqarlibit, the palace chefs had gone to great lengths to prepare a meal of vegetables and fruit they believed would appeal to Jenetta's Terran tastes. She learned later that Vertap had actually contacted the *Ares* after she arrived and spoken to the head nutritionist.

At the end of the meal, the king thanked Jenetta for stopping on her return trip and Jenetta thanked the king for allowing her to save days of travel by crossing through Hudeerac space. He told her that she was always welcome in his kingdom, and she told him that he would always be welcome if he chose to visit Quesann. She didn't really expect to ever see him there unless he got a ride aboard a Space Command vessel. The fastest Hudeerac vessels were only able to achieve Light-387, so it would take almost four years and four months to travel each way as opposed to the sixty-two days it took the *Ares* for each leg of the trip.

Vertap showed up as Jenetta and the king said their goodbyes. He escorted Jenetta to a waiting vehicle for the promised trip to the zoo. Her protection detail followed along in another vehicle.

The animals in the royal zoo represented not just species found on the Hudeerac home planet but from all the planets in their territory and beyond. The zoo was so massive and contained so many exhibits that had they not had the oh-gee cart they could never have seen a tenth of it in one afternoon. Halfway through the tour, they stopped at a building that was closed to the public.

"We don't normally allow visitors in here because the ferocity of this animal frightens most people," Vertap said as he punched in an access code and the door opened.

The air had a peculiar order, and Jenetta could see that it was having an effect on her pets. Vertap turned on the lights, and a cage at the end of the large building became somewhat visible. An animal in the dark recesses of the cage immediately began to growl ominously as they approached.

As they reached the cage, the animal suddenly sprang at the bars. The cage was well constructed, and in addition to the solid bars, a mesh of wire meant that nothing larger than three centimeters in width or height could get through, but the cage shook considerably. Vertap took an involuntary step backward, but Jenetta never moved from her spot two meters from the cage as the animal attacked the bars, snarling viciously.

Cayla and Tayna, who had seemed uneasy since entering the building, immediately moved protectively between Jenetta and the cage, snarling a warning back at the vicious animal. Their action caused the large animal to stop snarling. It stared at the two cats and seemed confused as it observed the way the two cats were protecting the strange-looking, two-legged creature with them.

As Jenetta stared at the large jumaka in the cage, she thought back to the day she had acquired Tayna and Cayla. They had behaved in pretty much the same way initially, a result of having been taunted, starved, and generally mistreated by cargo handlers. They too had jumped at anyone who approached their cage. Treating them with patience and kindness had turned them into cherished pets in a very short time. That spoke volumes about the intelligence of the species.

Unlike Cayla and Tayna, whose fur was black as space and whose yellow eyes seemed to glow, the jumaka in the cage had deep brown fur with dark green eyes. Information about jumakas was limited, so Jenetta didn't know if the differences were normal or if they indicated a different sub-species.

Since the building was closed to the public, Jenetta assumed that zookeepers were responsible for the animal's attitude. It would only take one unhappy guard or janitor to taunt an animal until it turned into a crazed beast. If the jumaka were out in the open, it would be difficult for an employee to torment the animal in a zoo environment, but anyone with access to this building could do it without being observed.

Jenetta squatted down where she had been standing. When the jumaka in the cage had stopped snarling, her cats had quieted down as well. They now began circling Jenetta uneasily. She reached out to Cayla and the jumaka stopped and licked her hand with its rough tongue, then pushed against Jenetta in a sign of affection. Tayna also stopped moving and nuzzled Jenetta. The jumaka in the cage quietly watched everything with great interest until Vertap took a step closer to the cage. As the large jumaka growled a warning, Vertap stepped back. The action quieted the animal.

"Vertap, please stay where you are," Jenetta said.

Rising up, Jenetta took two steps closer to the cage. The jumaka didn't make a sound or even move as she approached the cage bars to within the width of a hand. Cayla and Tayna moved with her.

"Has someone been mistreating you, fella?" Jenetta said to the jumaka in the cage. "Some people can be cruel at times, but we're not all like that."

The jumaka looked at Jenetta, then down at the cats by her legs. It suddenly took a step forward, but not in a threatening way, as it sniffed at her and her pets. Cayla and Tayna responded by sniffing back. The jumaka in the cage then walked calmly right up to the bars and looked at Jenetta. It seemed like a different animal than it had been when they entered.

Jenetta talked calmly and soothingly to the jumaka, and with each passing minute, it seemed to grow calmer. The presence of her two cats no doubt helped considerably by demonstrating to the caged jumaka that some people could be trusted by its species. Its mood change was further made evident when it pressed its muzzle against the wire mesh in an attempt to better capture her smell. She helped by placing the flat of her palm against the bars.

Taking their cue from Jenetta, Cayla and Tayna pressed their muzzles against the bars. The caged jumaka reciprocated and essentially established the first contact when it licked at the wire mesh that separated them.

After a few more minutes of talking to the caged jumaka, Jenetta took a step backward. The large jumaka emitted a sound like a mewl, as if it realized she was about to leave. She gave it one sad last look and then turned and walked towards Vertap.

"That was amazing, Admiral," the minister said. "If I hadn't seen it, I wouldn't have believed it."

"Jumakas are very intelligent animals. I think someone has been abusing yours. Like people, they don't respond well to abuse. Treat it well, and it will respond well."

"Shall we continue the tour?"

"Yes, by all means. The exhibits and species are wonderful."

As they started to leave, Jenetta realized that her cats were not at her side. She hadn't noticed it until they were almost to the door because she had never had to look before. Turning, she saw they were still at the cage.

"I guess I'll need another minute or two," she said to Vertap.

"I'll wait outside at the vehicle."

Jenetta walked back to the cage where all three cats were mewling and making assorted sounds. She stood there observing for a couple of minutes and then said, "Time to go, girls."

Cayla and Tayna turned to look at her, then turned back to the caged jumaka and mewled more sounds. Jenetta waited patiently while they said their goodbyes. This was the first time they had seen another jumaka since she had acquired them, and she knew it was an emotional moment. Finally, they pulled back and walked to Jenetta's side. For the caged jumaka, it had also been an emotional time. Taken from its family when just a newborn cub, it hadn't seen another jumaka since. It began to wail loudly as the trio left the building. The sound was heart-wrenching. The large jumaka instinctively knew it would never again see the two lovely females with whom it had shared those brief minutes.

The rest of the zoo was just as wonderful as the first half. It was a place where Jenetta could happily have spent long days learning about all the animals there. Despite the poor situation with the jumaka, no effort seemed to have been spared in providing exhibit conditions that, to the greatest degree possible, seemed to emulate the natural surroundings of the various species, and they seemed to be well cared for. Perhaps the problem with the care of the jumaka was owed to its being an off-world species about which little was known.

The tour made Jenetta think about Obotymot and the efforts to save as many species as possible after the meteor strike. On her next visit there, she promised herself that she would find out how that effort had gone and see if there was anything she could do to assist repopulation of the various species.

It was approaching suppertime when the tour ended back at the shuttle pad. Jenetta thanked the minister for the warm reception she had received on the planet and again expressed her appreciation for the intel he had provided in the past. She also expressed her hope that they would continue to work together for the betterment of both their nations. He echoed her sentiments and told her she would always be welcome in their kingdom.

As Jenetta climbed the shuttle ramp with Cayla and Tayna, the cats paused and looked back. Perhaps they expected

Jenetta to bring the large, caged jumaka with them. After a moment's hesitation, they continued on into the shuttle.

Chapter Twenty-Eight
~ March 15th, 2288 ~

Captain Gavin was waiting at the shuttle bay to welcome Jenetta back. The normal greeting protocol for visiting admirals had been extended to Jenetta when she first came aboard, but she had since modified it for those times she was aboard the ship for an extended stay. Now the protocol only required the captain to be present whenever an admiral came back aboard, unless an emergency required that the captain be elsewhere, at which time the second in command would greet the admiral.

"Welcome back, Admiral," Captain Gavin said formally.

"Thank you, Captain."

"I trust all went well on the surface."

"It was a very pleasant visit. I actually enjoyed myself, which I usually can't say with state visits."

"I understand," he said, smiling." Your package arrived a short time ago. We placed it in a secure hold— for safety's sake."

"My package?"

"It was addressed to you from Minister Aloyandro."

"I wasn't expecting anything."

"Really? Should we send it back?"

"Let's go take a look at it before I decide."

Two heavily armed Marine sentries at the entrance to the hold braced to attention as Jenetta and Gavin approached.

"What did he send— the crown jewels?" Jenetta asked.

"Not hardly," Gavin said, then nodded at one of the sentries. The sentry turned and entered the code that would open the hatchway.

As soon as Jenetta entered the hold, her pets left her side and raced to the large cage. A series of mewls then ensued between the animals. Jenetta couldn't help but smile.

"It seems your pets like it," Gavin said.

"They developed a quick friendship on the planet."

"Are there many jumakas down there?"

"This was the only one, as far as I know. I have no idea who brought it here. Taurentlus-Thur is in Region One of GA space.

"Only since the expansion in 2273. Before that, it was unclaimed space."

"Still, it must be twenty-five hundred light years from here. I suppose it's possible that a trader was breeding jumakas and selling them as security animals. I don't suppose we'll ever know."

"You're going to keep it, then?"

"I can't refuse a gift from the King of the Hudeerac Order," she said with a smile. "Besides, the animal was obviously miserable on the planet. They had it locked away in a warehouse at the zoo because it had attacked several zoo-keepers."

"It sure doesn't like Hudeera. It never stopped growling and snapping at the Hudeera cargo handlers. But as soon as they were out of sight, it calmed right down. Even when our people moved it into this hold, it just sat quietly in the cage."

"It must have been abused on the planet. Perhaps the zoo-keepers who were injured were responsible. It doesn't matter now. I could never send it back to that situation."

"Two jumakas was stretching things a bit. Can you really go about with three?"

"No, that would be too difficult. I'll have to figure out how to deal with the situation."

"Then you're definitely keeping it?"

"Definitely."

"Very well. I'll take the ship out of orbit and head us back towards Region Two. Uh— it's 1700 now. Dinner at 1800?"

"You're on. Tell my steward, please. I want to stay here for a few minutes."

As Gavin left the hold, Jenetta walked to the cage. The large jumaka looked up and mewled at her approach. Cayla and Tayna were pressing their muzzles against the cage and mewling also. Jenetta knelt with her cats and the bonding began in earnest.

Jenetta remained in the hold for half an hour, then had to leave for her dinner appointment with Gavin. Cayla and Tayna seemed reluctant to go, but she told them they'd come back later and bring food for the newest member of the family. That mollified them, and after a few more mewling sounds, Cayla and Tayna accompanied her to their quarters. She fed the cats first, then washed up for dinner. Her steward told her that dinner would be ready at six, so she relaxed in her sitting room until Gavin arrived. It was a few minutes before six, so they went to the dining room and took their usual seats.

"Everything go okay in the hold?" Gavin asked.

"Fine. My girls were a little reluctant to leave the new jumaka alone down there at first, but I told them we'd go back down after dinner."

"I've always been amazed that you can talk to them like you would another person, and they always seem to under-stand you."

"I wish I knew more about them, but there's almost nothing in the various databases. All they talk about is the basic physical attributes, such as length, height, and weight, and mention that they're used as guard animals. I suppose that Taurentlus-Thur is so far from Earth— and as you mentioned, it only recently became part of GA space— that no zoological parties have gotten to that area yet."

I've never seen any, apart from your two pets and now this new one."

"I've never even heard of anyone having one. And the new one is the first I'd ever heard of being in a zoo. I'm glad the Hudeerac King gave it to me. It's too intelligent an animal to be in a zoo. It would be like putting Terrans on exhibit behind bars. We'd react badly as well."

"Have you decided what you'll do with it?"

"I know Christa or Eliza would love to have one. The problem is deciding who gets it. I'm sure all of my brothers would love to have one as well."

"You might have hit on a solution earlier when we were down in the hold."

"Did I?"

"You suggested that a trader might have been breeding them. The large one in the hold looks like a male, and you already have two females. If the new one is healthy, you can have two litters in no time. What's the gestation period for jumakas?"

"I have no idea. I remember reading once that it's about one hundred days for jaguars."

"There you go. In about three to four months you could be up to your eyebrows in kittens."

"Just what I need right now. But I'm glad we discussed this. Somehow I'll have to figure out if my girls are in heat and keep them away from the male until they're past it. I'd hate to keep him locked in the cage all the time."

Gavin smiled and said, "If anybody ever says parenthood is easy, they're either crazy or lying."

With furrowed brow, Jenetta lowered her head and gave Gavin a hairy eyebrow stare.

* * *

"That was an interesting report you sent me," Gavin said the next day. "When did you receive it?"

"It arrived yesterday while I was with the Hudeerac King."

"What are you going to do about it?"

"Nothing."

"Nothing? We may be putting our people in danger."

"And then again, we may not. I believe our captains know their ship must not make contact with any other ship in the same envelope mode, whether single or double, but we can warn them again. As to whether they're in danger when passing through a ship that has an envelope in place— well, we'll leave that issue unstated for now. The physicists are divided, so there's no sense placing additional worries on the shoulders of our people until we know."

"Is that fair to them?" Gavin asked.

"Do you feel we should ignore an enemy ship traveling FTL because there *might* be a danger? Should we simply let the enemy ship get away? I don't have to warn you of the potential dangers these enemy ships represent."

"What if we try to stop it first? If it stops and drops its envelope to fight, then we'll know we're safe."

"There's one problem with that. The only way we'll know it hasn't cancelled an envelope is if it suddenly goes FTL. If it simply stops and doesn't cancel its envelope, we'll never know the envelope is still active."

"Then let's assume that if it stops, the envelope is down."

"I have no problem with that," Jenetta said, "but what if it won't stop?"

"Then— we attack and pray that the physicists who believe the scout-destroyer will lose its double envelope and reintegrate inside the enemy ship are wrong."

"Amen."

*   *   *

"Captain," the tac officer aboard the *Nile* said," I believe I saw something."

"Something?"

"I can't be any more definite than that. It was at maximum range and appeared only for an instant."

"Helm, turn us around for another look. Tac, provide the coordinates."

"Aye, sir," both officers said.

Five minutes later the ship had turned around and returned to the possible sighting area.

"Contact off the larboard side, sir," the tac officer said.

"Do you have their course and speed?"

Aye, sir. It's recorded, along with the sighting data from the DeTect system."

Commander Soren Mojica called up the images from the appropriate DeTect sensor and verified the presence. "Com, notify the others that we've found them. We have five solid contacts. Send them our coordinates."

"Aye, sir." A few seconds later the com chief said, "Message sent, sir."

"Helm, let's park and wait for the others."

* * *

"We just received a message from the *Nile*," Gavin said after establishing a com signal with Jenetta. It was first watch and she was in her office on the Admiral's Bridge. "They've found the Denubbewa mother ships."

"All of them?"

"It appears so. They report having five solid contacts."

"Five? Well, now we know what they were waiting for. I hope that's all of them. How long until we reach the *Nile's* location?"

"Almost two days. I've notified the *Ferdinand* and other SD's to meet at the new RP location."

Jenetta looked away from the com screen for a moment and said, "Once more unto the breach, dear friends, once more."

"Shakespeare?"

Jenetta nodded. "Henry V, Act Three."

"May we be as successful as King Henry was at Agincourt."

"I refuse to contemplate any other outcome. We will never stop fighting while we live— or they do."

* * *

It had only taken a few days of gentle treatment to get the new jumaka to calm down completely. Jenetta knew that Cayla and Tayna were largely responsible for the attitude change. Their display of affection for— and protection of— Jenetta had made the large male see her as not as a threat but as a friend.

"Good morning, Thor," Jenetta said as she entered the hold with the jumaka's breakfast. She opened the latch on the cage door and he jumped out and ran around the hold several times before returning to eat. She retrieved his water bowl from inside the cage and filled it to the brim, then put it back inside. She wished she didn't have to lock him in the cage when she wasn't there, but she was afraid to leave him loose so soon. The Marine sentries were still posted at the door to ensure no unauthorized person entered the hold, but Jenetta had to guarantee that no one would be injured. Thor, as she had named him, would be locked in the cage whenever she wasn't around until she was absolutely sure he wouldn't attack an innocent party. So far he had returned to the cage whenever she told him.

When Thor finished his food, he bounded over to where Jenetta was sitting on the deck. As she began pulling the grooming brush through his thick fur, he mewled with pleasure. Jenetta didn't know if it was the grooming or simply the attention that he enjoyed so much. But it didn't really matter. He had to be groomed anyway, and it was a good way of bonding with the jumaka.

After the brushing was finished, Jenetta ran laps around the hold. Thor enjoyed running alongside her, just as Cayla and Tayna did.

At 0800, Jenetta told Thor it was time for her to go. Without even telling him, he returned to the cage. After she locked the door, she said, "I'll see you at dinnertime."

Thor laid down quietly on the floor of the cage and watched her leave.

* * *

The *Ares*, along with the four SD's that had accompanied him into Ruwalchu space, finally arrived at the RP established by the *Nile*. The six ships involved in the search had been performing flybys of the Denubbewa mother ships every four hours while waiting for the *Ares* to arrive. The remainder of the bombers, targeting ships, and the *Ferdinand*, had arrived at the RP and were standing by ready for action.

"Ladies and gentlemen, good job locating the mother ships," Jenetta said as the twenty-eight-ship teleconference began. "We're about to enter the final phase of this undeclared war and avenge the crews of the *Yenisei*, the *Salado*, and the crewmembers we lost from the *Gambia* and *Vistula*. Have we determined where the quintet of mother ships is headed?"

"My navigator believes their destination is the planet Bludlow," Captain Zakir Singh of the *Duluth* said. "It was a vital part of the Milori Empire and is still an important trading partner with Milor."

"I'm familiar with it. Their principal export is titanium and, of course, tritanium."

"Yes, ma'am. According to reports, their ore deposits are enormous, and their foundries can turn out processed material almost faster than it can be prepared for shipment. If the Denubbewa are looking to build more mother ships, that's the place to go for raw materials."

"Yes, Maxxiloth relied on it to provide the tritanium for his massive shipbuilding operations. It would seem that the Denubbewa intend to greatly expand their presence here. We're going to see that doesn't happen.

"The ships engaged in searching for and then maintaining track of the mother ships have performed a great service to Space Command. Knowing that the Denubbewa hadn't begun open warfare against planets out here enabled those of us back at Quesann to concentrate our attentions on developing new weapons to use against this formidable enemy. Every scrap of information, including an analysis of the two destroyed hulls and the intact missile, has helped us develop our weapons and our plan of attack. I'm sure that, at times, you were frustrated with our non-action, but we needed that time to prepare. I know in my heart you've been anticipating the day when you could get some payback for what the Denubbewa have done, but most of you will have to take a backseat to other ships as we begin our efforts here today. The reason is simple. We're still too vulnerable to the missile barrages the Denubbewa are capable of launching. When we leave here to launch the attack, we will first travel to a new RP ten billion kilometers behind the position of the mother ships. Those not involved in the attack will remain there until they receive new orders.

"Ten of the SD's I brought with me have been modified to perform as bombers. Our plan is to bomb the Denubbewa into oblivion. I know that sounds a bit crazy at first, but when you think about it, it makes perfect sense. We can use our TW envelope technology to actually drop our 'eggs' *inside* their ships."

Jenetta paused as officers aboard the six ships on search-and-observe duty digested what she had said and had a few seconds to think about it.

"The speed at which our ships travel in TW envelope mode," Jenetta continued, "means that no bomber can operate independently. A lead ship, that we refer to as the targeting ship, leads the way to the enemy and actually takes helm-control of the bomber. It's responsible for sending the signal to drop the bomb or bombs once the optimal drop point is established. The targeting ships have had special equipment and software installed to accomplish this, because in the last few seconds of the run, picoseconds are critical.

"For our initial attack, it might improve targeting if we could halt the mother ships. The *Nile* will fly ahead and position itself directly in the path of the mother ships. It will not cancel its TW envelope, so there's almost no danger. If the mother ships halt to attack the *Nile*, the *Nile* will engage its drive and clear the area when ordered to do so by Captain Gavin. At that same instant, five of our bombing groups will start their run. All ships not part of the action will remain ten billion kilometers away to ensure that the Denubbewa DeTect screens remain perfectly clear."

"Admiral," Captain Singh asked, "what's the accuracy of the bombs? At Light-9790, we're traveling almost three billion kilometers per second."

"During testing, the minimum acceptable drop radius was established at fifteen meters. All ships achieved that mark with all bombs." When Jenetta saw several jaws drop slightly, she added, "You have to remember that this weapon was intended to also fight the support ships back when we only knew of one mother ship in GA space. Accuracy was and is paramount. Although the ships are traveling as fast as Captain Singh says, the bomb-release process actually begins when the ship is still billions of kilometers from the target. The timing sequence establishes precisely when the bomb will separate from the TW envelope. At that point, the bomb is instantly back in normal space while the ship continues on at Light-9790. It took a great deal of engineering effort to make the drops so precise.

"All bombs in the bomb cradles of ships making the initial assault have WOLaR payloads. The other five ships have a combination of WOLaR and standard 'torpedo' payloads. The *Ferdinand* is carrying substantial replacement quantities of both types.

"The size of the mother ships means that one WOLaR payload might be inadequate for causing crippling injuries, so the bombing teams will each drop three bombs on the initial run. The timing circuitry ensures they drop sufficiently distant from one another to achieve maximum damage.

"The bombing teams participating in the first run are the *Magdalena, Congo, Tigris, St. Lawrence,* and *Purus.* The targeting ships are the *Katanga, Murray, Ohio, Ottawa*, and *Rhine.* These ships have trained together, so they operate in specific pairs.

"At present, the Denubbewa mother ships are traveling in a 'V' formation. Numbering the ships from left to right, ship number three is out in front. The *Tigris* and its targeting ship, the *Ohio*, will take down mother ship number three. The *St. Lawrence* and the *Murray* drew number two, and number four goes to the *Purus* and the *Rhine*. The *Magdalena* and the

Katanga will take down number one, while the *Congo* and the *Ottawa* are assigned to number five.

"I'm sure you all know this, but let me remind everyone. While in a TW envelope, you can pass through any solid object in normal space. However, if you impact another ship enclosed in a TW envelope, it's as if both of you are in normal space. So keep to your lanes. When you prepare to attack, make sure your course will not cross that of another ship. After dropping your bombs, continue on in a straight line for sixty seconds, then stop for new orders.

"Ten seconds after the bombing teams complete their run, the *Mekong* will perform a flyby of the area to give us an initial view of the damage. If the damage appears considerable, the *Mekong* should make a second pass, halt, cancel its envelope, drop a sensor buoy, create a new envelope and then return to the RP. We'll be able to determine what additional action is required after we see the images."

"What if the mother ships don't halt when I stop my ship in front of them?" Commander Soren Mojica asked.

"Then you'll engage your drive and get out of the way to ensure you don't collide with the bombing teams. We can't cancel the operation if the mother ships don't stop, but there might be an additional danger, so only one ship will attempt the bomb run until we know. That ship must be crewed by volunteers."

"What's the danger, Admiral?" Commander Dillon Wilder of the *Tigris* asked. "We've all made solo drops during testing."

"Following my trip to the Ruwalchu home world, I received a report from Space Command that addressed the issue of a ship with a TW envelope in place passing through a ship with a single envelope. To the best of our knowledge, this has never been done before, and half the Space Command physicists participating in a discussion on the topic expressed concern that the TW envelope might be cancelled if this was attempted. If it did, the ship might reintegrate while inside the single-envelope ship."

Two minutes passed before anyone spoke. Jenetta gave them time to consider the ramifications.

"But only half believed that, Admiral?" Commander Shawn Fischer of the *Yukon* asked.

"Yes, the other half believe there will be no effect. Space Command was preparing to conduct tests, but we won't have the report for probably a year. We can't wait."

"I volunteer," Wilder said, "and I'm pretty sure every member of my crew will go also, but I'll put the question to them after the conference ends. We never expected to be totally safe during this attack."

Wilder's comment drew a chorus of assent statements from the other officers who had been designated to participate in the attack.

"Thank you, all. You make me proud to lead this fine group. If any member of your crew wishes not to participate, shuttle them to the *Ares* before we commence the operation. Their decision not to volunteer will not be held against them."

"If the mother ships don't stop, and the *Tigris* and *Ohio* make it through successfully, do we then proceed as well, Admiral?" Commander Myles Barley of the *St. Lawrence* asked.

"Yes, as soon as we hear from the *Tigris*, we'll know it's safe to proceed.

"Any other questions?"

Jenetta waited a few seconds before adding," Very well. Poll your crew and make sure everyone who remains behind is a volunteer. We'll leave for the new RP in two hours."

Chapter Twenty-Nine
~ March 24th, 2288 ~

"I thought you weren't going to tell them," Gavin said, following the teleconference.

"I had to. I couldn't keep that kind of information from them. They had a right to know."

"I knew you would tell them," Gavin said with a smile.

Jenetta looked at him for several long seconds before replying. "And I knew they would volunteer to a man, in spite of the danger."

"They trust you— implicitly. They know you wouldn't risk their lives unnecessarily. If you say it has to be done, it has to be done."

"Sending someone into harm's way is the toughest part of a commanding officer's job."

"If it ever gets easy, it's time to put in your papers."

Two hours later, the entire task force left to establish the new RP ten billion kilometers behind the mother ships' current location. The *Mekong* performed a flyby to verify the exact position of the Denubbewa ships, their course, and speed.

Within minutes of arriving at the new RP, the five teams that would attack the mother ships were in position and ready to begin their runs. The *Nile* sped to a position well ahead of the Denubbewa using a wide track that couldn't possibly show up on the DeTect screens of the mother ship or give them any impression that the ship hadn't simply been sitting there for some time.

The situation was tense as the mother ships bore down on the *Nile's* location. Every ship in the task force was projecting a view from the *Nile's* sensors and seeing exactly what the *Nile's* bridge crew saw as the mother ships closed the distance.

"They're not slowing," Commander Mojica's voice was heard saying over the open communication line.

When the mother ships were less than two seconds away, the *Nile* engaged their drive and disappeared from their previous location in a heartbeat.

"What do you make of that?" Gavin asked Jenetta on their direct line.

Gavin was on the command bridge of the *Ares* with a full bridge crew, while Jenetta was in her chair on the Admiral's Bridge with Cmdr. Ashraf on her left and a full complement of crewmembers at support consoles. Her bridge didn't have a helm console and had no access to the weapons control systems, but it was almost identical to the command bridge in most other respects. The image of Captain Gavin was on the monitor by her left hand, and a tiny image of every other captain was on the monitor on her right.

Jenetta touched the image of Gavin and said, "I guess they felt that stopping to swat a fly wasn't worth the effort. We'll have to go with plan B. Send in the *Ohio* and *Tigris*."

The tac officer changed the image on the main monitor to reflect the forward image being sent from the *Ohio*. Seconds after first appearing, the mother ships began increasing in size dramatically as the *Ohio*, with the *Tigris* following a set distance and under the control of the *Ohio's* helmsman, came up behind the Denubbewa ships. The image suddenly contorted and disappeared briefly as the *Ohio* and *Tigris* entered the lead mother ship.

* * *

The entire room suddenly shook violently. It was the first such occurrence since Marine corporal Beth Rondara and PFC Vincent Kilburn had been awakened from stasis sleep.

"Corporal, did you feel that?"

"Feel it? I'm lying on my face with the bed on top of me. What do *you* think?"

"I'm on the deck too. The bed is on its side and I'm still strapped to it."

"What do think that was?"

"I think a Space Command vessel has attacked."

"What makes you think that?"

"There's a thing that kinda looks like a torpedo stuck in the deck between us. It has Space Command markings on it."

With much difficulty, Rondara twisted her head to look towards Kilburn, hoping she could see the object he was referring to. She could, and it did have Space Command markings on it. And it *was* buried in the deck. But it didn't seem to have crashed through the deck. It seemed more like it had been built there.

"I see it," Rondara said. "It's not a torpedo though. It might be some sort of probe or perhaps a sensor buoy."

"I don't care what it is or how it got buried in the deck. I only know that our suffering is finally about to end."

"Space Command can't put us back the way we were, Kilburn. These monsters have pared our torso down so much that we probably can't even use prosthetics. We're going to be flat on our backs forever."

"Not me. Once we're out of here, I'm going to find a way to end it all. I've got some buddies in the Corps who will help me. I can't live like this, Corporal. And God only knows what diseases they've been pumping into us. Before I joined the Corps, I was a beach bum— of sorts. I worked evenings in a tee shirt factory on the boardwalk so I practically lived at the beach. I rode my board when the waves were right, swam, and played volleyball. I'll never do any of those things again, and I don't want to live if I can't."

"Yeah, I understand. I was into kickboxing. I was about to go pro when the Milori attacked the GA. I've always believed I'd return to that when the war was over. I'm quite a ways along with this pregnancy now and Space Command will probably expect me to go to full term. But who knows what sort of monster will come out— if flipping me over and smashing me into the deck hasn't killed it already. God, I wish the fall had simply broken my neck."

* * *

"We're through," Commander Wilder of the *Tigris* reported as the first pair completed their bombing run. "Someone tell Space Command that the group of physicists who predicted our demise were totally wrong. Our envelopes are intact. Unfortunately, one of our bombs didn't detonate."

"Roger, *Tigris*," the *Ares* tac officer said. "We were expecting that might happen. *Magdalena*, *Katanga*, *Congo* and *Ottawa*, you're a go."

"Roger, *Ares*. *Magdalena* and *Katanga* are on the move."

"*Congo* and *Ottawa* are moving as well."

The tac officer waited three seconds and then released the *St. Lawrence*, *Murray*, *Purus*, and *Rhine* for their runs.

"The *Magdalena* is in the clear," the tac officer heard after the bombing team had completed its run. A second later he heard, "The *Congo* is clear."

A few seconds later the last two pairs of ships reported that they also were clear of the Denubbewa ships.

"Bombing teams, any difficulties encountered?" Captain Gavin asked.

"Number five started to veer off as we approached," the *Ottawa* said, "but we adjusted our course to compensate."

"*Mekong*," Gavin said, "perform a flyby so we can see what's going on out there."

"Roger, sir. *Mekong* is on the move."

Unlike the flybys performed while the ships were monitoring the presence of the mother ships where the scout-destroyer flew by at the edge of the Detect Range, the *Mekong* passed just a thousand kilometers from the center of the battle zone. Image resolution was naturally incredible. Broadcast on an encrypted SC channel, the image was displayed on the bridge of every ship and available throughout every vessel on closed-circuit systems. The cheering in each area lasted for a full minute.

Everyone saw the gaping holes in each of the mother ships but also knew the enemy wasn't out of the fight yet. In fact, they were far from it. As they watched, small ships began streaming out of every mother ship, and the mother ships were rolling back the domes that protected their enormous missile platforms.

"We've stung them," Jenetta said to Gavin, but they're still able to fight. Send in the bombers for another run."

Gavin relayed the order and the images changed to show the view from the targeting ships as they approached the battle zone. Now that they knew the envelopes would not cancel during their flythrough, the five bombing pairs went in three seconds apart. To the Denubbewa, they weren't even visible. The invaders only knew that parts of their ships kept exploding. "Let's pull back," Jenetta said to Gavin. "Now that we've stopped them, we can establish an RP half a light-year away. Have the bombing groups continue to pound the Denubbewa until they run out of bombs, then join us."

"Aye, Admiral," Gavin said, then relayed the orders. Within minutes all of the ships not involved in the bombing effort were on their way to the new RP. One half light-year for the task force represented less than thirty minutes of travel, but it represented almost twelve days of travel for the Denubbewa. It was unlikely in the extreme that if the enemy spread out looking for Space Command vessels they would travel that far in the correct direction. If the Denubbewa were looking for enemies, they would exhaust themselves searching space nearby. At most they might travel a few trillion kilometers' distance. They would never find anything.

The images provided by the bombing groups after the last pass were startling. The mother ships could hardly be called 'ships' anymore. It appeared that at least half of the five hundred bombs dropped inside the ships had detonated. It was only their enormous size that accounted for the mother ships not having been blown out of existence. A hundred-twenty-six-kilometer-long spaceship has a lot of mass to destroy, even for WOLaR weapons. With huge holes everywhere in their bodies and enormous sections torn asunder, they would never be moving under their own power again. Like clouds of bees circling a hive, what seemed like thousands of warships, dwarfed by the size of the mother ships, filled the areas around the former mother ships. Despite their diminutive appearance, everyone in the task force knew they were full-sized warships, each with a deadly arsenal of missiles.

"Those mother ships will never move from this area under their own power," Gavin said as he and Jenetta examined the images.

"Anything can be made whole again, given time and the materials. We proved that after our first encounter with the Milori. What we have to do now is *deny* them the time and materials to accomplish repairs. Tomorrow we begin to work on those warships."

"Why not tonight?"

"If they're like us, they're on high alert right now. Let's give them a chance to stand down a little and begin picking up the pieces of their battle group. Then we'll hit them with everything we've got. Besides, we have to rearm the five ships that performed the bombing runs today."

"We still have the five bombing teams who didn't participate in today's runs."

"They'll be the first ships in when we begin operations again."

"There are thousands of those warships," Gavin said. "I hope that fifteen-meter bomb-drop radius holds. It's going to be a lot more critical now."

"We have fourteen thousand bombs in the *Ferdinand*. That should be enough, assuming we'll only need one bomb to destroy each ship."

"Assuming that half the bombs will land inside bulkheads and decks, and so won't denote, that means we can take out seven thousand of those ships. I hope that's enough."

"It'll have to be. That's all the bombs we have. I'm glad the AB increased my requisition. When I put it in, I sure wasn't thinking we'd have to fight five of those things. Hey, look at those small flashes in the images. They're everywhere."

"Yes, I didn't notice them at first."

"Do you think the Denubbewa are shooting at shadows?"

"That could be. We must have really spooked them with that attack. They never saw the ships that destroyed their mother ships. Ah, I think I know what they are. After the attack on the first mother ship, they all began opening up their missile platform domes. I bet those flashes are from missiles that got loose when platforms were blown apart. They're probably scattered all over the battle site."

"You might be right," Jenetta said as she increased the magnification of the image they were studying, then walked over to the monitor mounted on the bulkhead. "With luck, their own missiles will help us defeat them. And tomorrow our ships can cruise right through that area and place their bombs without worrying about the missiles." With a slight smile, she added, "If there are any ships left."

By first watch, the ordnance engineers responsible for rearming the SD Bombers had completed their tasks. Most of the bomb cradles of the ten ships were loaded with standard-load bombs, but each ship had just one WOLaR for this effort since the mother ships had been largely incapacitated. The SD's not part of the bombing effort had been performing flybys of the battle site every two hours to watch for significant changes. Little had seemed to change since the previous day's last images. Warships were still moving around the battle site, and pieces of the destroyed mother ships seemed to be everywhere.

"Today's mission," Gavin said as he addressed all senior officers in a teleconference, "is to destroy as many of the enemy's warships as possible. Our greatest danger is from contact with another of our own ships. As we begin today's mission, warships may begin to move to avoid our attacks, so we can't depend on having clear lanes for the runs. So each bombing pair will complete one pass, then wait until all ships have completed their run before starting the cycle over again.

This is not a 'clean' zone, so it's possible that some previously destroyed warships may be retargeted. That's not a problem, but we'd naturally prefer to concentrate on the ones that still pose a risk if they can be clearly identified. All ships are carrying ninety-nine standard bombs, so you have a full day ahead of you. Good luck and good shooting."

The half light-year distance to the battle site meant it would be thirty minutes before the bombing groups arrived and began their work, so Gavin joined Jenetta in her office.

"I'm really anxious to see the first images from the battle site," Gavin said. "I want to see how many of the warships have been damaged or destroyed by their own missiles overnight."

"That will be interesting. I hadn't considered that possibility while working on the weapon plans. We knew the detonation process began when the warhead shattered and the nuclear detonation had to occur once that happened, but we never considered that so many missiles would be flung from their racks by the explosions in the mother ships."

"The same might happen when we begin destroying their warships. After the bombing groups complete their task, the area might be littered with additional missiles."

"True. This might be their Achilles heel."

"There's an issue we've avoided but which must be discussed," Gavin said.

"You're referring to the missing crewmembers?"

"Yes."

Jenetta took a deep breath, held it for a second, then released it slowly. "I've given it a lot of thought and come to the conclusion that there's virtually nothing we can do while the Denubbewa can still fight. Their military power must be completely neutralized before we can try to locate our people. To do otherwise would put even more of our people in danger."

"That might be a death sentence for many if the ship they're in is destroyed."

"Yes, it might come to that. But without any idea of where they're being held or even if they were still alive before we attacked the mother ships, a search and recover operation would have been pointless."

"Okay. I agree completely, but I had to mention it. As you say, there was nothing we could do."

* * *

"Where is everyone?" Kilburn said. "We've been lying on this deck in total darkness forever."

"Quit complaining," Rondara said. "At least you don't have a bed on your back."

"Yeah, sorry, Corporal. Hey, I wonder if all the aliens on this ship were killed."

"I don't want to think about that."

"Why not? After what these bastards have done to us."

"If everyone is dead, we'll starve to death. It's not a nice way to go."

"I'm still hoping that this thing in the deck between us is a torpedo and that it blows up."

"It's not a torpedo, Kilburn. I've seen enough torpedoes to know that."

"Maybe it's a new type. It appeared when those explosions began and we were knocked onto the deck. I was *really* hoping one of those explosions ended our misery here."

"No more than me. No such luck. Now that the explosions have stopped, I guess the battle is over. I wonder who won."

Seconds later, the pain and suffering of Marine corporal Beth Rondara and PFC Vincent Kilburn was finally ended as a bomb destroyed the warship where the experiments on their bodies were being performed.

* * *

"Still up?" Gavin said as he entered Jenetta's office at 0136.

"I'm anxious to listen to the debriefings. It shouldn't be very much longer."

"One hundred bomb runs, probably averaging about ten minutes per run, means more than sixteen hours plus a half-hour out and a half-hour back. We may not see them until after 0300."

"I couldn't sleep anyway. What kind of commander could simply go to sleep while his or her people are involved in a known combat situation?"

"We've had periodic reports from the team leader. Everything was going well. The enemy hadn't been able to mount any kind of a defense. Our people should all be safe."

"In battle, the situation can change in a heartbeat."

"You have trouble letting go."

"Yes, I admit it. I've always had a problem with sending people into combat situations, especially where I can't be with them. I do my best to make sure they have the equipment and information they need to do the job, but I have this over-whelming desire to be there to help keep them safe if the situation changes."

Gavin chuckled. "That's one of the things I've always appreciated most. And the thing that inspires such loyalty in your people."

Jenetta smiled. "I once had an officer say that my crew would 'follow you down the cone of an active volcano on Io.'"

"I think that's true. And they'd know you wouldn't ask it of them, so they'd have to do it on their own."

"Perhaps it's related to an overinflated opinion of my ability to handle any situation. That's gotten me into trouble a couple of times."

"Perhaps," Gavin said with a smile, "but don't knock what works."

* * *

"Chairman Strauss has disappeared," former Lower Councilmember Erika Overgaard said to the council members assembled for the day's scheduled meeting. With Strauss's seat vacant, there were only seven members around the table. "Today's meeting is canceled, as are all meetings until a new Lower Council Chairman is selected. You'll be notified when that happens and meetings resume. I don't anticipate this taking longer than a week."

"Is there going to be a service?" Councilmember Flora Iversen asked. "We had one for Chairman Andrei Gagarin when *he* disappeared."

"No, no service. Chairman Gagarin didn't disappear. He— retired. Strauss has simply vanished. We have no idea where he is. He returned to his apartment after work on Friday and wasn't there this morning when his bodyguards arrived to pick him up. A lot of his clothes are gone, and he cleaned out his bank accounts last week. This appears to be a planned absence. That's all for today."

Later that afternoon, Overgaard reported to the office of the Upper Council Chairman. "I briefed the Lower Council members. Have you decided on a new chairman, ma'am?"

"Not yet. I've been too preoccupied with the search effort. This is so unlike Strauss— to just disappear like this."

"He seemed pretty upset that he wasn't chosen to sit on the Upper Council."

"We couldn't promote him. We need him to run the Lower Council. He's done a better job in that position than any other chairperson we've ever had. He was too good at what he did to promote."

"I understand, but that kind of business policy often fosters ill will in the people not promoted for the good of the organization without regard for the career of the individual."

"We doubled his salary and increased all his expense accounts. What more could he want?"

"A seat on the Upper Council, obviously. Now that we have the Age Prolongation formulas, there will be almost no chance for promotion."

"I want him found."

"Yes, ma'am. He knows all the secrets and where the skeletons are hidden. We shall retire him with extreme prejudice when we find him."

"Absolutely not! I want him found but not harmed. I want him returned to his job here. We need his firm hand on the Lower Council tiller. We'll find a way to make it up to him and make him want to stay in that job."

"Yes, ma'am. We'll find him."

Chapter Thirty
~ March 26th, 2288 ~

"We clobbered them again," Commander Katherine Jameson of the *Ohio* said during her debriefing session. "The warships were everywhere, milling around what was left of the mother ships and, I guess, trying to rescue trapped personnel. There were so many it made it hard to pick out a target. We've estimated that we took out at least four hundred warships during the day, but there were at least a thousand left. We might need three more trips to get them all."

All of the officers echoed essentially the same message. They insisted that the main threat from the Denubbewa mother ships seemed to be over, and all they had to do was keep attacking until all of the Denubbewa ships were destroyed. The images provided by the bombing groups seemed to confirm their statements. Many of the enemy ships never moved during the bombing run, leading to speculation that they were already dead. Analysts would examine the images carefully before the next attack and try to determine if certain ships should not be targeted because they had already been destroyed by the Denubbewa's own small missiles.

It was almost 0500 by the time the process was completed and the crews were allowed to retire to get some sleep after a very long day. The crews would stand down for the day and resume their bombing attacks with first watch tomorrow.

Jenetta had remained awake and listened to all of the debriefing sessions, which had been conducted by teleconference, although she didn't participate and was off camera the entire time. The official log noted her presence even though she was never observed during the recording. So it was with a heavy head that she finally turned in. Sleep should have come easily now that everyone had returned safely, but she couldn't get the images of the Space Command and Marine personnel taken prisoner by the Denubbewa out of her head. She kept telling herself there was nothing she could have done to rescue them before the attacks began and finally drifted off to sleep after several hours of tossing and turning.

"Going to feed the new kid?" Eliza asked as she encountered Jenetta in the corridor at the end of the first watch.

"Yes. And you can't come," Jenetta said.

"Why not? I want to see him."

"I'll send you a picture."

"I've already seen a picture. I want to see *him*."

"It's too early. I don't want to confuse him. I've barely begun to bond with him myself. He seems to trust me now and does whatever I tell him, but I want a little time to reinforce that before he meets someone who looks identical to me."

"You're afraid he may not know the difference?"

"Of course he would. My girls always know which of us is which. And he'd certainly know why one of us seemed different if he saw both of us at the same time."

"Well, when *can* I see him?"

"Perhaps in a couple of weeks. I'll let you know."

"Have you decided who's going to get him?"

"Is that what this is about? You want Thor for yourself?"

"Yes, I'd like to take him. You can't keep three of them for yourself."

"Who says?"

Eliza simply made a face at that remark.

"Okay, I agree. I can't keep all three on a continuing basis. But until I make a decision and I trust Thor to be around other people, I'm going to keep him isolated. I, alone, feed him twice a day, and my girls haven't even seen him since the first day he came aboard. I'm sure Thor smells them on my clothes, and they must detect his odor on me also since I groom him regularly. But neither has made a fuss yet. In time, I'll bring them down to see him again, and then you can see him."

"Okay," Eliza said with a grimace. "But make it soon, okay?"

*   *   *

The bombing groups left again the next day at 0900 with a full rack of standard payload bombs in their cradles. Fifty minutes later a message arrived from the bombing leader, Commander Jameson of the *Ohio*, that the battle site seemed to be clear of all ships still able to travel.

The one-half light-year distance meant that messages on the IDS band took just over ten minutes to travel between the RP and the battle site, so an interrogatory communication was impractical. Gavin, on instructions from Jenetta, immediately sent a message to the *Ohio* to have all ships begin a search for the missing enemy ships. The message also stated that the other five SD's and the *Duluth* would join the search as soon as they could reach the site.

The first report from the searchers was received seven hours after they began their efforts to track down the missing alien ships. The *Zambezi* had located a group of thirty-six Denubbewa warships headed away from the battle site at their top speed of Light-462. The *Zambezi* was ordered to perform a flyby every hour to verify their continued flight and course.

The next report came from the *Purus*. It had located another forty-three Denubbewa warships. As with the ships in the other group, they were not headed out of GA space.

Over the next twelve hours, the search teams located a total of seven hundred forty-two warships. Estimates from analysts aboard the *Ares* who had studied images of the battle site were convinced there could be as many as seven hundred more that were unaccounted for, but all available ships other than the *Ares* and the *Ferdinand* were busy tracking the groups they had found.

A tactical team put together aboard the *Ares* formulated a plan of attack that would produce the highest possible number of kills with a minimum waste of time and resources. Jenetta issued orders for the ten bombing groups to rendezvous and commence the attack on the first group whenever they were ready. The ships that were not part of the bombing groups were assigned to watch the largest six groups not targeted for the first attack. When every ship was in position, the attacks began.

Six hours later, the *Ares* received a message that the first group had been completely destroyed. According to the report filed, ten Denubbewa warships had been destroyed during the first run, but then the others had scattered in every direction. It had taken hours to chase them down and destroy them, but the final count was one hundred sixteen enemy warships destroyed.

The bombing groups headed to where the next closest group should be, but they had changed course and were nowhere in the area. That was consistent with what the six ships still trailing Denubbewa warships reported. After the bombing group had made their first run, the enemy ships being tailed had changed course, no doubt the result of communication messages from the attacked group.

Since there was no danger of losing the six alien groups being watched, the bombing groups took a break to eat and relax a little before attacking the next group.

Over the course of twenty-eight days, the Space Command bombing groups destroyed seven hundred three of the Denubbewa warships that had fled the battle zone. A full day had been spent with the *Ares* and *Ferdinand* while the bomb cradles were reloaded, and the bombing groups had been allowed to stand down for two days while the *Duluth* and five SD's searched for new targets. When several more groups of Denubbewa warships had been found, the bombers went back to work.

After two full weeks had passed without locating any more enemy ships, Jenetta ended the searches. The *Artemis*, the newest *Ares*-class battleship in the fleet, had arrived with the transport ships *Winston* and *Sebastian*, plus additional SD's and DS destroyers. They would begin the massive cleanup effort at the original battle site and the multiple locations where the warships had been destroyed. Intelligence personnel who would try to learn everything possible about the Denubbewa were still on the way. But before that work could even start, the battle areas would have to be cleared of Denubbewa missiles. Some of the ordnance engineers were estimating that the complete cleanup could take years, but Space Command couldn't simply leave the broken hulls and loose missiles that could destroy SC ships for scavengers.

Believing that her job was done in that part of space, Jenetta decided to return to Quesann. She was looking forward to the downtime during the sixty-day trip.

Two weeks into the trip, Jenetta invited Eliza to her quarters for dinner at the end of the first watch.

"I don't smell anything cooking," Eliza said as she sniffed towards the steward's kitchen. Cayla and Tayna busied themselves sniffing Eliza and she bent to pet them.

"Dinner will be ready at 1900. First we have to exercise Thor and feed him."

"I'm finally going to see the new kid?"

"Yes. I believe he can be trusted to have more freedom."

"What about the girls?"

"They haven't seen him since he came aboard, so we're all going down together. If they get a little too amorous, you'll have to help me keep them separated."

Eliza giggled. "So I'm here as a jumaka chaperon?"

"We both are. And it might take both of us to keep them apart if my girls are in the *mood*."

"Why risk it at all?'

"They've been wanting to see Thor even more than you have. And I'm sure he wants to see them."

"So we have to make sure it's just a meeting of minds."

"Platonic affection would sure save a lot of headaches later."

As soon as the two women entered the hold with Cayla and Tayna, Thor started bouncing excitedly around in his cage. Jenetta had to tell him to calm down just so she could open the door.

As the door opened, Thor rushed out and then stopped cold. He had been so fixated on Cayla and Tayna that he hadn't even noticed Eliza. He turned his head and looked at Jenetta, then looked at Eliza again, then back to Jenetta and back to Eliza. While Cayla and Tayna nuzzled him, he pushed his way to Eliza and sniffed. He was confused. She had almost the same smell as the other one. But the scent of Cayla and Tayna wasn't as strong on Eliza.

"Thor," Jenetta said. "This is my sister." She knew he wouldn't understand cloning, so she said, "We come from the same litter."

That seemed to get through. He smelled her again to remember her, then turned to Cayla and Tayna. A second later he spun and ran as fast as he could around the hold. The two female jumakas stayed right with him. If anything, they were more fit because they ran with Jenetta every day and were able to move around her quarters, whereas he had spent his days in the cage.

The cats ran, rolled around on the deck together like kittens, and nuzzled each other while mewling almost constantly. Jenetta then fed all three together. While Thor was wolfing his food down, a small chunk fell onto the deck. When he lowered his head to retrieve it, Cayla growled at him. He was startled and stopped, then looked at her. She mewled a series of different sounds at him and then continued eating. Thor lowered his head and finished the food in his bowl, then took a long drink but never touched the food on the deck.

While Jenetta was cleaning up after they had finished eating, Eliza asked, "Did Cayla just give Thor a lesson in table manners?"

Jenetta picked up the piece of food and tossed it in the trash. "I think it was a lesson in security. Cayla and Tayna were trained never to eat anything that's not in their bowl. Security animals are usually trained that way to keep them from being poisoned or drugged by outsiders. I guess in their mind that even includes dropped food that lands outside their bowl."

"And Cayla was able to communicate that to Thor?"

"It seemed that way. Each time Tayna and Cayla have been with Thor, they've made a lot sounds that remind me of conversing. I think their spoken language abilities are far greater than I suspected. Well, the kids are exercised and fed, so now it's time for us to go eat."

* * *

"General Ardlessel, we've been waiting for many weeks for your report regarding the Galactic Alliance," Prime Minister Pemillisa said. "Are you finally prepared to present it?"

Ardlessel stood at his seat. The enormous room in the Ruwalchu War Conference Center was packed with government officials and military officers either seated at the table, sitting in the gallery, or lining the walls.

"Mr. Prime Minister, honorable members of the Gilesset, and my fellow officers, I apologize for keeping you waiting so long for this report. We are a considerable distance from Uthlarigasset, and I was waiting for a response from my contact there. Yes, I am prepared to present my information today. First, I must report that my Uthlaro contact continues to maintain that the Galactic Alliance has definite plans to take over our territory three annuals from now. We are stronger now, militarily, than we've ever been, and I know that if we continue to build ships at the current rate and our recruitment continues as it is now, we will definitely be in a position to repel them when they come."

"That's all, General?"

"Yes, sir. That's all of the new information I have to offer."

"I assume you're open to questioning now?"

"Yes, sir. I am."

"Fine. I'd like to go first. Admiral Carver recently arrived just outside our solar system. She came peacefully, but I question how she got here at all without being detected."

"I can't answer that, Prime Minister."

"You don't know?"

"We're still investigating."

"You've had many weeks. How much longer is your investigation going to take?"

"I can't answer that, Prime Minister."

"Will you know in a month?"

"Again, I can't answer that, Prime Minister."

"You must have some idea. What leads are you following?"

"Uh— it seems inconceivable that she could have gotten past all our sensor systems completely undetected. We're still working on finding out how that happened."

"Okay, let's move on. The Director of Planetary Defense filed a report that when Admiral Carver was here, our systems couldn't fix her exact position. Are you aware of that?"

"Yes, sir. We looked into that and tested the systems. Everything appears to have been working fine."

"Then how do you account for the fact that our systems couldn't establish exact positions for her ship or the other ships with her?"

"I can't answer that, sir."

"You're saying you have no idea?"

"We've reviewed the recorded data and it appears that she was there some of the time but not there at others. We're trying to determine the reason for the anomalies."

"So, you say that she was not there some of the time, yet we clearly communicated with her. Are you telling us we were watching some sort of long-distance projected hologram?"

"No, sir, it was not a hologram. The vid signal was definitely emanating from the immediate area where we believe she must have been."

"Could it have been a relay satellite?"

"No, sir. That would have shown clearly."

"Then how do you explain this?"

"We're still investigating, sir."

"So at this time you can't establish exactly where she was located?"

"Uh, we can't, Prime Minister. At least not yet."

"Okay, let's move on. When Admiral Carver was preparing to leave, I told her we would order our ships not to attack her on her way out of our space. She replied that it wasn't necessary because our weapons couldn't hurt them."

"Obvious bravado, Prime Minister."

"Bravado?"

"Yes, sir. Our weapons are among the most powerful known and can destroy any ship."

"Did your command center watch Admiral Carver's progress as she left our territory?"

"I can't answer that, sir."

"You don't know if your people watched her leave?"

"Uh— we tried to, sir."

"And what did you see?"

"She, uh, didn't show up on any of our systems."

"A battleship and five smaller ships didn't appear on any of our sensors. Not on the way in or on the way out?"

Ardlessel hesitated for a couple of seconds before saying, "We only know that one second she was there, communicating with the Council, and the next she was gone."

"And that doesn't seem strange to you?"

"It is *very* strange, and we continue to examine the systems to find out how she did it."

"So let me summarize. You didn't see her arrive, couldn't see her while she was here, and didn't see her leave. Is that accurate?"

"We *will* find out sir. We simply don't know at this time how she did it. I've previously brought unconfirmed reports about incredible speed advances by the GA to your attention. It's possible that whatever allows them to achieve those speeds is responsible for masking their travel and presence."

"So is my statement accurate, at this time?"

"At this time, yes, sir."

"So if she returned tomorrow, you probably wouldn't see her arrival either?"

"We might, sir."

"And you might not?"

"Uh— that's a possibility."

"And if she showed up with a thousand warships tomorrow, you might not see her until she was in orbit over our planet?"

"I doubt we could miss a thousand warships, sir."

"Why? You missed six warships, and one of them was larger than anything we have."

"The sheer numbers would make the difference."

"Suppose she approached in groups of five?"

"We're talking about speculation, sir."

"So speculate."

"Uh— it's possible we might see them."

"And possible you might not?"

"I— uh— suppose that's a possibility."

"So all of the technological marvels we have at our disposal might not be able to see their approach. Tell us, General, if a thousand warships suddenly appeared around our planet and began targeting key locations, how long would it take to devastate our planet?"

"That's impossible to say, sir. Naturally, our planetary defense ships would attack immediately."

"And how many ships are close enough to make an immediate difference?"

"Uh— perhaps as many as five are close enough to make an immediate difference."

"Five? And how long would five last against the most powerful military force in this part of space?"

"Other ships would be on their way immediately, sir. We simply don't keep a large number of ships in orbit around the planet."

"But before those other ships could reach us, we could be devastated?"

"That would depend on the ships attacking us, sir."

"Are you aware that Admiral Carver devastated the Milori home world with just two of the small ships like those she had with her?"

"More bravado, sir."

"Yet that bravado is confirmed by all of our spies."

"The GA obviously has tight control over their media."

"Okay, let's assume that their ships *are* the most powerful ever built. Could we be devastated?"

"I— uh— suppose, sir."

"So why should Space Command wait three years to attack and give you time to build up our forces when they could destroy us today?"

"Perhaps they're not ready to take control of our territory, sir."

"So they should wait until they have some extra free time and possibly face a much more powerful space force?"

"Perhaps they're not looking at it that way."

"And perhaps they know themselves to be so powerful that facing a larger force wouldn't make any difference?"

"I wouldn't say that, sir."

"You don't have to say it, General. I said it."

Ardlessel bit his tongue to keep from responding with anger or disrespect.

"General, how many nations has the Galactic Alliance attacked that did not first begin the hostilities by attacking the GA?"

"I don't have that information, sir."

"I do. I was interested enough to check. Take a guess."

"I don't know of any, sir."

"That's the correct answer. They have *never* attacked anyone who didn't attack them first. With Milor, they even ordered the enemy ships out of their space after defeating them and then didn't attack Milor until Maxxiloth attacked the GA a second time. That makes it sound like they don't want war with their neighbors, which reinforces what Admiral Carver said."

"I can't imagine that anyone would have spent so much money and effort building up their military forces if they didn't have eyes on conquering other nations."

"What nations do we intend to conquer?"

"Uh, none," Ardlessel said, clearly confused by the question.

"Then why have we spent years building up our military?"

General Ardlessel finally understood the reason for the question and the trap laid by the PM. He didn't respond. He just stared at the Prime Minister.

"Exactly, General. There are often good and valid reasons for creating a strong military even when a nation doesn't covet the territory of its neighbors. The Galactic Alliance seems to fit that description. Uthlarigasset, on the other hand, had attacked a neighbor with intent to steal its territory. So I ask you now, whom should we be listening to and believing?"

When General Ardlessel continued his silence, Prima Minister Pemillisa asked, "Are you familiar with the enemy Admiral Carver mentioned— the Denubbewa?"

"Following her assertions that they had entered GA space, I did some investigating. I learned that their home territory is over ten thousand light-years beyond our border. It's unlikely that they have invaded GA space."

"But if they have, what are their chances of defeating Space Command?"

"Their chances are excellent, if all accounts are true. But it seems unlikely that they would bypass us to attack the GA. For that reason, I think her statements were simply more bravado."

"You don't seem to have very much respect for Admiral Carver or her accomplishments."

"No, sir, I don't. I think her claims are merely to frighten everyone into submission. She's all talk and no action."

"Interesting, general. She defeated the Milori— twice, defeated the Tsgardi, Gondusans, Hudeerac, and the Uthlaro. All of that is verifiable. Yet you believe she's all talk and no action." The Prime Minister was silent for a few seconds, then added, "Tomorrow, at the regular session of the Gilesset, I'm going to propose that we establish diplomatic relations with the Galactic Alliance. If the Denubbew Dominancy is indeed moving in this direction, we want to be allied with a peaceful nation most able to help halt their advance. Further, I'm going to propose that we alter the military budget with an eye towards spending more on technological advances and less on increasing the number of personnel and new ships."

Chapter Thirty-One

~ July 18th, 2288 ~

Jenetta spent as much time as possible with Thor during the two months' time it took to return to Quesann. By the time they reached the base, Jenetta was confident that Thor wouldn't attack anyone unless that individual was threatening her. She no longer locked him in the cage, but he remained in the hold and only saw Cayla and Tayna when Eliza was there to help chaperon because Jenetta wasn't ready to have jumaka kittens underfoot just yet. But Thor was happy because he could run around or leap up on the cage or the containers stored in the hold when he had an urge to stretch his legs. Jenetta had tested him twice by 'accidently' dropping a piece of food outside his bowl at feeding time. When she returned that evening, or the following day, the food was still where it had fallen. It proved both that he had learned from Cayla and that he was getting enough to eat. Whenever Jenetta arrived at the hold, Thor greeted her with the same enthusiasm she got from Cayla and Tayna.

When Jenetta stepped from the shuttle at the palace shuttle pad, she was greeted by a large welcoming party of Space Command and Marine officers. The greeting, actually required by protocol, had been orchestrated by Admiral Holt.

"Welcome to the conquering heroine," Holt said as she stepped off the shuttle ramp with Cayla and Tayna. The sounds of applause from the crowd filled her ears.

"Thank you, Admiral," Jenetta said graciously. She then smiled, waved, and said loudly, "Thank you, everyone."

"After what you've accomplished, it was the least we could do. The west conference hall is set up with food and beverages."

"Then let's all go inside. I could use a cup of coffee— and perhaps a piece of cake."

The welcome-back party lasted for about an hour. Jenetta stayed for the first half-hour, making the rounds and accepting congratulatory sentiments from her officers, then headed to her palace office with Admiral Holt.

"It's good to be back," Jenetta said. "I can't wait to jump into my fighter and spend an hour cruising around the planet."

"I understand you picked up another jumaka."

"Who told you that? Larry?"

"Yes. We talked after the *Ares* arrived a few hours ago."

"It was a present from the King of the Hudeera. I suspect the Intelligence Director was the main force behind the gift. They had the poor animal hidden away inside a zoo building because he had attacked a number of people."

"Is he dangerous?"

"I believe he might have been mistreated, much as my girls were before I acquired them."

At the statement, both Cayla and Tayna raised their heads, then laid back down.

"So it's safe to have him here in the palace?"

"Perfectly. Except to someone who might be planning to attack me."

"Why didn't you bring him down?"

"Eliza will bring him down later. I didn't want to subject him to crowds just yet. He might not understand the difference between applause and danger. He'll have to get used to us and our customs before I trust him in all situations. My girls have been immensely helpful in training him so far."

"It's always good to have a role model."

"It's more than that. I've always believed they have a rudimentary language— like dolphins. And lately I've become convinced that it's much more than that."

"I know you've always talked to your jumakas as if they were people, and they always seem to understand, but I didn't know they conversed among themselves."

"It's only since Thor joined us that I've seen it so openly manifested. It's almost seemed like they were explaining things to him. And he instantly picked up on whatever they were explaining and changed his behavior."

"That *is* interesting. Are you going to travel around with three jumakas now?"

"No, two is the maximum."

"So what of— what did you call him— Thor?"

"I haven't made a decision yet. Eliza would love to have him, naturally, and I'm sure Christa or my brothers would take him in a heartbeat. Larry suggested that I allow them to breed, but I've kept them apart so far."

"That might serve to satisfy all the family members who'd like to have a jumaka of their own."

"We'll have to see. I know that the gestation period for house cats is just sixty days and for large cats it runs from ninety to a hundred twenty days. But that could be meaningless. Even within some species on earth, the time is radically different depending on the subspecies. For example, I once read that some scorpion species gestate at ninety days, while with others it takes as long as a year and half."

"You're covering new ground here. You may just have to learn by doing."

"It's beginning to look that way, but you can see why I'm holding off. I've even considered taking a leave of absence and taking the kids to Obotymot where the event can have as much, or as little, time as it takes to happen."

"You can't take a leave of absence."

"Of course I can. The Denubbewa are pretty much on the ropes, even if a number of their warships did slip through our fingers. They don't have a mother ship to return to for food, ordnance, and repairs, so that will hamper any efforts to make trouble. We'll resume normal patrols and keep looking for them. The bomber groups will all remain in that part of

Region Two and travel in pairs so that when we find Denubbewa we're ready to take them down.

"In my report to the AB following the destruction of the mother ships, I stated that I'd like to receive enough bomb cradles to modify every DS ship in my fleet and suggested that all new warships have the cradles installed during construction, with internal reload capability. Also, I want every DS ship to have targeting capability. That would make our response capability as flexible as possible. We wouldn't be limited to specific bomber/targeting pairs.

"While the Denubbewa ships that escaped our net still present a significant danger to individual planets and colonies, the main threat is ended. And we have the tools now to take the rest out when we find them, with minimal danger to our ships.

"All in all, I'd say that the GA is about as safe as it has been in years, even if things continue to heat up on the Clidepp border."

"But you can't possibly take leave now. The GA Senate and the Admiralty Board are on their way here now that their complex is finished and the Denubbewa threat is over. We're pushing to get their housing done, but the official meeting halls and office buildings are ready for occupancy. I reported that to you."

"You reported that the government buildings and offices were completed. You never said that the Senate and AB were on their way here."

"I just received that message today. They left yesterday, and they'll be here in fifty days. You probably have a copy in your queue."

Jenetta walked to her desk and checked the queue, then read the announcement. She returned to her informal seating area afterwards.

"Then I have all the more reason to take a leave of absence. I can be gone long before they arrive."

"You can't leave. You didn't read any of the other messages, did you?"

"No, just the one."

"In another message, it's stated that the GA Senate, in their final legislative act yesterday before leaving to board their ships, passed a resolution that named you as the replacement for out-going Admiral of the Fleet, Richard Edward Moore."

Jenetta just stared at him, sure that he was joking. His expression never changed as he stared back at her.

"You're joking, right?" she finally said.

"I'm perfectly serious. You're the new Admiral of the Fleet, ma'am."

"No," she said, shaking her head. "Richard told me he intends to remain in the service as long as he can."

"His wife refused to leave Earth, so after turning over command to you, he'll retire and return to earth."

"No. No, No. I won't do it. I won't take the job."

"Too late. You've already been confirmed by the GA Senate, unanimously."

"It's doesn't matter. I will not, not now— not ever, take that job. It's not me. I won't do it. I let them stick these stars on me because there was a job to be done, and they convinced me I was the best qualified. And I've allowed them to keep kicking me upstairs because there was always a more important job to be done. But I won't allow them to stick me in the AB Hall for the rest of my days in the service. I refuse."

"Then you'll have to resign, because even with a leave of absence, you're the Admiral of the Fleet."

"How could you let them do that to me, Brian?"

"I swear I didn't know. I had no idea that Richard was going to retire. I believe even he didn't know until he told his wife to start packing. She refuses to leave her children, grandchildren, great grandchildren, and now a great, great grandchild."

"I can appreciate Richard's situation, but I'm still not taking the job." Jenetta sighed. "I've been afraid of something like this happening. I suppose I'll have to send in my papers. I entered the Academy in 2252, so I have thirty-six years in. That's enough for retirement, even though I don't need the money. My estate on Obotymot is beginning to turn a profit finally."

"Jenetta Carver can't leave the service. For many people, you *are* the service."

"A long time ago I was told by someone who was present to overhear your own words when you commented on Space Command not having just one Jenetta Carver anymore. As quoted to me, you said, 'Now we have three.' That's still true, Eliza and Christa can fill my shoes, although I doubt you'll ever get them to accept admiral's stars."

"Do you really think you can just sit around and get fat on Obotymot? You'll be bored to death and climbing the walls in a month."

"For one thing, I can't get fat. The DNA Manipulation process performed on me while I was in the Raider jail makes that impossible. For another, I might get involved in freight operations. I might even start my own freight company. Brian, while I was off fighting the Denubbewa, my sister-in-law Regina gave birth to a beautiful baby boy at my house on Obotymot. I missed her wedding, and that of Marisa, and I really wanted to be there for the blessed event. Now Marisa is pregnant, and I'm not going to miss that birth as well. This might be the right time to submit my papers, before any other critical problems develop."

"What about the Denubbewa?"

"They're under control, and this command can handle the rest as they're located."

"What about the ones that are coming? You surely don't believe they expected to take over all of GA space with just five mother ships."

"Space Command has a weapon now which can defeat them. The others may not even come now."

"If we were talking about the Uthlaro, would you think that?"

"No. The Uthlaro wouldn't stop. They'd send everyone and every ship they had. But they may not arrive here for years if all they have is Light-462 and their home system is twelve thousand light-years away."

"And what about the Uthlaro?"

"You can handle that. What I've been thinking of doing is sending a small task force to destroy the three warships guarding the new shipyards, then having a fleet of tugs drag everything back here. The loss of their entire investment should be enough to oust the leaders behind the plan. Besides, it will save us from having to build a shipyard."

"But it's in unclaimed territory. We don't have jurisdiction there. Can we just commandeer it?"

"Who are they going to complain to? They surrendered unconditionally to the GA and have been prohibited from ever again building warships. If they file a complaint with anyone about us commandeering the secret shipyard they established to build warships, they're admitting to sedition."

"That's true. Look, Jen, I'm sorry I dropped all of this on you today. I think you should take time to think about it. Please don't submit your papers until you've thought it through. Perhaps a leave of absence would be best. It'll give you a chance to see if retirement from the service is really for you."

Jenetta sighed. "Okay. Since both the AB and the GA Senate are out of session for almost two months, I'll grant myself an official LOA as the most senior officer in Space Command. You did say I've been confirmed as Admiral of the Fleet, so technically I outrank Admiral Platt on Earth who had me on seniority as a four-star. I will not, however, under any circumstances agree to assume Richard's duties with the GA Senate and AB. If they attempt to push me into that role, I will submit my papers for sure. There is nothing they can say or do that will induce me to accept that job. All they'll manage to do is drive me from the service, permanently."

~ finis ~

*** *The exciting adventures of the Carver sisters* ***
*** *will continue* ***

Watch for new books on Amazon and other fine booksellers,
check my website - www.deprima.com
or, sign up for my free newsletter to receive email
announcements about future book releases.

Appendix

This chart is offered to assist readers who may be unfamiliar with military rank and the reporting structure. Newly commissioned officers begin at either ensign or second lieutenant rank.

Space Command	Space Marine Corps
Admiral of the Fleet	
Admiral	General
Vice-Admiral	Lieutenant General
Rear Admiral - Upper	Major General
Rear Admiral - Lower	Brigadier General
Captain	Colonel
Commander	Lieutenant Colonel
Lieutenant Commander	Major
Lieutenant	Captain
Lieutenant(jg) 'Junior Grade'	First Lieutenant
Ensign	Second Lieutenant

The commanding officer on a ship is always referred to as Captain, regardless of his or her official military rank. Even an Ensign could be a Captain of the Ship, although that would only occur as the result of an unusual situation or emergency where no senior officers survived.

On Space Command ships and bases, time is measured according to a twenty-four-hour clock, normally referred to as military time. For example, 8:42 PM would be referred to as 2042 hours. Chronometers are always set to agree with the date and time at Space Command Supreme Headquarters on Earth. This is known as GST, or Galactic System Time.

A

Admiralty Board:

Moore, Richard E.	Admiral of the Fleet
Platt, Evelyn S.	Admiral - Director of Fleet Operations
Bradlee, Roger T.	Admiral - Director of Intelligence (SCI)
Ressler, Shana E.	Admiral - Director of Budget & Accounting
Hillaire, Arnold H.	Admiral - Director of Academies
Burke, Raymond A.	Vice-Admiral – Dir. of GSC Base Management
Ahmed, Raihana L.	Vice-Admiral - Dir. of Quartermaster Supply
Woo, Lon C.	Vice-Admiral - Dir. of Scientific & Expeditionary Forces
Plimley, Loretta J.	Rear-Admiral, (U) - Dir. of Weapons R&D
Yuthkotl, Lesbolh	Rear-Admiral, (U) - Dir. of Nordakian Forces Integration

Ship Speed Terminology	Speed
Plus-1	1 kps
Sub-Light-1	1,000 kps
Light-1 (*c*) (speed of light in a vacuum)	299,792.458 kps
Light-9790 or **9790 c**	9790 times the speed of light

Hyper-Space Factors	
IDS Communications Band	.0513 light years each minute (8.09 billion kps)
DeTect Range	4 billion kilometers

Sample Distances	
Earth to Mars (Mean)	78 million kilometers
Nearest star to our Sun	4 light-years (Proxima Centauri)
Milky Way Galaxy diameter	100,000 light-years
Thickness of M'Way at Sun	2,000 light-years
Stars in Milky Way	200 billion (est.)
Nearest galaxy (Andromeda)	2 million light-years from M'Way
A light-year (in a vacuum)	9,460,730,472,580.8 kilometers
A light-second (in vacuum)	299,792.458 km
Grid Unit	1,000 light-years^2 (1,000,000 Sq. LY)
Deca-Sector	100 light-years^2 (10,000 Sq. LY)
Sector	10 light-years^2 (100 Sq. LY)
Section	94,607,304,725 km^2
Sub-section	946,073,047 km^2

The two-dimensional representation that follows is offered to provide the reader with a feel for the spatial relationships between bases, systems, and celestial events referenced in the novels of this series. The reader should remember that GA territory extends through the entire depth of the Milky Way galaxy when the galaxy is viewed on edge.

The millions of stars, planets, moons, and celestial phenomena in this small part of the galaxy would only confuse, and therefore have been omitted from the image.

This map shows Galactic Alliance space after maps were redrawn following the end of hostilities with the Milori, and the war with the Tsgardi, Hudeerac, Uthlaro, and Gondusans. Unclaimed territories between the three regions were claimed in order to have one contiguous area. Regions Two and Three are so vast that exercising control and maintaining law and order has been largely impossible to this date.

Should the maps be unreadable, or should you desire additional imagery, .jpg and .pdf versions of all maps are available for free downloading at:

www.deprima.com/ancillary/maps.html

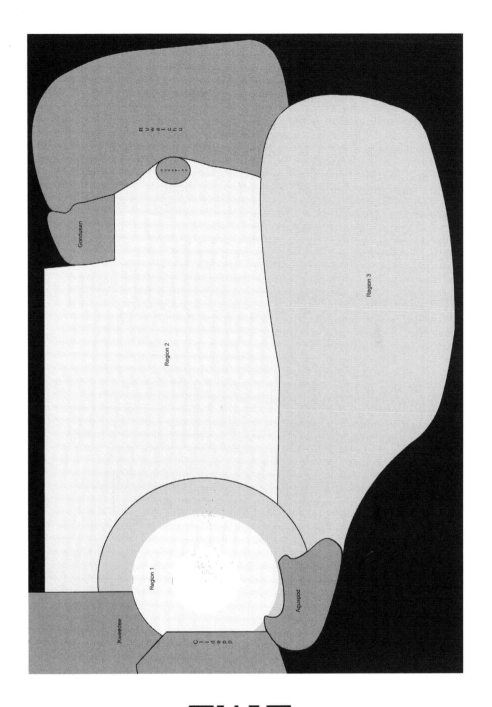

Region 1

Region 2

Region 3

Gordusan

Kneebdee

Aguspod

4503284R00223

Printed in Germany
by Amazon Distribution
GmbH, Leipzig